DISNEY MASTERS

MICKEY MOUSE:
THE PHANTOM BLOT'S
DOUBLE MYSTERY

by Romano Scarpa

Publisher: GARY GROTH
Series Editor: J. MICHAEL CATRON
Archival Editor: DAVID GERSTEIN
Designer: KEELI McCARTHY
Production: PAUL BARESH
Associate Publisher: ERIC REYNOLDS

Disney Masters showcases the work of internationally acclaimed Disney artists. Many of the stories presented in the *Disney Masters* series appear in English for the first time. This is *Disney Masters* Volume 5. Permission to quote or reproduce material for reviews must be obtained from the publisher.

Fantagraphics Books, Inc.
7563 Lake City Way NE
Seattle WA 98115
(800) 657-1100

Visit us at fantagraphics.com. Follow us on Twitter at @fantagraphics and on Facebook at facebook.com/fantagraphics.

Cover and title page art by Giorgio Cavazzano and Sandro Zemolin
Special thanks to Arianna Marchione and Anne Marie Mersing

First printing: December 2018
ISBN 978-1-68396-136-9
Printed in The Republic of Korea
Library of Congress Control Number: 2018936470

The stories in this volume were originally published in Italy. "The Eternal Flame of Kalhoa" and the complete version of "The Phantom Blot's Double Mystery" appear here for the first time in English.

"The Phantom Blot's Double Mystery" ("Topolino e il doppio segreto di Macchia Nera") in *Topolino* #116-119, June 10, June 25, July 10, and June 25, 1955 (I TL 116-AP). "The Last Balaboo" ("Zio Paperone e l'ultimo balabù") in *Topolino* #243, July 24, 1960 (I TL 243-A). "The Eternal Flame of Kalhoa" ("Topolino e la fiamma eterna di Kalhoa") in *Topolino* #303-304, September 17 and September 24, 1961 (I TL 303-AP).

These stories were created during an earlier time and may include cartoon violence, historically dated content, or gags that depict smoking, drinking, gunplay, or ethnic stereotypes. We present them here with their original flaws with a caution to the reader that they reflect a bygone era.

Walt Disney

MICKEY MOUSE

The Phantom Blot's
DOUBLE MYSTERY

FANTAGRAPHICS BOOKS

SEATTLE

CONTENTS

WALT DISNEY

MICKEY MOUSE

IN *The Phantom Blot's*

DOUBLE MYSTERY

CHAPTER 1

MIDNIGHT, AND A BLANKET OF SNOW COVERS THE SLEEPING CITY! NOTHING STIRS IN THE VAST WHITENESS -- EXCEPT FOR A SLINKY SILHOUETTE THAT GLIDES UPON MICKEY MOUSE'S ROOF!

MY TIMING IS IMPECCABLE! THE LITTLE RAT IS GLUED TO HIS TV ... PROBABLY WATCHING THE LATE SHOW!

STORY BY GUIDO MARTINA • ART BY ROMANO SCARPA
TRANSLATION AND DIALOGUE BY DWIGHT DECKER WITH DAVID GERSTEIN

1

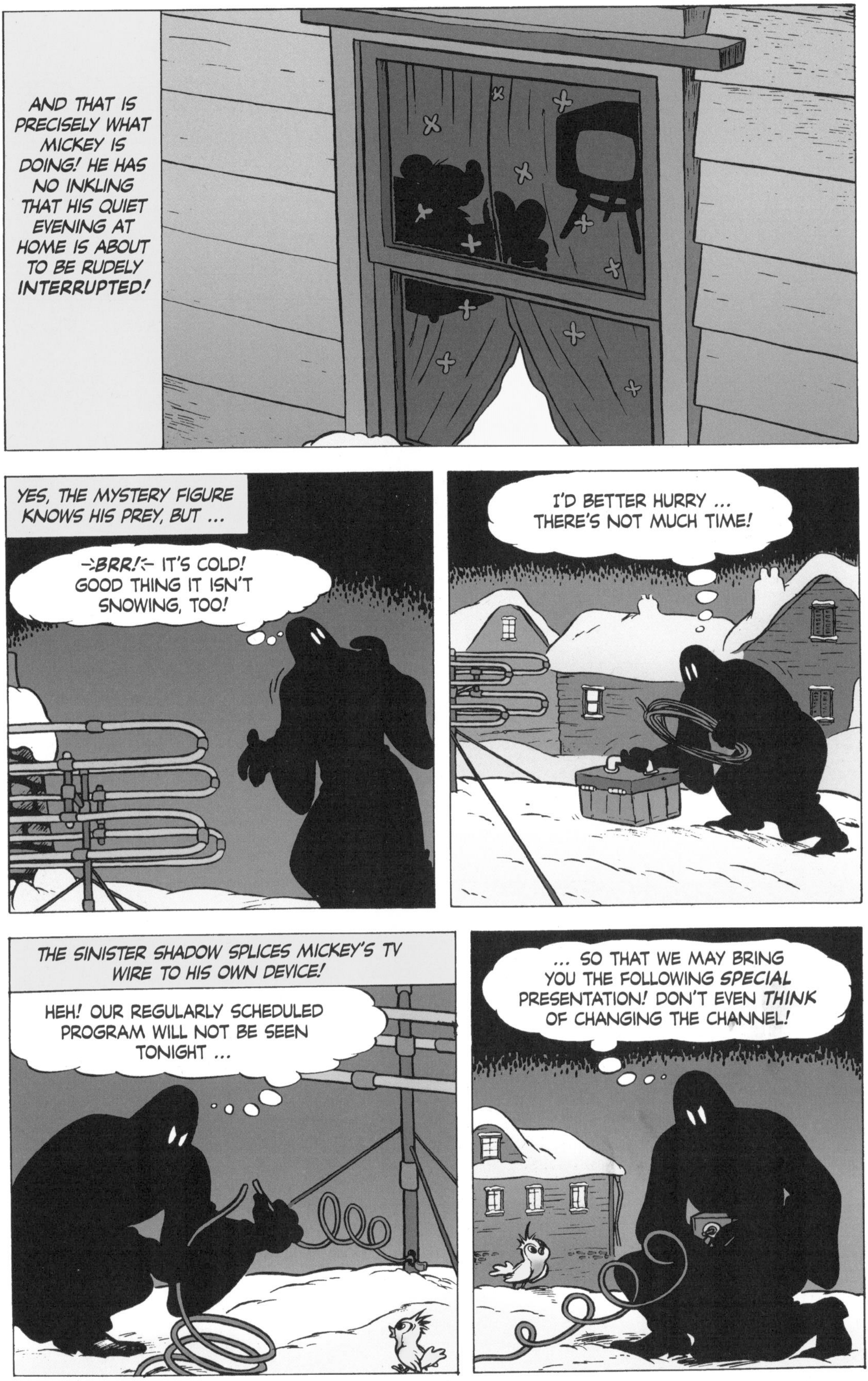
AND THAT IS PRECISELY WHAT MICKEY IS DOING! HE HAS NO INKLING THAT HIS QUIET EVENING AT HOME IS ABOUT TO BE RUDELY INTERRUPTED!
YES, THE MYSTERY FIGURE KNOWS HIS PREY, BUT ...
-BRR!- IT'S COLD! GOOD THING IT ISN'T SNOWING, TOO!
I'D BETTER HURRY ... THERE'S NOT MUCH TIME!
THE SINISTER SHADOW SPLICES MICKEY'S TV WIRE TO HIS OWN DEVICE!
HEH! OUR REGULARLY SCHEDULED PROGRAM WILL NOT BE SEEN TONIGHT ...
... SO THAT WE MAY BRING YOU THE FOLLOWING SPECIAL PRESENTATION! DON'T EVEN THINK OF CHANGING THE CHANNEL!

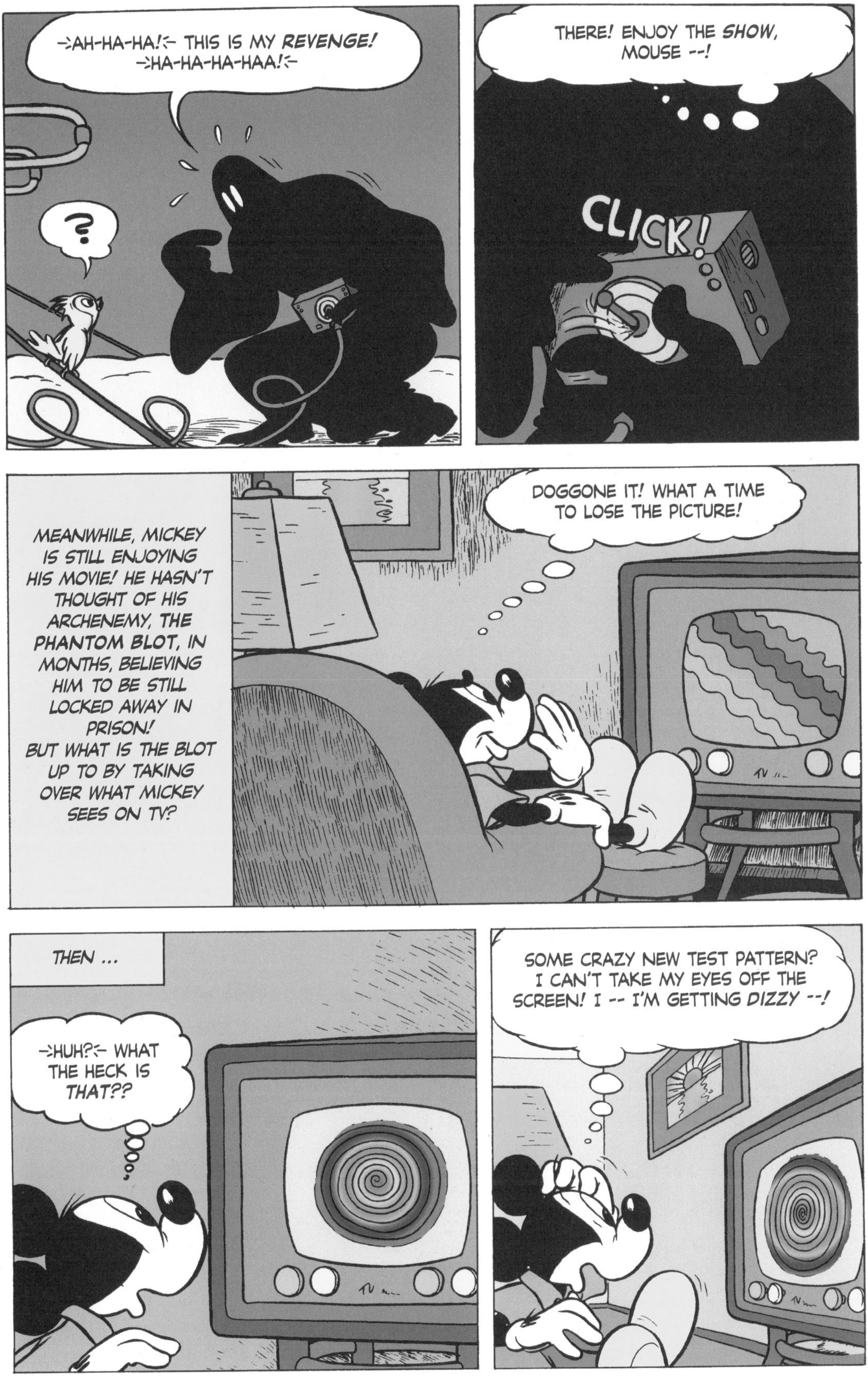
-AH-HA-HA!- THIS IS MY *REVENGE!*
-HA-HA-HA-HAA!-
?
THERE! ENJOY THE *SHOW,* MOUSE --!
CLICK!
MEANWHILE, MICKEY IS STILL ENJOYING HIS MOVIE! HE HASN'T THOUGHT OF HIS ARCHENEMY, THE PHANTOM BLOT, IN MONTHS, BELIEVING HIM TO BE STILL LOCKED AWAY IN PRISON!
BUT WHAT IS THE BLOT UP TO BY TAKING OVER WHAT MICKEY SEES ON TV?
DOGGONE IT! WHAT A TIME TO LOSE THE PICTURE!
THEN ...
-HUH?- WHAT THE HECK IS *THAT??*
SOME CRAZY NEW TEST PATTERN? I CAN'T TAKE MY EYES OFF THE SCREEN! I -- I'M GETTING *DIZZY* --!

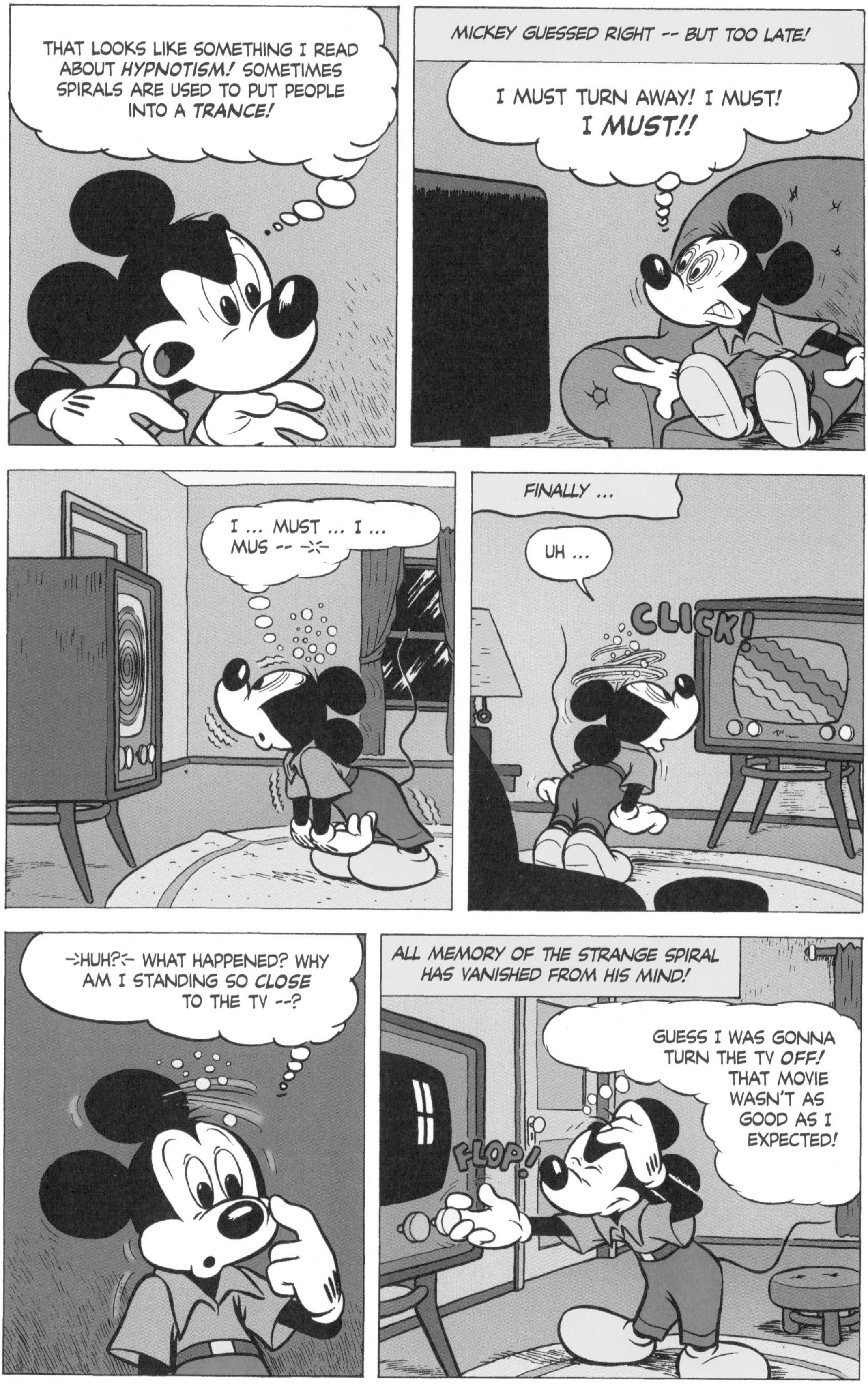
THAT LOOKS LIKE SOMETHING I READ ABOUT HYPNOTISM! SOMETIMES SPIRALS ARE USED TO PUT PEOPLE INTO A TRANCE!
MICKEY GUESSED RIGHT -- BUT TOO LATE!
I MUST TURN AWAY! I MUST! I MUST!!
I ... MUST ... I ... MUS --
FINALLY ...
UH ...
CLICK!
HUH? WHAT HAPPENED? WHY AM I STANDING SO CLOSE TO THE TV --?
ALL MEMORY OF THE STRANGE SPIRAL HAS VANISHED FROM HIS MIND!
GUESS I WAS GONNA TURN THE TV OFF! THAT MOVIE WASN'T AS GOOD AS I EXPECTED!
FLOP!

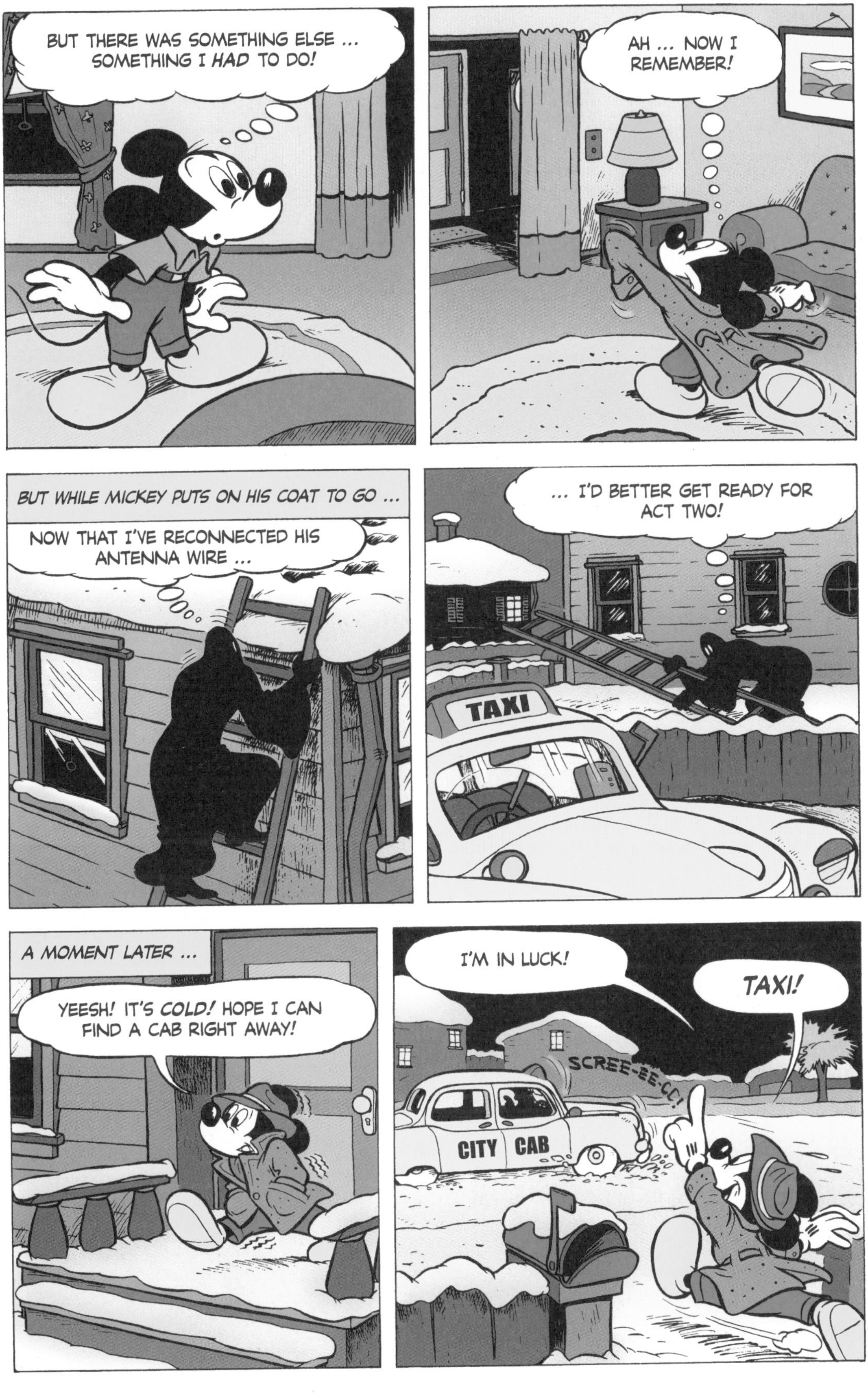
BUT THERE WAS SOMETHING ELSE ... SOMETHING I HAD TO DO!
AH ... NOW I REMEMBER!
BUT WHILE MICKEY PUTS ON HIS COAT TO GO ...
NOW THAT I'VE RECONNECTED HIS ANTENNA WIRE ...
... I'D BETTER GET READY FOR ACT TWO!
TAXI
A MOMENT LATER ...
YEESH! IT'S COLD! HOPE I CAN FIND A CAB RIGHT AWAY!
I'M IN LUCK!
TAXI!
SCREE-EE-CC!
CITY CAB

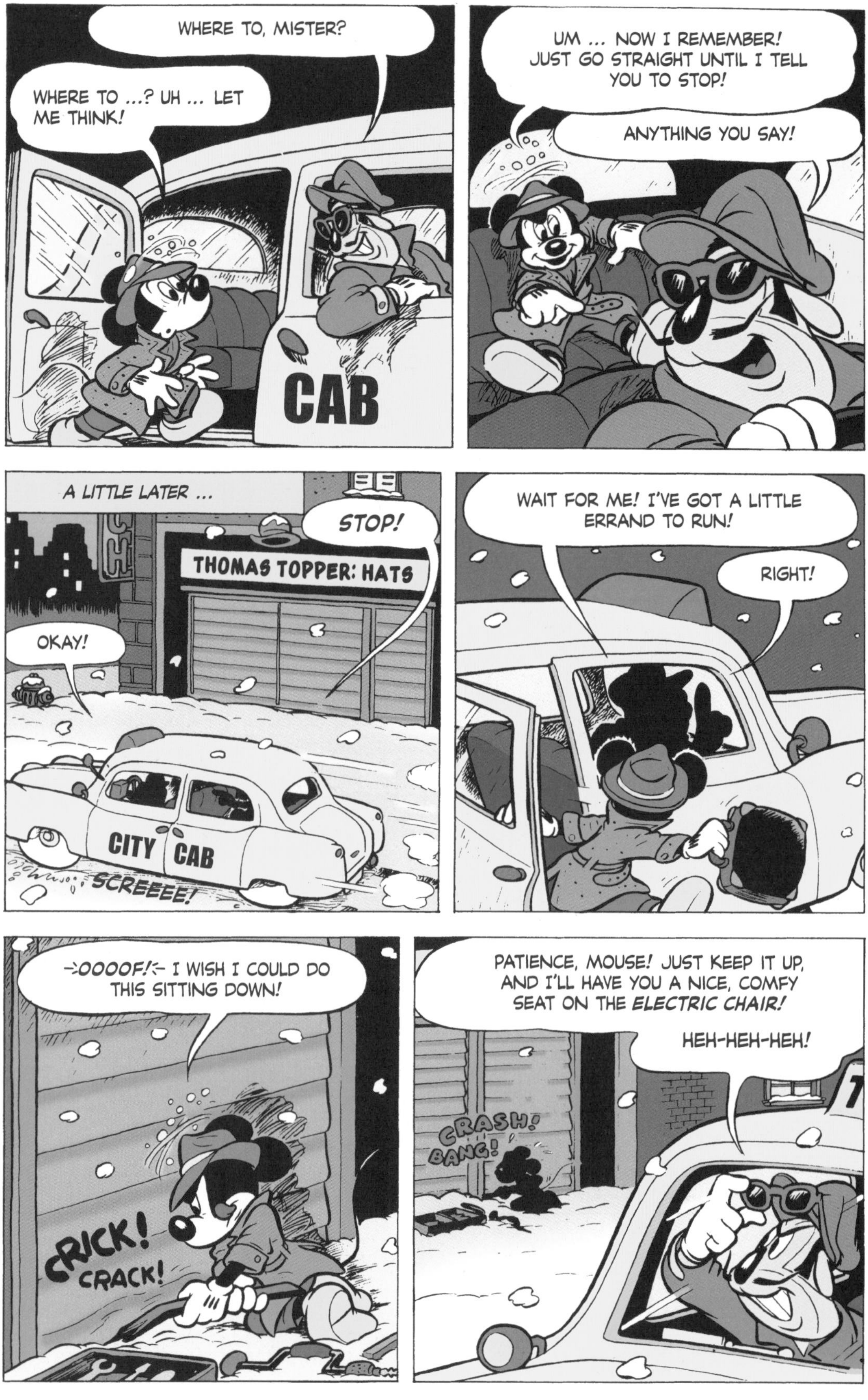
WHERE TO, MISTER?
WHERE TO ...? UH ... LET ME THINK!
CAB
UM ... NOW I REMEMBER! JUST GO STRAIGHT UNTIL I TELL YOU TO STOP!
ANYTHING YOU SAY!
A LITTLE LATER ...
STOP!
THOMAS TOPPER: HATS
OKAY!
CITY CAB
SCREEEEE!
WAIT FOR ME! I'VE GOT A LITTLE ERRAND TO RUN!
RIGHT!
OOOOF! I WISH I COULD DO THIS SITTING DOWN!
CRICK!
CRACK!
PATIENCE, MOUSE! JUST KEEP IT UP, AND I'LL HAVE YOU A NICE, COMFY SEAT ON THE *ELECTRIC CHAIR!*
HEH-HEH-HEH!
CRASH!
BANG!

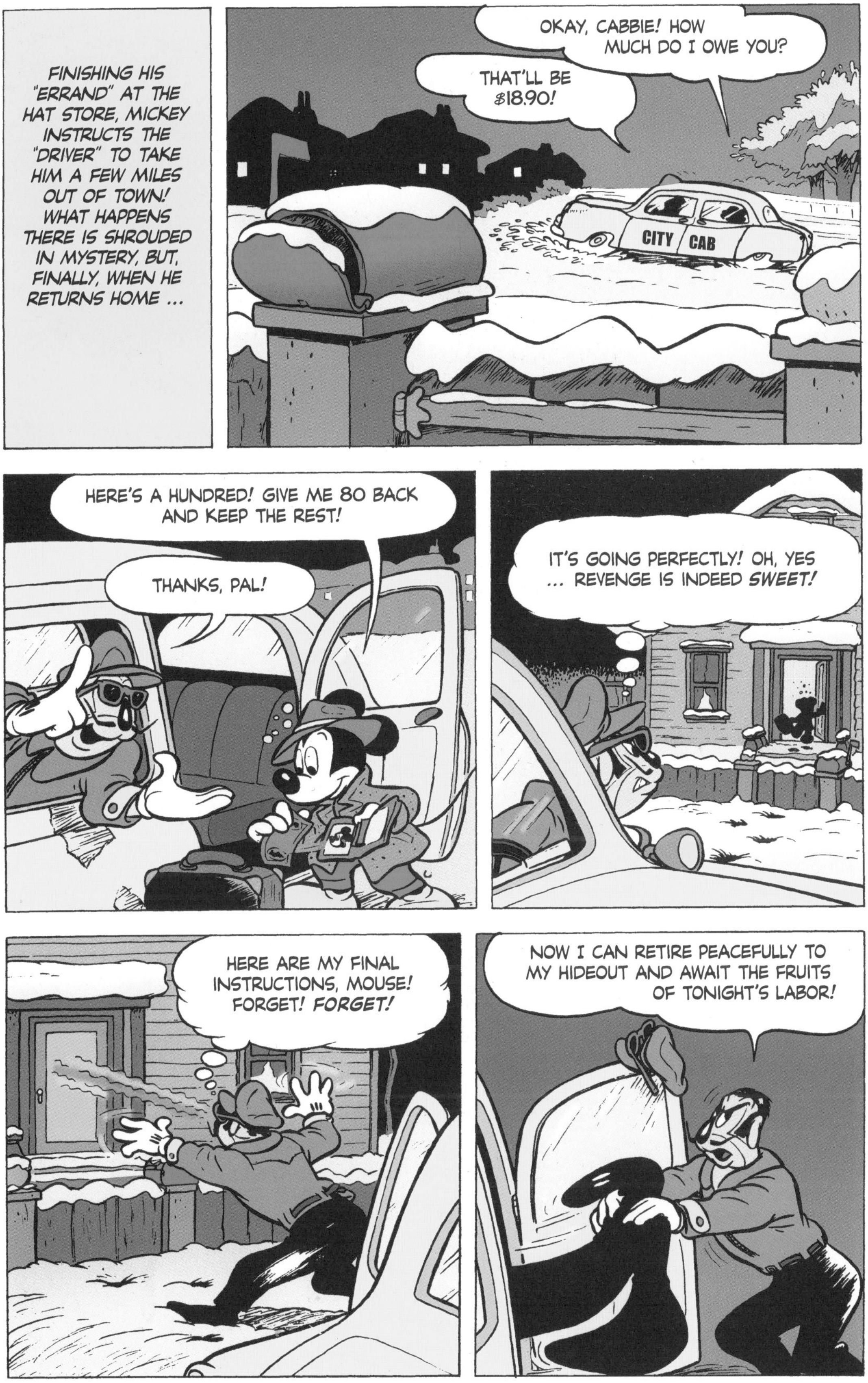
FINISHING HIS "ERRAND" AT THE HAT STORE, MICKEY INSTRUCTS THE "DRIVER" TO TAKE HIM A FEW MILES OUT OF TOWN! WHAT HAPPENS THERE IS SHROUDED IN MYSTERY, BUT, FINALLY, WHEN HE RETURNS HOME ...
OKAY, CABBIE! HOW MUCH DO I OWE YOU?
THAT'LL BE $18.90!
CITY CAB
HERE'S A HUNDRED! GIVE ME 80 BACK AND KEEP THE REST!
THANKS, PAL!
IT'S GOING PERFECTLY! OH, YES ... REVENGE IS INDEED *SWEET!*
HERE ARE MY FINAL INSTRUCTIONS, MOUSE! FORGET! *FORGET!*
NOW I CAN RETIRE PEACEFULLY TO MY HIDEOUT AND AWAIT THE FRUITS OF TONIGHT'S LABOR!

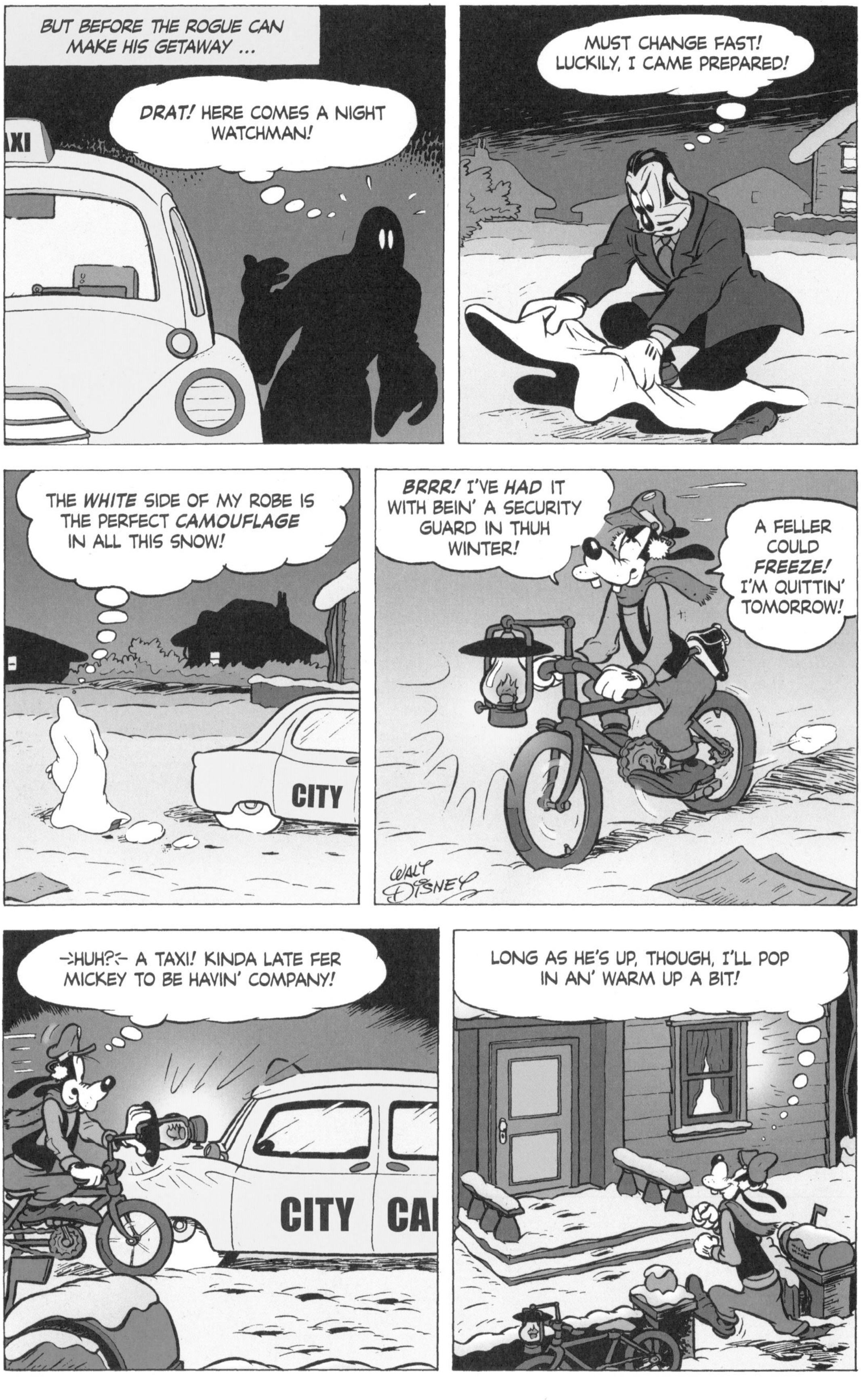
BUT BEFORE THE ROGUE CAN MAKE HIS GETAWAY ...
DRAT! HERE COMES A NIGHT WATCHMAN!
TAXI
MUST CHANGE FAST! LUCKILY, I CAME PREPARED!
THE WHITE SIDE OF MY ROBE IS THE PERFECT CAMOUFLAGE IN ALL THIS SNOW!
CITY
BRRR! I'VE HAD IT WITH BEIN' A SECURITY GUARD IN THUH WINTER!
A FELLER COULD FREEZE! I'M QUITTIN' TOMORROW!
WALT DISNEY
HUH? A TAXI! KINDA LATE FER MICKEY TO BE HAVIN' COMPANY!
CITY CA
LONG AS HE'S UP, THOUGH, I'LL POP IN AN' WARM UP A BIT!

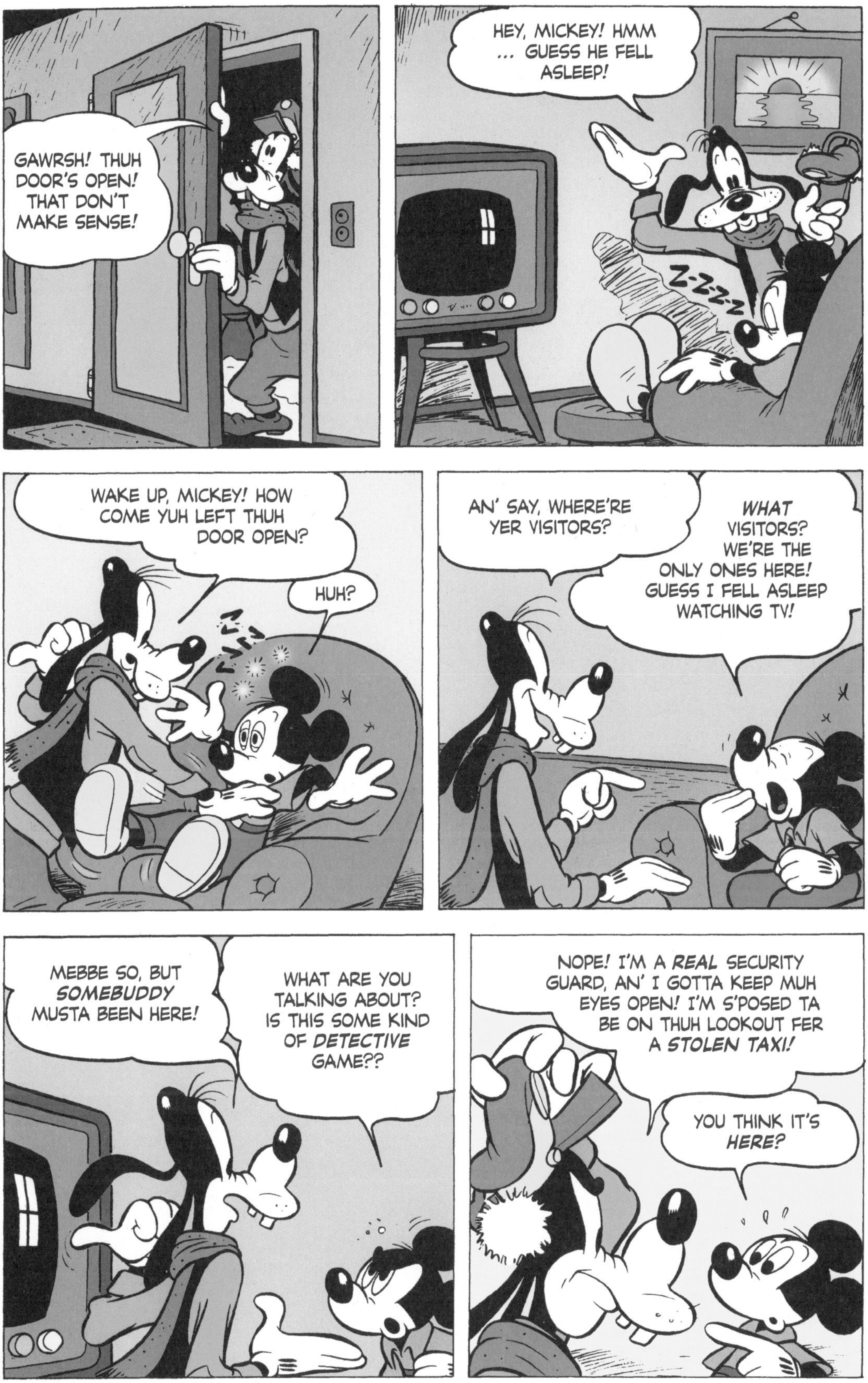
GAWRSH! THUH DOOR'S OPEN! THAT DON'T MAKE SENSE!
HEY, MICKEY! HMM ... GUESS HE FELL ASLEEP!
Z-Z-Z-Z-Z
WAKE UP, MICKEY! HOW COME YUH LEFT THUH DOOR OPEN?
HUH?
AN' SAY, WHERE'RE YER VISITORS?
WHAT VISITORS? WE'RE THE ONLY ONES HERE! GUESS I FELL ASLEEP WATCHING TV!
MEBBE SO, BUT *SOMEBUDDY* MUSTA BEEN HERE!
WHAT ARE YOU TALKING ABOUT? IS THIS SOME KIND OF *DETECTIVE* GAME??
NOPE! I'M A *REAL* SECURITY GUARD, AN' I GOTTA KEEP MUH EYES OPEN! I'M S'POSED TA BE ON THUH LOOKOUT FER A *STOLEN TAXI!*
YOU THINK IT'S *HERE?*

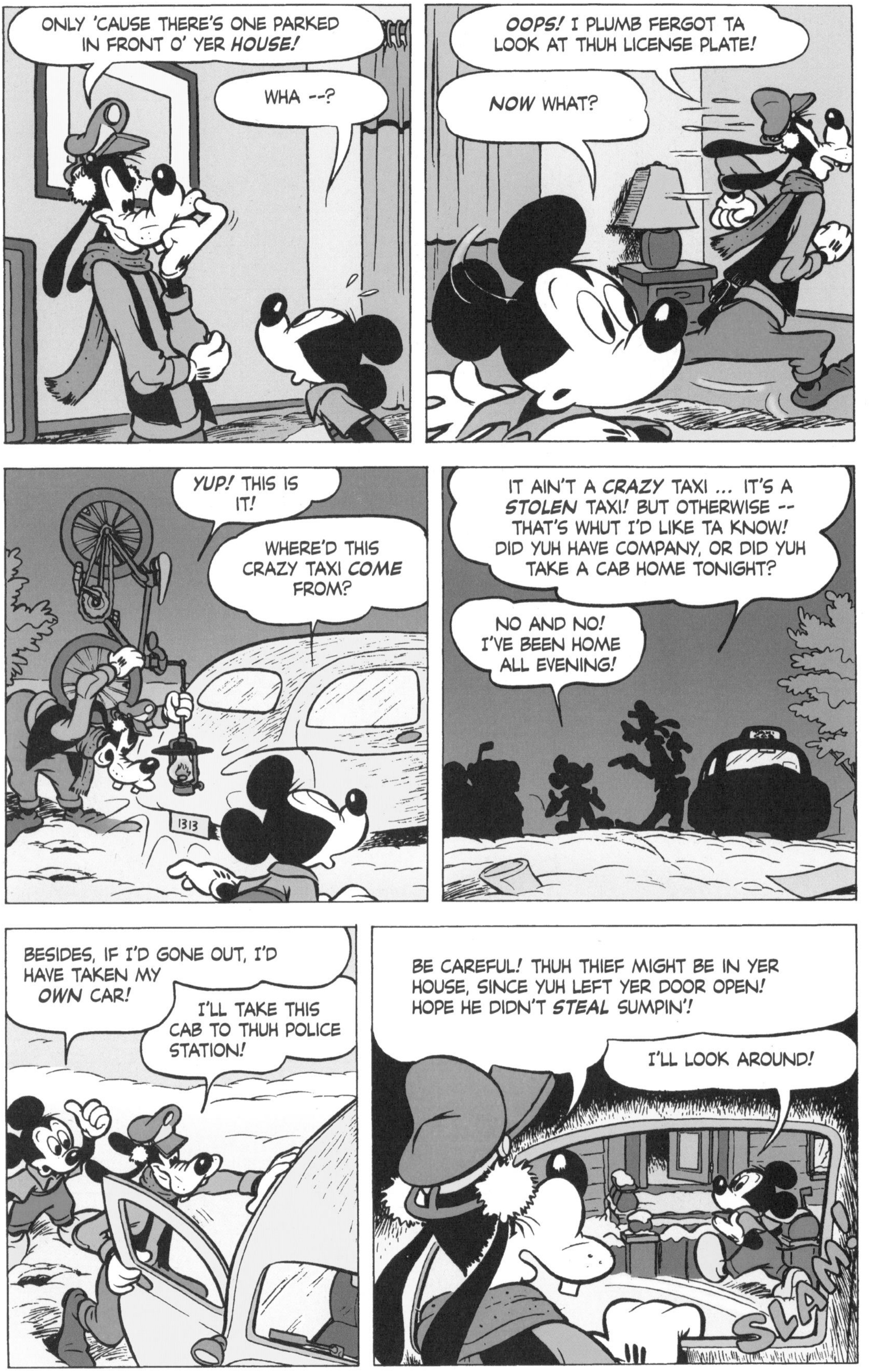
ONLY 'CAUSE THERE'S ONE PARKED IN FRONT O' YER HOUSE!
WHA --?
OOPS! I PLUMB FERGOT TA LOOK AT THUH LICENSE PLATE!
NOW WHAT?
YUP! THIS IS IT!
WHERE'D THIS CRAZY TAXI COME FROM?
1313
IT AIN'T A CRAZY TAXI ... IT'S A STOLEN TAXI! BUT OTHERWISE -- THAT'S WHUT I'D LIKE TA KNOW! DID YUH HAVE COMPANY, OR DID YUH TAKE A CAB HOME TONIGHT?
NO AND NO! I'VE BEEN HOME ALL EVENING!
BESIDES, IF I'D GONE OUT, I'D HAVE TAKEN MY OWN CAR!
I'LL TAKE THIS CAB TO THUH POLICE STATION!
BE CAREFUL! THUH THIEF MIGHT BE IN YER HOUSE, SINCE YUH LEFT YER DOOR OPEN! HOPE HE DIDN'T STEAL SUMPIN'!
I'LL LOOK AROUND!
SLAM!

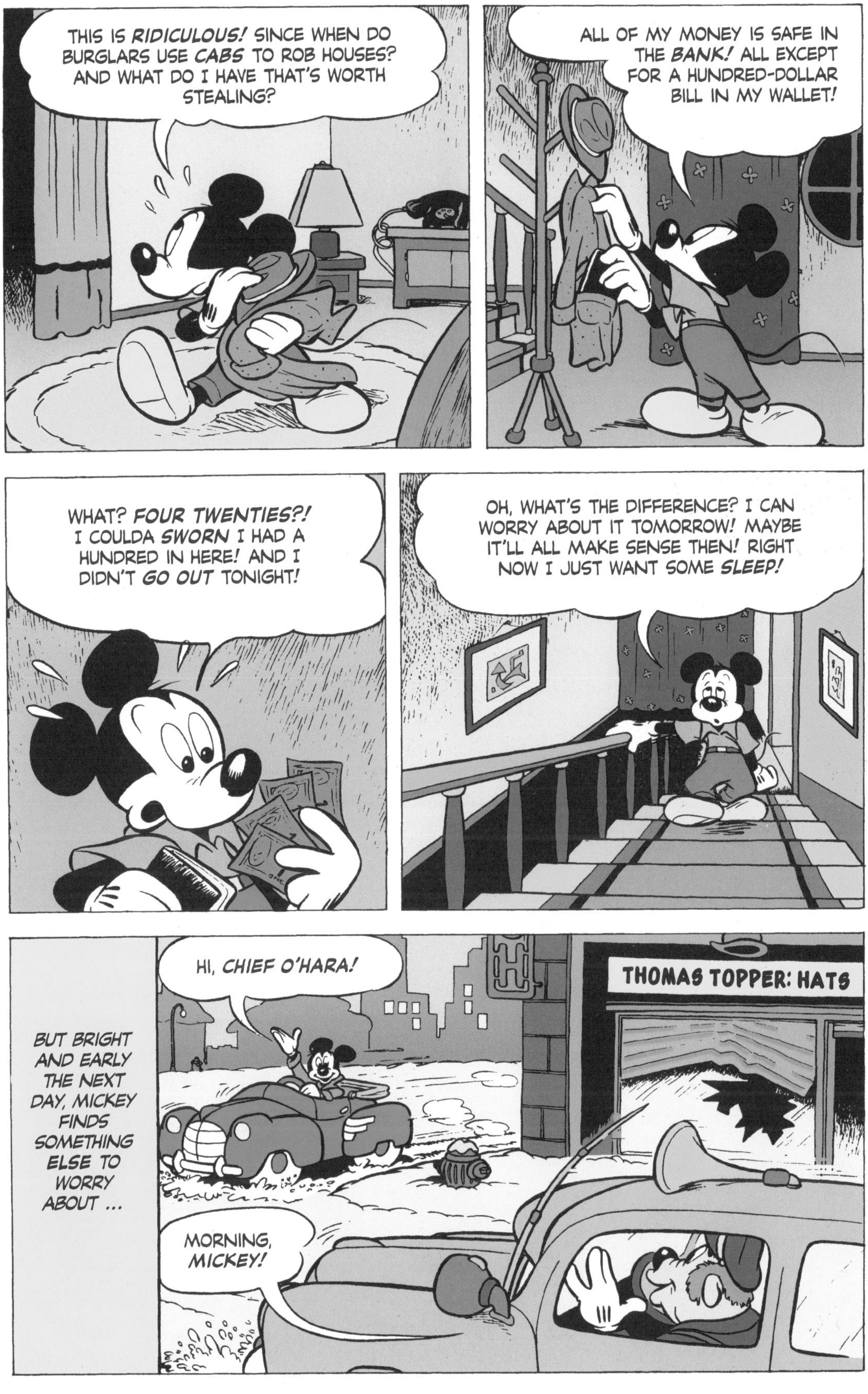
THIS IS RIDICULOUS! SINCE WHEN DO BURGLARS USE CABS TO ROB HOUSES? AND WHAT DO I HAVE THAT'S WORTH STEALING?
ALL OF MY MONEY IS SAFE IN THE BANK! ALL EXCEPT FOR A HUNDRED-DOLLAR BILL IN MY WALLET!
WHAT? FOUR TWENTIES?! I COULDA SWORN I HAD A HUNDRED IN HERE! AND I DIDN'T GO OUT TONIGHT!
OH, WHAT'S THE DIFFERENCE? I CAN WORRY ABOUT IT TOMORROW! MAYBE IT'LL ALL MAKE SENSE THEN! RIGHT NOW I JUST WANT SOME SLEEP!
BUT BRIGHT AND EARLY THE NEXT DAY, MICKEY FINDS SOMETHING ELSE TO WORRY ABOUT ...
HI, CHIEF O'HARA!
THOMAS TOPPER: HATS
MORNING, MICKEY!

AS YOU CAN SEE, I'M TAKIN' THIS LITTLE BREAK-IN *SERIOUSLY!* I CAME AS SOON AS I GOT THE CALL!

ME, TOO! LET'S FIND OUT WHAT'S UP!

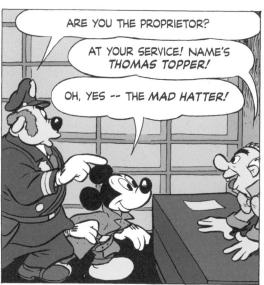

ARE YOU THE PROPRIETOR?

AT YOUR SERVICE! NAME'S *THOMAS TOPPER!*

OH, YES -- THE *MAD HATTER!*

PLEASE TELL US WHAT HAPPENED!

WHEN I CAME TO OPEN UP THIS MORNING, I NOTICED THE LOCK HAD BEEN FORCED!

THAT'S PUTTING IT MILDLY!

WHEN DID YOU REALIZE ALL YOUR HATS WERE MISSING?

THAT'S JUST IT! *NOTHING* IS MISSING!

TAKE A LOOK FOR YOURSELF!

BUT ALL THE SHELVES ARE *EMPTY!*

THERE ISN'T A SINGLE HAT LEFT!

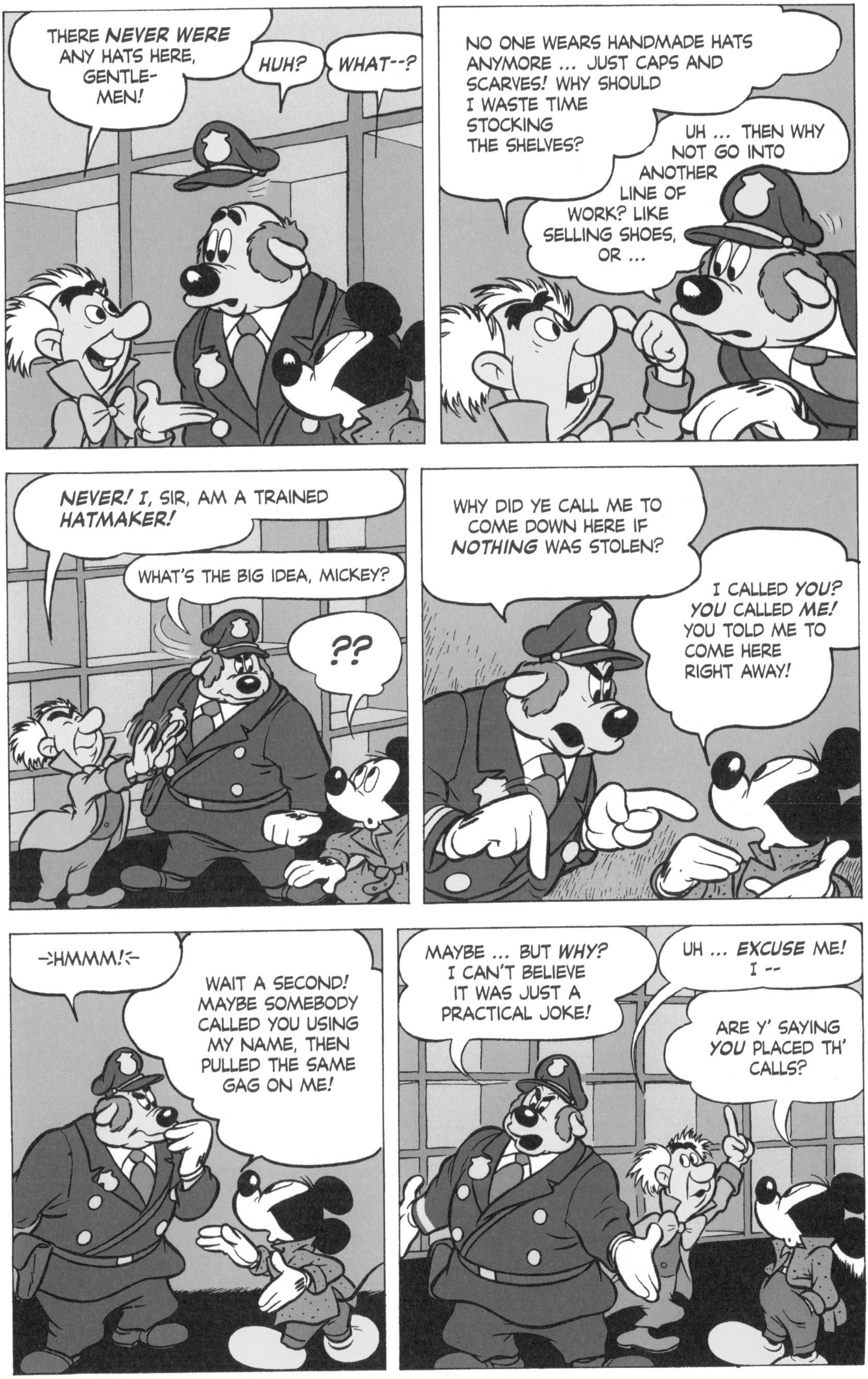
THERE NEVER WERE ANY HATS HERE, GENTLE- MEN!
HUH?
WHAT--?
NO ONE WEARS HANDMADE HATS ANYMORE ... JUST CAPS AND SCARVES! WHY SHOULD I WASTE TIME STOCKING THE SHELVES?
UH ... THEN WHY NOT GO INTO ANOTHER LINE OF WORK? LIKE SELLING SHOES, OR ...
NEVER! I, SIR, AM A TRAINED HATMAKER!
WHAT'S THE BIG IDEA, MICKEY?
??
WHY DID YE CALL ME TO COME DOWN HERE IF NOTHING WAS STOLEN?
I CALLED YOU? YOU CALLED ME! YOU TOLD ME TO COME HERE RIGHT AWAY!
HMMM!
WAIT A SECOND! MAYBE SOMEBODY CALLED YOU USING MY NAME, THEN PULLED THE SAME GAG ON ME!
MAYBE ... BUT WHY? I CAN'T BELIEVE IT WAS JUST A PRACTICAL JOKE!
UH ... EXCUSE ME! I --
ARE Y' SAYING YOU PLACED TH' CALLS?

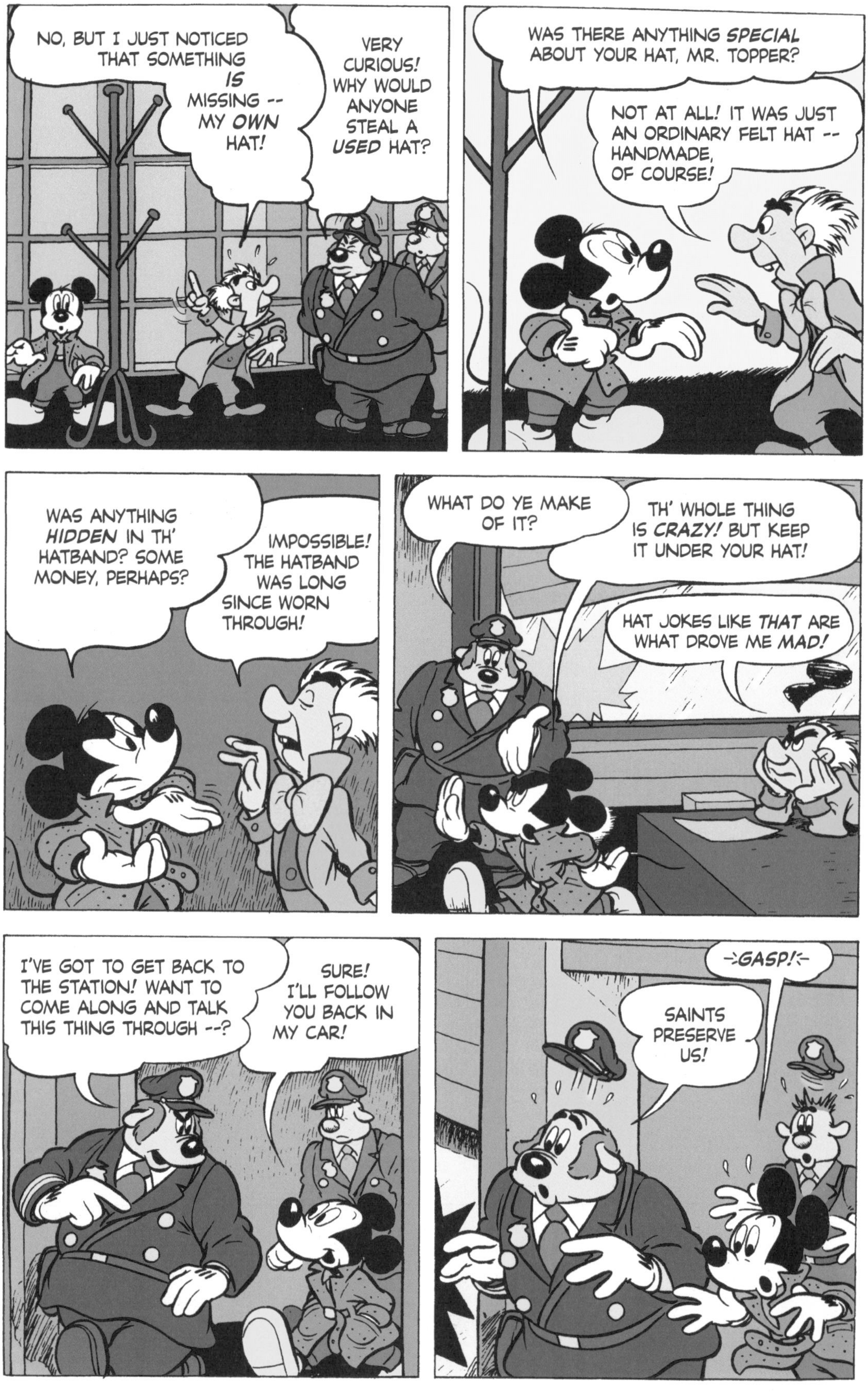
NO, BUT I JUST NOTICED THAT SOMETHING IS MISSING -- MY OWN HAT!
VERY CURIOUS! WHY WOULD ANYONE STEAL A USED HAT?
WAS THERE ANYTHING SPECIAL ABOUT YOUR HAT, MR. TOPPER?
NOT AT ALL! IT WAS JUST AN ORDINARY FELT HAT -- HANDMADE, OF COURSE!
WAS ANYTHING HIDDEN IN TH' HATBAND? SOME MONEY, PERHAPS?
IMPOSSIBLE! THE HATBAND WAS LONG SINCE WORN THROUGH!
WHAT DO YE MAKE OF IT?
TH' WHOLE THING IS CRAZY! BUT KEEP IT UNDER YOUR HAT!
HAT JOKES LIKE THAT ARE WHAT DROVE ME MAD!
I'VE GOT TO GET BACK TO THE STATION! WANT TO COME ALONG AND TALK THIS THING THROUGH --?
SURE! I'LL FOLLOW YOU BACK IN MY CAR!
-GASP!-
SAINTS PRESERVE US!

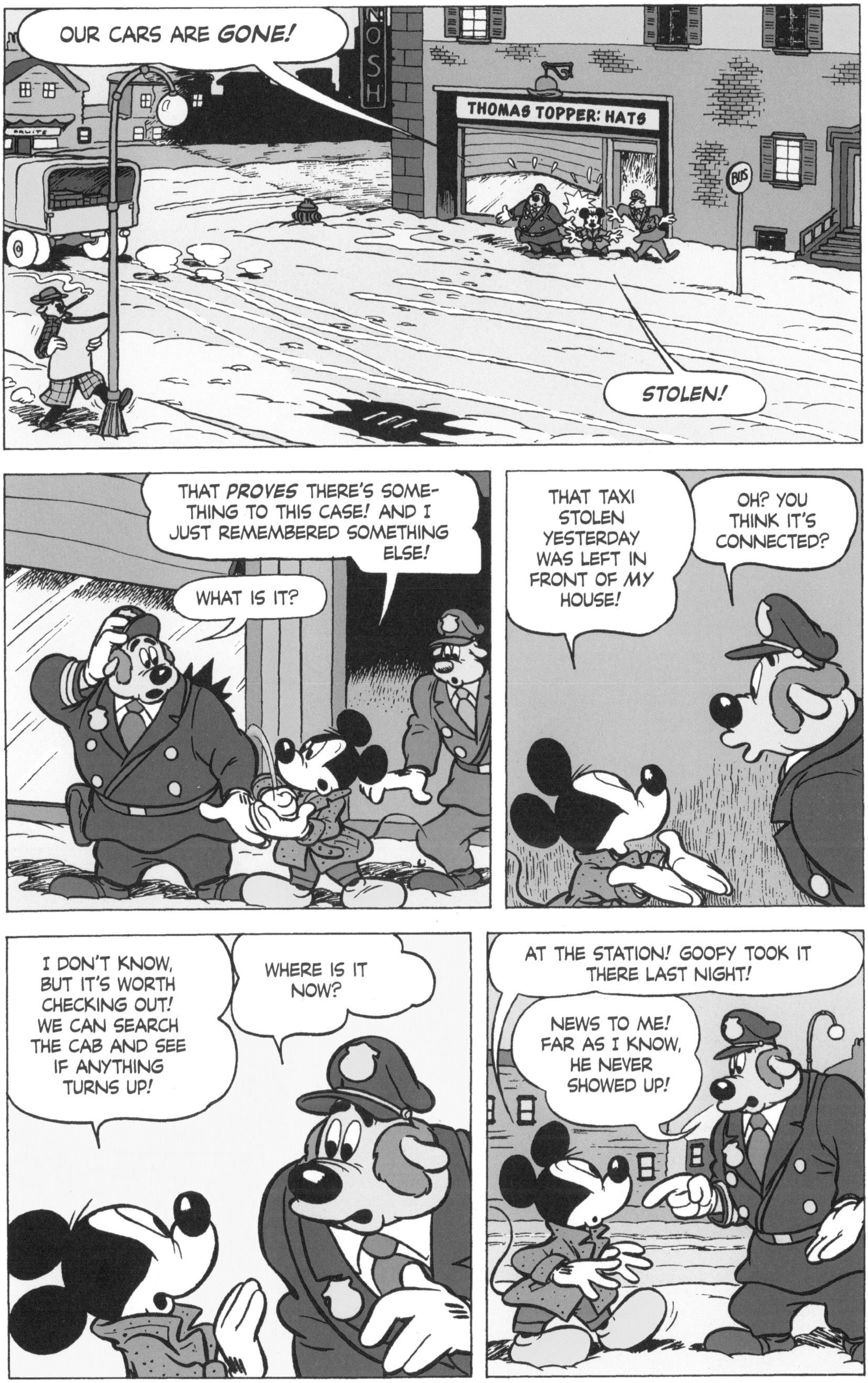
OUR CARS ARE *GONE!*
NOSH
THOMAS TOPPER: HATS
BUS
STOLEN!
THAT *PROVES* THERE'S SOMETHING TO THIS CASE! AND I JUST REMEMBERED SOMETHING ELSE!
WHAT IS IT?
THAT TAXI STOLEN YESTERDAY WAS LEFT IN FRONT OF *MY* HOUSE!
OH? YOU THINK IT'S CONNECTED?
I DON'T KNOW, BUT IT'S WORTH CHECKING OUT! WE CAN SEARCH THE CAB AND SEE IF ANYTHING TURNS UP!
WHERE IS IT NOW?
AT THE STATION! GOOFY TOOK IT THERE LAST NIGHT!
NEWS TO ME! FAR AS I KNOW, HE NEVER SHOWED UP!

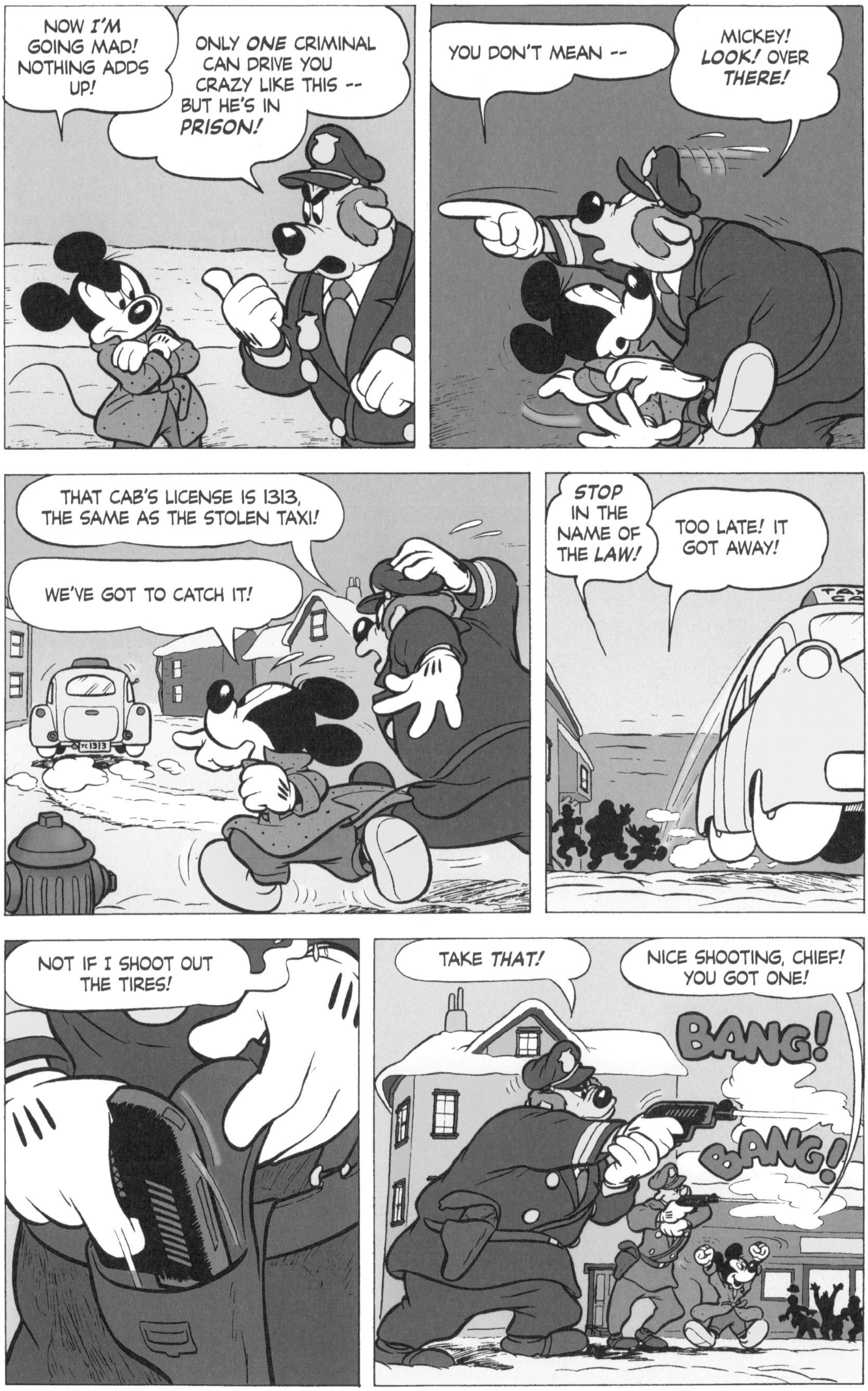
NOW I'M GOING MAD! NOTHING ADDS UP!
ONLY ONE CRIMINAL CAN DRIVE YOU CRAZY LIKE THIS -- BUT HE'S IN PRISON!
YOU DON'T MEAN --
MICKEY! LOOK! OVER THERE!
THAT CAB'S LICENSE IS 1313, THE SAME AS THE STOLEN TAXI!
WE'VE GOT TO CATCH IT!
STOP IN THE NAME OF THE LAW!
TOO LATE! IT GOT AWAY!
NOT IF I SHOOT OUT THE TIRES!
TAKE THAT!
NICE SHOOTING, CHIEF! YOU GOT ONE!
BANG!
BANG!

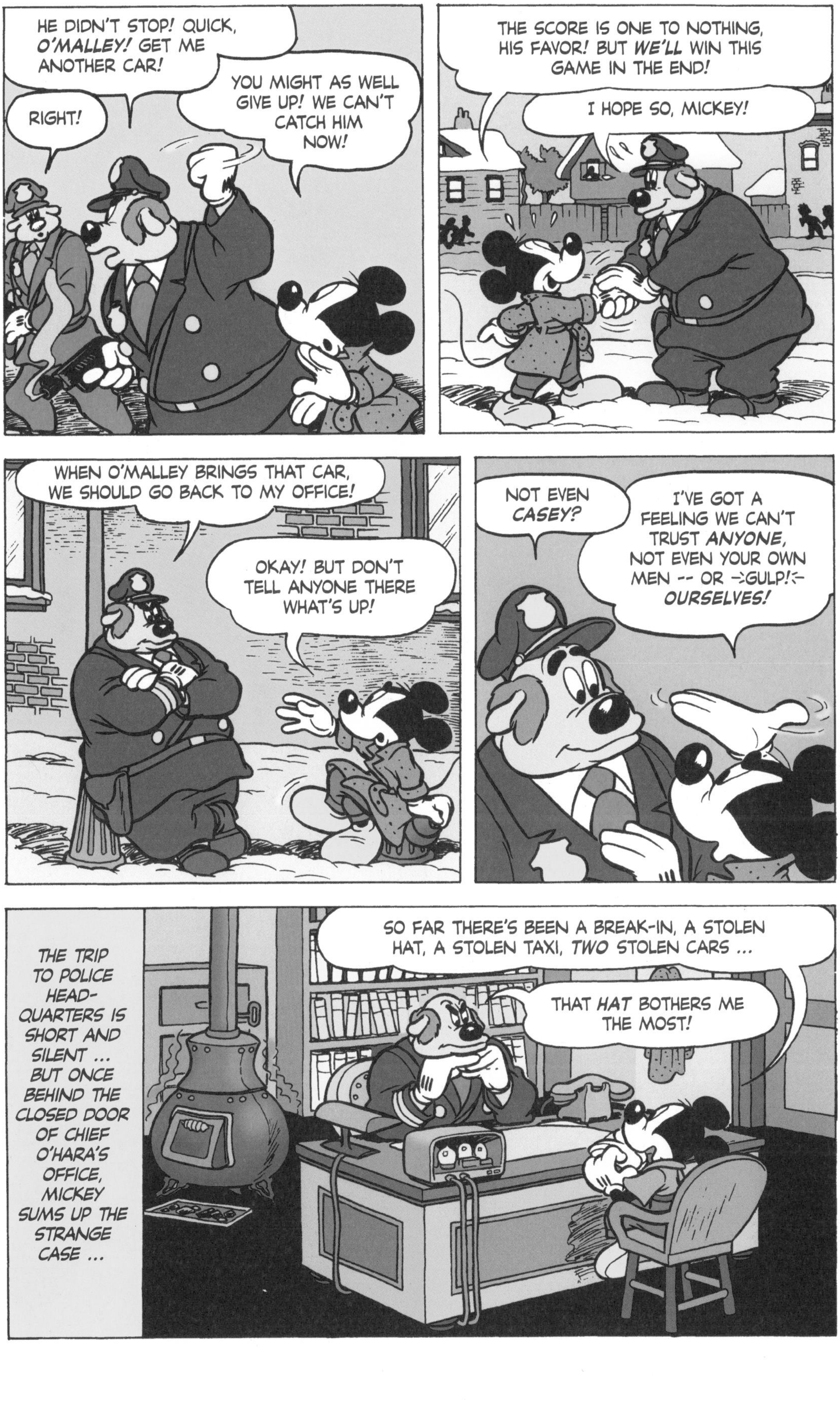

HE DIDN'T STOP! QUICK, O'MALLEY! GET ME ANOTHER CAR!
RIGHT!
YOU MIGHT AS WELL GIVE UP! WE CAN'T CATCH HIM NOW!
THE SCORE IS ONE TO NOTHING, HIS FAVOR! BUT WE'LL WIN THIS GAME IN THE END!
I HOPE SO, MICKEY!
WHEN O'MALLEY BRINGS THAT CAR, WE SHOULD GO BACK TO MY OFFICE!
OKAY! BUT DON'T TELL ANYONE THERE WHAT'S UP!
NOT EVEN CASEY?
I'VE GOT A FEELING WE CAN'T TRUST ANYONE, NOT EVEN YOUR OWN MEN -- OR -GULP!- OURSELVES!
THE TRIP TO POLICE HEAD-QUARTERS IS SHORT AND SILENT ... BUT ONCE BEHIND THE CLOSED DOOR OF CHIEF O'HARA'S OFFICE, MICKEY SUMS UP THE STRANGE CASE ...
SO FAR THERE'S BEEN A BREAK-IN, A STOLEN HAT, A STOLEN TAXI, TWO STOLEN CARS ...
THAT HAT BOTHERS ME THE MOST!

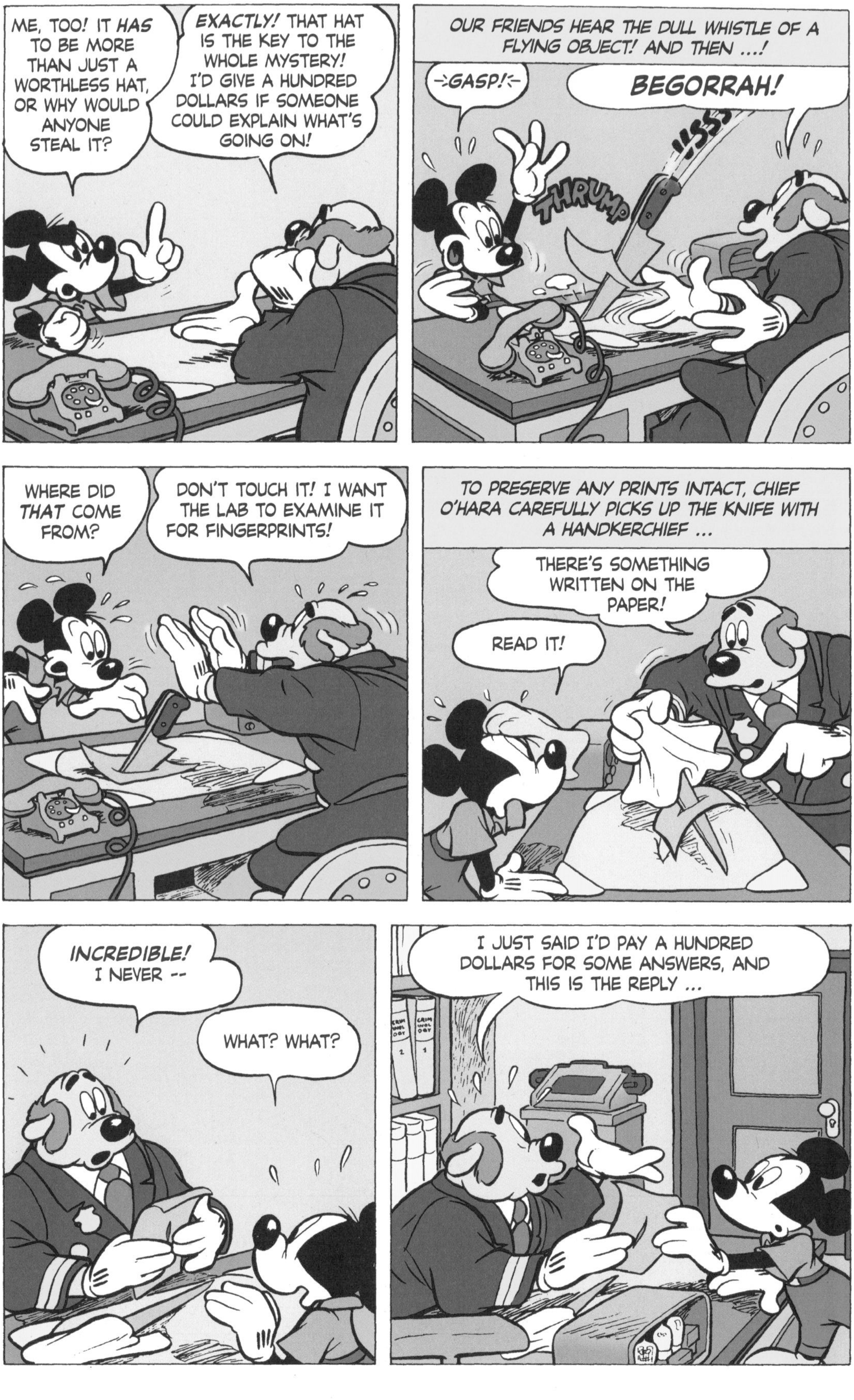

ME, TOO! IT *HAS* TO BE MORE THAN JUST A WORTHLESS HAT, OR WHY WOULD ANYONE STEAL IT?
EXACTLY! THAT HAT IS THE KEY TO THE WHOLE MYSTERY! I'D GIVE A HUNDRED DOLLARS IF SOMEONE COULD EXPLAIN WHAT'S GOING ON!
OUR FRIENDS HEAR THE DULL WHISTLE OF A FLYING OBJECT! AND THEN ...!
GASP!
BEGORRAH!
THRUMP
WHERE DID *THAT* COME FROM?
DON'T TOUCH IT! I WANT THE LAB TO EXAMINE IT FOR FINGERPRINTS!
TO PRESERVE ANY PRINTS INTACT, CHIEF O'HARA CAREFULLY PICKS UP THE KNIFE WITH A HANDKERCHIEF ...
THERE'S SOMETHING WRITTEN ON THE PAPER!
READ IT!
INCREDIBLE! I NEVER --
WHAT? WHAT?
I JUST SAID I'D PAY A HUNDRED DOLLARS FOR SOME ANSWERS, AND THIS IS THE REPLY ...

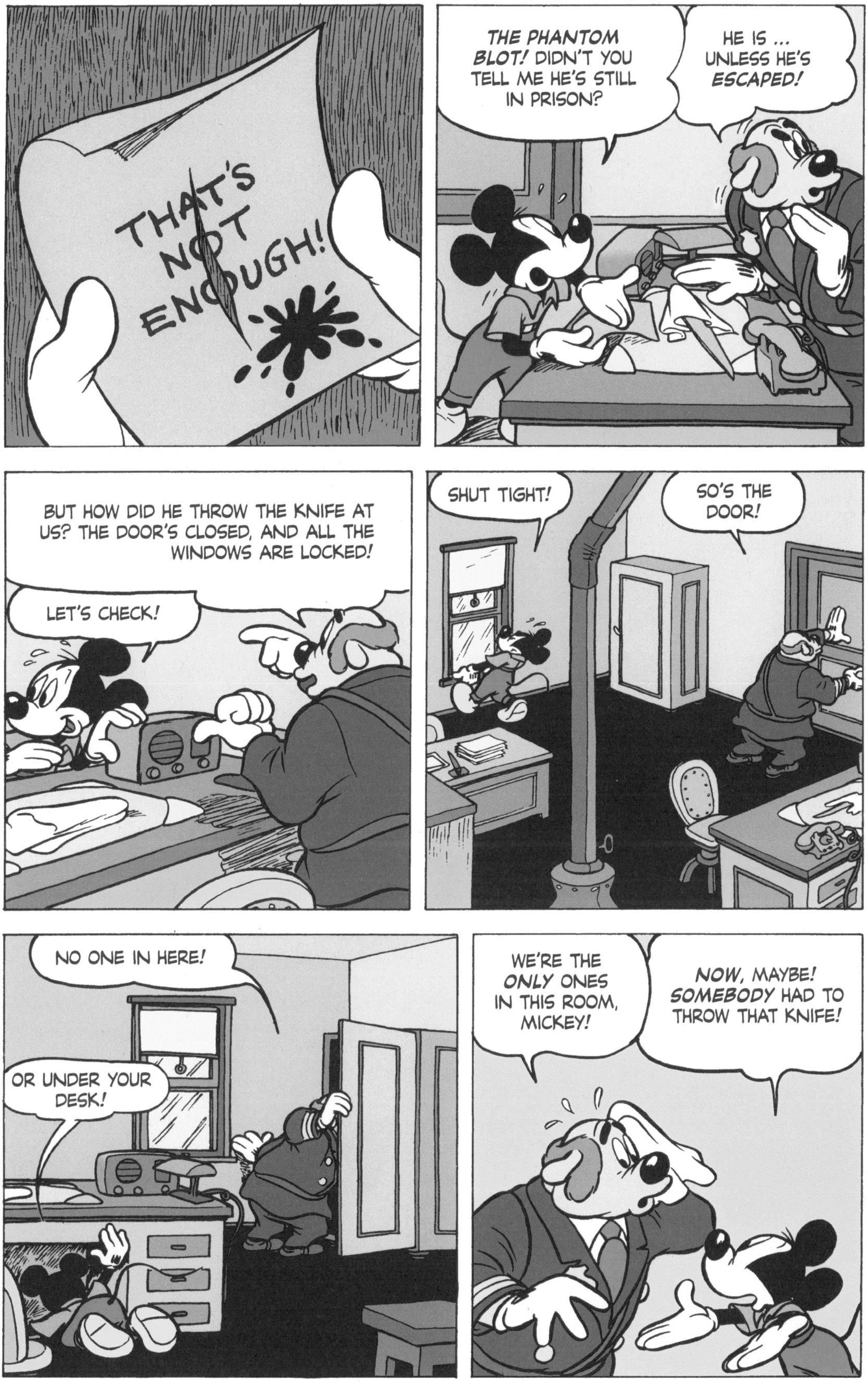
THAT'S NOT ENOUGH!
THE PHANTOM BLOT! DIDN'T YOU TELL ME HE'S STILL IN PRISON?
HE IS ... UNLESS HE'S ESCAPED!
BUT HOW DID HE THROW THE KNIFE AT US? THE DOOR'S CLOSED, AND ALL THE WINDOWS ARE LOCKED!
LET'S CHECK!
SHUT TIGHT!
SO'S THE DOOR!
NO ONE IN HERE!
OR UNDER YOUR DESK!
WE'RE THE ONLY ONES IN THIS ROOM, MICKEY!
NOW, MAYBE! SOMEBODY HAD TO THROW THAT KNIFE!

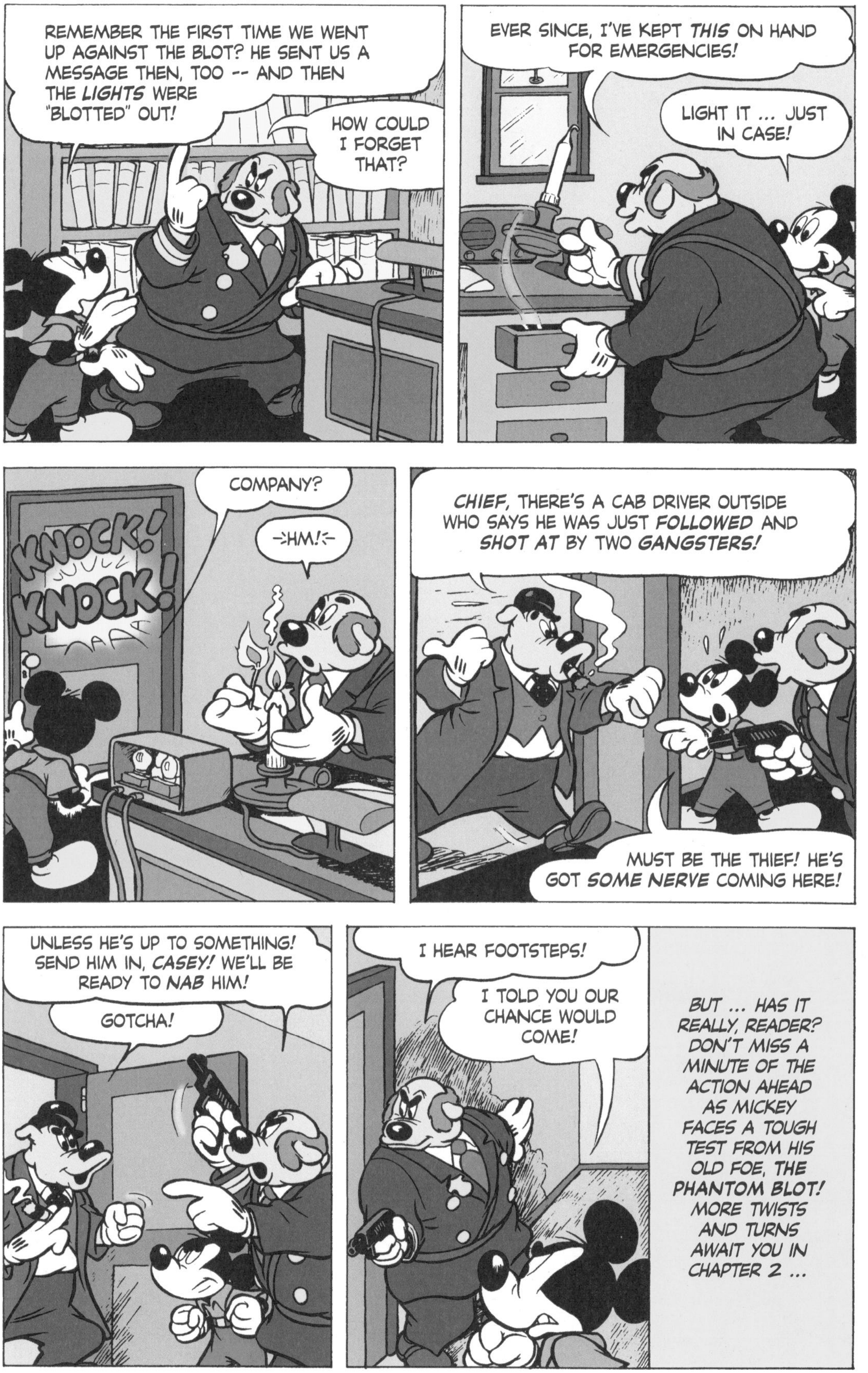
REMEMBER THE FIRST TIME WE WENT UP AGAINST THE BLOT? HE SENT US A MESSAGE THEN, TOO -- AND THEN THE LIGHTS WERE "BLOTTED" OUT!
HOW COULD I FORGET THAT?
EVER SINCE, I'VE KEPT THIS ON HAND FOR EMERGENCIES!
LIGHT IT ... JUST IN CASE!
KNOCK! KNOCK!
COMPANY?
HM!
CHIEF, THERE'S A CAB DRIVER OUTSIDE WHO SAYS HE WAS JUST FOLLOWED AND SHOT AT BY TWO GANGSTERS!
MUST BE THE THIEF! HE'S GOT SOME NERVE COMING HERE!
UNLESS HE'S UP TO SOMETHING! SEND HIM IN, CASEY! WE'LL BE READY TO NAB HIM!
GOTCHA!
I HEAR FOOTSTEPS!
I TOLD YOU OUR CHANCE WOULD COME!
BUT ... HAS IT REALLY, READER? DON'T MISS A MINUTE OF THE ACTION AHEAD AS MICKEY FACES A TOUGH TEST FROM HIS OLD FOE, THE PHANTOM BLOT! MORE TWISTS AND TURNS AWAIT YOU IN CHAPTER 2 ...

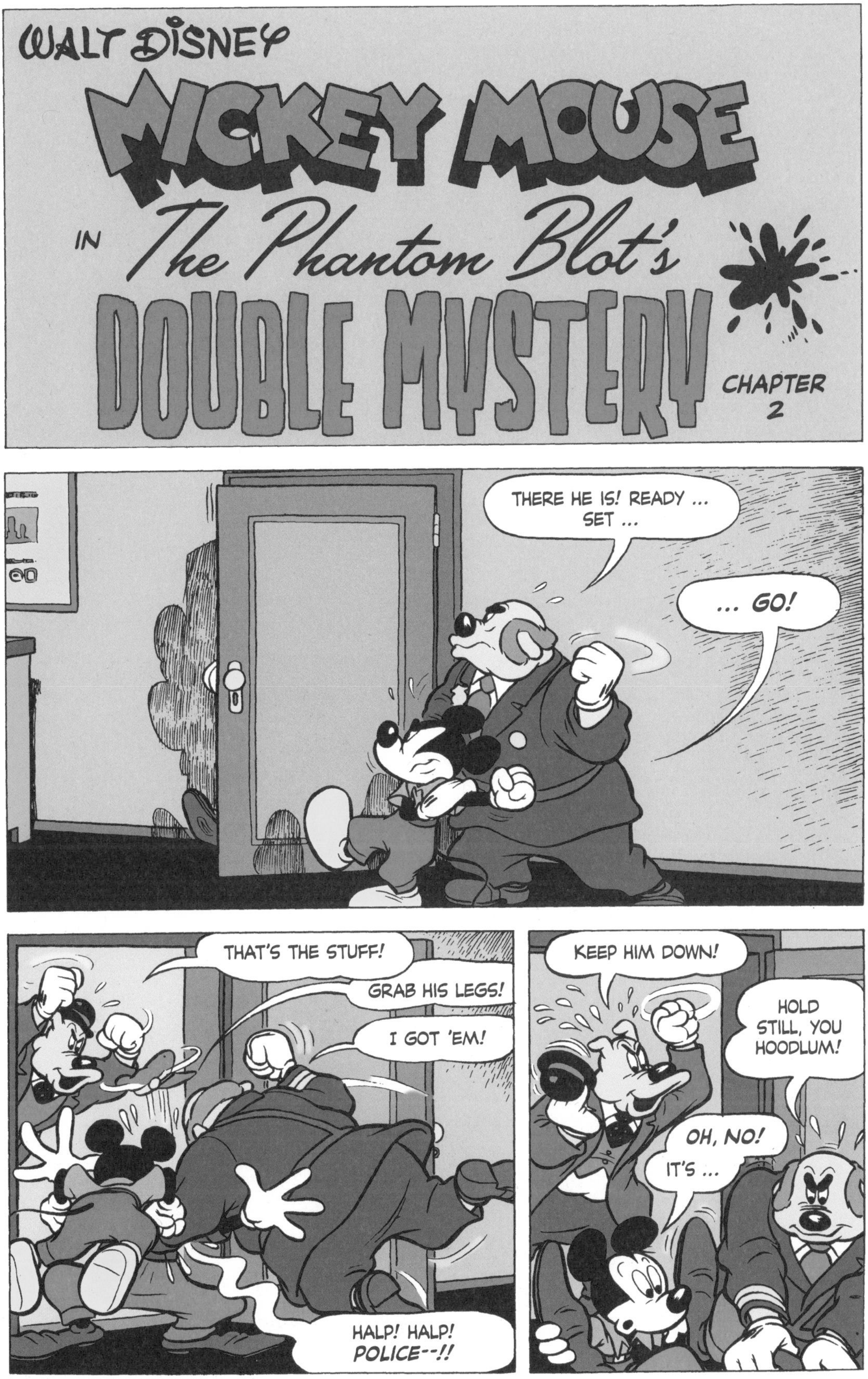
WALT DISNEY
MICKEY MOUSE
IN The Phantom Blot's
DOUBLE MYSTERY
CHAPTER 2
THERE HE IS! READY ... SET ...
... GO!
THAT'S THE STUFF!
GRAB HIS LEGS!
I GOT 'EM!
HALP! HALP! POLICE--!!
KEEP HIM DOWN!
HOLD STILL, YOU HOODLUM!
OH, NO!
IT'S ...

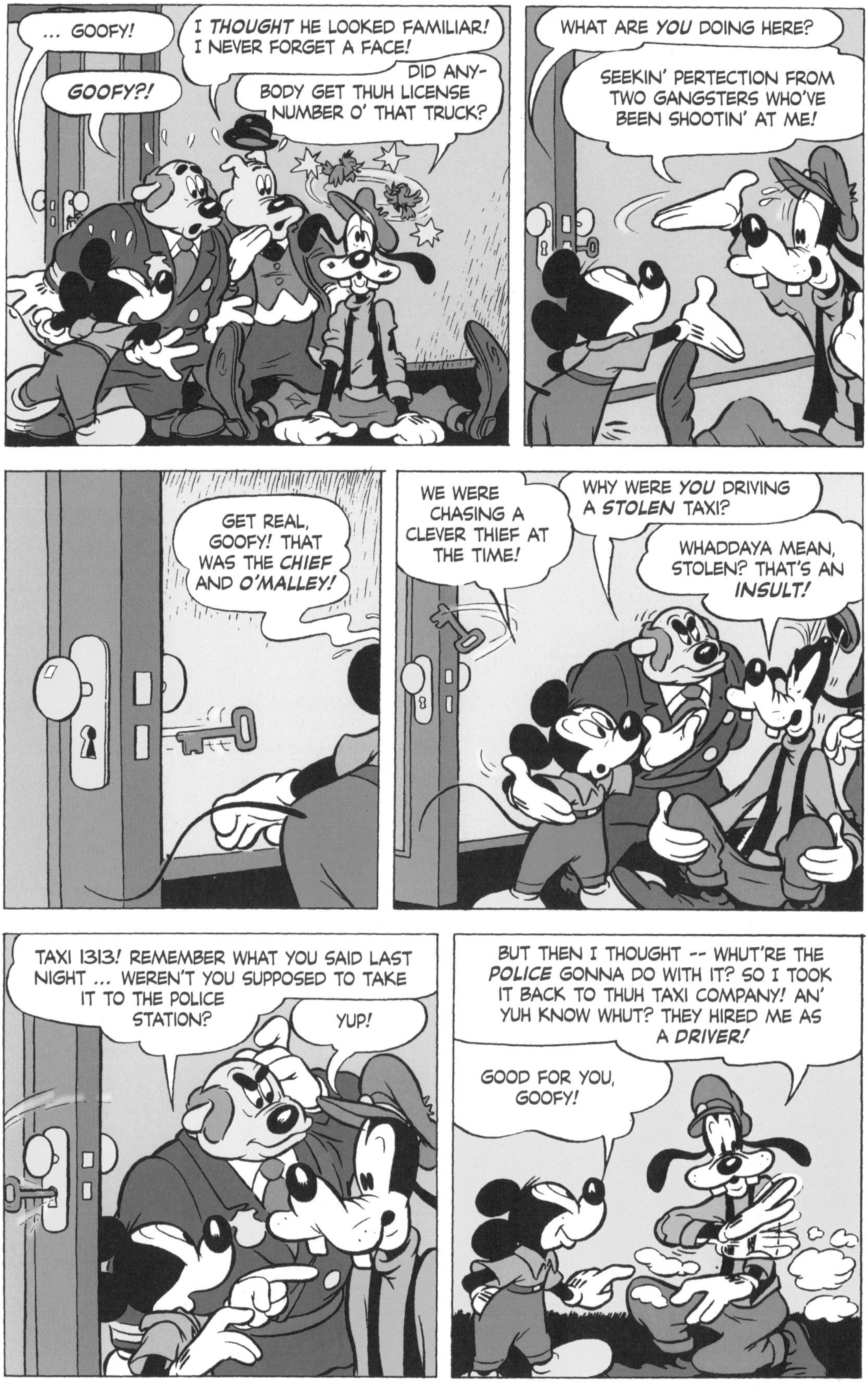
... GOOFY!
GOOFY?!
I THOUGHT HE LOOKED FAMILIAR! I NEVER FORGET A FACE!
DID ANYBODY GET THUH LICENSE NUMBER O' THAT TRUCK?
WHAT ARE YOU DOING HERE?
SEEKIN' PERTECTION FROM TWO GANGSTERS WHO'VE BEEN SHOOTIN' AT ME!
GET REAL, GOOFY! THAT WAS THE CHIEF AND O'MALLEY!
WE WERE CHASING A CLEVER THIEF AT THE TIME!
WHY WERE YOU DRIVING A STOLEN TAXI?
WHADDAYA MEAN, STOLEN? THAT'S AN INSULT!
TAXI 1313! REMEMBER WHAT YOU SAID LAST NIGHT ... WEREN'T YOU SUPPOSED TO TAKE IT TO THE POLICE STATION?
YUP!
BUT THEN I THOUGHT -- WHUT'RE THE POLICE GONNA DO WITH IT? SO I TOOK IT BACK TO THUH TAXI COMPANY! AN' YUH KNOW WHUT? THEY HIRED ME AS A DRIVER!
GOOD FOR YOU, GOOFY!

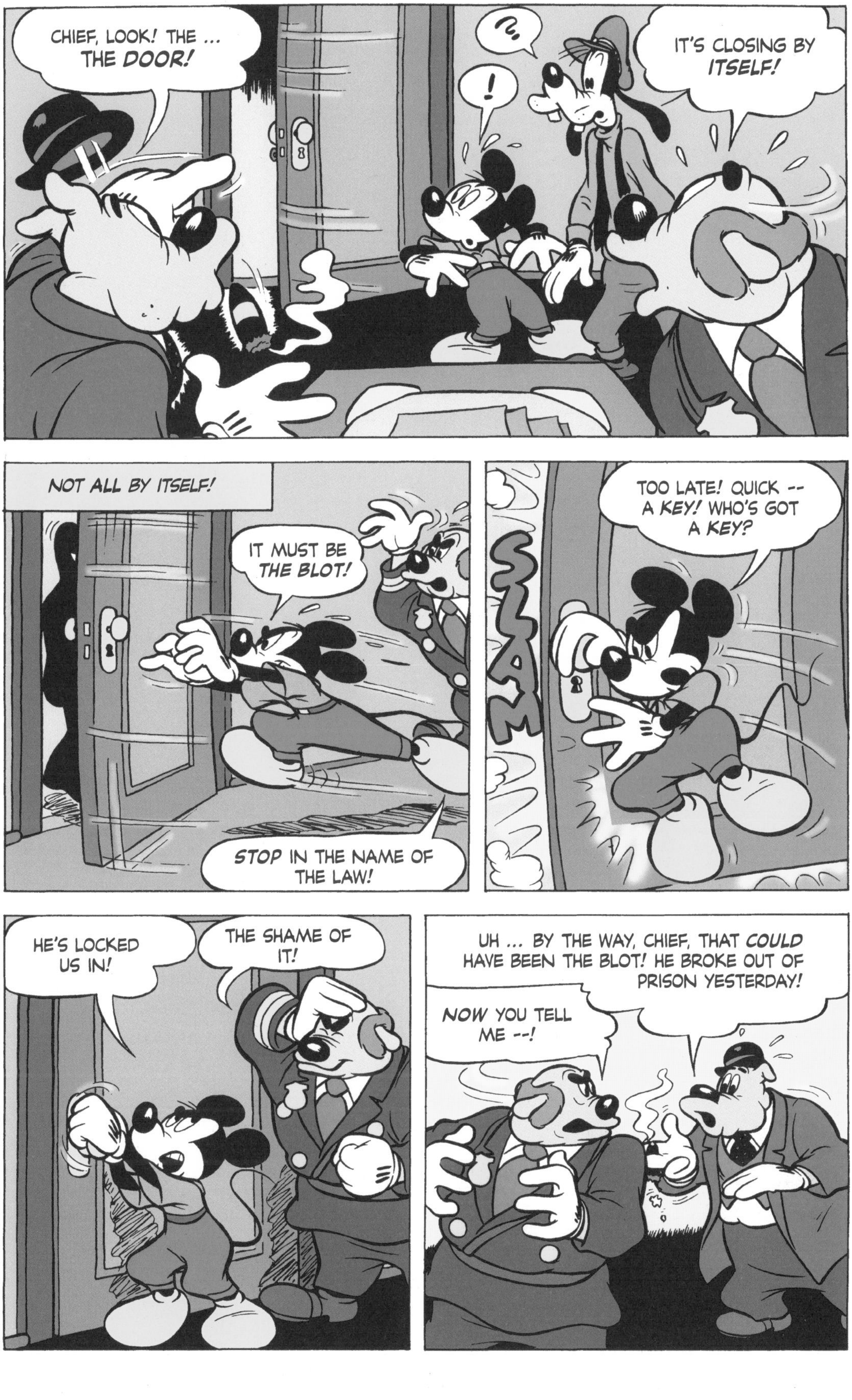

CHIEF, LOOK! THE ... THE DOOR!
?
!
IT'S CLOSING BY ITSELF!
NOT ALL BY ITSELF!
IT MUST BE THE BLOT!
STOP IN THE NAME OF THE LAW!
SLAM
TOO LATE! QUICK -- A KEY! WHO'S GOT A KEY?
HE'S LOCKED US IN!
THE SHAME OF IT!
UH ... BY THE WAY, CHIEF, THAT COULD HAVE BEEN THE BLOT! HE BROKE OUT OF PRISON YESTERDAY!
NOW YOU TELL ME --!

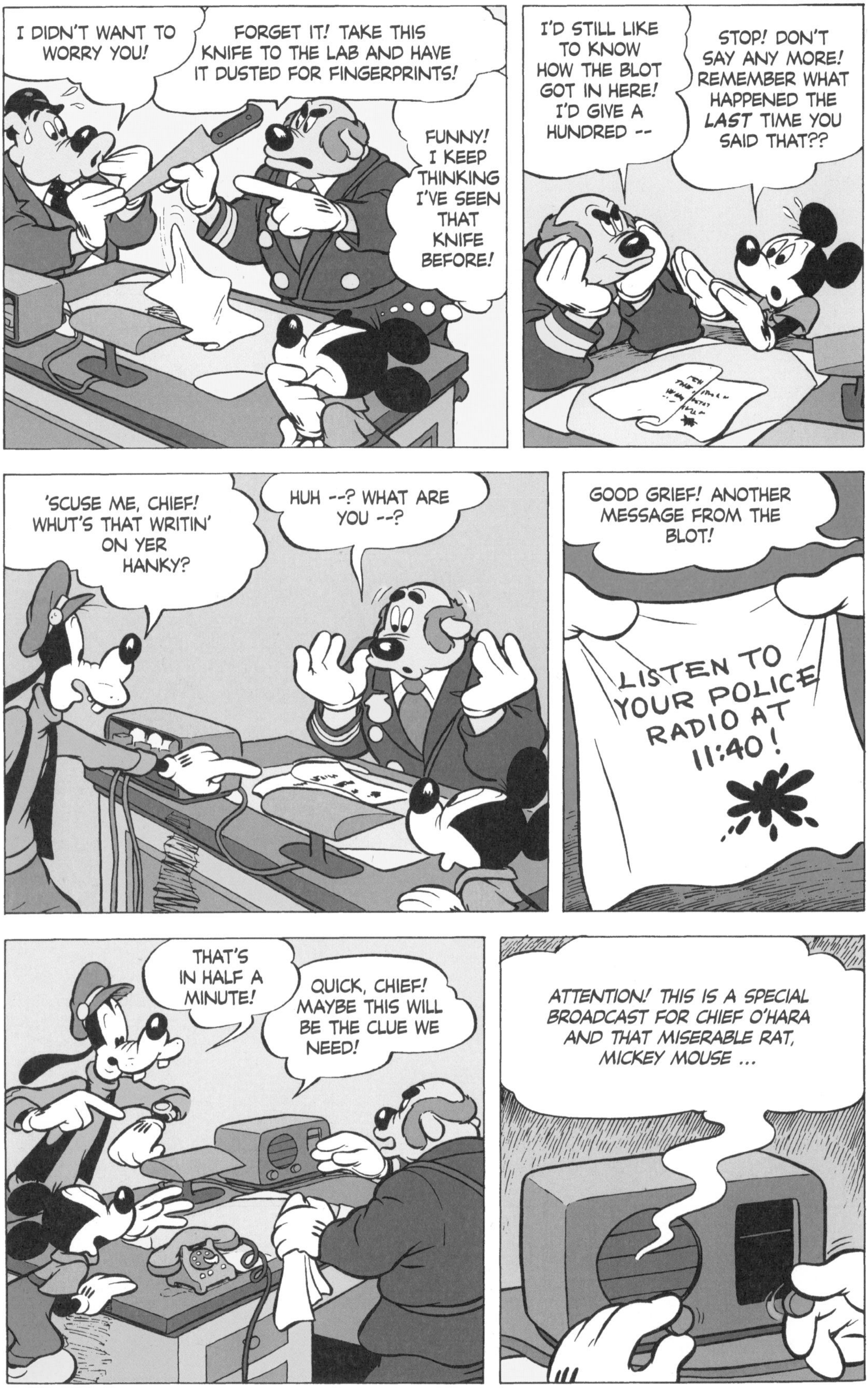
I DIDN'T WANT TO WORRY YOU!
FORGET IT! TAKE THIS KNIFE TO THE LAB AND HAVE IT DUSTED FOR FINGERPRINTS!
FUNNY! I KEEP THINKING I'VE SEEN THAT KNIFE BEFORE!
I'D STILL LIKE TO KNOW HOW THE BLOT GOT IN HERE! I'D GIVE A HUNDRED --
STOP! DON'T SAY ANY MORE! REMEMBER WHAT HAPPENED THE LAST TIME YOU SAID THAT??
'SCUSE ME, CHIEF! WHUT'S THAT WRITIN' ON YER HANKY?
HUH --? WHAT ARE YOU --?
GOOD GRIEF! ANOTHER MESSAGE FROM THE BLOT!
LISTEN TO YOUR POLICE RADIO AT 11:40!
THAT'S IN HALF A MINUTE!
QUICK, CHIEF! MAYBE THIS WILL BE THE CLUE WE NEED!
ATTENTION! THIS IS A SPECIAL BROADCAST FOR CHIEF O'HARA AND THAT MISERABLE RAT, MICKEY MOUSE ...

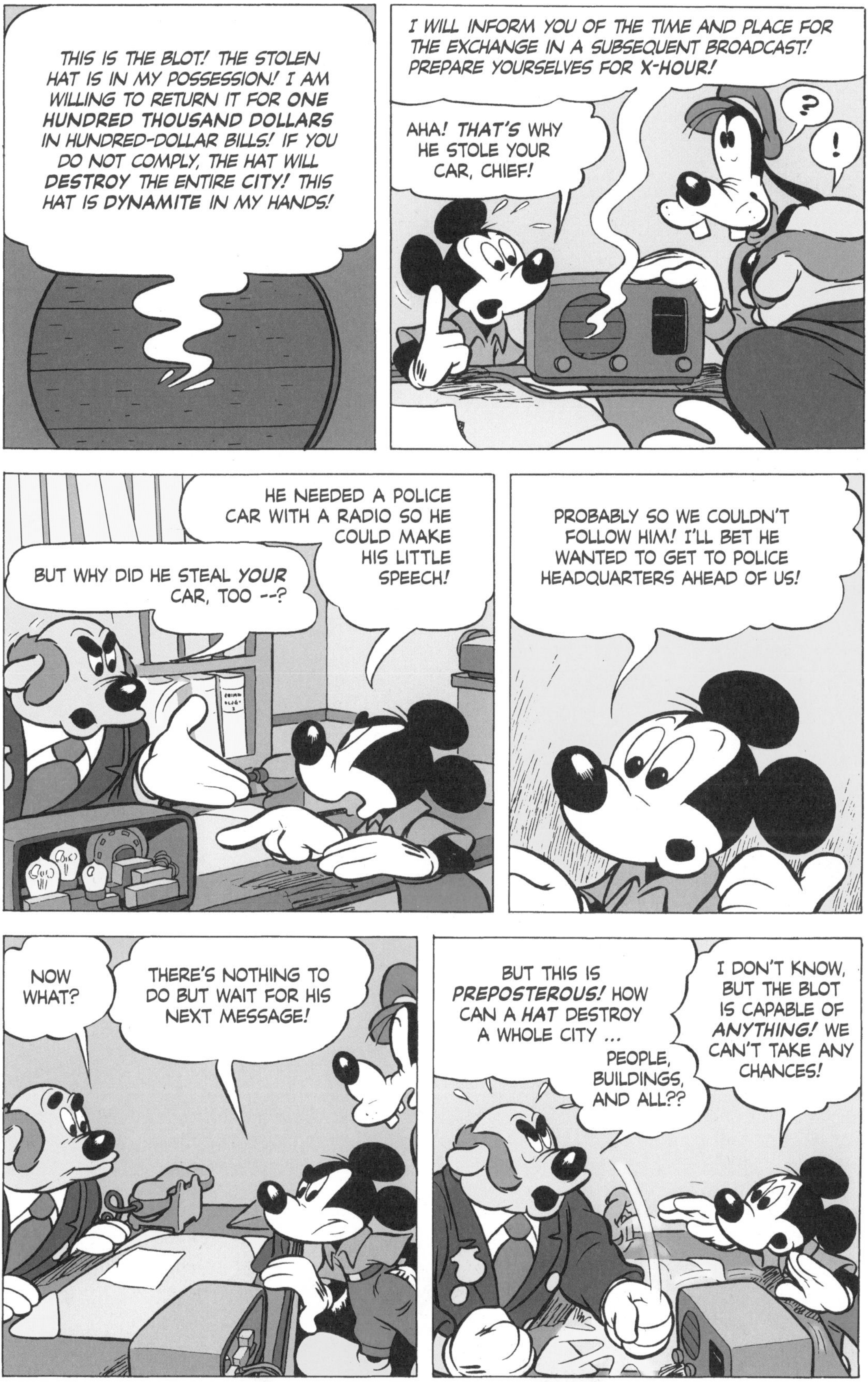
THIS IS THE BLOT! THE STOLEN HAT IS IN MY POSSESSION! I AM WILLING TO RETURN IT FOR ONE HUNDRED THOUSAND DOLLARS IN HUNDRED-DOLLAR BILLS! IF YOU DO NOT COMPLY, THE HAT WILL DESTROY THE ENTIRE CITY! THIS HAT IS DYNAMITE IN MY HANDS!
I WILL INFORM YOU OF THE TIME AND PLACE FOR THE EXCHANGE IN A SUBSEQUENT BROADCAST! PREPARE YOURSELVES FOR X-HOUR!
AHA! THAT'S WHY HE STOLE YOUR CAR, CHIEF!
?
!
BUT WHY DID HE STEAL YOUR CAR, TOO --?
HE NEEDED A POLICE CAR WITH A RADIO SO HE COULD MAKE HIS LITTLE SPEECH!
PROBABLY SO WE COULDN'T FOLLOW HIM! I'LL BET HE WANTED TO GET TO POLICE HEADQUARTERS AHEAD OF US!
NOW WHAT?
THERE'S NOTHING TO DO BUT WAIT FOR HIS NEXT MESSAGE!
BUT THIS IS PREPOSTEROUS! HOW CAN A HAT DESTROY A WHOLE CITY ...
PEOPLE, BUILDINGS, AND ALL??
I DON'T KNOW, BUT THE BLOT IS CAPABLE OF ANYTHING! WE CAN'T TAKE ANY CHANCES!

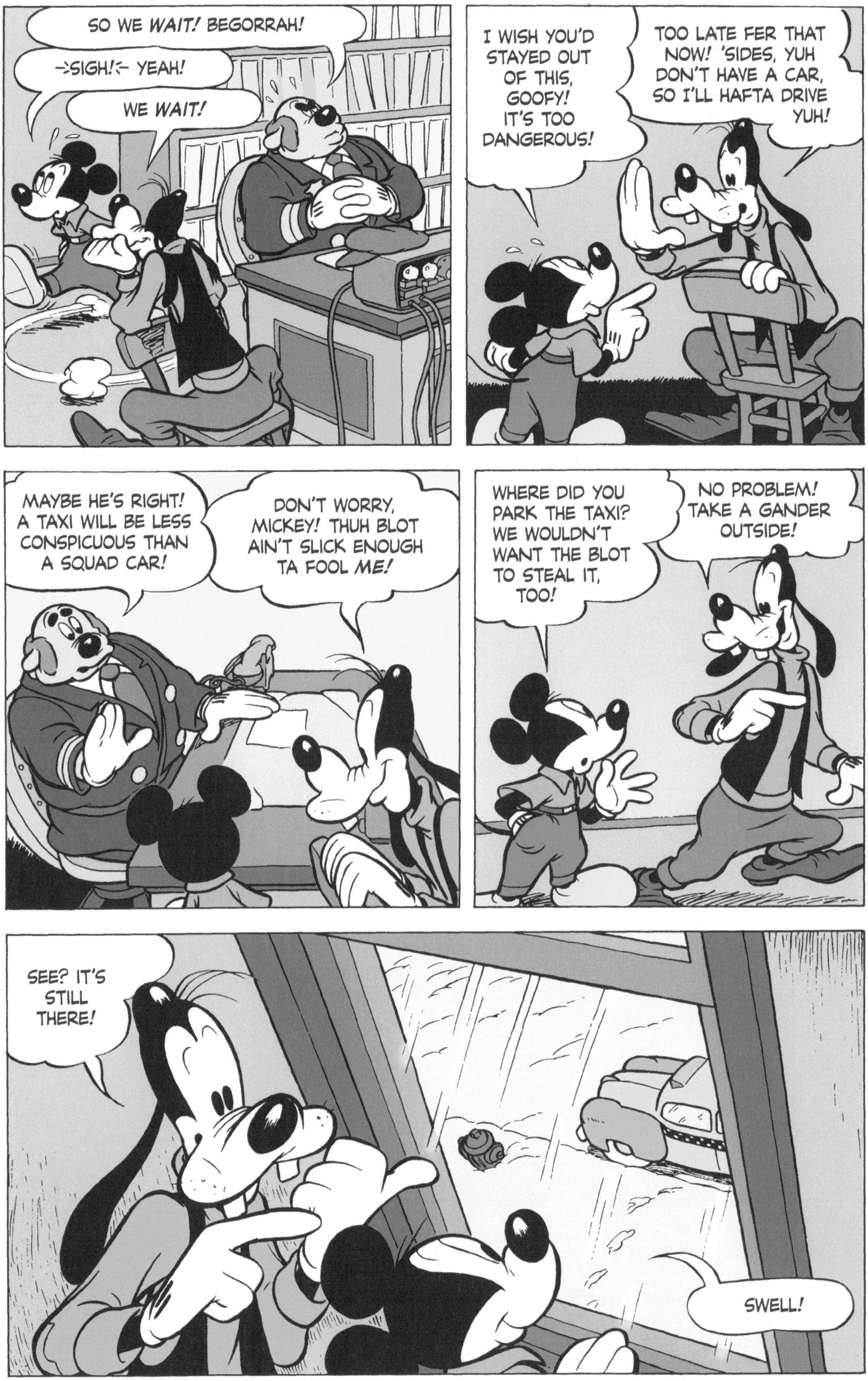
SO WE WAIT! BEGORRAH!
-SIGH!- YEAH!
WE WAIT!
I WISH YOU'D STAYED OUT OF THIS, GOOFY! IT'S TOO DANGEROUS!
TOO LATE FER THAT NOW! 'SIDES, YUH DON'T HAVE A CAR, SO I'LL HAFTA DRIVE YUH!
MAYBE HE'S RIGHT! A TAXI WILL BE LESS CONSPICUOUS THAN A SQUAD CAR!
DON'T WORRY, MICKEY! THUH BLOT AIN'T SLICK ENOUGH TA FOOL ME!
WHERE DID YOU PARK THE TAXI? WE WOULDN'T WANT THE BLOT TO STEAL IT, TOO!
NO PROBLEM! TAKE A GANDER OUTSIDE!
SEE? IT'S STILL THERE!
SWELL!

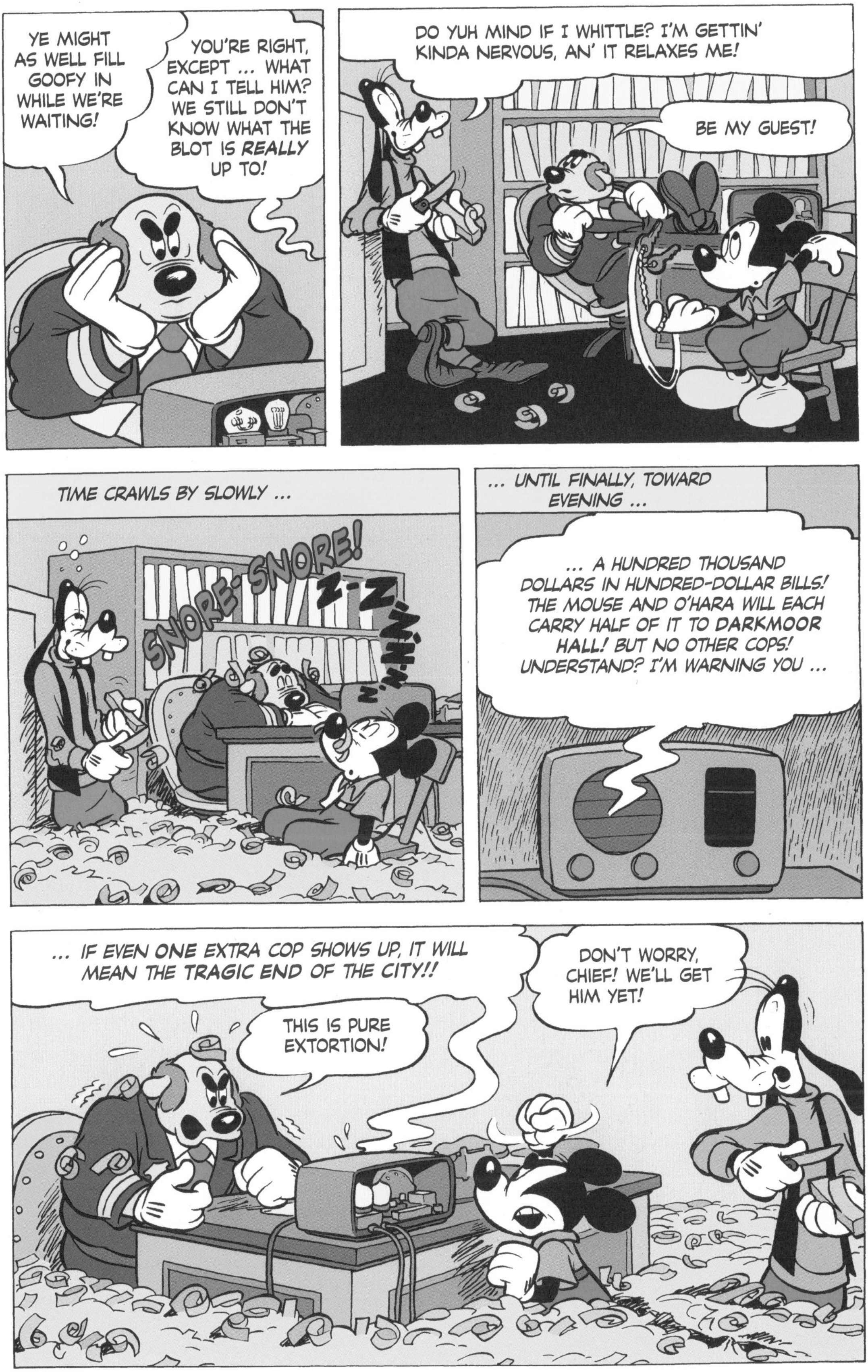
YE MIGHT AS WELL FILL GOOFY IN WHILE WE'RE WAITING!
YOU'RE RIGHT, EXCEPT ... WHAT CAN I TELL HIM? WE STILL DON'T KNOW WHAT THE BLOT IS REALLY UP TO!
DO YUH MIND IF I WHITTLE? I'M GETTIN' KINDA NERVOUS, AN' IT RELAXES ME!
BE MY GUEST!
TIME CRAWLS BY SLOWLY ...
SNORE-SNORE!
Z-Z
... UNTIL FINALLY, TOWARD EVENING ...
... A HUNDRED THOUSAND DOLLARS IN HUNDRED-DOLLAR BILLS! THE MOUSE AND O'HARA WILL EACH CARRY HALF OF IT TO DARKMOOR HALL! BUT NO OTHER COPS! UNDERSTAND? I'M WARNING YOU ...
... IF EVEN ONE EXTRA COP SHOWS UP, IT WILL MEAN THE TRAGIC END OF THE CITY!!
THIS IS PURE EXTORTION!
DON'T WORRY, CHIEF! WE'LL GET HIM YET!

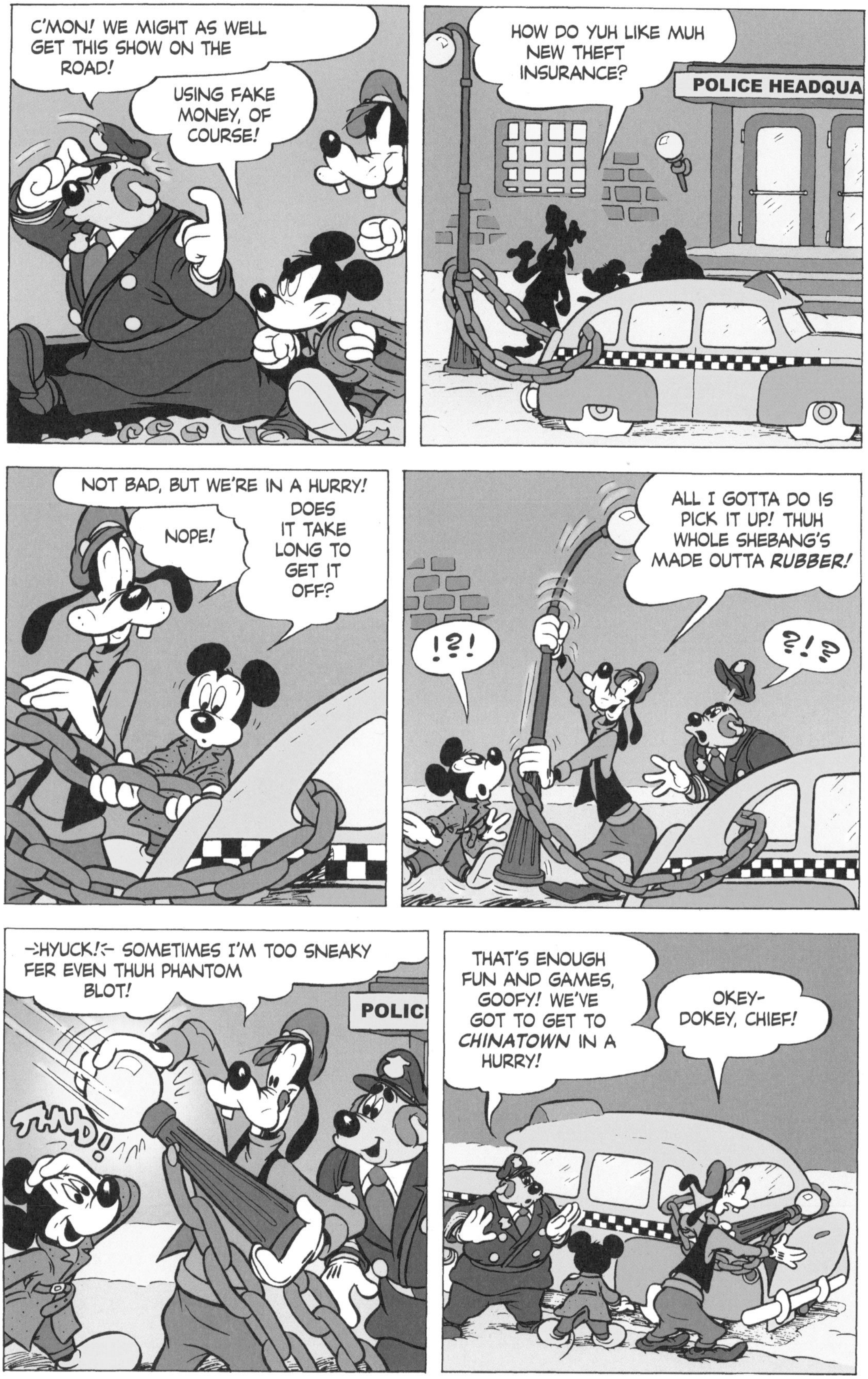

C'MON! WE MIGHT AS WELL GET THIS SHOW ON THE ROAD!
USING FAKE MONEY, OF COURSE!
HOW DO YUH LIKE MUH NEW THEFT INSURANCE?
POLICE HEADQUA
NOT BAD, BUT WE'RE IN A HURRY! DOES IT TAKE LONG TO GET IT OFF?
NOPE!
ALL I GOTTA DO IS PICK IT UP! THUH WHOLE SHEBANG'S MADE OUTTA *RUBBER!*
!?!
?!?
–HYUCK!– SOMETIMES I'M TOO SNEAKY FER EVEN THUH PHANTOM BLOT!
POLIC
THUD!
THAT'S ENOUGH FUN AND GAMES, GOOFY! WE'VE GOT TO GET TO *CHINATOWN* IN A HURRY!
OKEY-DOKEY, CHIEF!

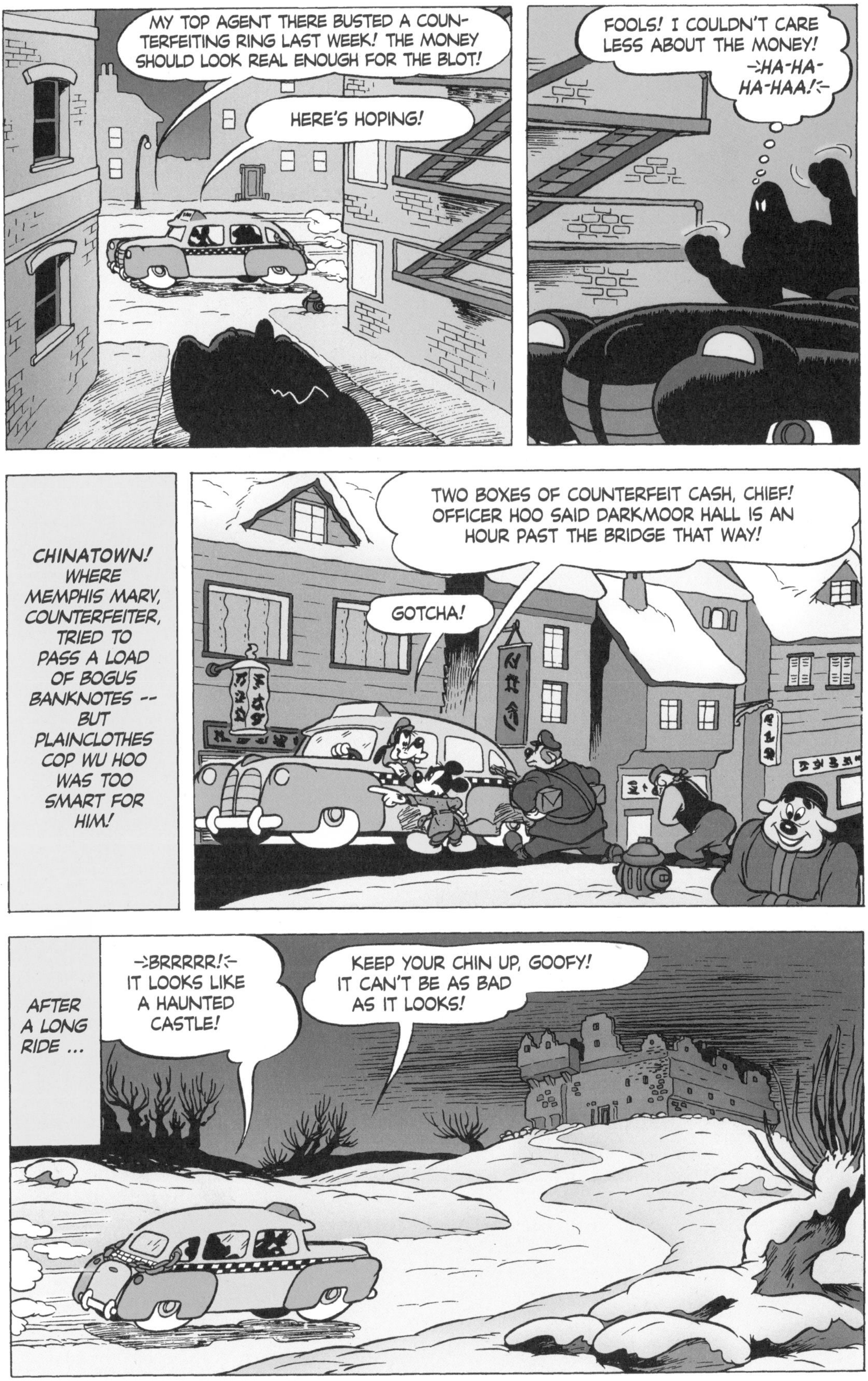

MY TOP AGENT THERE BUSTED A COUNTERFEITING RING LAST WEEK! THE MONEY SHOULD LOOK REAL ENOUGH FOR THE BLOT!
HERE'S HOPING!
FOOLS! I COULDN'T CARE LESS ABOUT THE MONEY!
-HA-HA-HA-HAA!-
CHINATOWN! WHERE MEMPHIS MARY, COUNTERFEITER, TRIED TO PASS A LOAD OF BOGUS BANKNOTES -- BUT PLAINCLOTHES COP WU HOO WAS TOO SMART FOR HIM!
TWO BOXES OF COUNTERFEIT CASH, CHIEF! OFFICER HOO SAID DARKMOOR HALL IS AN HOUR PAST THE BRIDGE THAT WAY!
GOTCHA!
AFTER A LONG RIDE ...
-BRRRRR!- IT LOOKS LIKE A HAUNTED CASTLE!
KEEP YOUR CHIN UP, GOOFY! IT CAN'T BE AS BAD AS IT LOOKS!

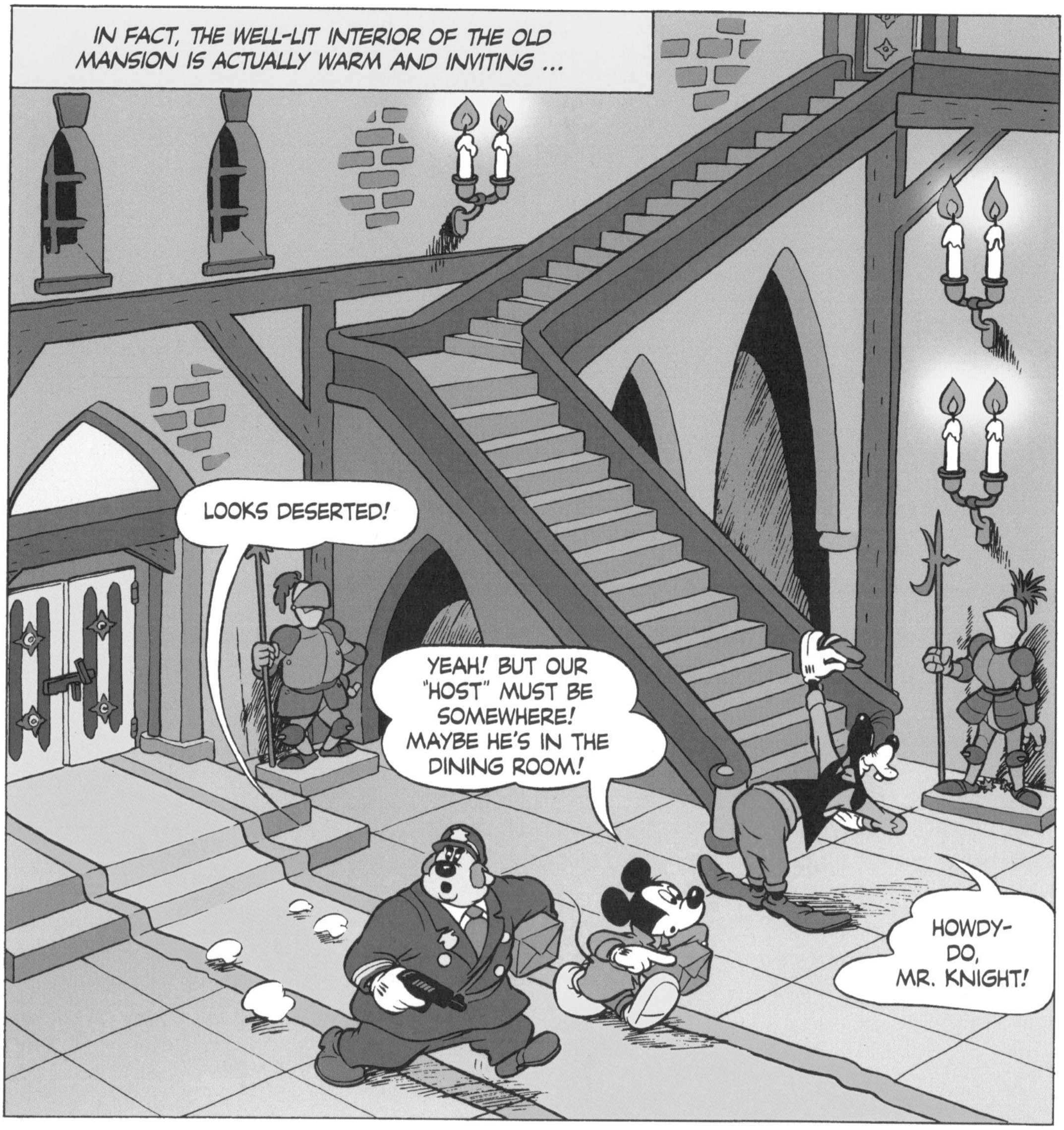
IN FACT, THE WELL-LIT INTERIOR OF THE OLD MANSION IS ACTUALLY WARM AND INVITING ...
LOOKS DESERTED!
YEAH! BUT OUR "HOST" MUST BE SOMEWHERE! MAYBE HE'S IN THE DINING ROOM!
HOWDY-DO, MR. KNIGHT!

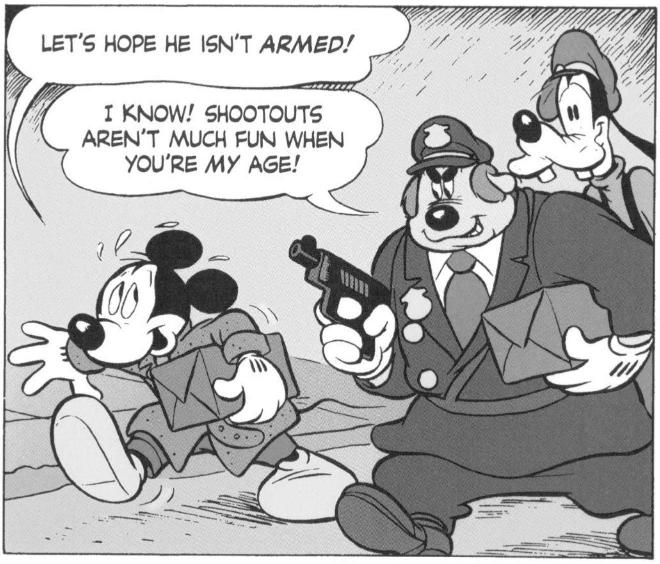
LET'S HOPE HE ISN'T *ARMED!*
I KNOW! SHOOTOUTS AREN'T MUCH FUN WHEN YOU'RE *MY* AGE!

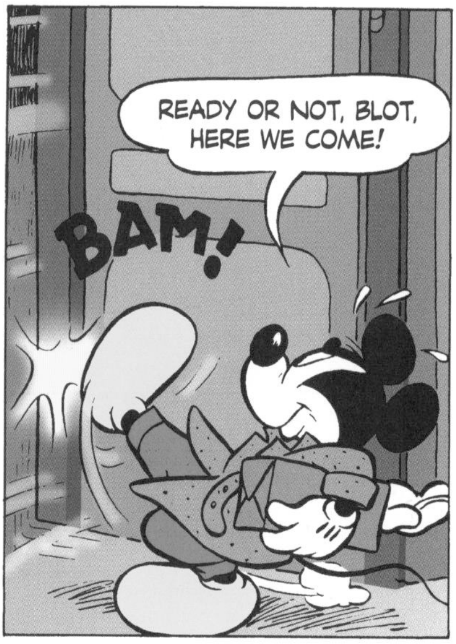
READY OR NOT, BLOT, HERE WE COME!
BAM!

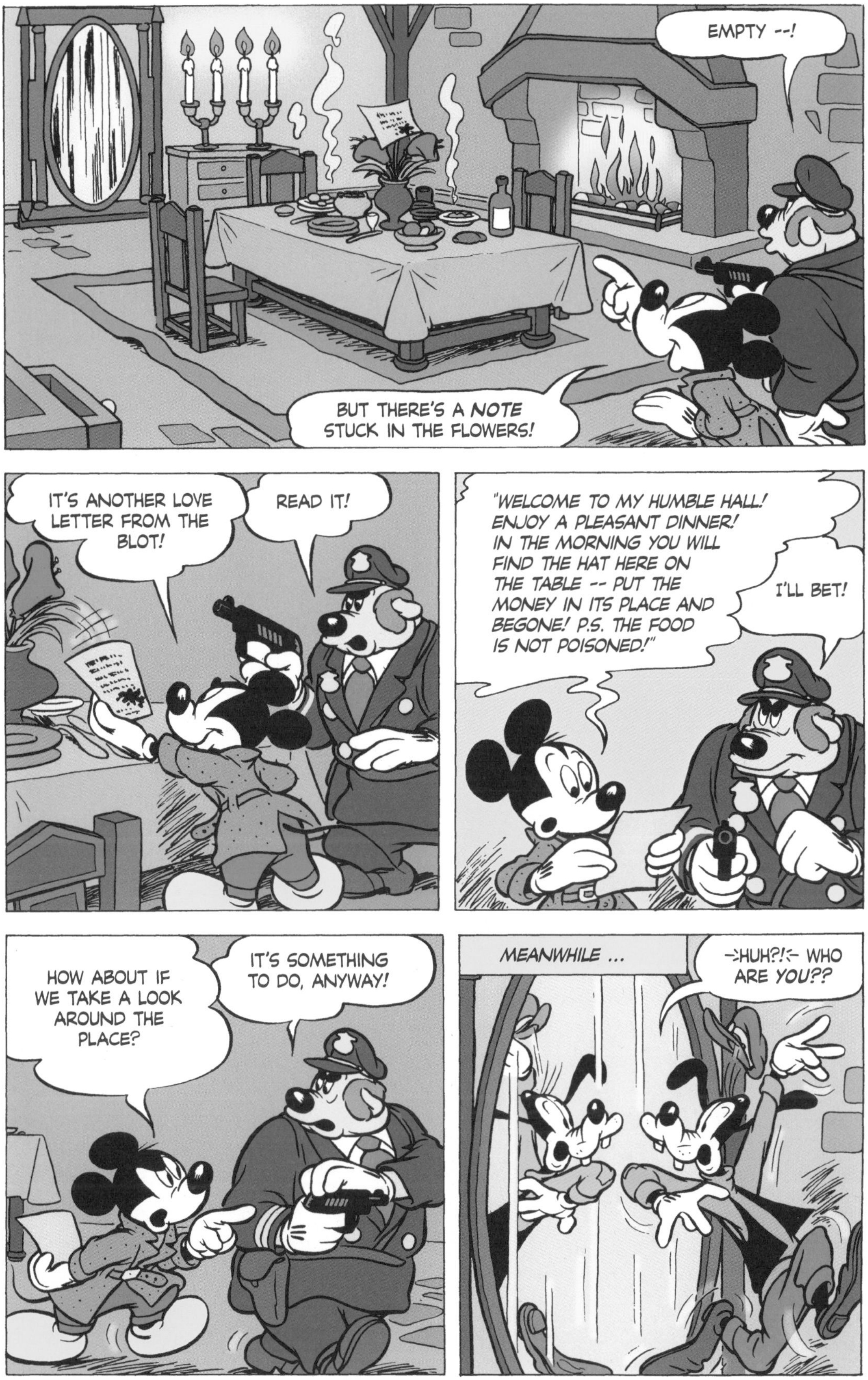
EMPTY --!
BUT THERE'S A *NOTE* STUCK IN THE FLOWERS!
IT'S ANOTHER LOVE LETTER FROM THE BLOT!
READ IT!
"WELCOME TO MY HUMBLE HALL! ENJOY A PLEASANT DINNER! IN THE MORNING YOU WILL FIND THE HAT HERE ON THE TABLE -- PUT THE MONEY IN ITS PLACE AND BEGONE! P.S. THE FOOD IS NOT POISONED!"
I'LL BET!
HOW ABOUT IF WE TAKE A LOOK AROUND THE PLACE?
IT'S SOMETHING TO DO, ANYWAY!
MEANWHILE ...
-HUH?!- WHO ARE *YOU*??

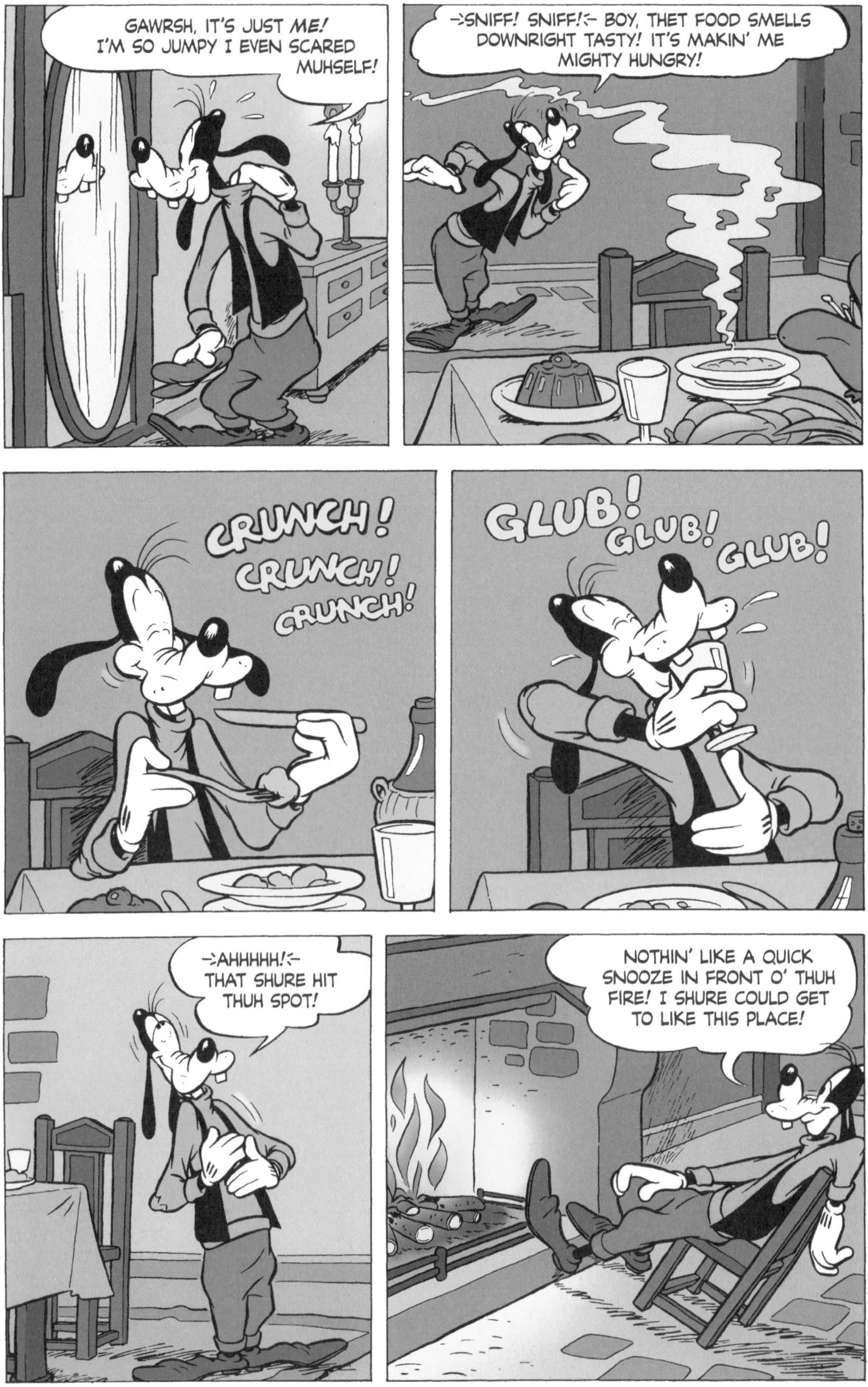
GAWRSH, IT'S JUST *ME!* I'M SO JUMPY I EVEN SCARED MUHSELF!
-SNIFF! SNIFF!- BOY, THET FOOD SMELLS DOWNRIGHT TASTY! IT'S MAKIN' ME MIGHTY HUNGRY!
CRUNCH! CRUNCH! CRUNCH!
GLUB! GLUB! GLUB!
-AHHHHH!- THAT SHURE HIT THUH SPOT!
NOTHIN' LIKE A QUICK SNOOZE IN FRONT O' THUH FIRE! I SHURE COULD GET TO LIKE THIS PLACE!

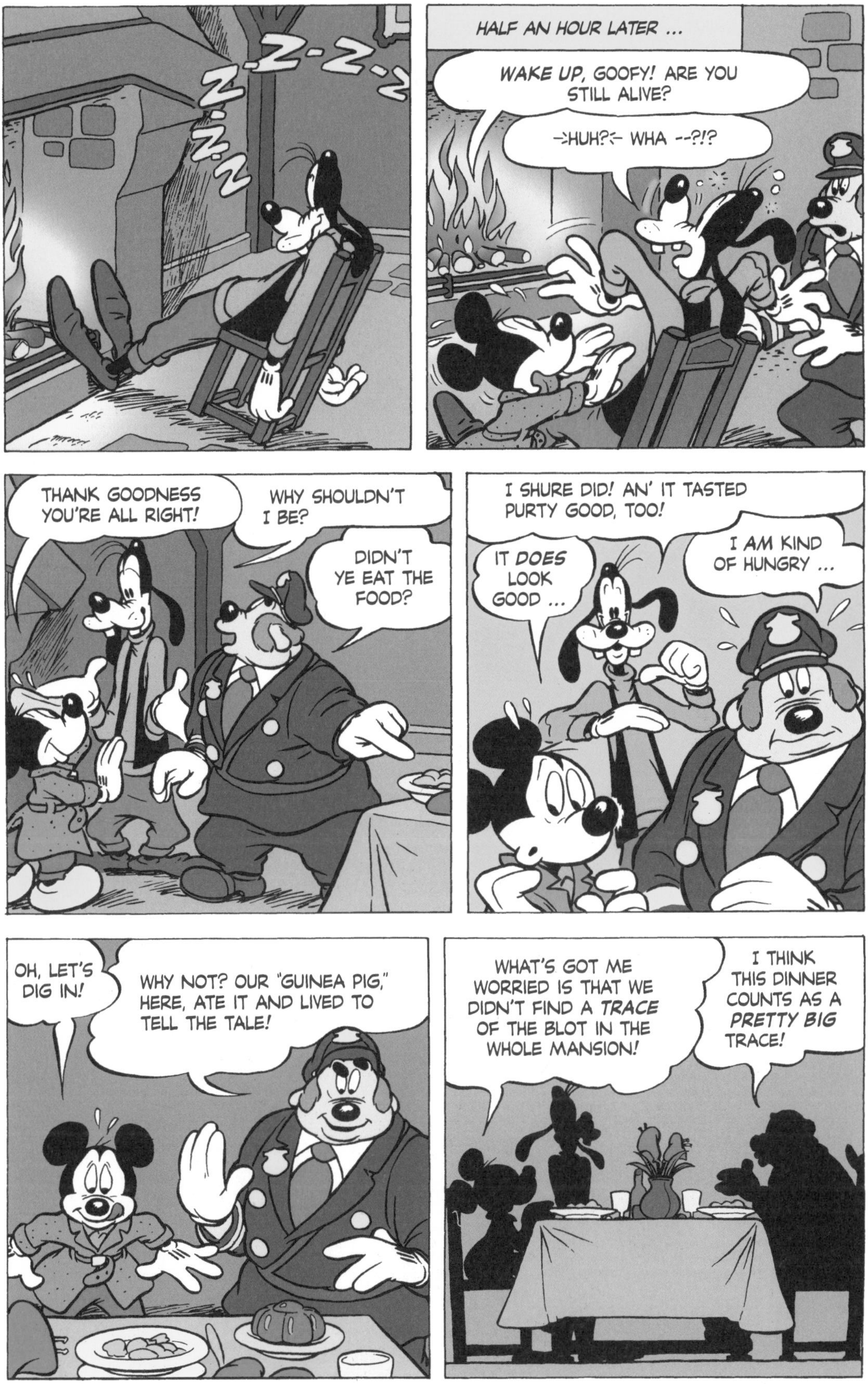
Z-Z-Z-Z-Z-Z-Z
HALF AN HOUR LATER ...
WAKE UP, GOOFY! ARE YOU STILL ALIVE?
–>HUH?<– WHA --?!?
THANK GOODNESS YOU'RE ALL RIGHT!
WHY SHOULDN'T I BE?
DIDN'T YE EAT THE FOOD?
I SHURE DID! AN' IT TASTED PURTY GOOD, TOO!
IT DOES LOOK GOOD ...
I AM KIND OF HUNGRY ...
OH, LET'S DIG IN!
WHY NOT? OUR "GUINEA PIG," HERE, ATE IT AND LIVED TO TELL THE TALE!
WHAT'S GOT ME WORRIED IS THAT WE DIDN'T FIND A TRACE OF THE BLOT IN THE WHOLE MANSION!
I THINK THIS DINNER COUNTS AS A PRETTY BIG TRACE!

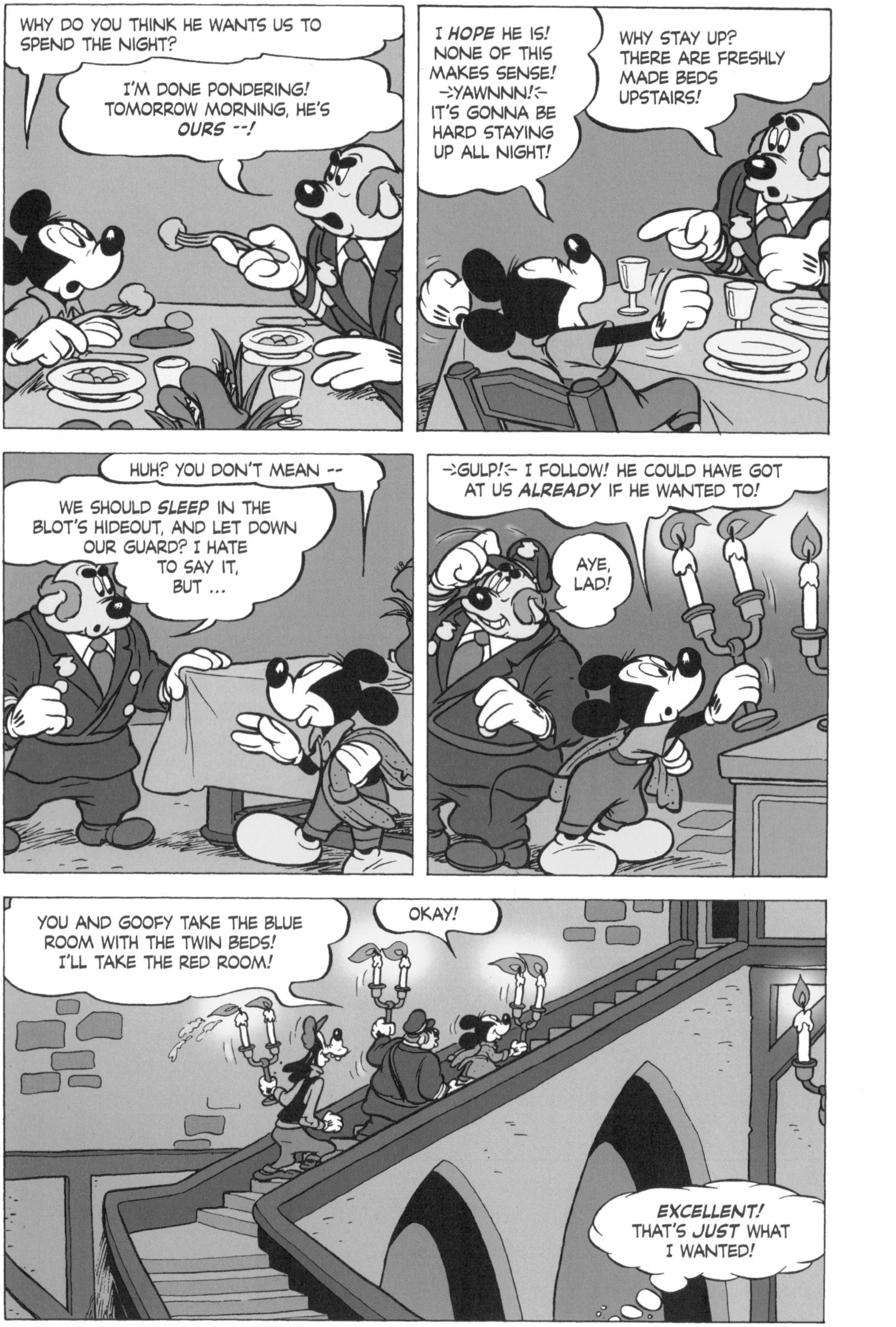
WHY DO YOU THINK HE WANTS US TO SPEND THE NIGHT?
I'M DONE PONDERING! TOMORROW MORNING, HE'S *OURS* --!
I *HOPE* HE IS! NONE OF THIS MAKES SENSE! -YAWNNN!- IT'S GONNA BE HARD STAYING UP ALL NIGHT!
WHY STAY UP? THERE ARE FRESHLY MADE BEDS UPSTAIRS!
HUH? YOU DON'T MEAN --
WE SHOULD *SLEEP* IN THE BLOT'S HIDEOUT, AND LET DOWN OUR GUARD? I HATE TO SAY IT, BUT ...
-GULP!- I FOLLOW! HE COULD HAVE GOT AT US *ALREADY* IF HE WANTED TO!
AYE, LAD!
YOU AND GOOFY TAKE THE BLUE ROOM WITH THE TWIN BEDS! I'LL TAKE THE RED ROOM!
OKAY!
EXCELLENT! THAT'S *JUST* WHAT I WANTED!

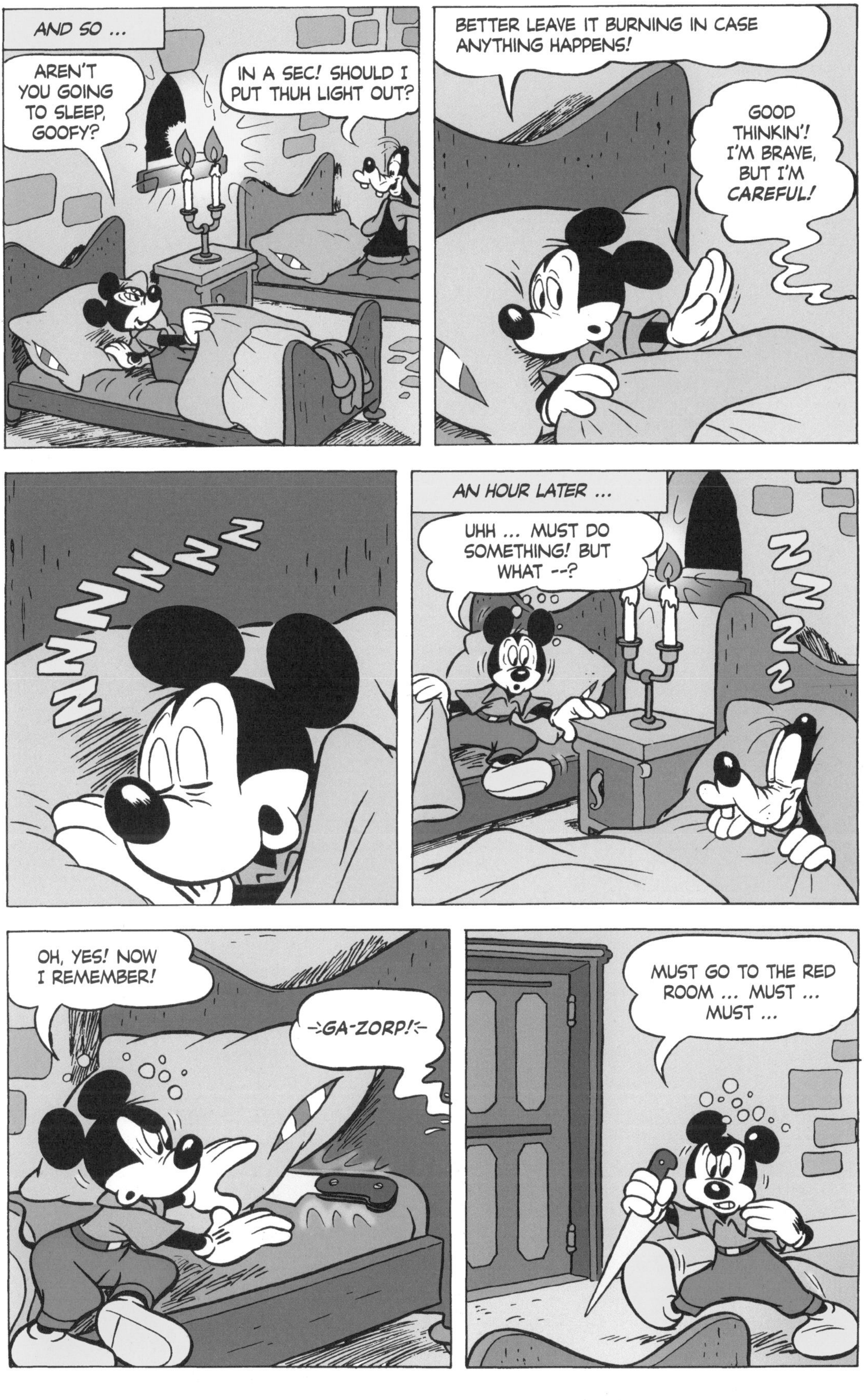
AND SO ...
AREN'T YOU GOING TO SLEEP, GOOFY?
IN A SEC! SHOULD I PUT THUH LIGHT OUT?
BETTER LEAVE IT BURNING IN CASE ANYTHING HAPPENS!
GOOD THINKIN'! I'M BRAVE, BUT I'M CAREFUL!
NNNNNNZZZ
AN HOUR LATER ...
UHH ... MUST DO SOMETHING! BUT WHAT --?
ZZZZ
OH, YES! NOW I REMEMBER!
-GA-ZORP!-
MUST GO TO THE RED ROOM ... MUST ... MUST ...

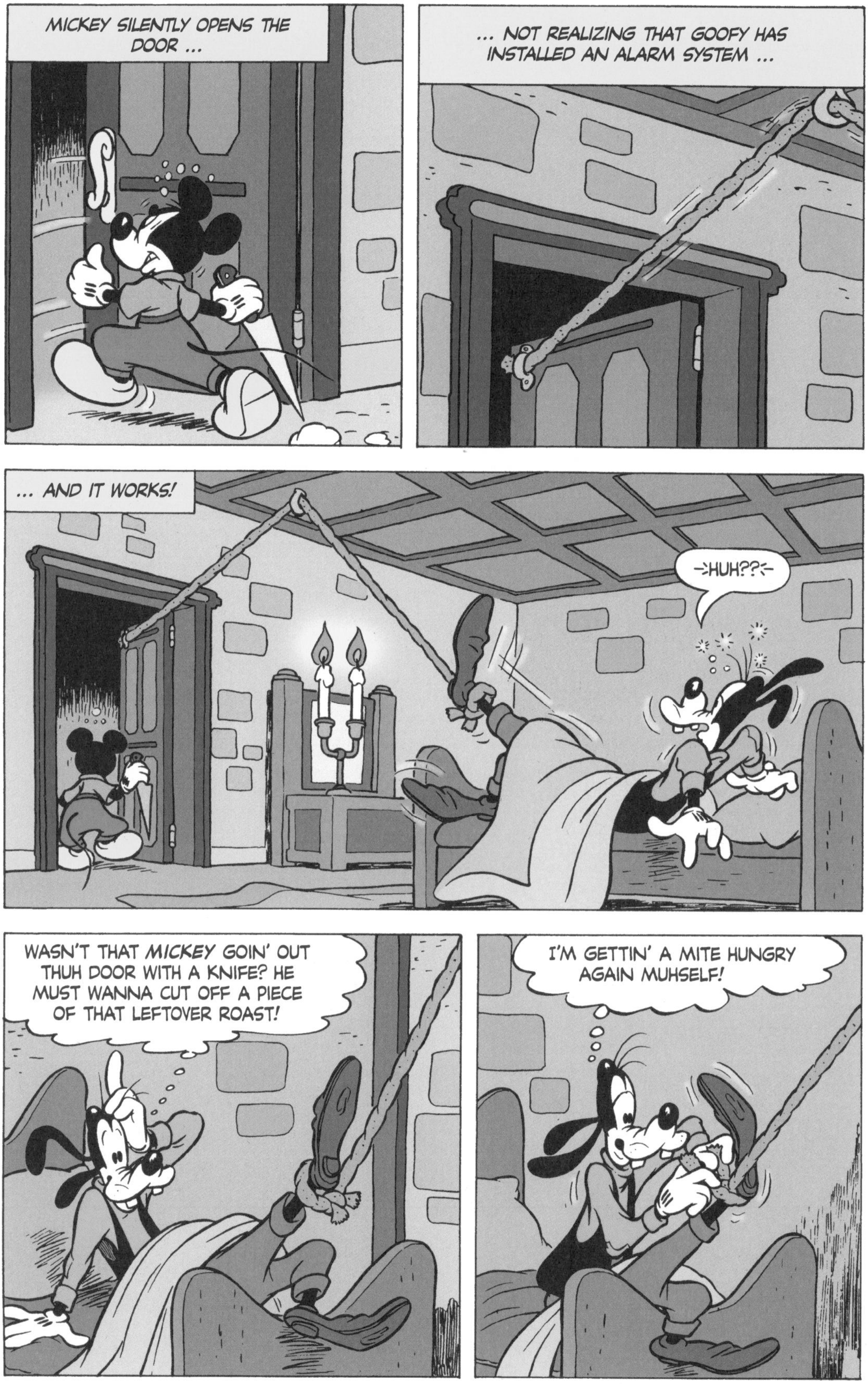
MICKEY SILENTLY OPENS THE DOOR ...
... NOT REALIZING THAT GOOFY HAS INSTALLED AN ALARM SYSTEM ...
... AND IT WORKS!
HUH??
WASN'T THAT *MICKEY* GOIN' OUT THUH DOOR WITH A KNIFE? HE MUST WANNA CUT OFF A PIECE OF THAT LEFTOVER ROAST!
I'M GETTIN' A MITE HUNGRY AGAIN MUHSELF!

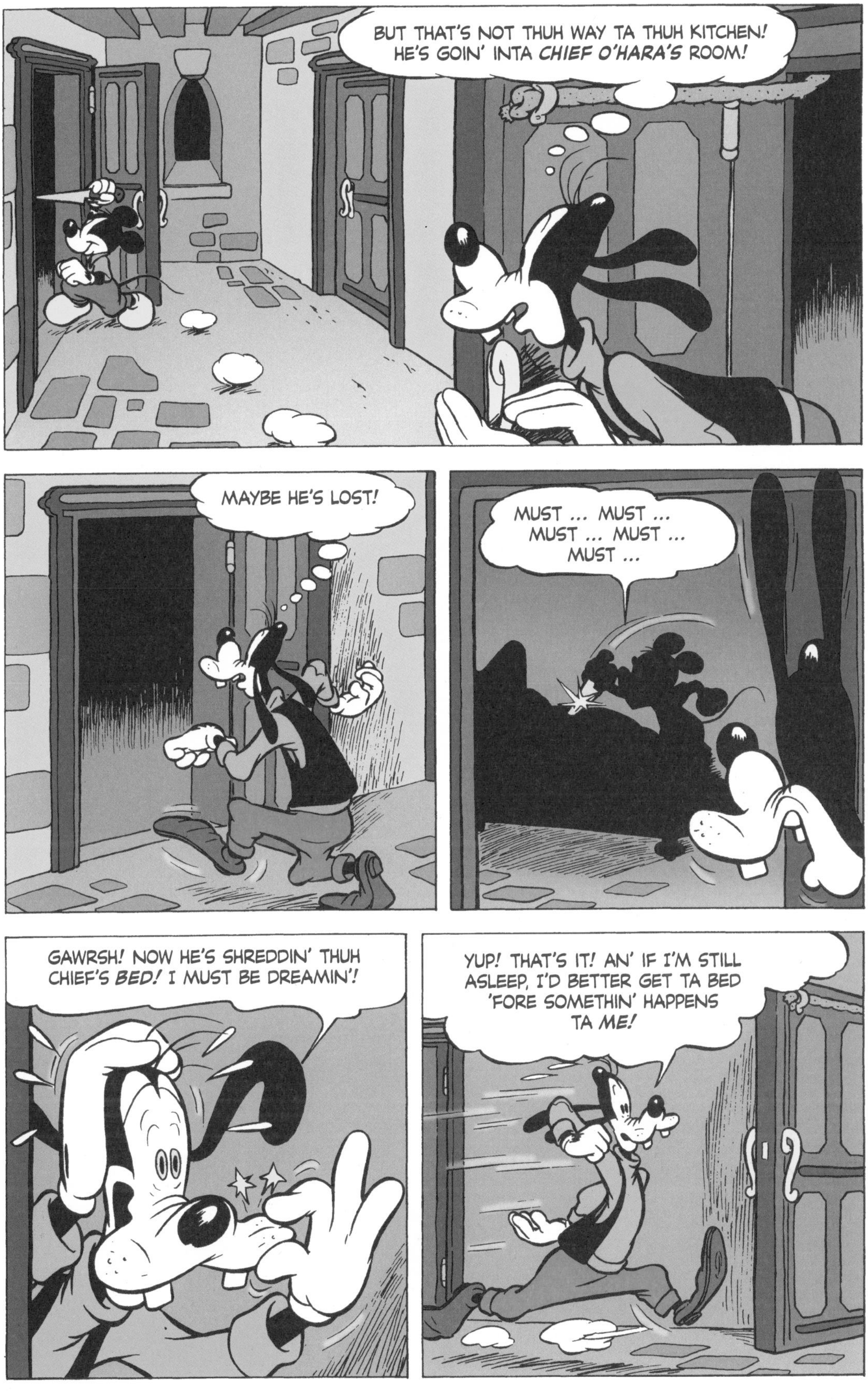
BUT THAT'S NOT THUH WAY TA THUH KITCHEN! HE'S GOIN' INTA *CHIEF O'HARA'S* ROOM!
MAYBE HE'S LOST!
MUST ... MUST ... MUST ... MUST ... MUST ...
GAWRSH! NOW HE'S SHREDDIN' THUH CHIEF'S *BED!* I MUST BE DREAMIN'!
YUP! THAT'S IT! AN' IF I'M STILL ASLEEP, I'D BETTER GET TA BED 'FORE SOMETHIN' HAPPENS TA *ME!*

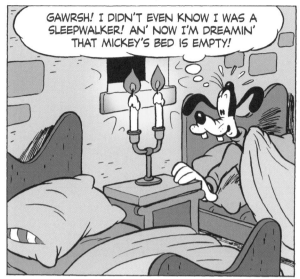

GAWRSH! I DIDN'T EVEN KNOW I WAS A SLEEPWALKER! AN' NOW I'M DREAMIN' THAT MICKEY'S BED IS EMPTY!

IN THUH MORNIN' I'D BETTER SEE ME A *PSYCHOLO-TRIST!*

THAT TAKES CARE OF *THAT!* NOW I CAN SLEEP IN PEACE!

THE NEXT MORNING ...

ALL RIGHT, MICKEY! YOU'D BETTER GET UP!

NOW WHAT?!

THE CASE IS *SOLVED!*

REALLY? THEN THE BLOT BROUGHT THE HAT BACK, AND ...

I DIDN'T SAY THAT! JUST COME DOWNSTAIRS WITH ME!

BOY! YOU'VE REALLY GOT ME CURIOUS!

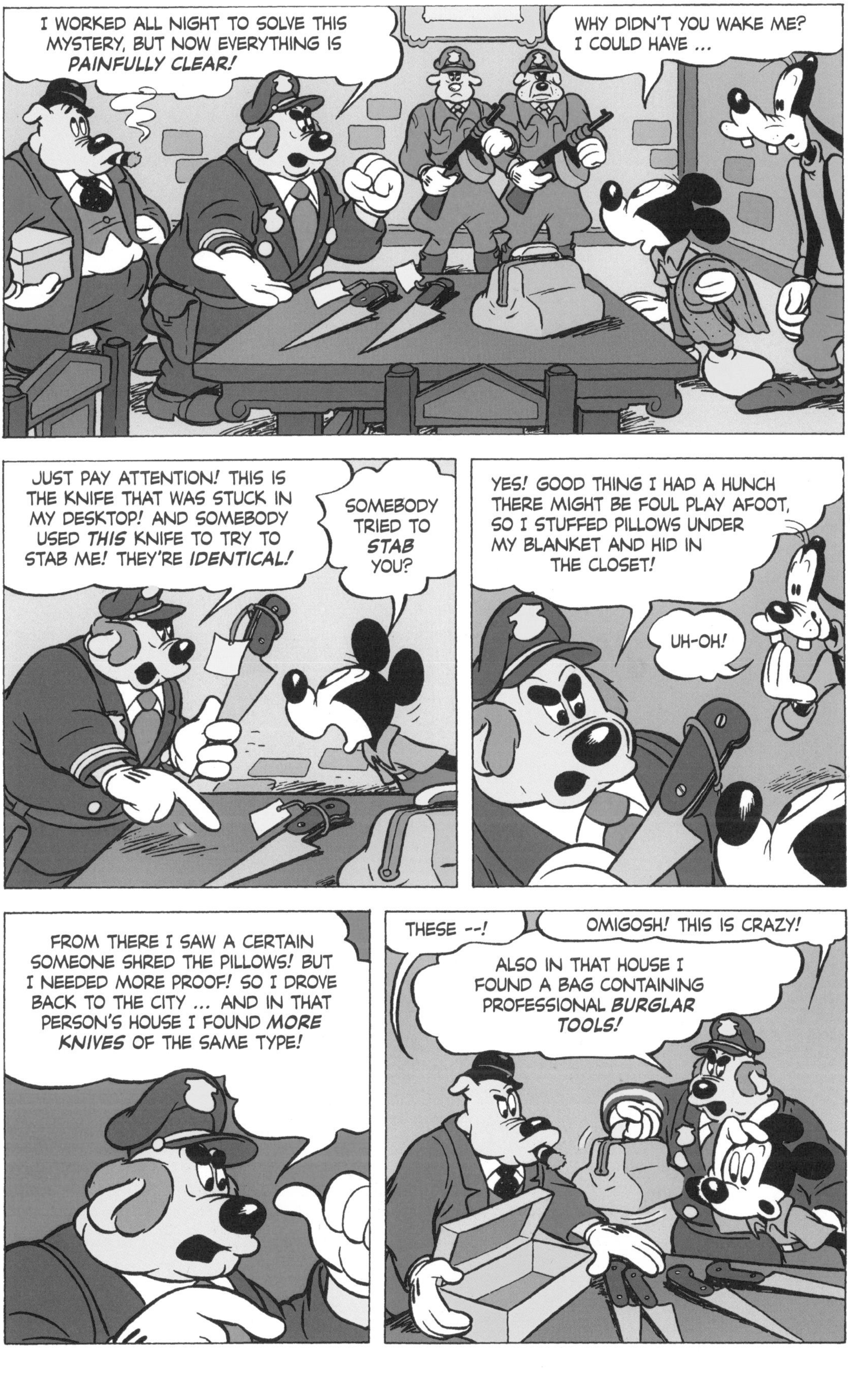

I WORKED ALL NIGHT TO SOLVE THIS MYSTERY, BUT NOW EVERYTHING IS PAINFULLY CLEAR!
WHY DIDN'T YOU WAKE ME? I COULD HAVE ...
JUST PAY ATTENTION! THIS IS THE KNIFE THAT WAS STUCK IN MY DESKTOP! AND SOMEBODY USED THIS KNIFE TO TRY TO STAB ME! THEY'RE IDENTICAL!
SOMEBODY TRIED TO STAB YOU?
YES! GOOD THING I HAD A HUNCH THERE MIGHT BE FOUL PLAY AFOOT, SO I STUFFED PILLOWS UNDER MY BLANKET AND HID IN THE CLOSET!
UH-OH!
FROM THERE I SAW A CERTAIN SOMEONE SHRED THE PILLOWS! BUT I NEEDED MORE PROOF! SO I DROVE BACK TO THE CITY ... AND IN THAT PERSON'S HOUSE I FOUND MORE KNIVES OF THE SAME TYPE!
THESE --!
OMIGOSH! THIS IS CRAZY!
ALSO IN THAT HOUSE I FOUND A BAG CONTAINING PROFESSIONAL BURGLAR TOOLS!

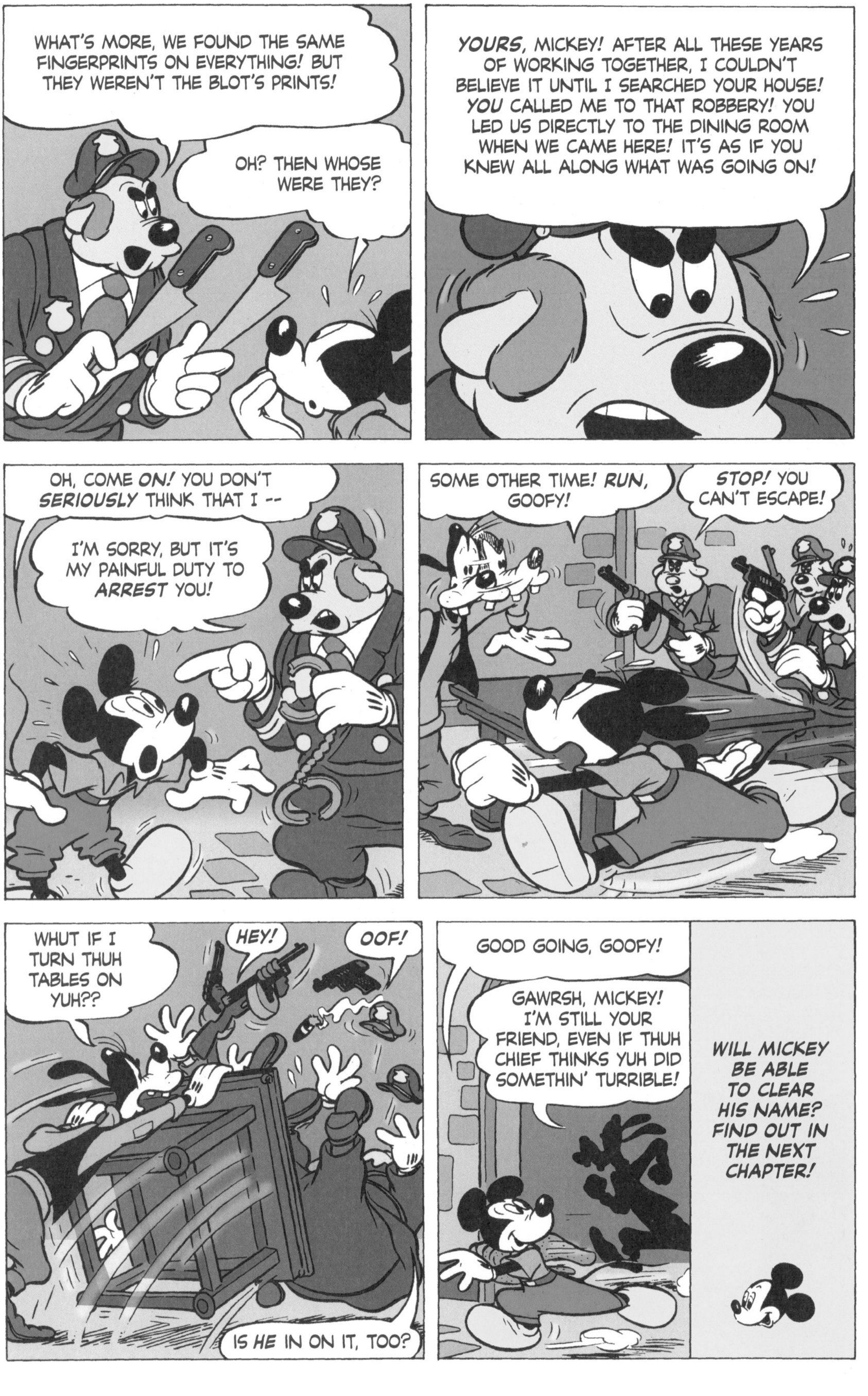
WHAT'S MORE, WE FOUND THE SAME FINGERPRINTS ON EVERYTHING! BUT THEY WEREN'T THE BLOT'S PRINTS!
OH? THEN WHOSE WERE THEY?
YOURS, MICKEY! AFTER ALL THESE YEARS OF WORKING TOGETHER, I COULDN'T BELIEVE IT UNTIL I SEARCHED YOUR HOUSE! YOU CALLED ME TO THAT ROBBERY! YOU LED US DIRECTLY TO THE DINING ROOM WHEN WE CAME HERE! IT'S AS IF YOU KNEW ALL ALONG WHAT WAS GOING ON!
OH, COME ON! YOU DON'T SERIOUSLY THINK THAT I --
I'M SORRY, BUT IT'S MY PAINFUL DUTY TO ARREST YOU!
SOME OTHER TIME! RUN, GOOFY!
STOP! YOU CAN'T ESCAPE!
WHUT IF I TURN THUH TABLES ON YUH??
HEY!
OOF!
IS HE IN ON IT, TOO?
GOOD GOING, GOOFY!
GAWRSH, MICKEY! I'M STILL YOUR FRIEND, EVEN IF THUH CHIEF THINKS YUH DID SOMETHIN' TURRIBLE!
WILL MICKEY BE ABLE TO CLEAR HIS NAME? FIND OUT IN THE NEXT CHAPTER!

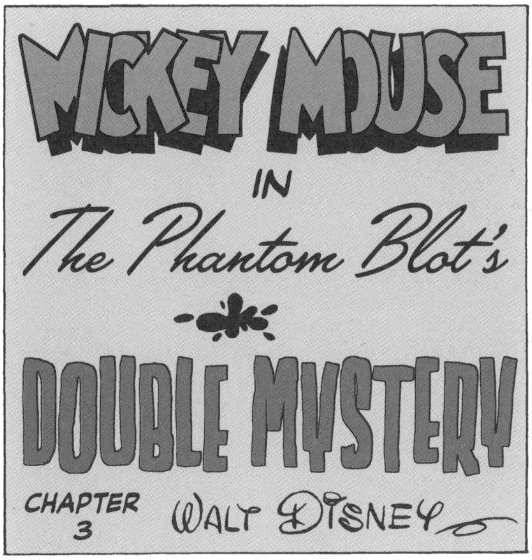
MICKEY MOUSE
IN
The Phantom Blot's
DOUBLE MYSTERY
CHAPTER 3
WALT DISNEY

THE PHANTOM BLOT ESCAPES FROM PRISON ... HATMAKER THOMAS TOPPER IS ROBBED OF HIS FAVORITE SILK HAT ... AND THE "HATNAPPER" DEMANDS A $100,000 RANSOM!

IF HE DOESN'T GET IT, HE SAYS HE'LL USE THE HAT TO DESTROY THE CITY! BUT ... HOW? IS THE HAT THIEF THE PHANTOM BLOT??

MAYBE NOT! THE CLUES POINT TO MICKEY MOUSE ... AND WHEN MICKEY AND GOOFY JOIN CHIEF O'HARA TO STAKE OUT THE BLOT'S HIDEOUT AT DARKMOOR HALL, MICKEY APPEARS TO ATTACK THE CHIEF!

BUT MICKEY HAS BEEN SECRETLY HYPNOTIZED! THE BLOT IS PUTTING HIM UP TO THIS VILLAINOUS BEHAVIOR -- BUT EVEN MICKEY DOESN'T KNOW IT ...

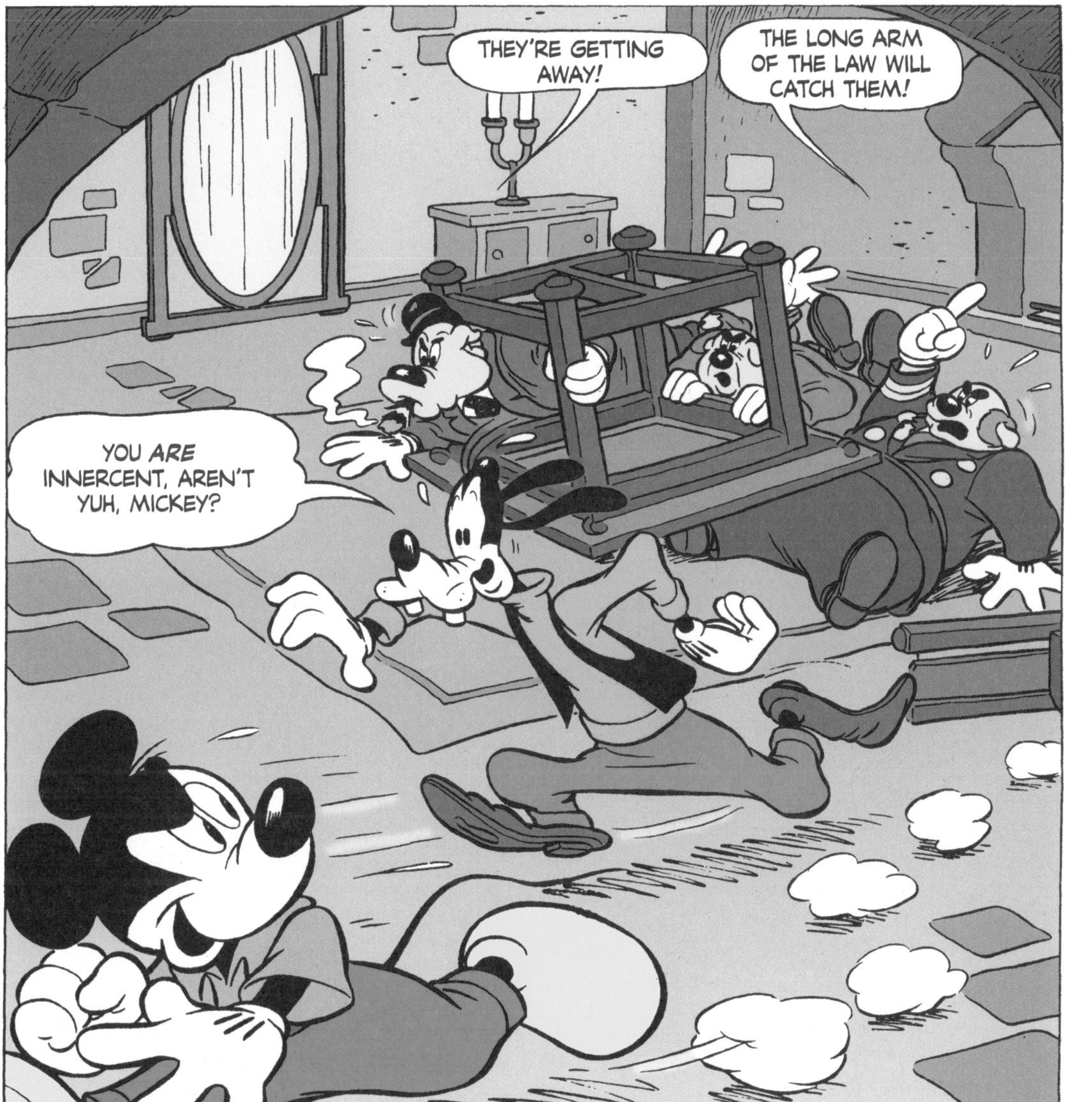
THEY'RE GETTING AWAY!
THE LONG ARM OF THE LAW WILL CATCH THEM!
YOU *ARE* INNERCENT, AREN'T YUH, MICKEY?

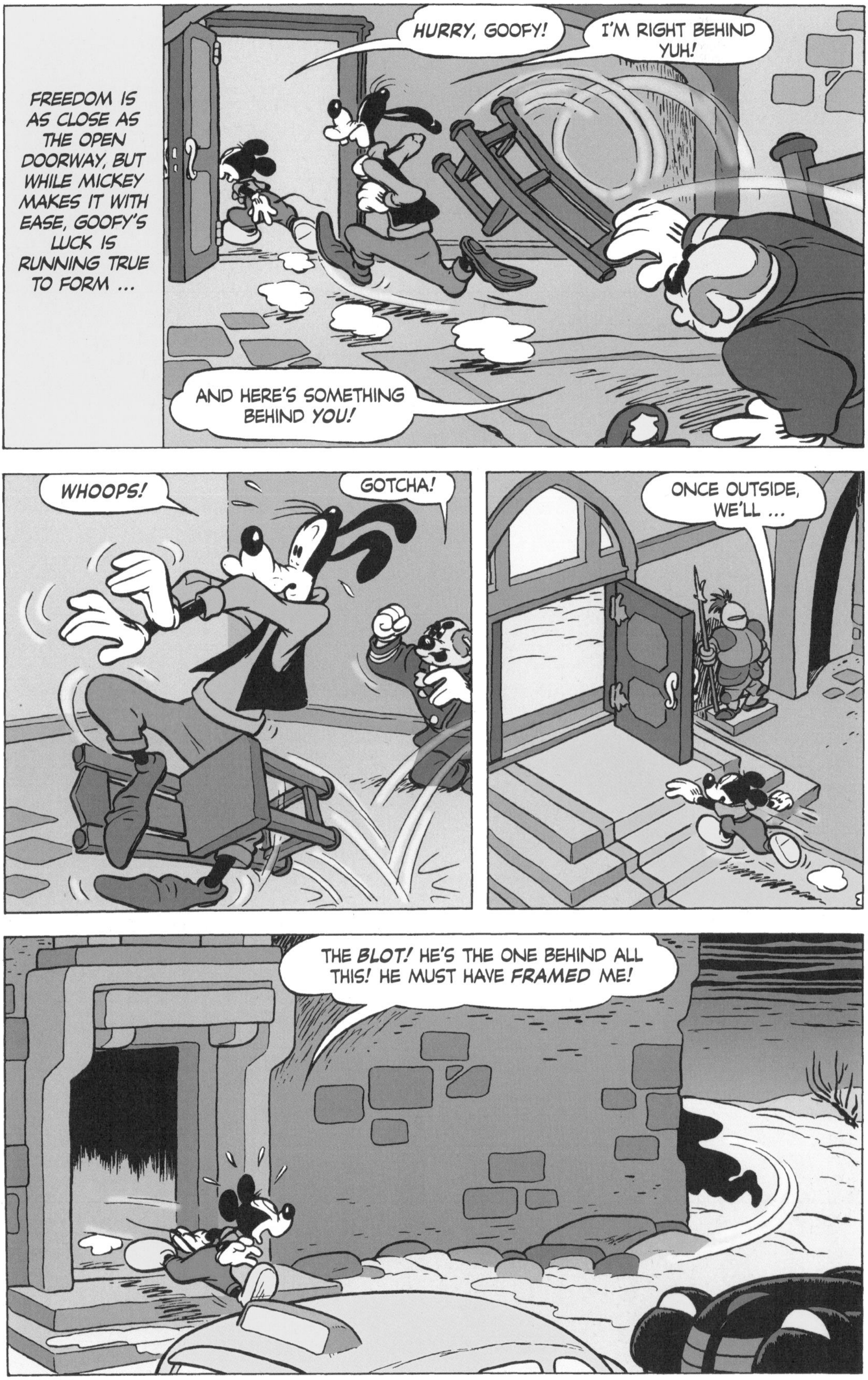
FREEDOM IS AS CLOSE AS THE OPEN DOORWAY, BUT WHILE MICKEY MAKES IT WITH EASE, GOOFY'S LUCK IS RUNNING TRUE TO FORM ...
HURRY, GOOFY!
I'M RIGHT BEHIND YUH!
AND HERE'S SOMETHING BEHIND YOU!
WHOOPS!
GOTCHA!
ONCE OUTSIDE, WE'LL ...
THE BLOT! HE'S THE ONE BEHIND ALL THIS! HE MUST HAVE FRAMED ME!

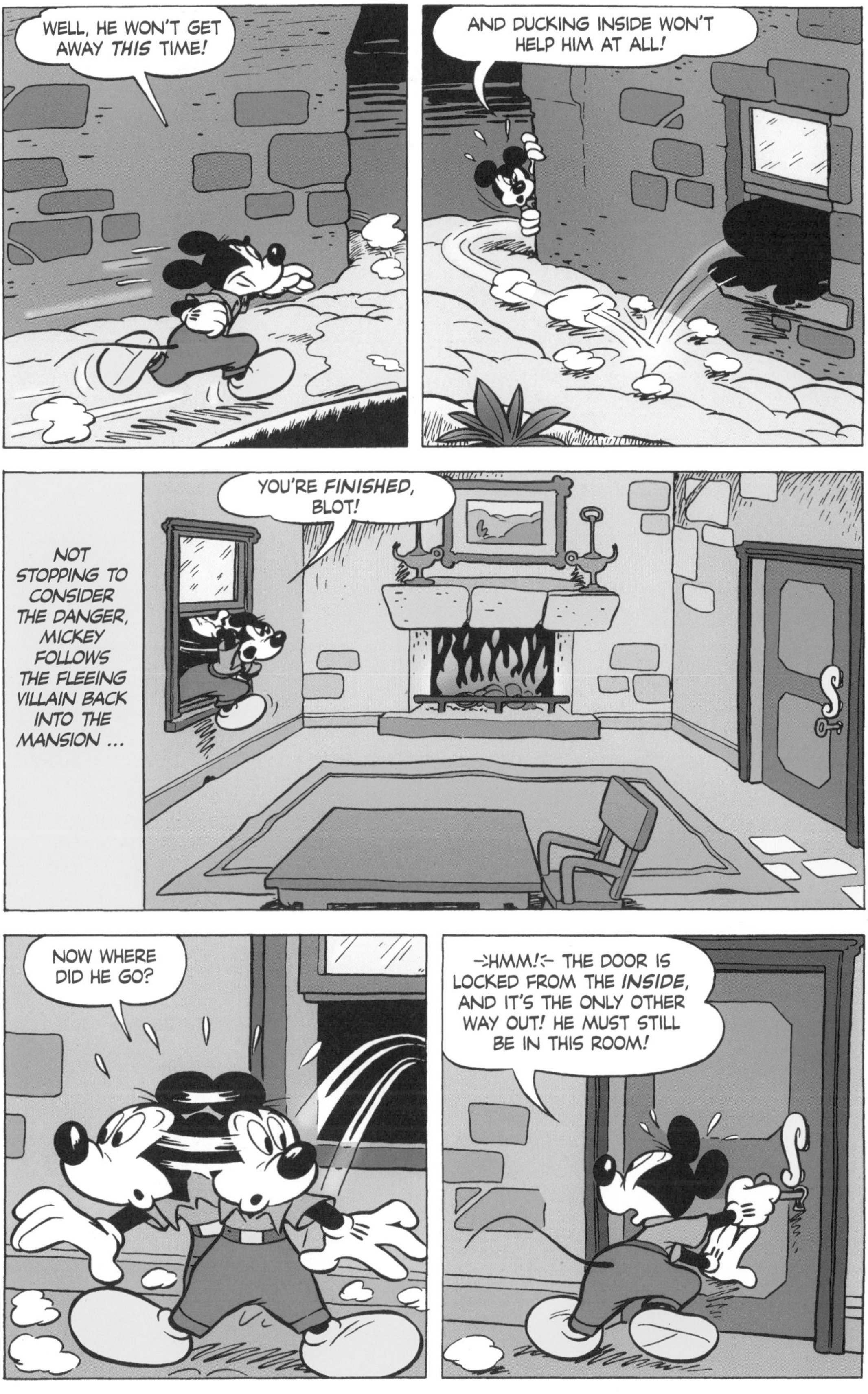
WELL, HE WON'T GET AWAY *THIS* TIME!
AND DUCKING INSIDE WON'T HELP HIM AT ALL!
NOT STOPPING TO CONSIDER THE DANGER, MICKEY FOLLOWS THE FLEEING VILLAIN BACK INTO THE MANSION ...
YOU'RE *FINISHED*, BLOT!
NOW WHERE DID HE GO?
-HMM!- THE DOOR IS LOCKED FROM THE *INSIDE*, AND IT'S THE ONLY OTHER WAY OUT! HE MUST STILL BE IN THIS ROOM!

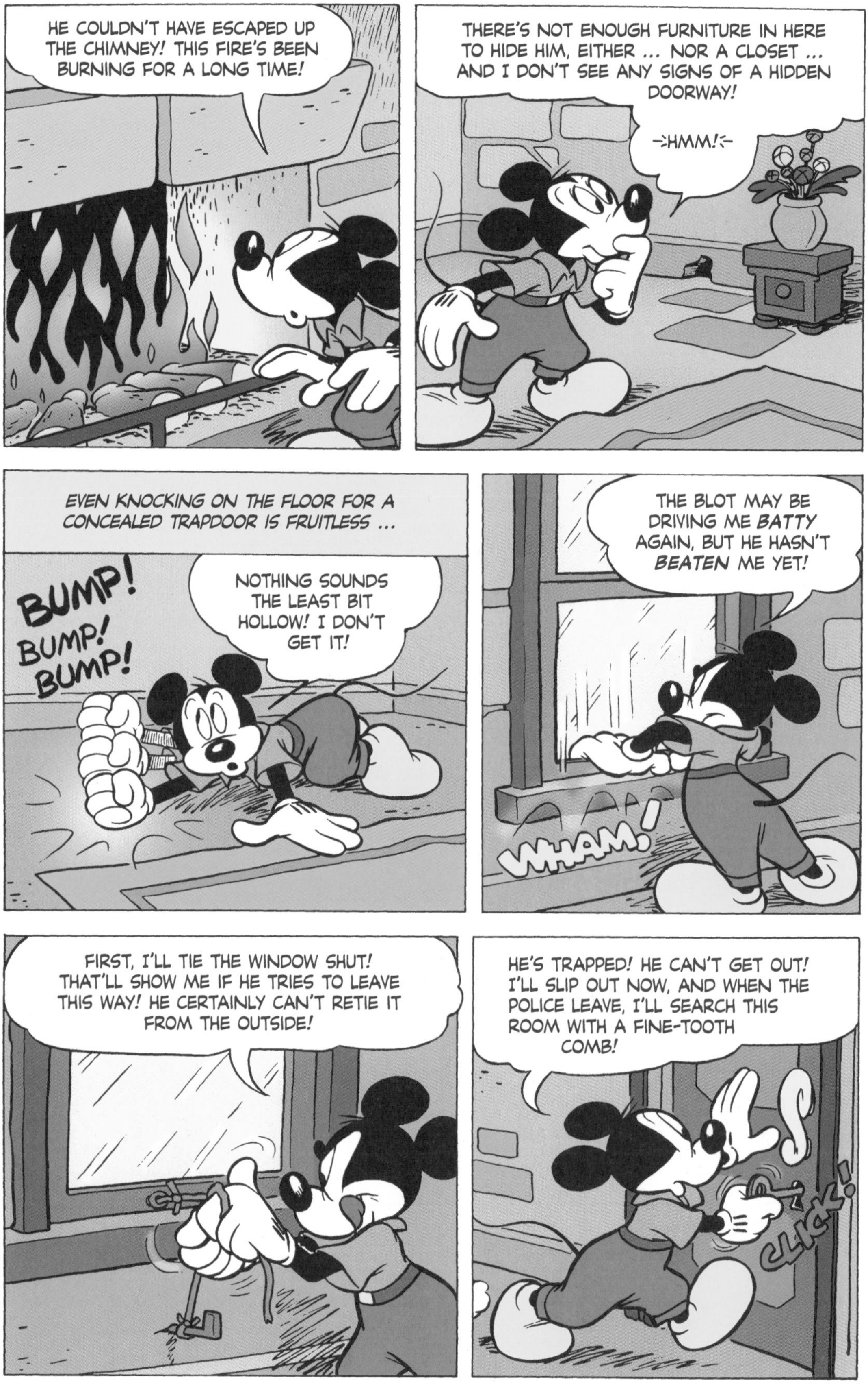
HE COULDN'T HAVE ESCAPED UP THE CHIMNEY! THIS FIRE'S BEEN BURNING FOR A LONG TIME!
THERE'S NOT ENOUGH FURNITURE IN HERE TO HIDE HIM, EITHER ... NOR A CLOSET ... AND I DON'T SEE ANY SIGNS OF A HIDDEN DOORWAY!
-HMM!-
EVEN KNOCKING ON THE FLOOR FOR A CONCEALED TRAPDOOR IS FRUITLESS ...
BUMP! BUMP! BUMP!
NOTHING SOUNDS THE LEAST BIT HOLLOW! I DON'T GET IT!
THE BLOT MAY BE DRIVING ME BATTY AGAIN, BUT HE HASN'T BEATEN ME YET!
WHAM!
FIRST, I'LL TIE THE WINDOW SHUT! THAT'LL SHOW ME IF HE TRIES TO LEAVE THIS WAY! HE CERTAINLY CAN'T RETIE IT FROM THE OUTSIDE!
HE'S TRAPPED! HE CAN'T GET OUT! I'LL SLIP OUT NOW, AND WHEN THE POLICE LEAVE, I'LL SEARCH THIS ROOM WITH A FINE-TOOTH COMB!
CLICK!

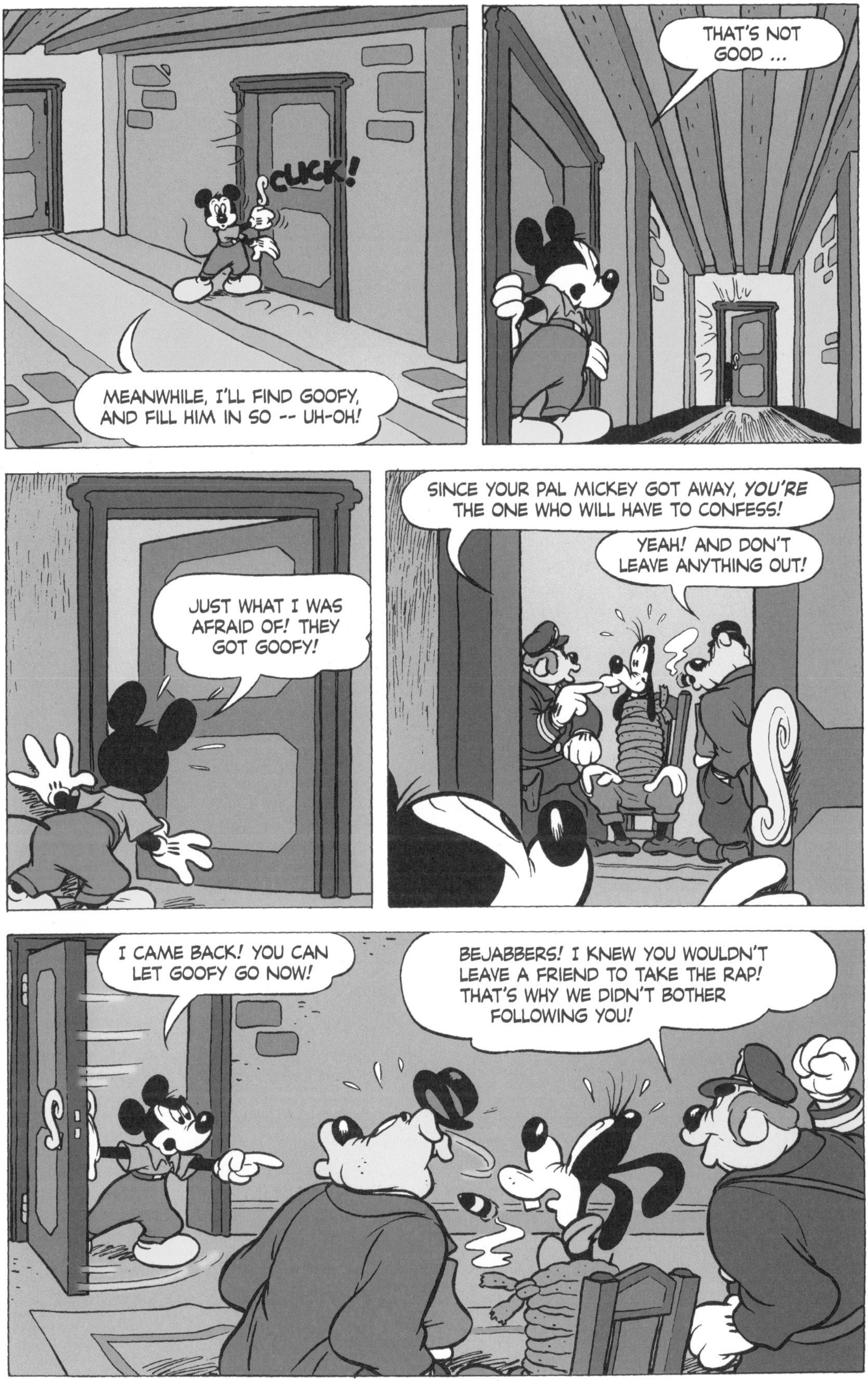
CLICK!
MEANWHILE, I'LL FIND GOOFY, AND FILL HIM IN SO -- UH-OH!
THAT'S NOT GOOD ...
JUST WHAT I WAS AFRAID OF! THEY GOT GOOFY!
SINCE YOUR PAL MICKEY GOT AWAY, *YOU'RE* THE ONE WHO WILL HAVE TO CONFESS!
YEAH! AND DON'T LEAVE ANYTHING OUT!
I CAME BACK! YOU CAN LET GOOFY GO NOW!
BEJABBERS! I KNEW YOU WOULDN'T LEAVE A FRIEND TO TAKE THE RAP! THAT'S WHY WE DIDN'T BOTHER FOLLOWING YOU!

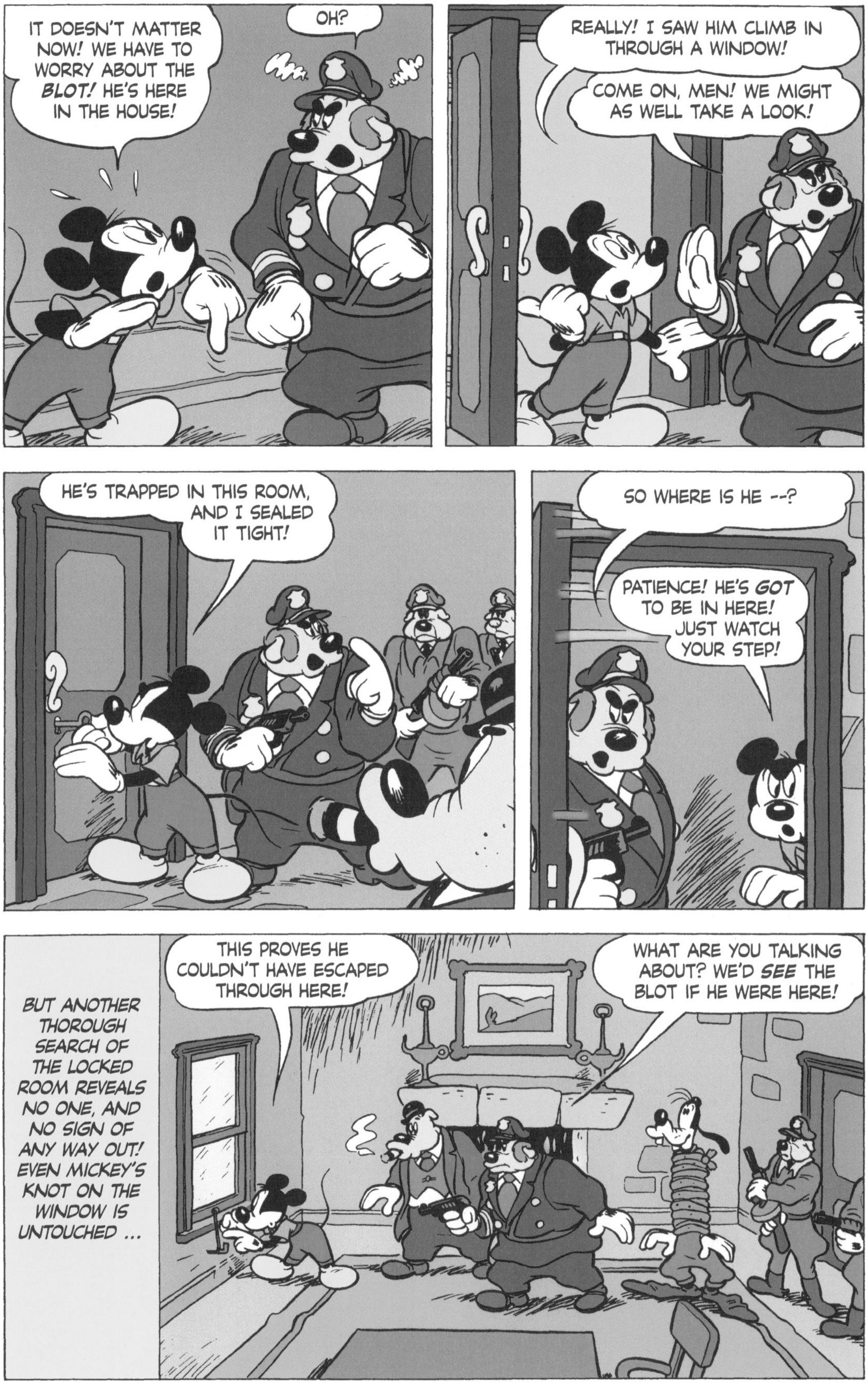

IT DOESN'T MATTER NOW! WE HAVE TO WORRY ABOUT THE *BLOT!* HE'S HERE IN THE HOUSE!
OH?
REALLY! I SAW HIM CLIMB IN THROUGH A WINDOW!
COME ON, MEN! WE MIGHT AS WELL TAKE A LOOK!
HE'S TRAPPED IN THIS ROOM, AND I SEALED IT TIGHT!
SO WHERE IS HE --?
PATIENCE! HE'S *GOT* TO BE IN HERE! JUST WATCH YOUR STEP!
BUT ANOTHER THOROUGH SEARCH OF THE LOCKED ROOM REVEALS NO ONE, AND NO SIGN OF ANY WAY OUT! EVEN MICKEY'S KNOT ON THE WINDOW IS UNTOUCHED ...
THIS PROVES HE COULDN'T HAVE ESCAPED THROUGH HERE!
WHAT ARE YOU TALKING ABOUT? WE'D *SEE* THE BLOT IF HE WERE HERE!

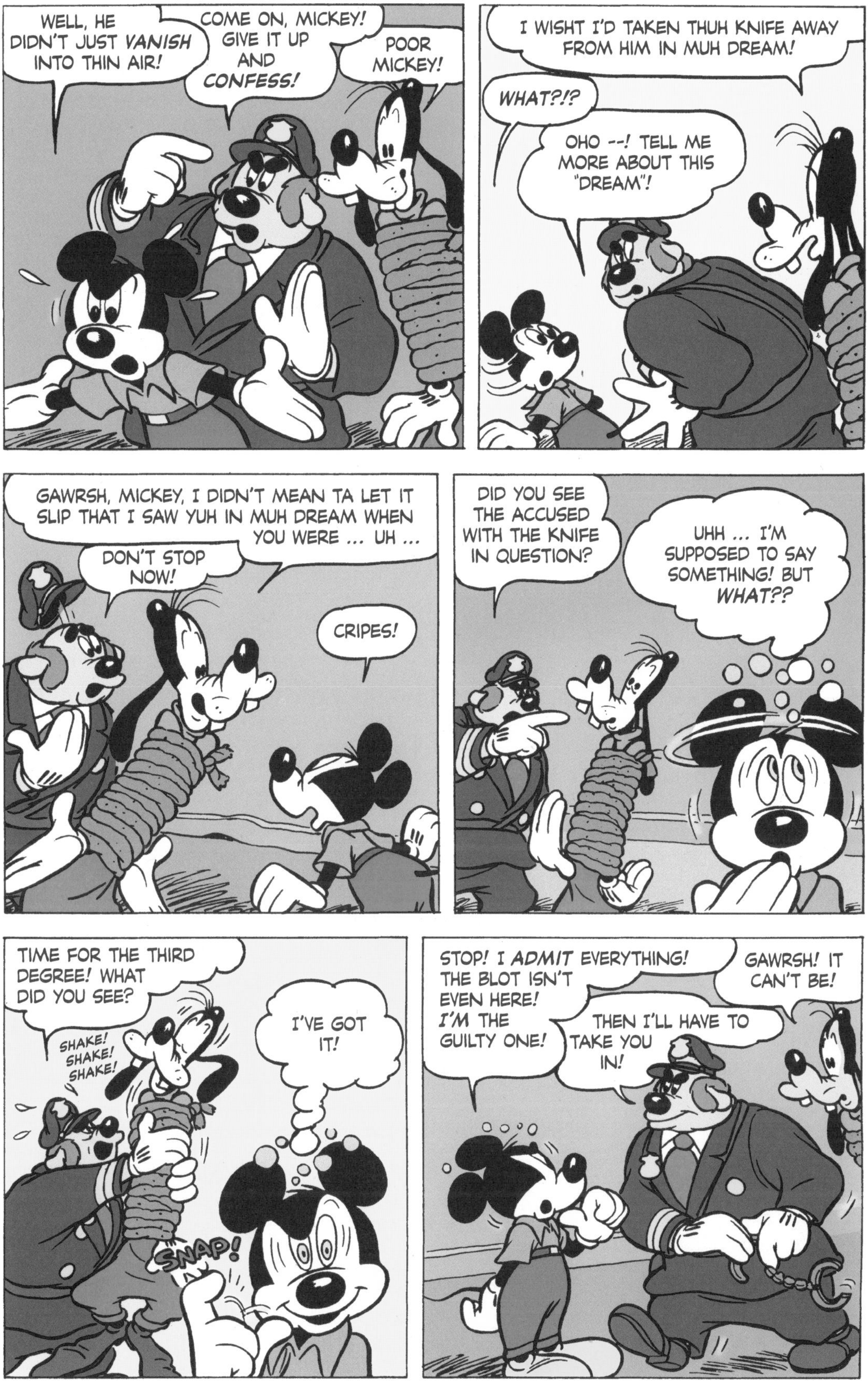
WELL, HE DIDN'T JUST VANISH INTO THIN AIR!
COME ON, MICKEY! GIVE IT UP AND CONFESS!
POOR MICKEY!
I WISHT I'D TAKEN THUH KNIFE AWAY FROM HIM IN MUH DREAM!
WHAT?!?
OHO --! TELL ME MORE ABOUT THIS "DREAM"!
GAWRSH, MICKEY, I DIDN'T MEAN TA LET IT SLIP THAT I SAW YUH IN MUH DREAM WHEN YOU WERE ... UH ...
DON'T STOP NOW!
CRIPES!
DID YOU SEE THE ACCUSED WITH THE KNIFE IN QUESTION?
UHH ... I'M SUPPOSED TO SAY SOMETHING! BUT WHAT??
TIME FOR THE THIRD DEGREE! WHAT DID YOU SEE?
SHAKE! SHAKE! SHAKE!
I'VE GOT IT!
SNAP!
STOP! I ADMIT EVERYTHING! THE BLOT ISN'T EVEN HERE! I'M THE GUILTY ONE!
GAWRSH! IT CAN'T BE!
THEN I'LL HAVE TO TAKE YOU IN!

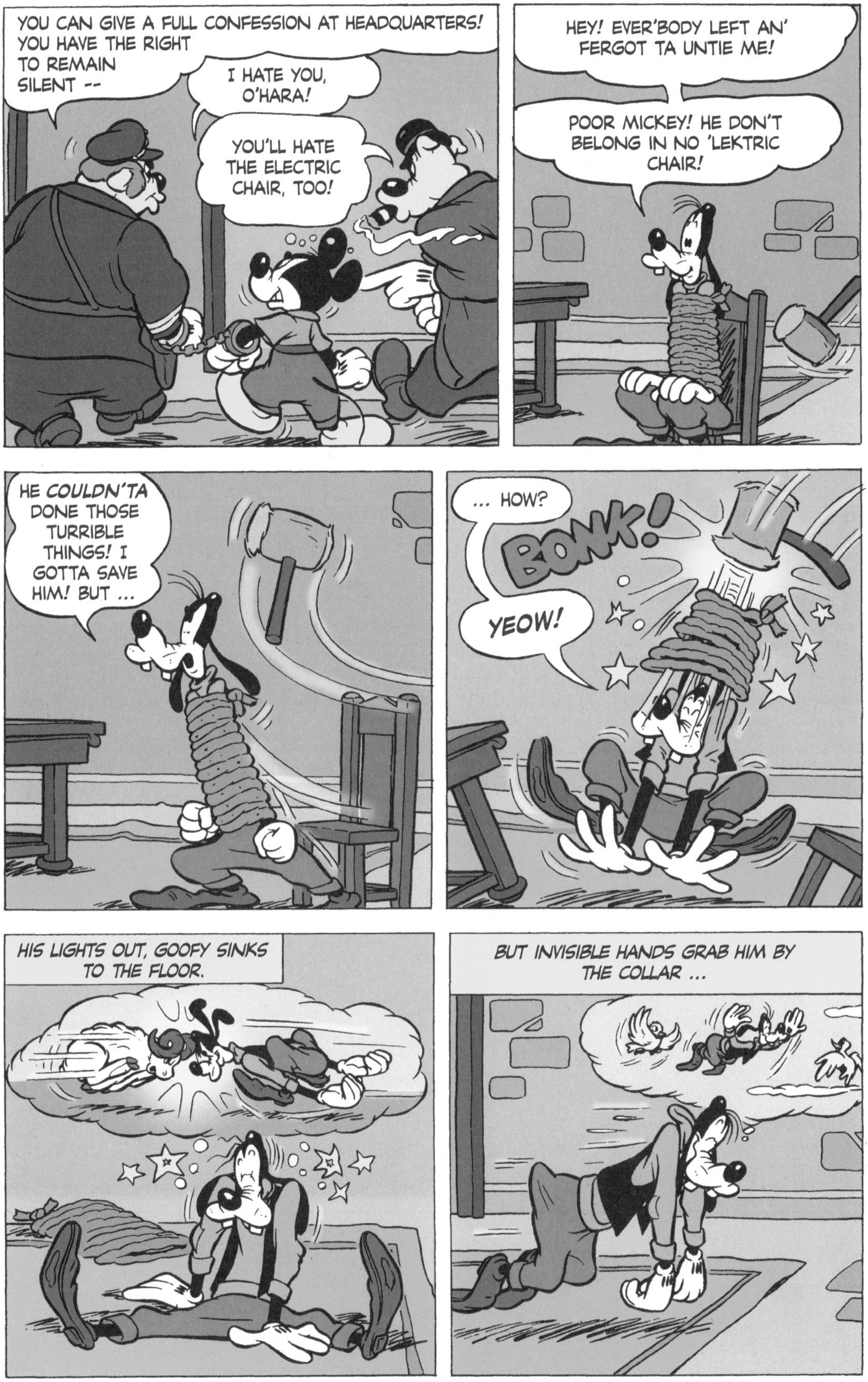

YOU CAN GIVE A FULL CONFESSION AT HEADQUARTERS! YOU HAVE THE RIGHT TO REMAIN SILENT --
I HATE YOU, O'HARA!
YOU'LL HATE THE ELECTRIC CHAIR, TOO!
HEY! EVER'BODY LEFT AN' FERGOT TA UNTIE ME!
POOR MICKEY! HE DON'T BELONG IN NO 'LEKTRIC CHAIR!
HE COULDN'TA DONE THOSE TURRIBLE THINGS! I GOTTA SAVE HIM! BUT ...
... HOW?
BONK!
YEOW!
HIS LIGHTS OUT, GOOFY SINKS TO THE FLOOR.
BUT INVISIBLE HANDS GRAB HIM BY THE COLLAR ...

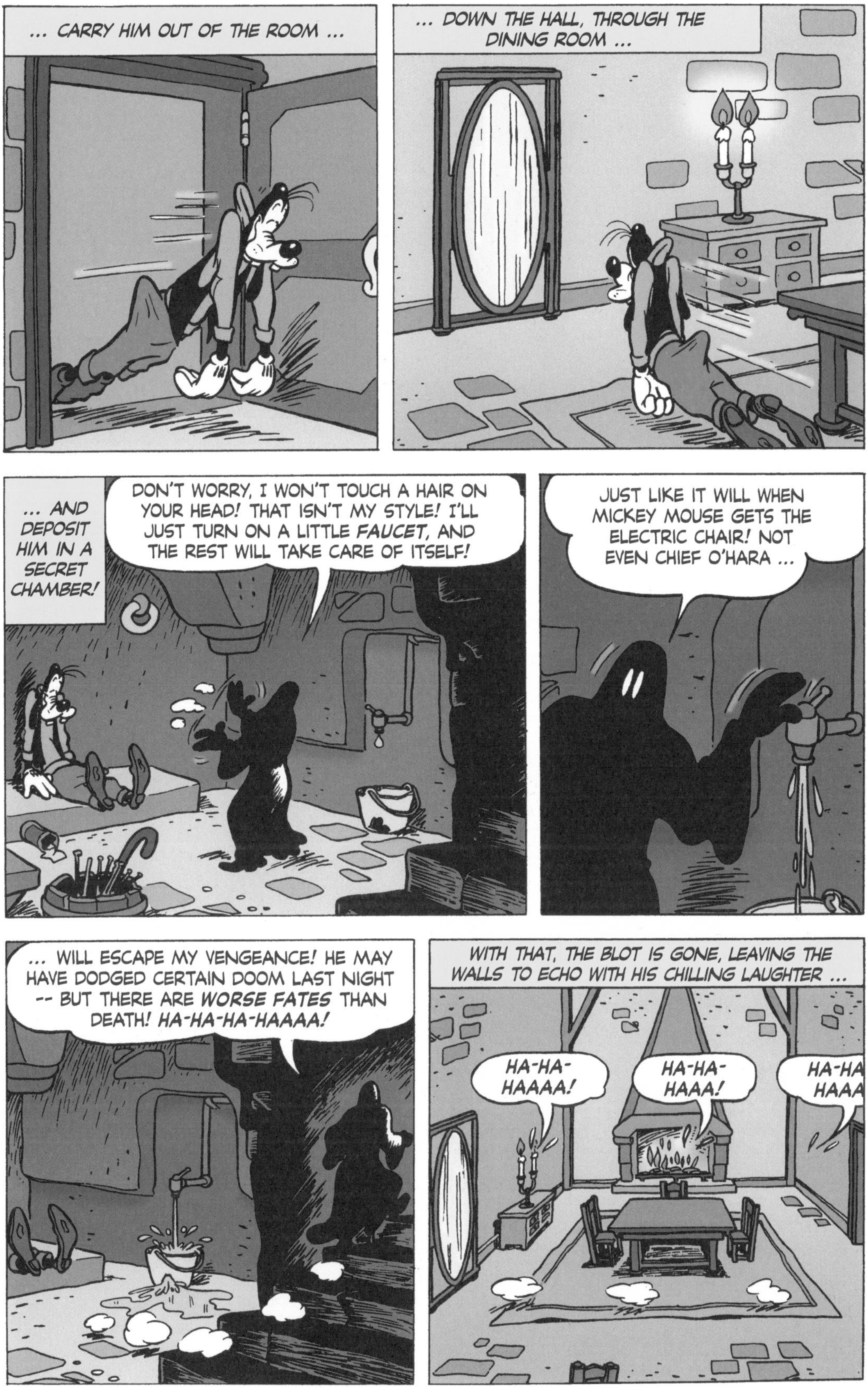
... CARRY HIM OUT OF THE ROOM ...
... DOWN THE HALL, THROUGH THE DINING ROOM ...
... AND DEPOSIT HIM IN A SECRET CHAMBER!
DON'T WORRY, I WON'T TOUCH A HAIR ON YOUR HEAD! THAT ISN'T MY STYLE! I'LL JUST TURN ON A LITTLE FAUCET, AND THE REST WILL TAKE CARE OF ITSELF!
JUST LIKE IT WILL WHEN MICKEY MOUSE GETS THE ELECTRIC CHAIR! NOT EVEN CHIEF O'HARA ...
... WILL ESCAPE MY VENGEANCE! HE MAY HAVE DODGED CERTAIN DOOM LAST NIGHT -- BUT THERE ARE WORSE FATES THAN DEATH! HA-HA-HA-HAAAA!
WITH THAT, THE BLOT IS GONE, LEAVING THE WALLS TO ECHO WITH HIS CHILLING LAUGHTER ...
HA-HA-HAAAA!
HA-HA-HAAA!

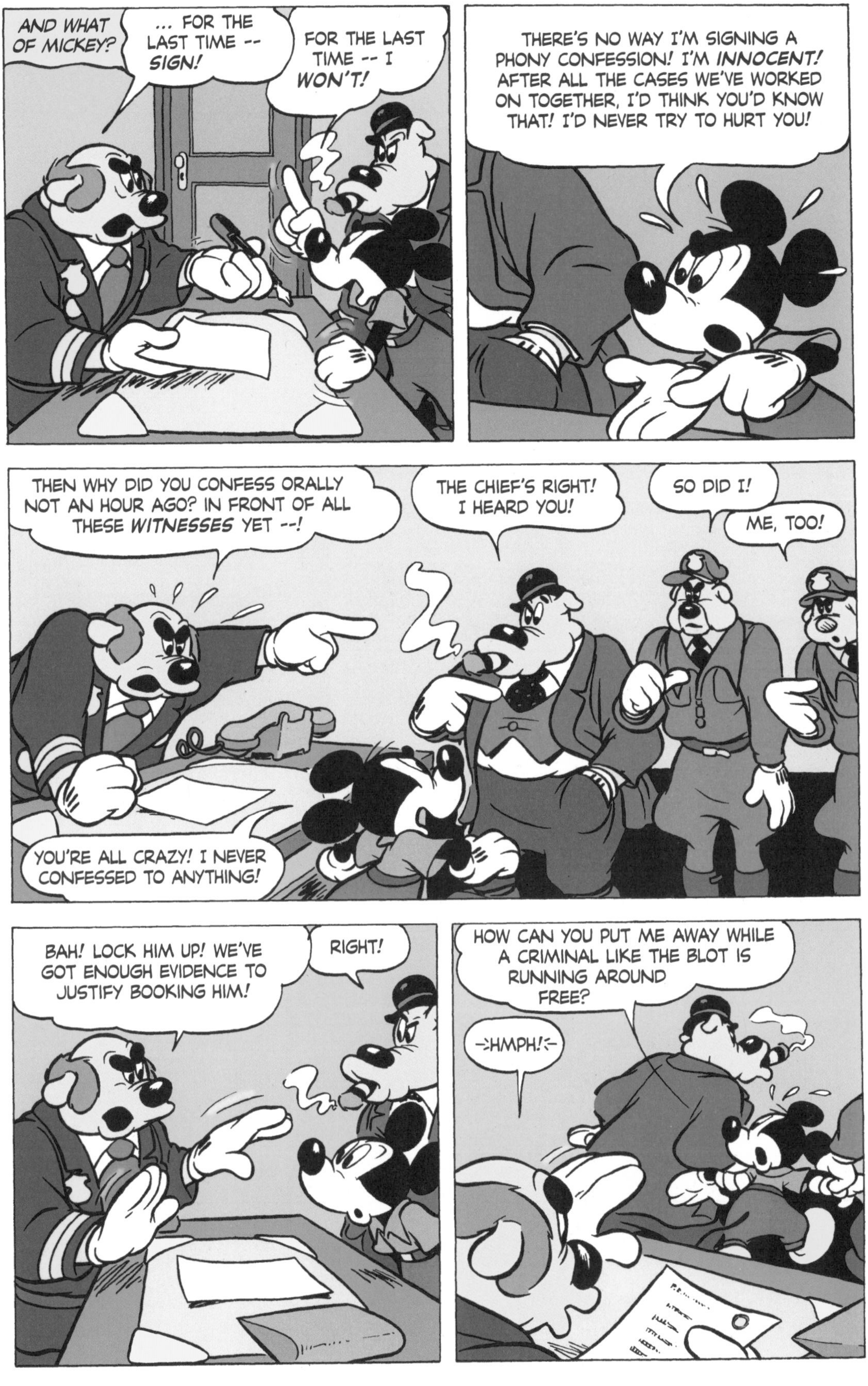
AND WHAT OF MICKEY?
... FOR THE LAST TIME -- SIGN!
FOR THE LAST TIME -- I WON'T!
THERE'S NO WAY I'M SIGNING A PHONY CONFESSION! I'M INNOCENT! AFTER ALL THE CASES WE'VE WORKED ON TOGETHER, I'D THINK YOU'D KNOW THAT! I'D NEVER TRY TO HURT YOU!
THEN WHY DID YOU CONFESS ORALLY NOT AN HOUR AGO? IN FRONT OF ALL THESE WITNESSES YET --!
THE CHIEF'S RIGHT! I HEARD YOU!
SO DID I!
ME, TOO!
YOU'RE ALL CRAZY! I NEVER CONFESSED TO ANYTHING!
BAH! LOCK HIM UP! WE'VE GOT ENOUGH EVIDENCE TO JUSTIFY BOOKING HIM!
RIGHT!
HOW CAN YOU PUT ME AWAY WHILE A CRIMINAL LIKE THE BLOT IS RUNNING AROUND FREE?
HMPH!

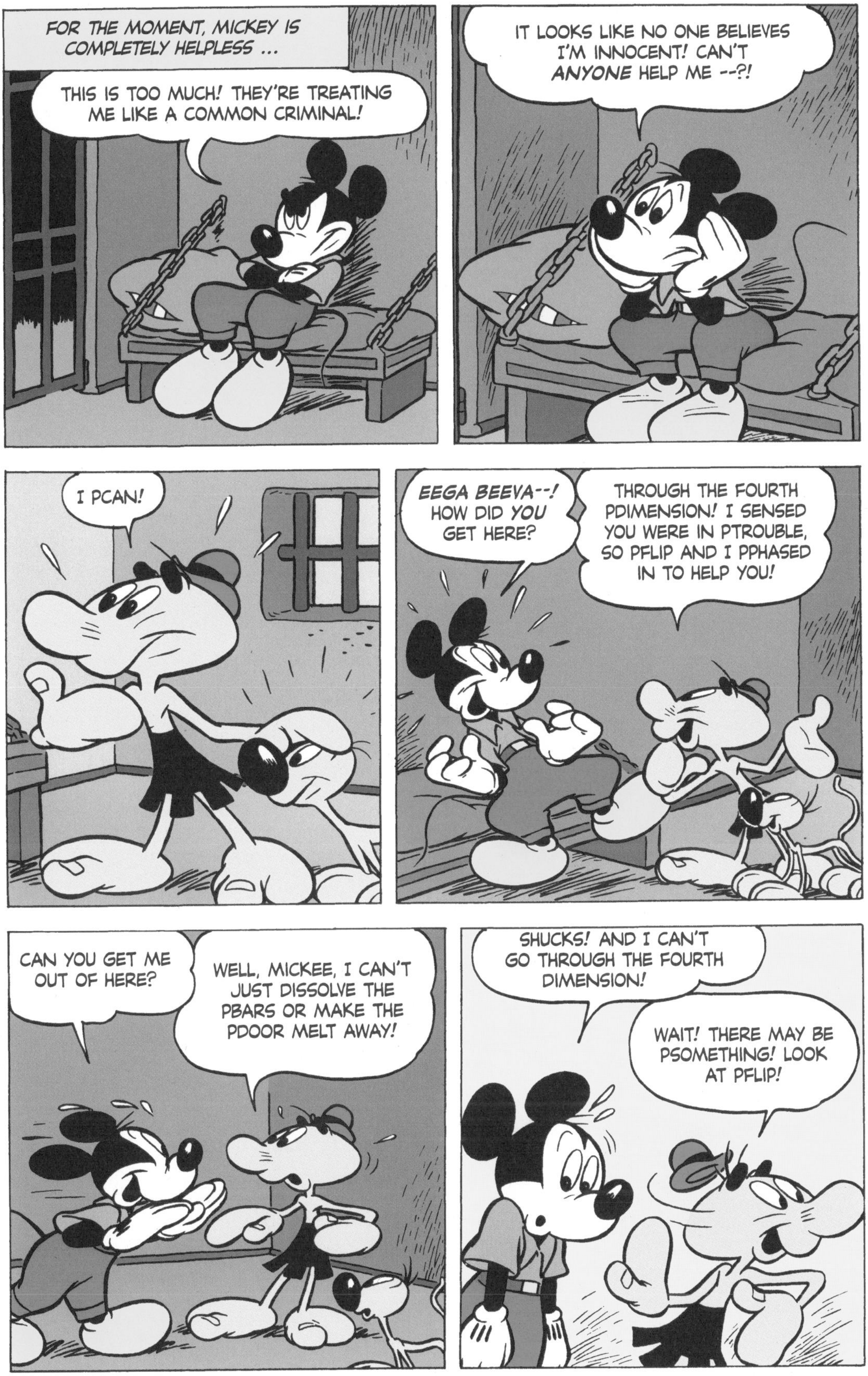
FOR THE MOMENT, MICKEY IS COMPLETELY HELPLESS ...
THIS IS TOO MUCH! THEY'RE TREATING ME LIKE A COMMON CRIMINAL!
IT LOOKS LIKE NO ONE BELIEVES I'M INNOCENT! CAN'T ANYONE HELP ME --?!
I PCAN!
EEGA BEEVA--! HOW DID YOU GET HERE?
THROUGH THE FOURTH PDIMENSION! I SENSED YOU WERE IN PTROUBLE, SO PFLIP AND I PPHASED IN TO HELP YOU!
CAN YOU GET ME OUT OF HERE?
WELL, MICKEE, I CAN'T JUST DISSOLVE THE PBARS OR MAKE THE PDOOR MELT AWAY!
SHUCKS! AND I CAN'T GO THROUGH THE FOURTH DIMENSION!
WAIT! THERE MAY BE PSOMETHING! LOOK AT PFLIP!

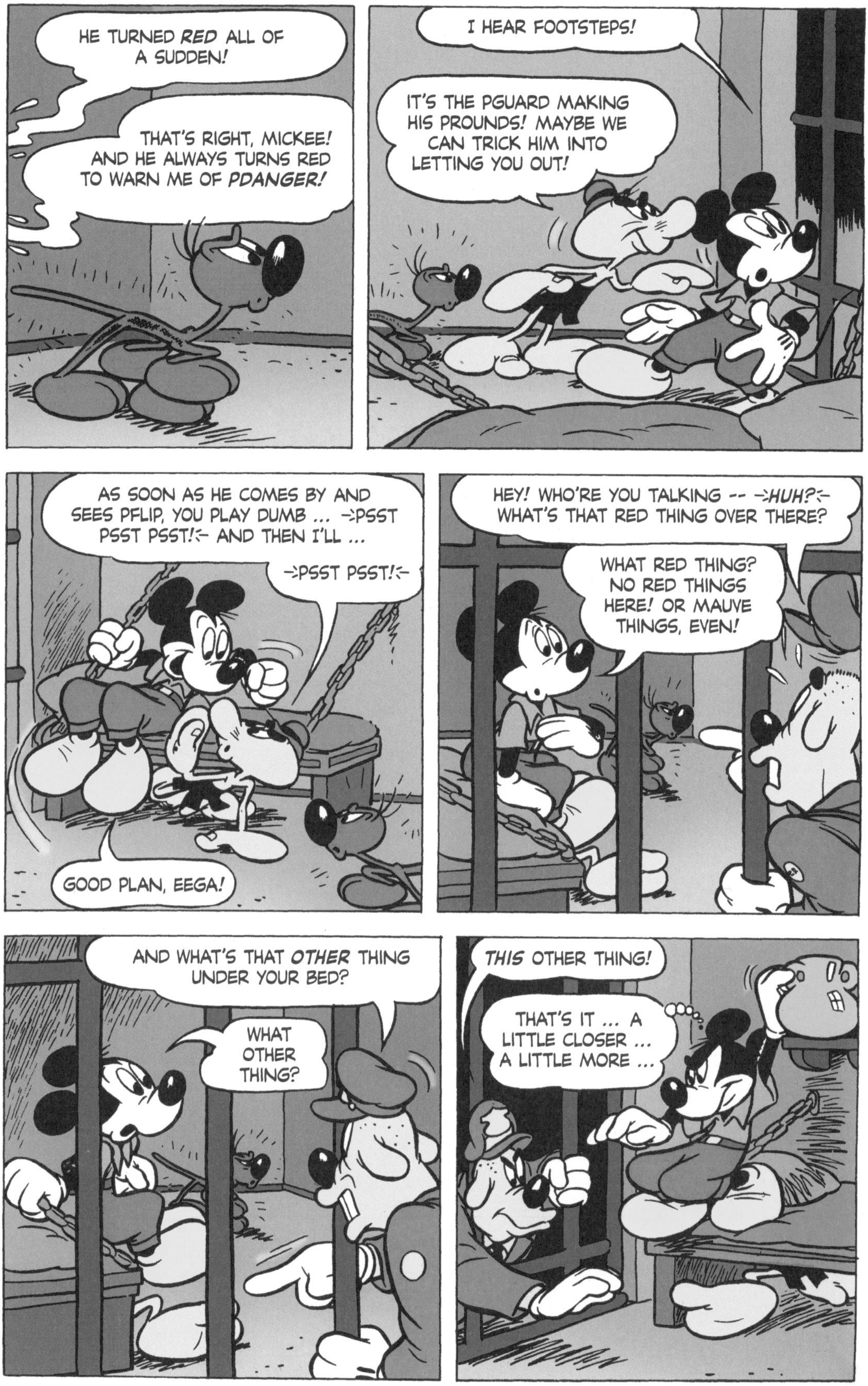
HE TURNED *RED* ALL OF A SUDDEN!
THAT'S RIGHT, MICKEE! AND HE ALWAYS TURNS RED TO WARN ME OF *PDANGER!*
I HEAR FOOTSTEPS!
IT'S THE PGUARD MAKING HIS PROUNDS! MAYBE WE CAN TRICK HIM INTO LETTING YOU OUT!
AS SOON AS HE COMES BY AND SEES PFLIP, YOU PLAY DUMB ... →PSST PSST PSST!← AND THEN I'LL ...
→PSST PSST!←
GOOD PLAN, EEGA!
HEY! WHO'RE YOU TALKING -- →*HUH?*← WHAT'S THAT RED THING OVER THERE?
WHAT RED THING? NO RED THINGS HERE! OR MAUVE THINGS, EVEN!
AND WHAT'S THAT *OTHER* THING UNDER YOUR BED?
WHAT OTHER THING?
THIS OTHER THING!
THAT'S IT ... A LITTLE CLOSER ... A LITTLE MORE ...

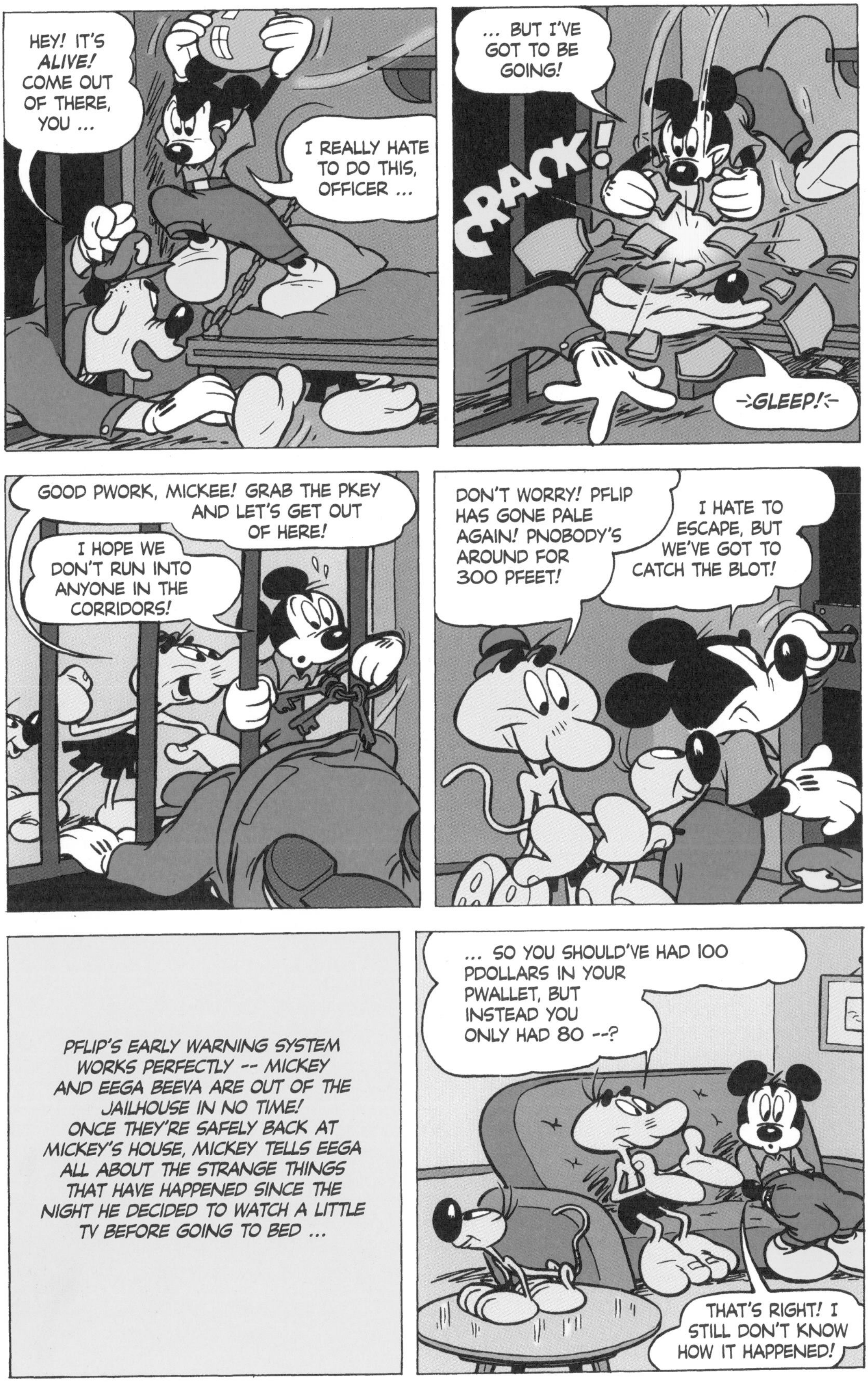
HEY! IT'S ALIVE! COME OUT OF THERE, YOU ...
I REALLY HATE TO DO THIS, OFFICER ...
... BUT I'VE GOT TO BE GOING!
CRACK!
-GLEEP!-
GOOD PWORK, MICKEE! GRAB THE PKEY AND LET'S GET OUT OF HERE!
I HOPE WE DON'T RUN INTO ANYONE IN THE CORRIDORS!
DON'T WORRY! PFLIP HAS GONE PALE AGAIN! PNOBODY'S AROUND FOR 300 PFEET!
I HATE TO ESCAPE, BUT WE'VE GOT TO CATCH THE BLOT!
PFLIP'S EARLY WARNING SYSTEM WORKS PERFECTLY -- MICKEY AND EEGA BEEVA ARE OUT OF THE JAILHOUSE IN NO TIME! ONCE THEY'RE SAFELY BACK AT MICKEY'S HOUSE, MICKEY TELLS EEGA ALL ABOUT THE STRANGE THINGS THAT HAVE HAPPENED SINCE THE NIGHT HE DECIDED TO WATCH A LITTLE TV BEFORE GOING TO BED ...
... SO YOU SHOULD'VE HAD 100 PDOLLARS IN YOUR PWALLET, BUT INSTEAD YOU ONLY HAD 80 --?
THAT'S RIGHT! I STILL DON'T KNOW HOW IT HAPPENED!

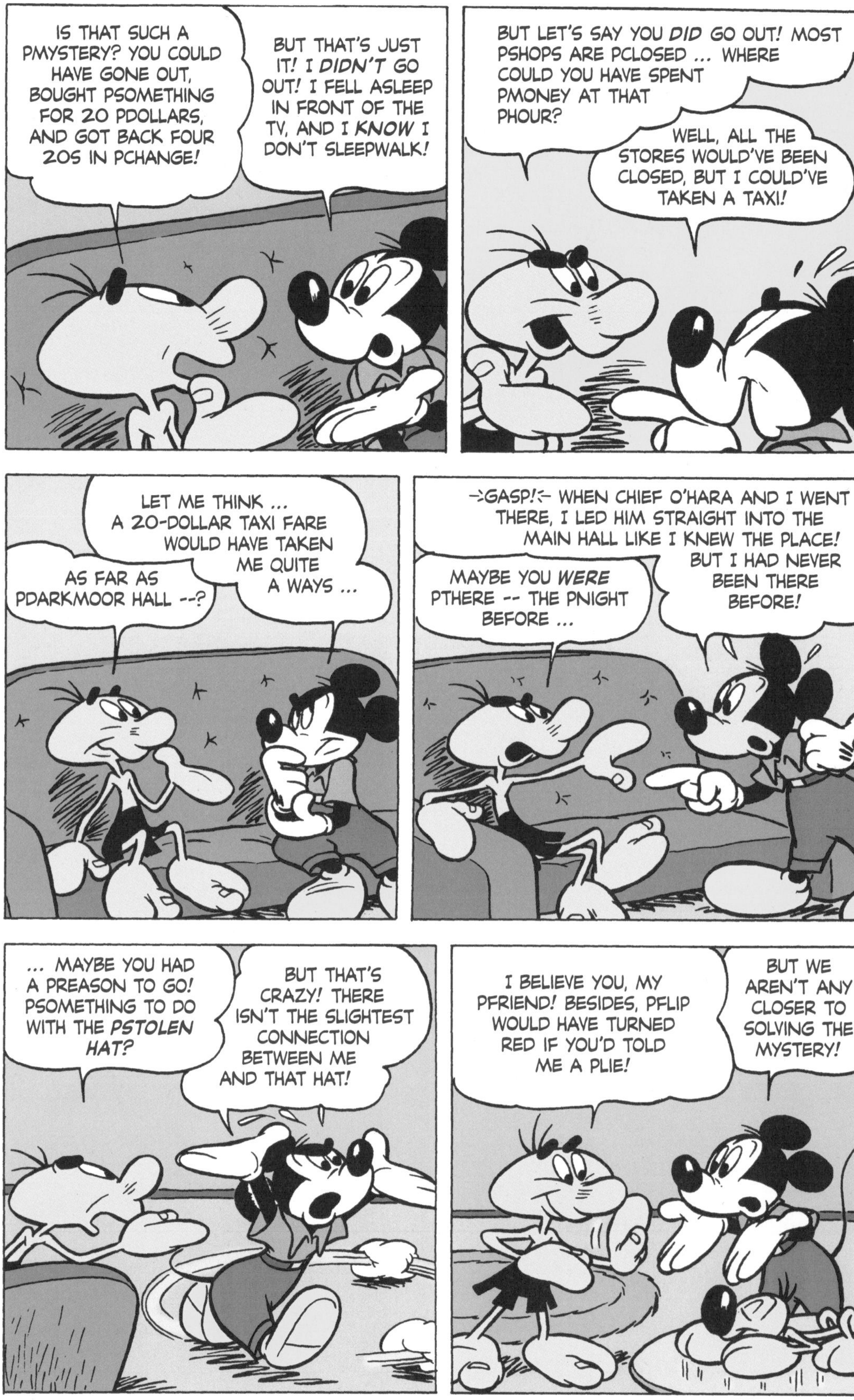
IS THAT SUCH A PMYSTERY? YOU COULD HAVE GONE OUT, BOUGHT PSOMETHING FOR 20 PDOLLARS, AND GOT BACK FOUR 20S IN PCHANGE!
BUT THAT'S JUST IT! I *DIDN'T* GO OUT! I FELL ASLEEP IN FRONT OF THE TV, AND I *KNOW* I DON'T SLEEPWALK!
BUT LET'S SAY YOU *DID* GO OUT! MOST PSHOPS ARE PCLOSED ... WHERE COULD YOU HAVE SPENT PMONEY AT THAT PHOUR?
WELL, ALL THE STORES WOULD'VE BEEN CLOSED, BUT I COULD'VE TAKEN A TAXI!
LET ME THINK ... A 20-DOLLAR TAXI FARE WOULD HAVE TAKEN ME QUITE A WAYS ...
AS FAR AS PDARKMOOR HALL --?
–GASP!– WHEN CHIEF O'HARA AND I WENT THERE, I LED HIM STRAIGHT INTO THE MAIN HALL LIKE I KNEW THE PLACE!
BUT I HAD NEVER BEEN THERE BEFORE!
MAYBE YOU *WERE* PTHERE -- THE PNIGHT BEFORE ...
... MAYBE YOU HAD A PREASON TO GO! PSOMETHING TO DO WITH THE *PSTOLEN HAT*?
BUT THAT'S CRAZY! THERE ISN'T THE SLIGHTEST CONNECTION BETWEEN ME AND THAT HAT!
I BELIEVE YOU, MY PFRIEND! BESIDES, PFLIP WOULD HAVE TURNED RED IF YOU'D TOLD ME A PLIE!
BUT WE AREN'T ANY CLOSER TO SOLVING THE MYSTERY!

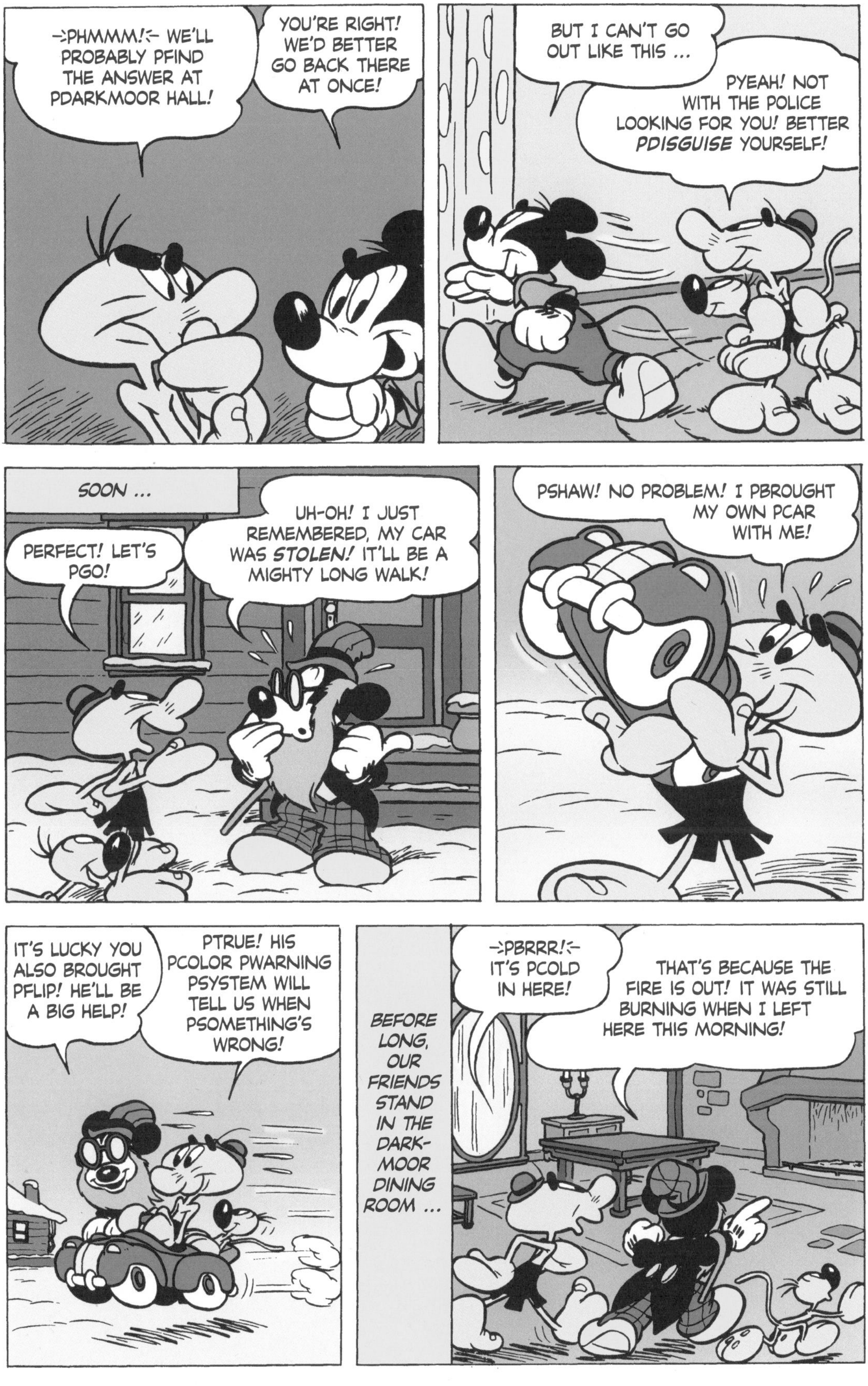
-PHMMM!- WE'LL PROBABLY PFIND THE ANSWER AT PDARKMOOR HALL!
YOU'RE RIGHT! WE'D BETTER GO BACK THERE AT ONCE!
BUT I CAN'T GO OUT LIKE THIS ...
PYEAH! NOT WITH THE POLICE LOOKING FOR YOU! BETTER *PDISGUISE* YOURSELF!
SOON ...
PERFECT! LET'S PGO!
UH-OH! I JUST REMEMBERED, MY CAR WAS *STOLEN!* IT'LL BE A MIGHTY LONG WALK!
PSHAW! NO PROBLEM! I PBROUGHT MY OWN PCAR WITH ME!
IT'S LUCKY YOU ALSO BROUGHT PFLIP! HE'LL BE A BIG HELP!
PTRUE! HIS PCOLOR PWARNING PSYSTEM WILL TELL US WHEN PSOMETHING'S WRONG!
BEFORE LONG, OUR FRIENDS STAND IN THE DARKMOOR DINING ROOM ...
-PBRRR!- IT'S PCOLD IN HERE!
THAT'S BECAUSE THE FIRE IS OUT! IT WAS STILL BURNING WHEN I LEFT HERE THIS MORNING!

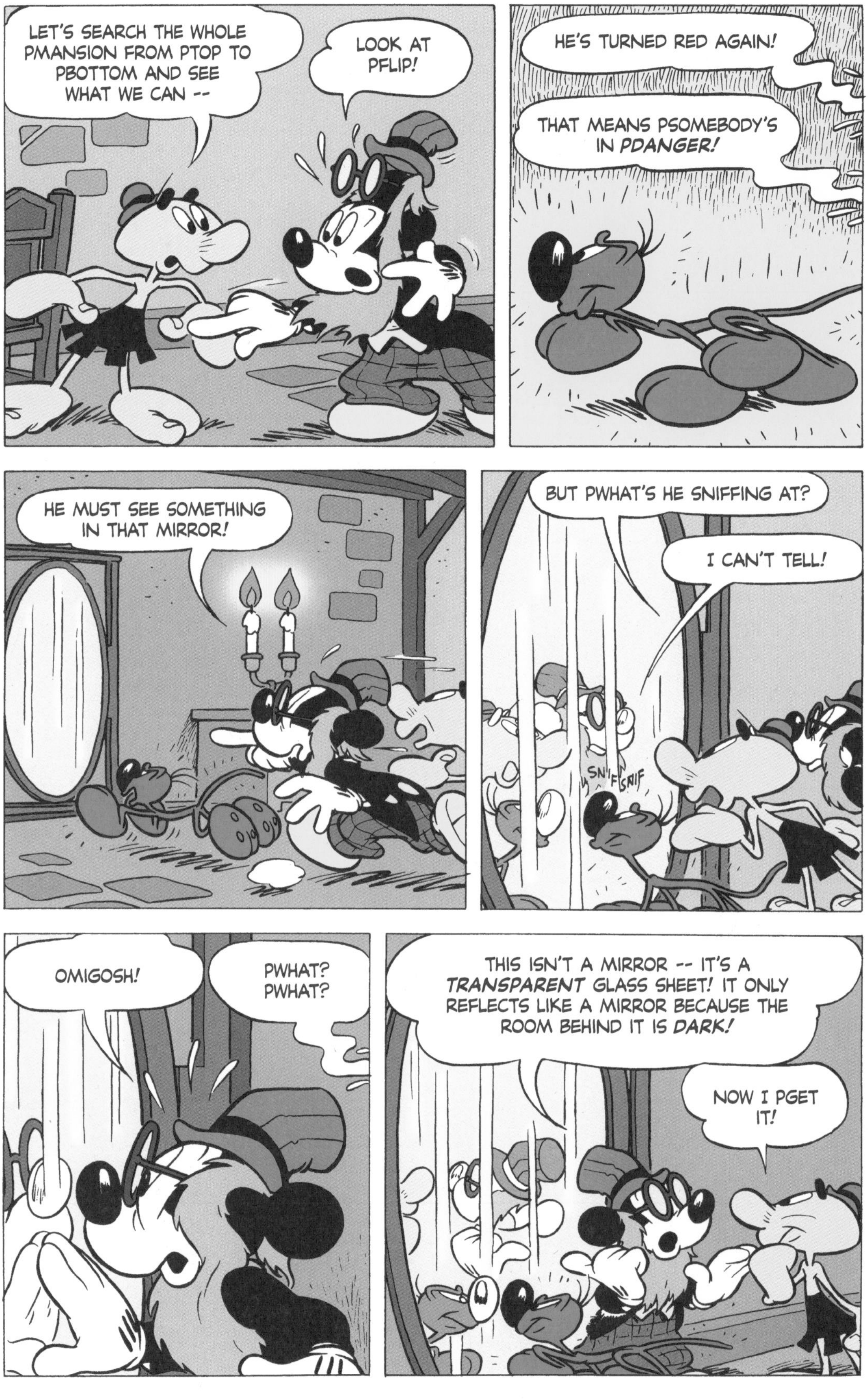
LET'S SEARCH THE WHOLE PMANSION FROM PTOP TO PBOTTOM AND SEE WHAT WE CAN --
LOOK AT PFLIP!
HE'S TURNED RED AGAIN!
THAT MEANS PSOMEBODY'S IN PDANGER!
HE MUST SEE SOMETHING IN THAT MIRROR!
BUT PWHAT'S HE SNIFFING AT?
I CAN'T TELL!
SNIF SNIF
OMIGOSH!
PWHAT? PWHAT?
THIS ISN'T A MIRROR -- IT'S A TRANSPARENT GLASS SHEET! IT ONLY REFLECTS LIKE A MIRROR BECAUSE THE ROOM BEHIND IT IS DARK!
NOW I PGET IT!

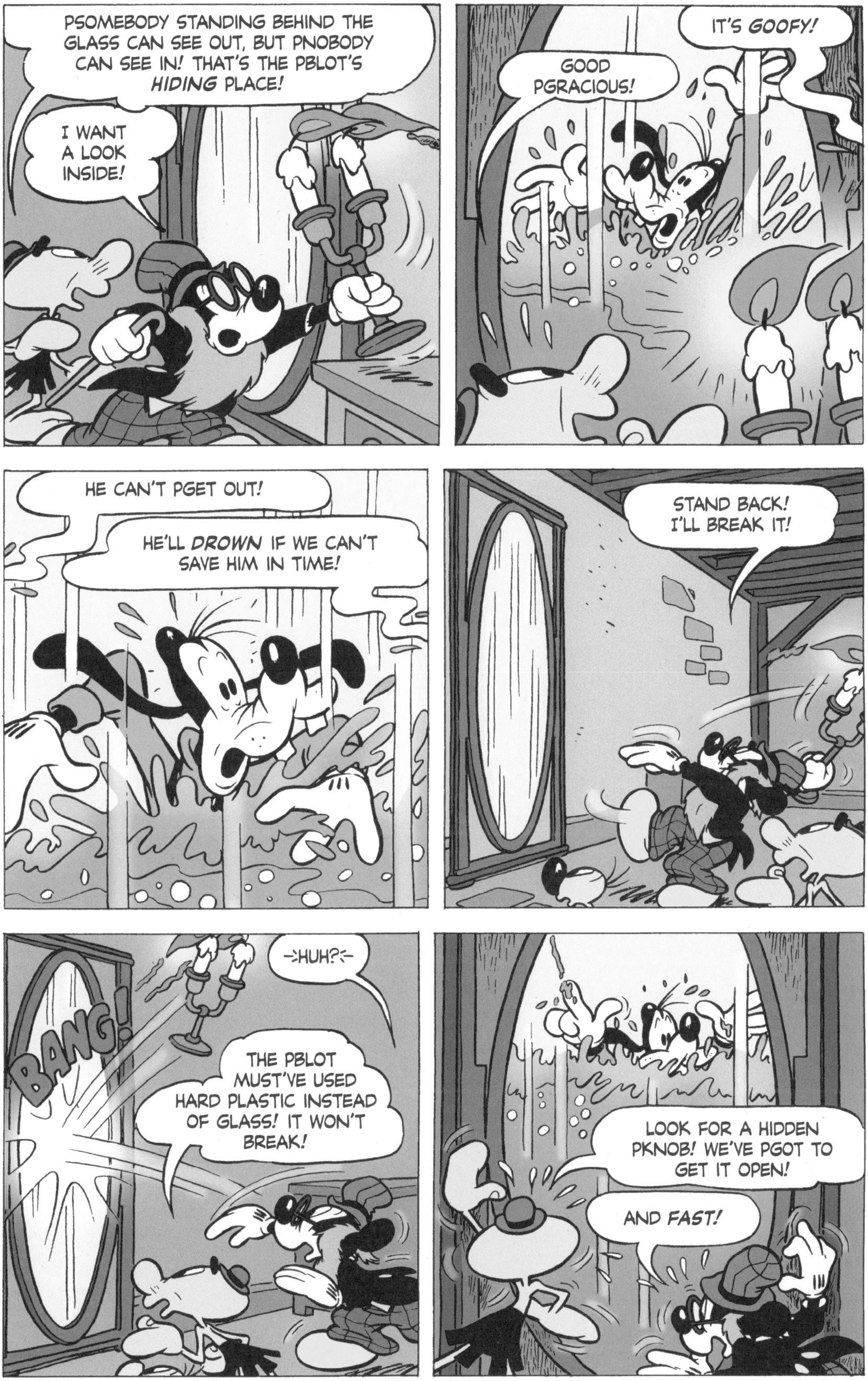

PSOMEBODY STANDING BEHIND THE GLASS CAN SEE OUT, BUT PNOBODY CAN SEE IN! THAT'S THE PBLOT'S *HIDING* PLACE!
I WANT A LOOK INSIDE!
IT'S *GOOFY!*
GOOD PGRACIOUS!
HE CAN'T PGET OUT!
HE'LL *DROWN* IF WE CAN'T SAVE HIM IN TIME!
STAND BACK! I'LL BREAK IT!
BANG!
HUH?
THE PBLOT MUST'VE USED HARD PLASTIC INSTEAD OF GLASS! IT WON'T BREAK!
LOOK FOR A HIDDEN PKNOB! WE'VE PGOT TO GET IT OPEN!
AND *FAST!*

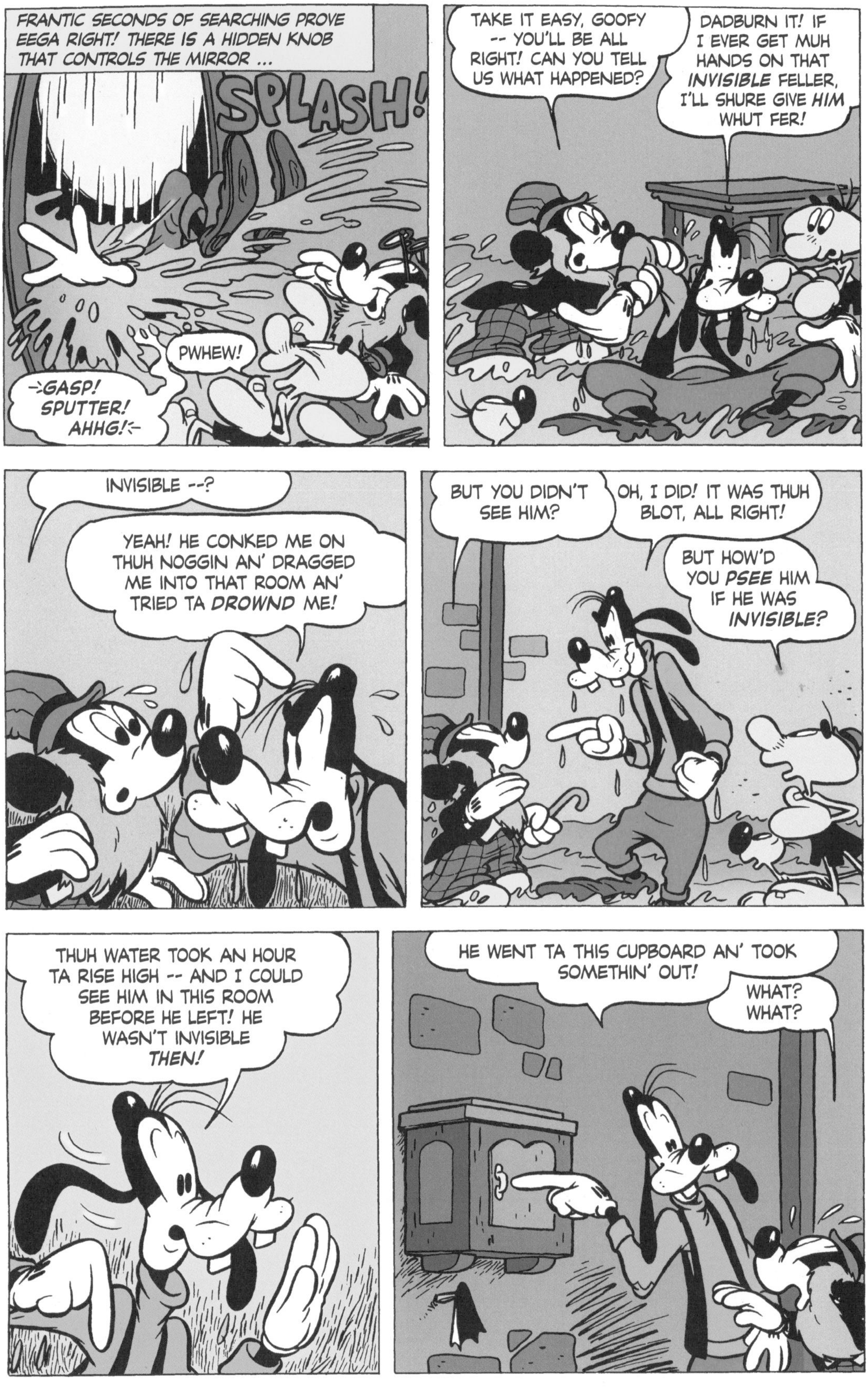

FRANTIC SECONDS OF SEARCHING PROVE EEGA RIGHT! THERE IS A HIDDEN KNOB THAT CONTROLS THE MIRROR ...
SPLASH!
PWHEW!
GASP! SPUTTER! AHHG!
TAKE IT EASY, GOOFY -- YOU'LL BE ALL RIGHT! CAN YOU TELL US WHAT HAPPENED?
DADBURN IT! IF I EVER GET MUH HANDS ON THAT INVISIBLE FELLER, I'LL SHURE GIVE HIM WHUT FER!
INVISIBLE --?
YEAH! HE CONKED ME ON THUH NOGGIN AN' DRAGGED ME INTO THAT ROOM AN' TRIED TA DROWND ME!
BUT YOU DIDN'T SEE HIM?
OH, I DID! IT WAS THUH BLOT, ALL RIGHT!
BUT HOW'D YOU PSEE HIM IF HE WAS INVISIBLE?
THUH WATER TOOK AN HOUR TA RISE HIGH -- AND I COULD SEE HIM IN THIS ROOM BEFORE HE LEFT! HE WASN'T INVISIBLE THEN!
HE WENT TA THIS CUPBOARD AN' TOOK SOMETHIN' OUT!
WHAT? WHAT?

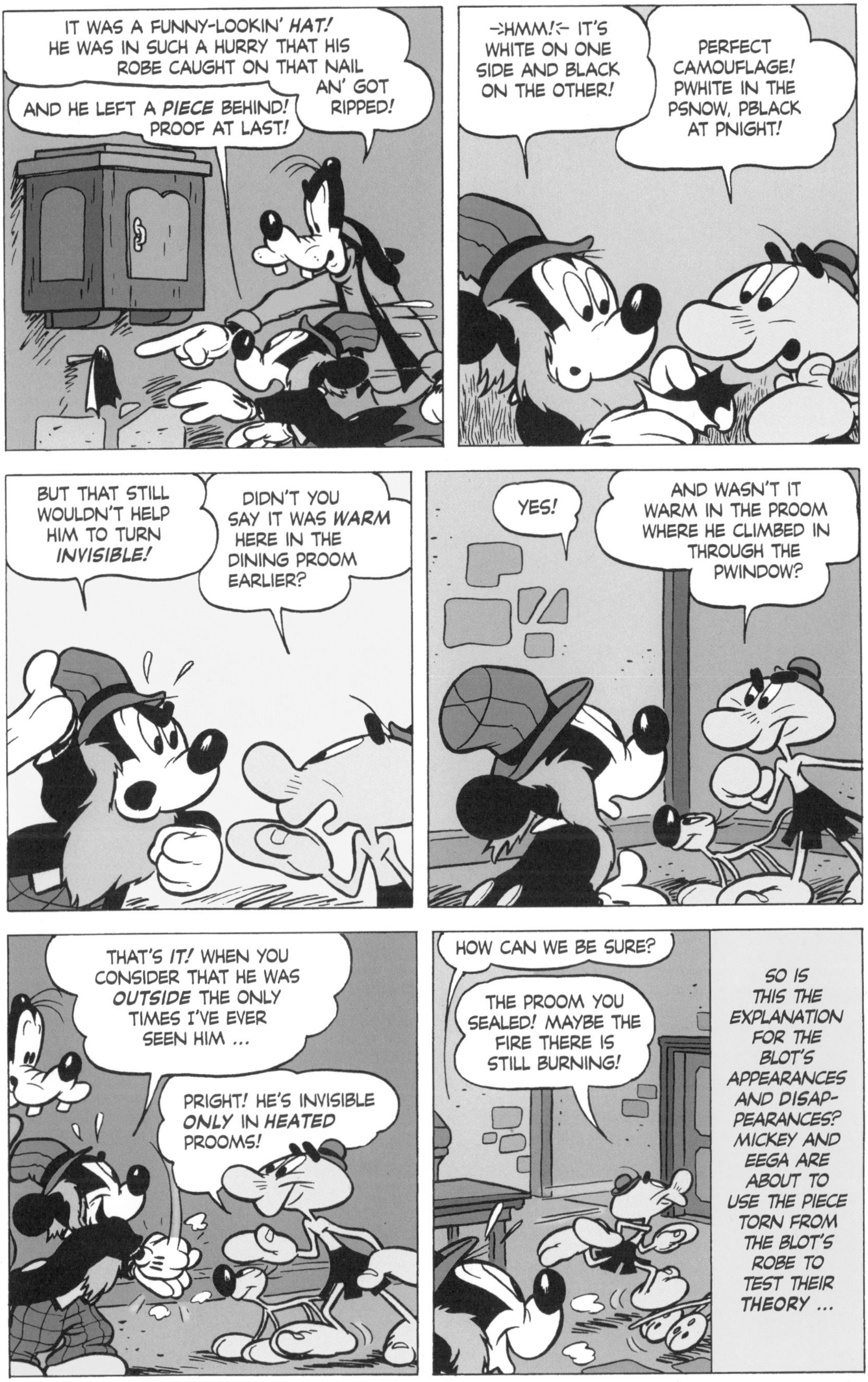
IT WAS A FUNNY-LOOKIN' HAT! HE WAS IN SUCH A HURRY THAT HIS ROBE CAUGHT ON THAT NAIL AN' GOT RIPPED!
AND HE LEFT A PIECE BEHIND! PROOF AT LAST!
-HMM!- IT'S WHITE ON ONE SIDE AND BLACK ON THE OTHER!
PERFECT CAMOUFLAGE! PWHITE IN THE PSNOW, PBLACK AT PNIGHT!
BUT THAT STILL WOULDN'T HELP HIM TO TURN INVISIBLE!
DIDN'T YOU SAY IT WAS WARM HERE IN THE DINING PROOM EARLIER?
YES!
AND WASN'T IT WARM IN THE PROOM WHERE HE CLIMBED IN THROUGH THE PWINDOW?
THAT'S IT! WHEN YOU CONSIDER THAT HE WAS OUTSIDE THE ONLY TIMES I'VE EVER SEEN HIM ...
PRIGHT! HE'S INVISIBLE ONLY IN HEATED PROOMS!
HOW CAN WE BE SURE?
THE PROOM YOU SEALED! MAYBE THE FIRE THERE IS STILL BURNING!
SO IS THIS THE EXPLANATION FOR THE BLOT'S APPEARANCES AND DISAPPEARANCES? MICKEY AND EEGA ARE ABOUT TO USE THE PIECE TORN FROM THE BLOT'S ROBE TO TEST THEIR THEORY ...

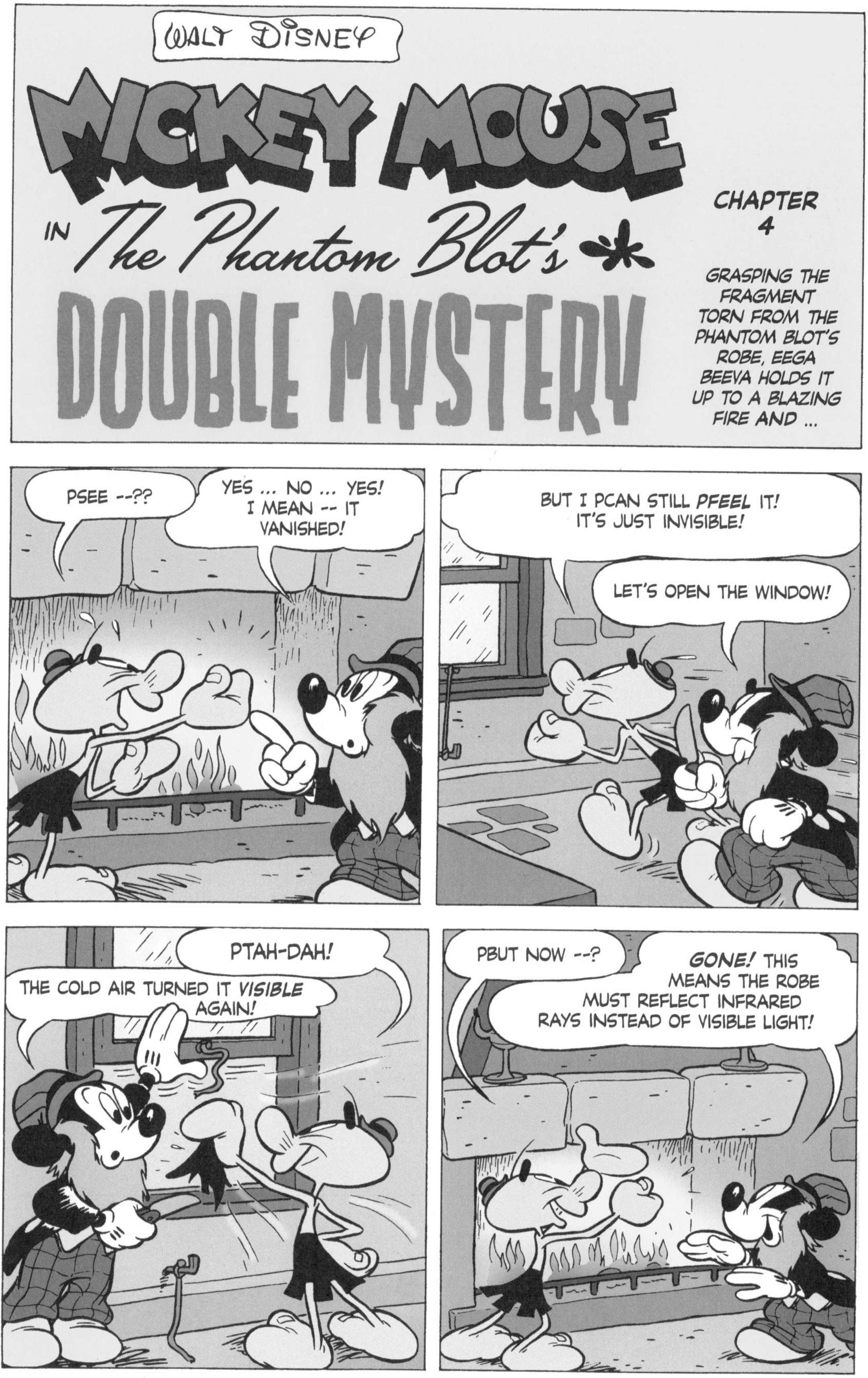
WALT DISNEY
MICKEY MOUSE
IN The Phantom Blot's DOUBLE MYSTERY
CHAPTER 4
GRASPING THE FRAGMENT TORN FROM THE PHANTOM BLOT'S ROBE, EEGA BEEVA HOLDS IT UP TO A BLAZING FIRE AND ...
PSEE --??
YES ... NO ... YES! I MEAN -- IT VANISHED!
BUT I PCAN STILL PFEEL IT! IT'S JUST INVISIBLE!
LET'S OPEN THE WINDOW!
PTAH-DAH!
THE COLD AIR TURNED IT VISIBLE AGAIN!
PBUT NOW --?
GONE! THIS MEANS THE ROBE MUST REFLECT INFRARED RAYS INSTEAD OF VISIBLE LIGHT!

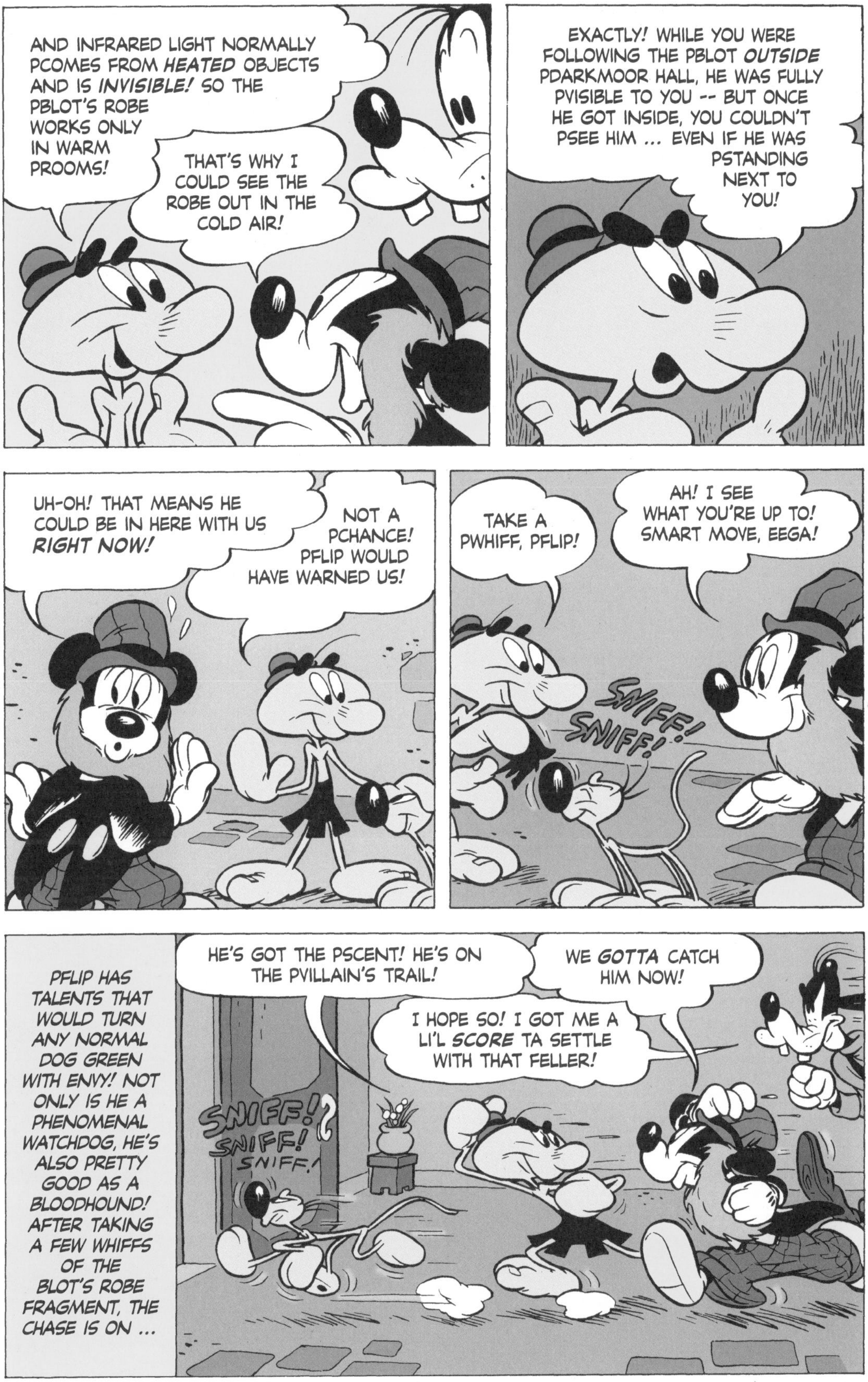
AND INFRARED LIGHT NORMALLY PCOMES FROM HEATED OBJECTS AND IS INVISIBLE! SO THE PBLOT'S ROBE WORKS ONLY IN WARM PROOMS!
THAT'S WHY I COULD SEE THE ROBE OUT IN THE COLD AIR!
EXACTLY! WHILE YOU WERE FOLLOWING THE PBLOT OUTSIDE PDARKMOOR HALL, HE WAS FULLY PVISIBLE TO YOU -- BUT ONCE HE GOT INSIDE, YOU COULDN'T PSEE HIM ... EVEN IF HE WAS PSTANDING NEXT TO YOU!
UH-OH! THAT MEANS HE COULD BE IN HERE WITH US RIGHT NOW!
NOT A PCHANCE! PFLIP WOULD HAVE WARNED US!
TAKE A PWHIFF, PFLIP!
AH! I SEE WHAT YOU'RE UP TO! SMART MOVE, EEGA!
SNIFF! SNIFF!
PFLIP HAS TALENTS THAT WOULD TURN ANY NORMAL DOG GREEN WITH ENVY! NOT ONLY IS HE A PHENOMENAL WATCHDOG, HE'S ALSO PRETTY GOOD AS A BLOODHOUND! AFTER TAKING A FEW WHIFFS OF THE BLOT'S ROBE FRAGMENT, THE CHASE IS ON ...
HE'S GOT THE PSCENT! HE'S ON THE PVILLAIN'S TRAIL!
WE GOTTA CATCH HIM NOW!
I HOPE SO! I GOT ME A LI'L SCORE TA SETTLE WITH THAT FELLER!
SNIFF! SNIFF! SNIFF!

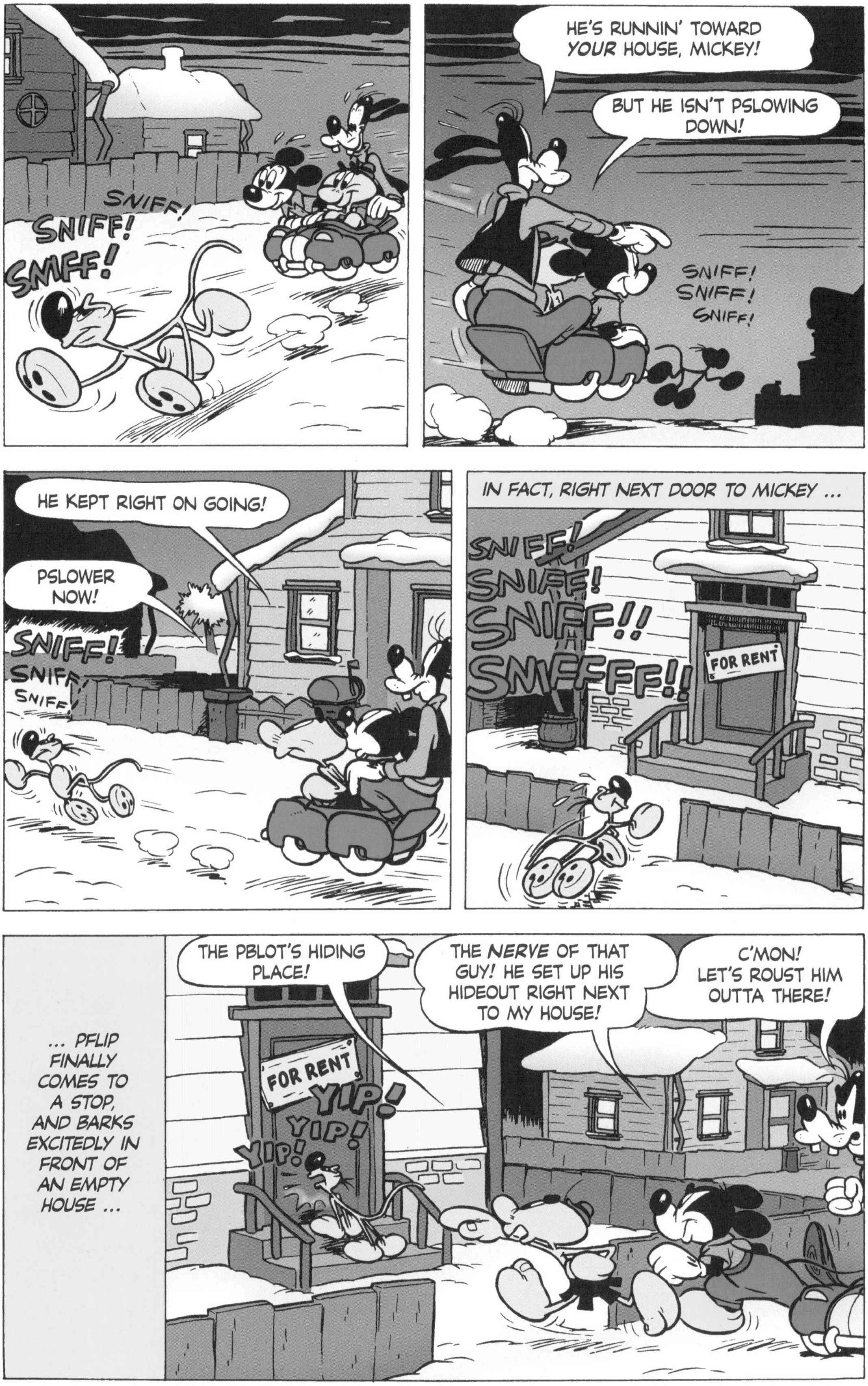

SNIFF!
SNIFF!
SNIFF!
HE'S RUNNIN' TOWARD YOUR HOUSE, MICKEY!
BUT HE ISN'T PSLOWING DOWN!
SNIFF! SNIFF! SNIFF!
HE KEPT RIGHT ON GOING!
PSLOWER NOW!
SNIFF!
SNIFF!
SNIFF!
IN FACT, RIGHT NEXT DOOR TO MICKEY ...
SNIFF!
SNIFF!
SNIFF!!
SNIFFFFF!!
FOR RENT
... PFLIP FINALLY COMES TO A STOP, AND BARKS EXCITEDLY IN FRONT OF AN EMPTY HOUSE ...
THE PBLOT'S HIDING PLACE!
THE NERVE OF THAT GUY! HE SET UP HIS HIDEOUT RIGHT NEXT TO MY HOUSE!
C'MON! LET'S ROUST HIM OUTTA THERE!
FOR RENT
YIP!
YIP!
YIP!

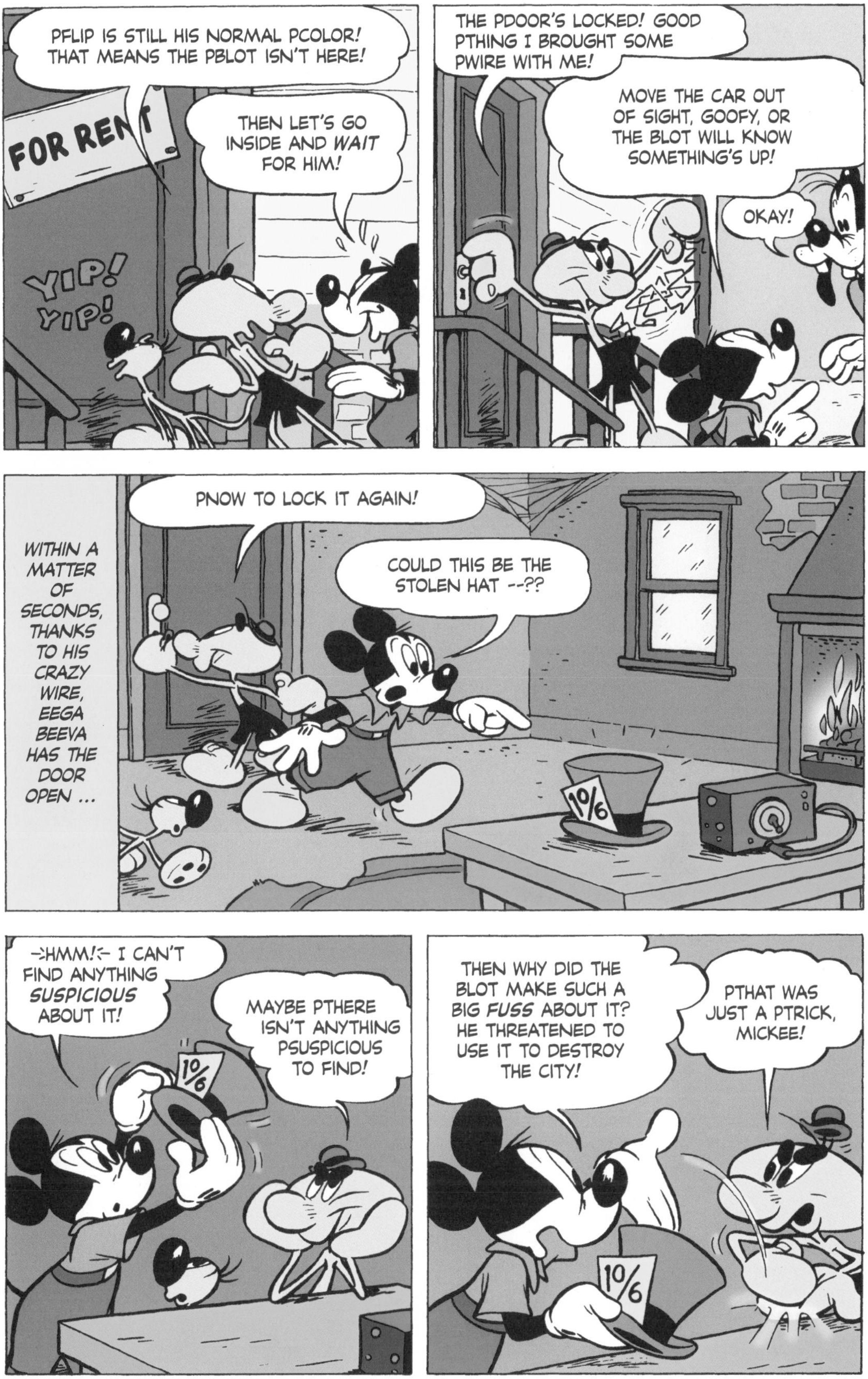
PFLIP IS STILL HIS NORMAL PCOLOR! THAT MEANS THE PBLOT ISN'T HERE!
FOR RENT
THEN LET'S GO INSIDE AND *WAIT* FOR HIM!
YIP! YIP!
THE PDOOR'S LOCKED! GOOD PTHING I BROUGHT SOME PWIRE WITH ME!
MOVE THE CAR OUT OF SIGHT, GOOFY, OR THE BLOT WILL KNOW SOMETHING'S UP!
OKAY!
WITHIN A MATTER OF SECONDS, THANKS TO HIS CRAZY WIRE, EEGA BEEVA HAS THE DOOR OPEN ...
PNOW TO LOCK IT AGAIN!
COULD THIS BE THE STOLEN HAT --??
10/6
-HMM!- I CAN'T FIND ANYTHING *SUSPICIOUS* ABOUT IT!
MAYBE PTHERE ISN'T ANYTHING PSUSPICIOUS TO FIND!
THEN WHY DID THE BLOT MAKE SUCH A BIG *FUSS* ABOUT IT? HE THREATENED TO USE IT TO DESTROY THE CITY!
PTHAT WAS JUST A PTRICK, MICKEE!

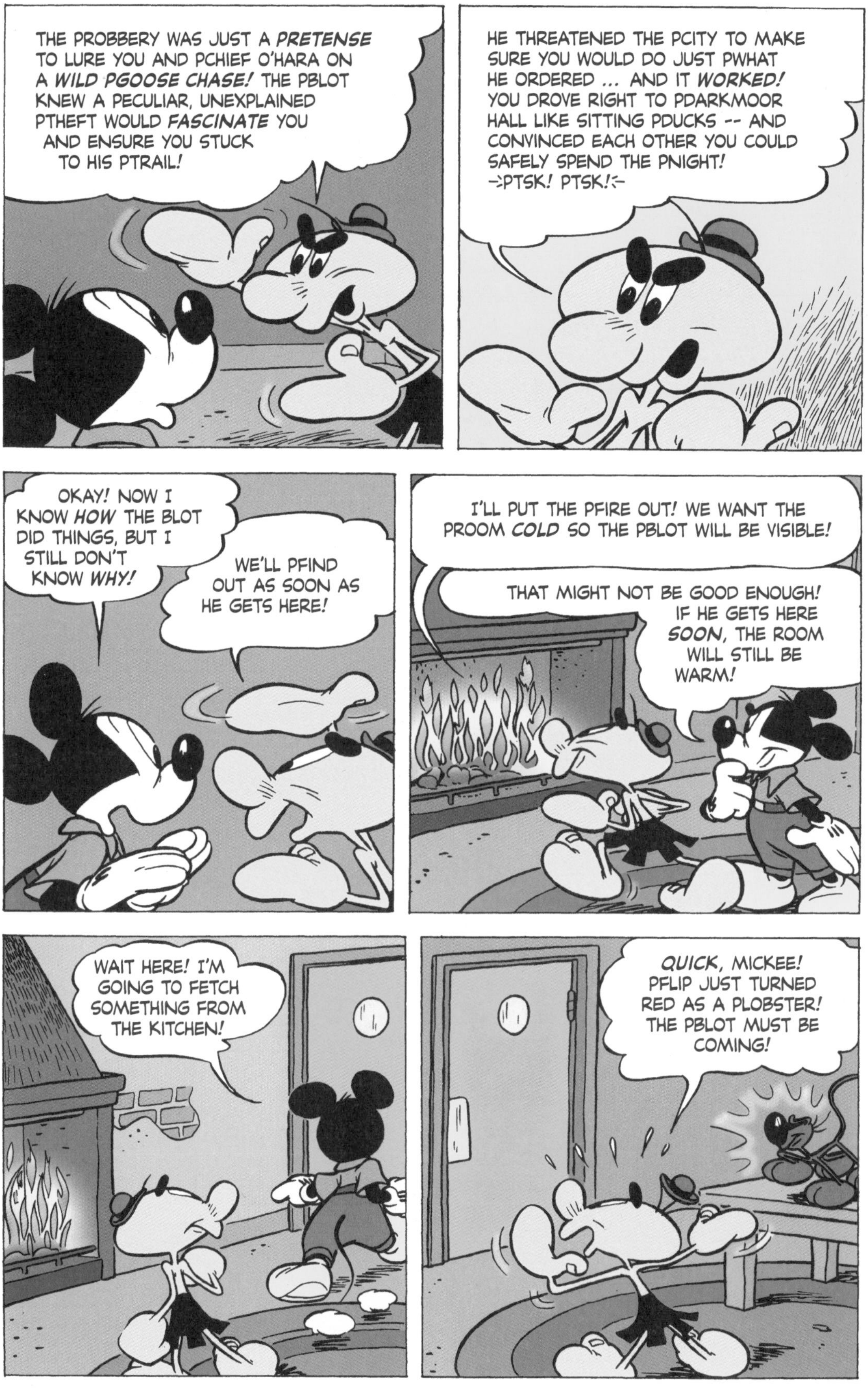
THE PROBBERY WAS JUST A PRETENSE TO LURE YOU AND PCHIEF O'HARA ON A WILD PGOOSE CHASE! THE PBLOT KNEW A PECULIAR, UNEXPLAINED PTHEFT WOULD FASCINATE YOU AND ENSURE YOU STUCK TO HIS PTRAIL!
HE THREATENED THE PCITY TO MAKE SURE YOU WOULD DO JUST PWHAT HE ORDERED ... AND IT WORKED! YOU DROVE RIGHT TO PDARKMOOR HALL LIKE SITTING PDUCKS -- AND CONVINCED EACH OTHER YOU COULD SAFELY SPEND THE PNIGHT! —PTSK! PTSK!—
OKAY! NOW I KNOW HOW THE BLOT DID THINGS, BUT I STILL DON'T KNOW WHY!
WE'LL PFIND OUT AS SOON AS HE GETS HERE!
I'LL PUT THE PFIRE OUT! WE WANT THE PROOM COLD SO THE PBLOT WILL BE VISIBLE!
THAT MIGHT NOT BE GOOD ENOUGH! IF HE GETS HERE SOON, THE ROOM WILL STILL BE WARM!
WAIT HERE! I'M GOING TO FETCH SOMETHING FROM THE KITCHEN!
QUICK, MICKEE! PFLIP JUST TURNED RED AS A PLOBSTER! THE PBLOT MUST BE COMING!

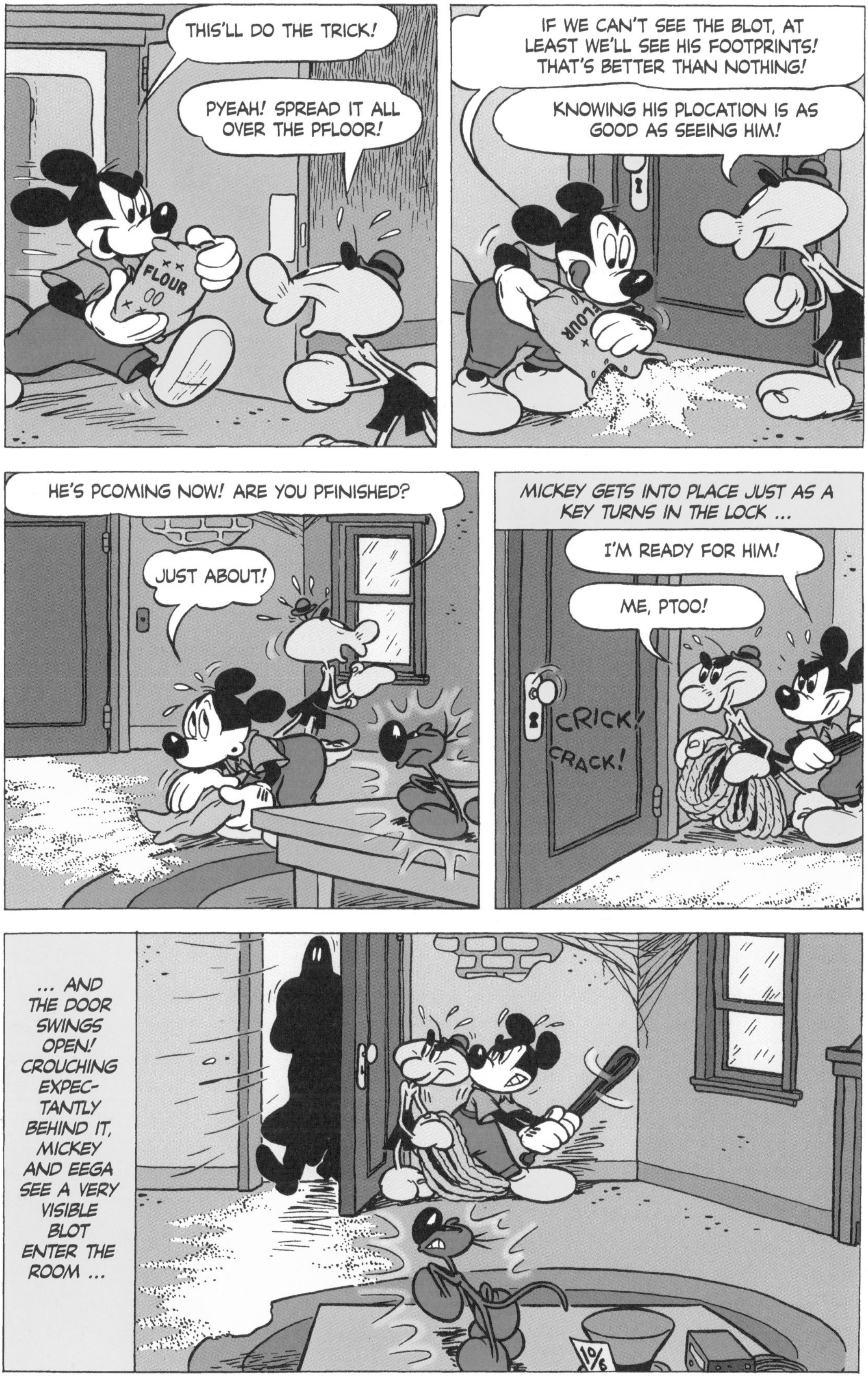
THIS'LL DO THE TRICK!
PYEAH! SPREAD IT ALL OVER THE PFLOOR!
FLOUR
IF WE CAN'T SEE THE BLOT, AT LEAST WE'LL SEE HIS FOOTPRINTS! THAT'S BETTER THAN NOTHING!
KNOWING HIS PLOCATION IS AS GOOD AS SEEING HIM!
FLOUR
HE'S PCOMING NOW! ARE YOU PFINISHED?
JUST ABOUT!
MICKEY GETS INTO PLACE JUST AS A KEY TURNS IN THE LOCK ...
I'M READY FOR HIM!
ME, PTOO!
CRICK!
CRACK!
... AND THE DOOR SWINGS OPEN! CROUCHING EXPEC-TANTLY BEHIND IT, MICKEY AND EEGA SEE A VERY VISIBLE BLOT ENTER THE ROOM ...

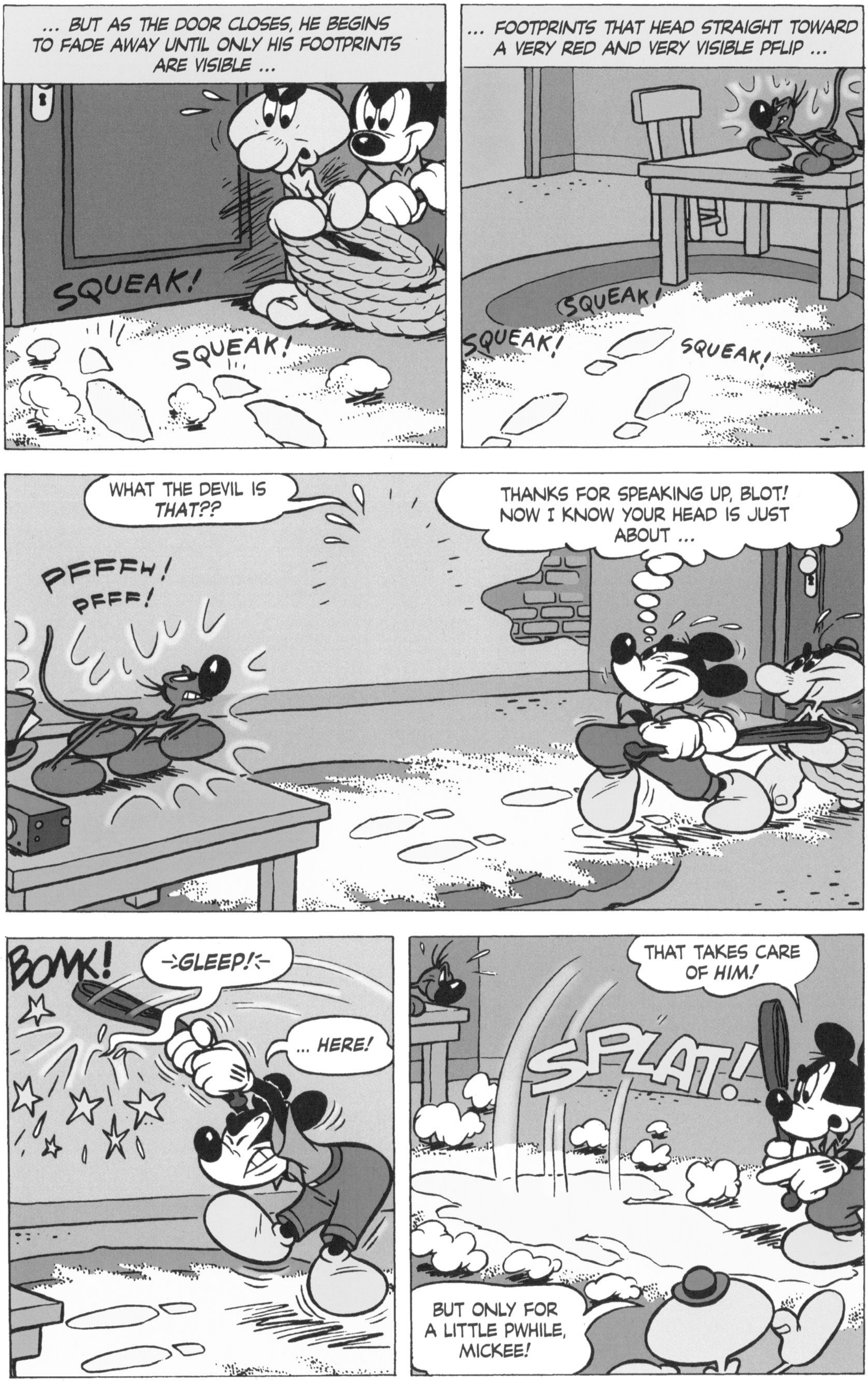
... BUT AS THE DOOR CLOSES, HE BEGINS TO FADE AWAY UNTIL ONLY HIS FOOTPRINTS ARE VISIBLE ...
SQUEAK!
SQUEAK!
... FOOTPRINTS THAT HEAD STRAIGHT TOWARD A VERY RED AND VERY VISIBLE PFLIP ...
SQUEAK!
SQUEAK!
SQUEAK!
WHAT THE DEVIL IS THAT??
THANKS FOR SPEAKING UP, BLOT! NOW I KNOW YOUR HEAD IS JUST ABOUT ...
PFFFH!
PFFF!
BONK!
GLEEP!
... HERE!
THAT TAKES CARE OF HIM!
SPLAT!
BUT ONLY FOR A LITTLE PWHILE, MICKEE!

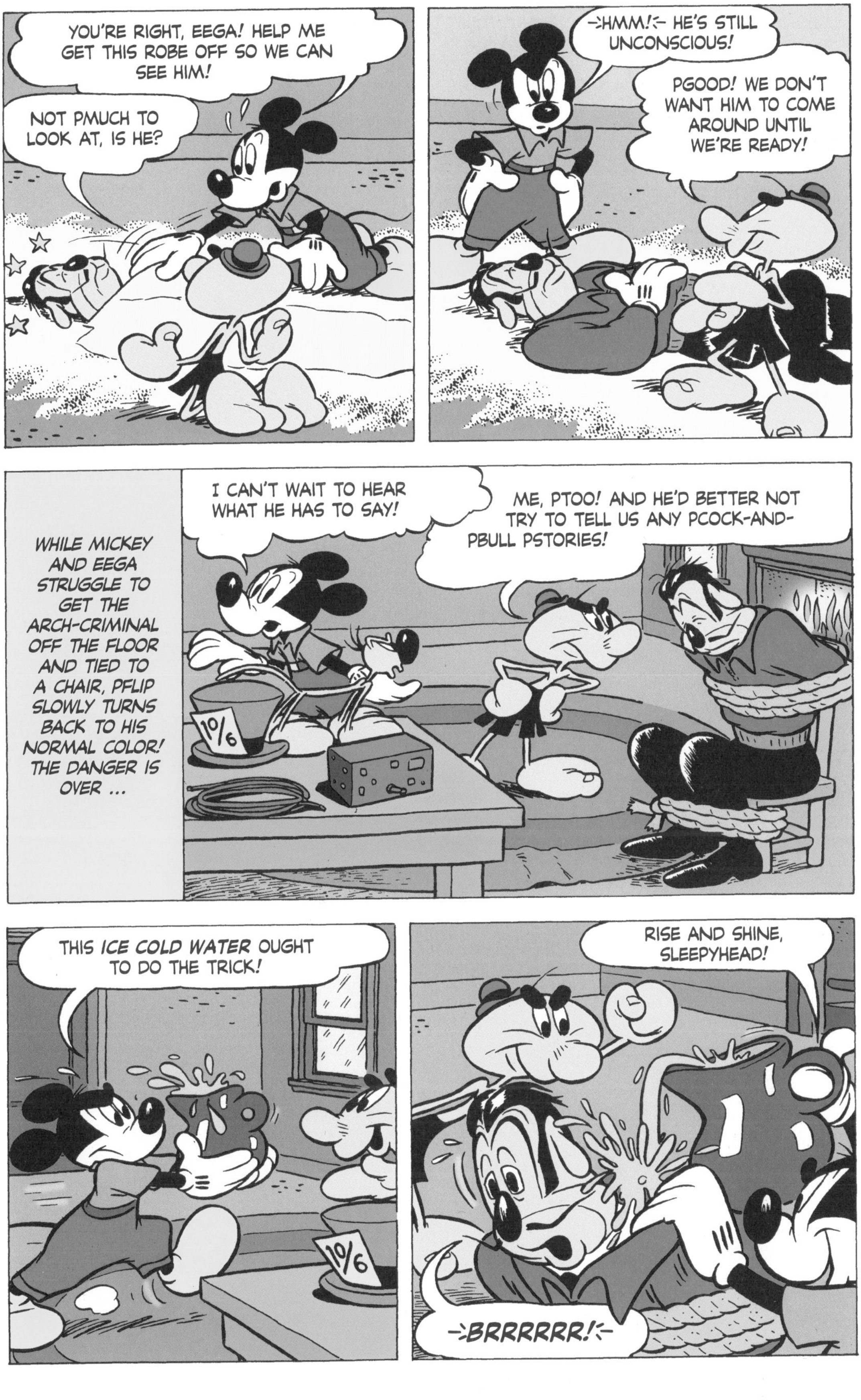
YOU'RE RIGHT, EEGA! HELP ME GET THIS ROBE OFF SO WE CAN SEE HIM!
NOT PMUCH TO LOOK AT, IS HE?
-HMM!- HE'S STILL UNCONSCIOUS!
PGOOD! WE DON'T WANT HIM TO COME AROUND UNTIL WE'RE READY!
WHILE MICKEY AND EEGA STRUGGLE TO GET THE ARCH-CRIMINAL OFF THE FLOOR AND TIED TO A CHAIR, PFLIP SLOWLY TURNS BACK TO HIS NORMAL COLOR! THE DANGER IS OVER ...
I CAN'T WAIT TO HEAR WHAT HE HAS TO SAY!
ME, PTOO! AND HE'D BETTER NOT TRY TO TELL US ANY PCOCK-AND-PBULL PSTORIES!
10/6
THIS ICE COLD WATER OUGHT TO DO THE TRICK!
10/6
RISE AND SHINE, SLEEPYHEAD!
-BRRRRRR!-

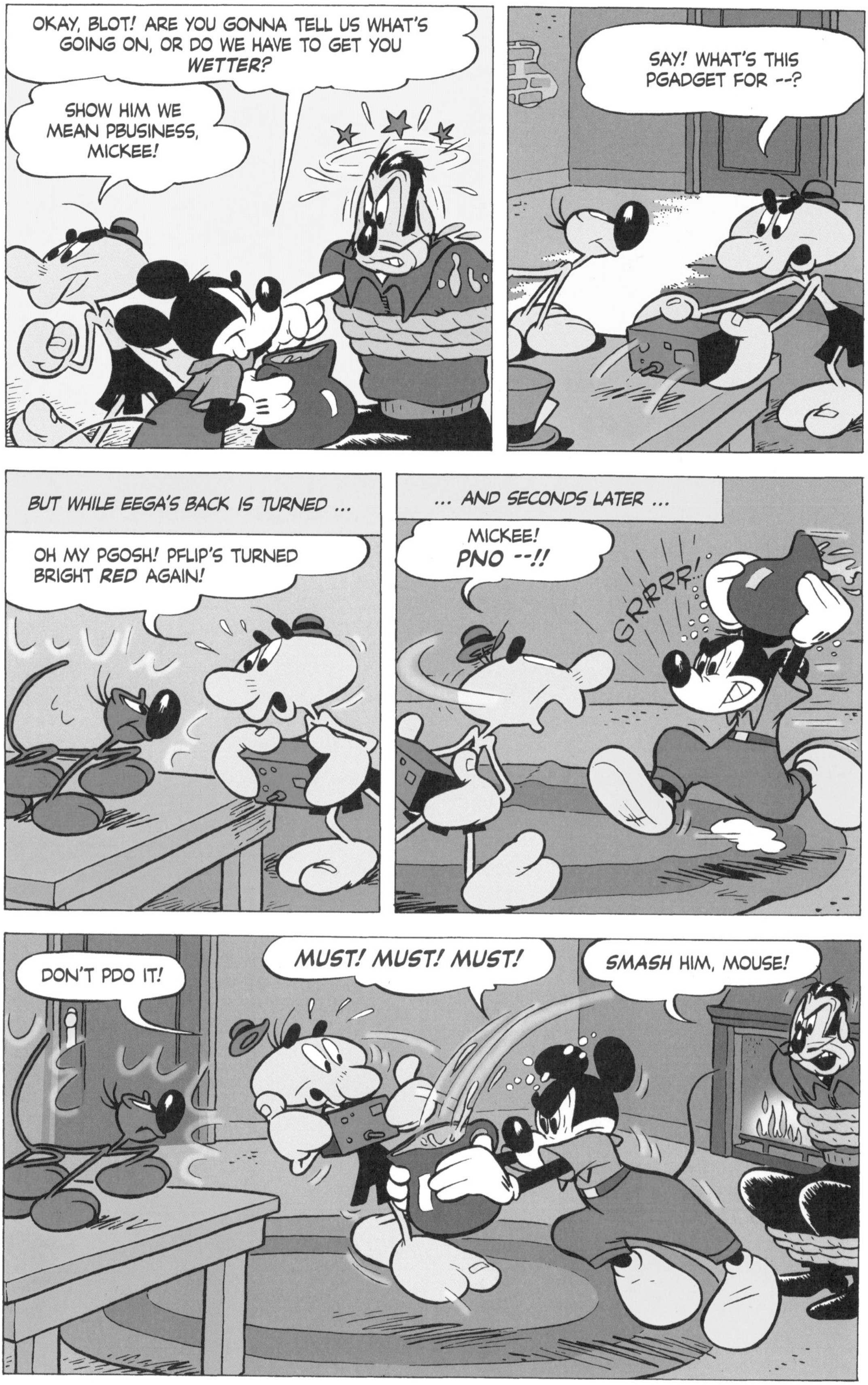

OKAY, BLOT! ARE YOU GONNA TELL US WHAT'S GOING ON, OR DO WE HAVE TO GET YOU *WETTER?*
SHOW HIM WE MEAN PBUSINESS, MICKEE!
SAY! WHAT'S THIS PGADGET FOR --?
BUT WHILE EEGA'S BACK IS TURNED ...
OH MY PGOSH! PFLIP'S TURNED BRIGHT *RED* AGAIN!
... AND SECONDS LATER ...
MICKEE! **PNO --!!**
GRRRR!
DON'T PDO IT!
MUST! MUST! MUST!
SMASH HIM, MOUSE!

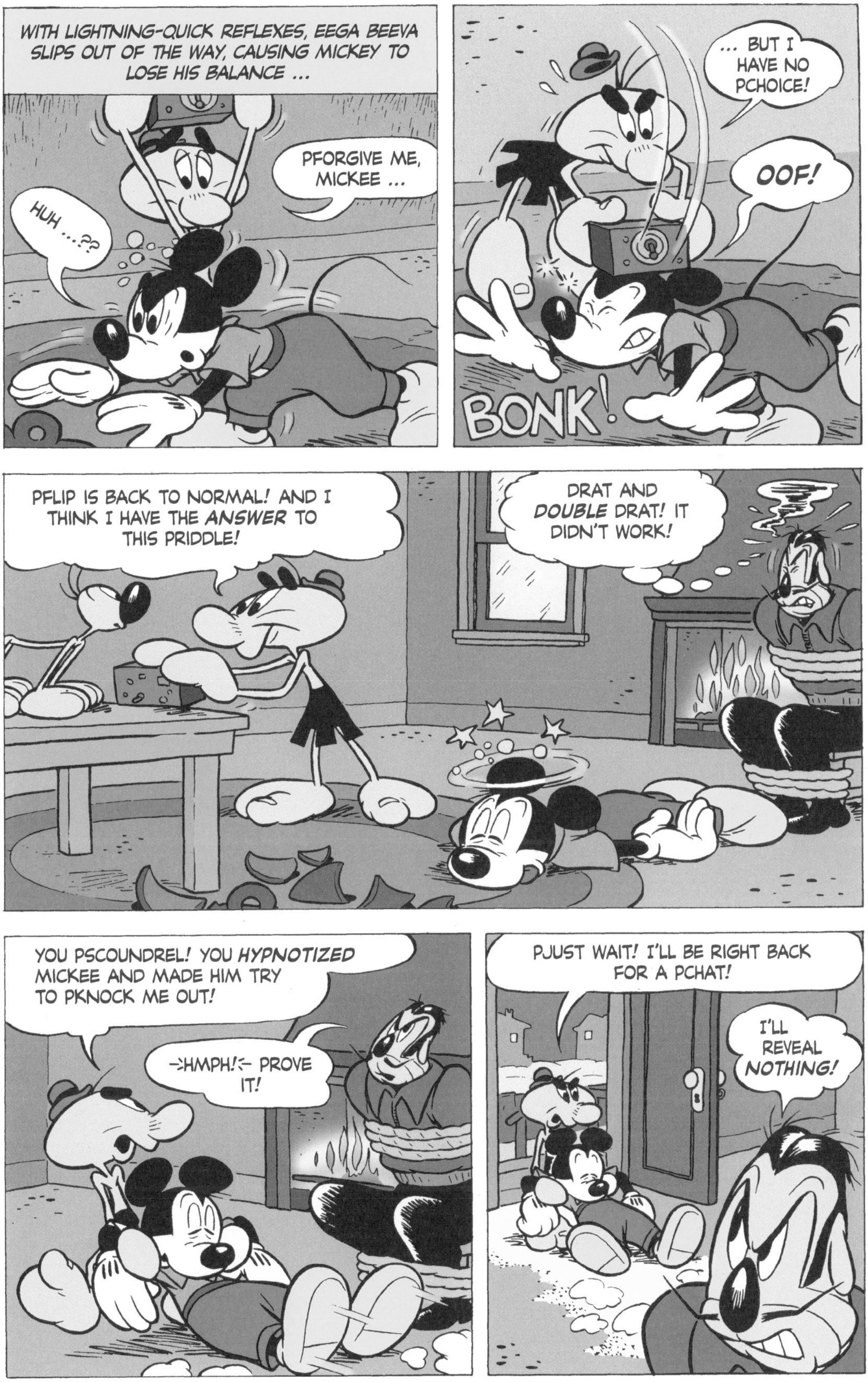
WITH LIGHTNING-QUICK REFLEXES, EEGA BEEVA SLIPS OUT OF THE WAY, CAUSING MICKEY TO LOSE HIS BALANCE ...
PFORGIVE ME, MICKEE ...
HUH ...??
... BUT I HAVE NO PCHOICE!
OOF!
BONK!
PFLIP IS BACK TO NORMAL! AND I THINK I HAVE THE *ANSWER* TO THIS PRIDDLE!
DRAT AND *DOUBLE* DRAT! IT DIDN'T WORK!
YOU PSCOUNDREL! YOU *HYPNOTIZED* MICKEE AND MADE HIM TRY TO PKNOCK ME OUT!
HMPH! PROVE IT!
PJUST WAIT! I'LL BE RIGHT BACK FOR A PCHAT!
I'LL REVEAL *NOTHING!*

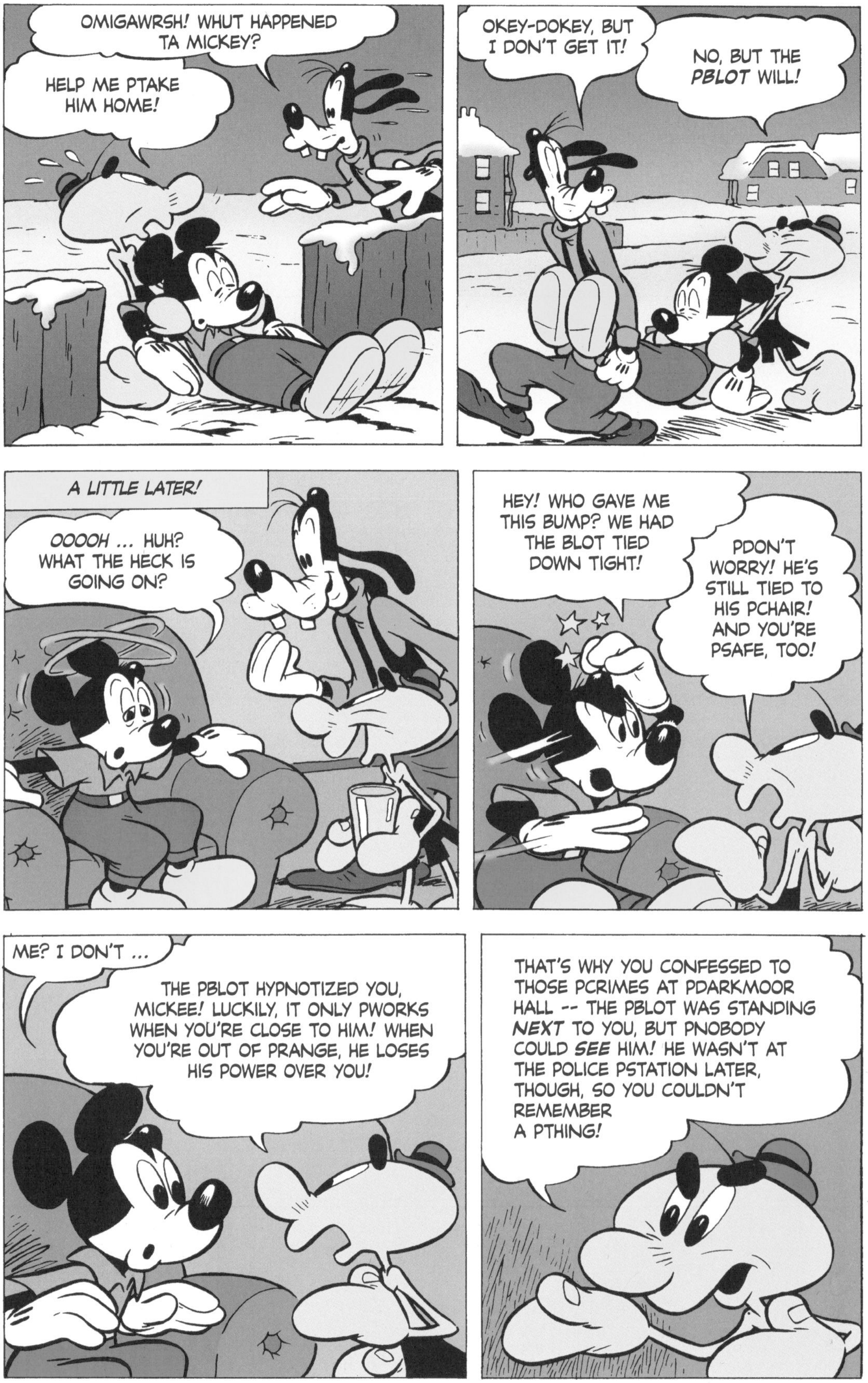
OMIGAWRSH! WHUT HAPPENED TA MICKEY?
HELP ME PTAKE HIM HOME!
OKEY-DOKEY, BUT I DON'T GET IT!
NO, BUT THE PBLOT WILL!
A LITTLE LATER!
OOOOH ... HUH? WHAT THE HECK IS GOING ON?
HEY! WHO GAVE ME THIS BUMP? WE HAD THE BLOT TIED DOWN TIGHT!
PDON'T WORRY! HE'S STILL TIED TO HIS PCHAIR! AND YOU'RE PSAFE, TOO!
ME? I DON'T ...
THE PBLOT HYPNOTIZED YOU, MICKEE! LUCKILY, IT ONLY PWORKS WHEN YOU'RE CLOSE TO HIM! WHEN YOU'RE OUT OF PRANGE, HE LOSES HIS POWER OVER YOU!
THAT'S WHY YOU CONFESSED TO THOSE PCRIMES AT PDARKMOOR HALL -- THE PBLOT WAS STANDING NEXT TO YOU, BUT PNOBODY COULD SEE HIM! HE WASN'T AT THE POLICE PSTATION LATER, THOUGH, SO YOU COULDN'T REMEMBER A PTHING!

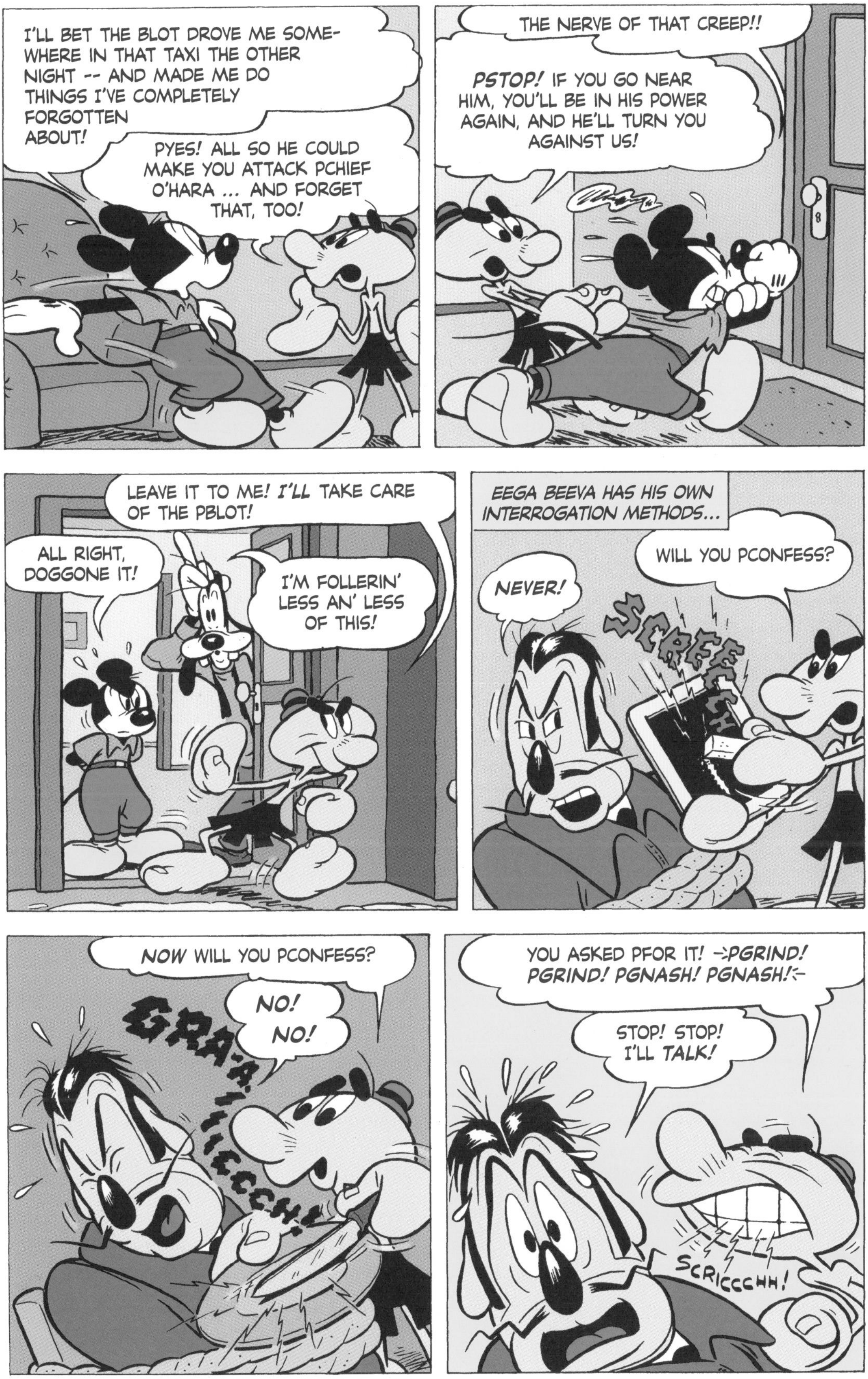

I'LL BET THE BLOT DROVE ME SOMEWHERE IN THAT TAXI THE OTHER NIGHT -- AND MADE ME DO THINGS I'VE COMPLETELY FORGOTTEN ABOUT!
PYES! ALL SO HE COULD MAKE YOU ATTACK PCHIEF O'HARA ... AND FORGET THAT, TOO!
THE NERVE OF THAT CREEP!!
PSTOP! IF YOU GO NEAR HIM, YOU'LL BE IN HIS POWER AGAIN, AND HE'LL TURN YOU AGAINST US!
LEAVE IT TO ME! I'LL TAKE CARE OF THE PBLOT!
ALL RIGHT, DOGGONE IT!
I'M FOLLERIN' LESS AN' LESS OF THIS!
EEGA BEEVA HAS HIS OWN INTERROGATION METHODS...
WILL YOU PCONFESS?
NEVER!
SCREEECH
NOW WILL YOU PCONFESS?
NO! NO!
GRA-A-IIICCCH!
YOU ASKED PFOR IT! PGRIND! PGRIND! PGNASH! PGNASH!
STOP! STOP! I'LL TALK!
SCRICCCHH!

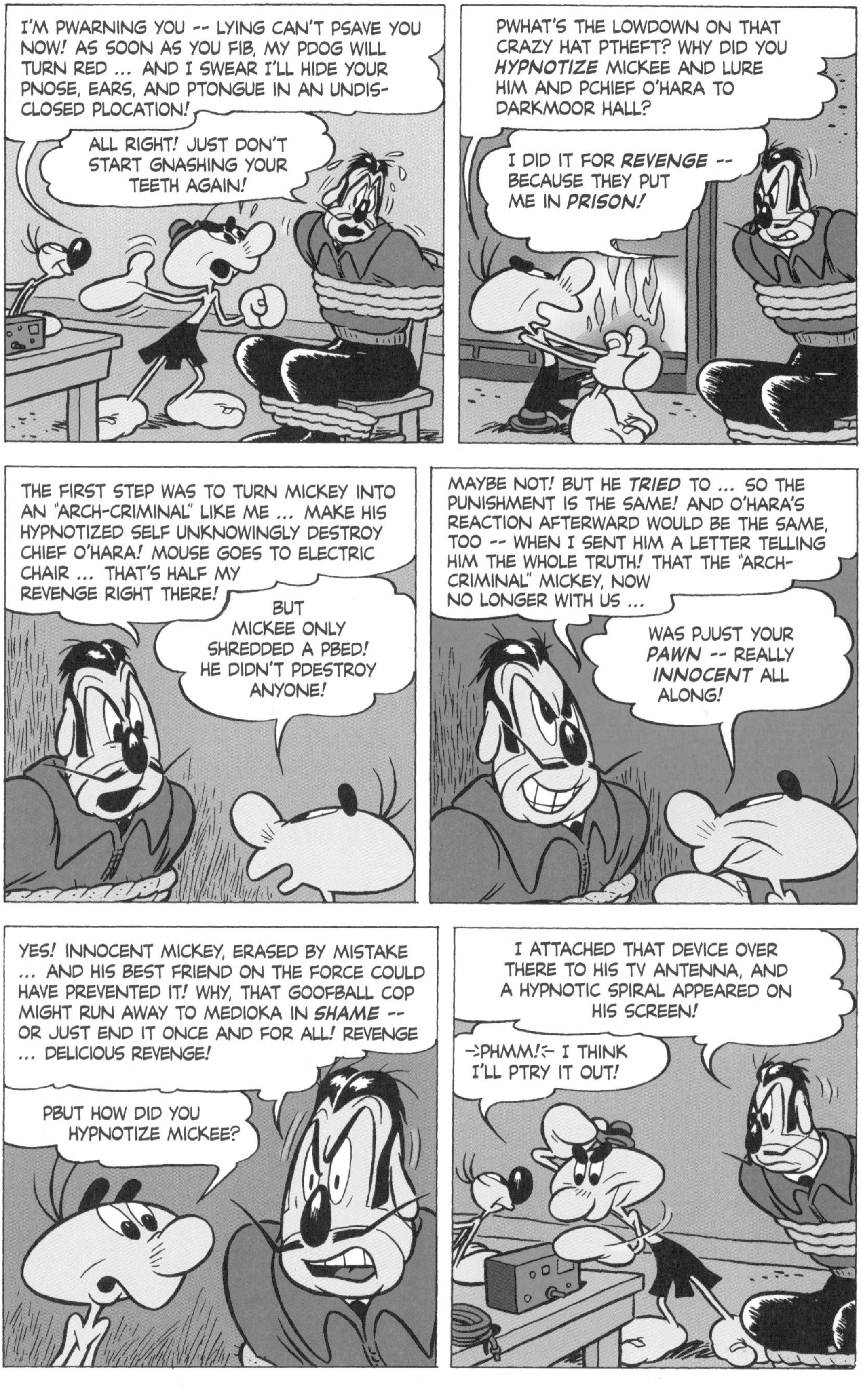
I'M PWARNING YOU -- LYING CAN'T PSAVE YOU NOW! AS SOON AS YOU FIB, MY PDOG WILL TURN RED ... AND I SWEAR I'LL HIDE YOUR PNOSE, EARS, AND PTONGUE IN AN UNDISCLOSED PLOCATION!
ALL RIGHT! JUST DON'T START GNASHING YOUR TEETH AGAIN!
PWHAT'S THE LOWDOWN ON THAT CRAZY HAT PTHEFT? WHY DID YOU HYPNOTIZE MICKEE AND LURE HIM AND PCHIEF O'HARA TO DARKMOOR HALL?
I DID IT FOR REVENGE -- BECAUSE THEY PUT ME IN PRISON!
THE FIRST STEP WAS TO TURN MICKEY INTO AN "ARCH-CRIMINAL" LIKE ME ... MAKE HIS HYPNOTIZED SELF UNKNOWINGLY DESTROY CHIEF O'HARA! MOUSE GOES TO ELECTRIC CHAIR ... THAT'S HALF MY REVENGE RIGHT THERE!
BUT MICKEE ONLY SHREDDED A PBED! HE DIDN'T PDESTROY ANYONE!
MAYBE NOT! BUT HE TRIED TO ... SO THE PUNISHMENT IS THE SAME! AND O'HARA'S REACTION AFTERWARD WOULD BE THE SAME, TOO -- WHEN I SENT HIM A LETTER TELLING HIM THE WHOLE TRUTH! THAT THE "ARCH-CRIMINAL" MICKEY, NOW NO LONGER WITH US ...
WAS PJUST YOUR PAWN -- REALLY INNOCENT ALL ALONG!
YES! INNOCENT MICKEY, ERASED BY MISTAKE ... AND HIS BEST FRIEND ON THE FORCE COULD HAVE PREVENTED IT! WHY, THAT GOOFBALL COP MIGHT RUN AWAY TO MEDIOKA IN SHAME -- OR JUST END IT ONCE AND FOR ALL! REVENGE ... DELICIOUS REVENGE!
PBUT HOW DID YOU HYPNOTIZE MICKEE?
I ATTACHED THAT DEVICE OVER THERE TO HIS TV ANTENNA, AND A HYPNOTIC SPIRAL APPEARED ON HIS SCREEN!
-PHMM!- I THINK I'LL PTRY IT OUT!

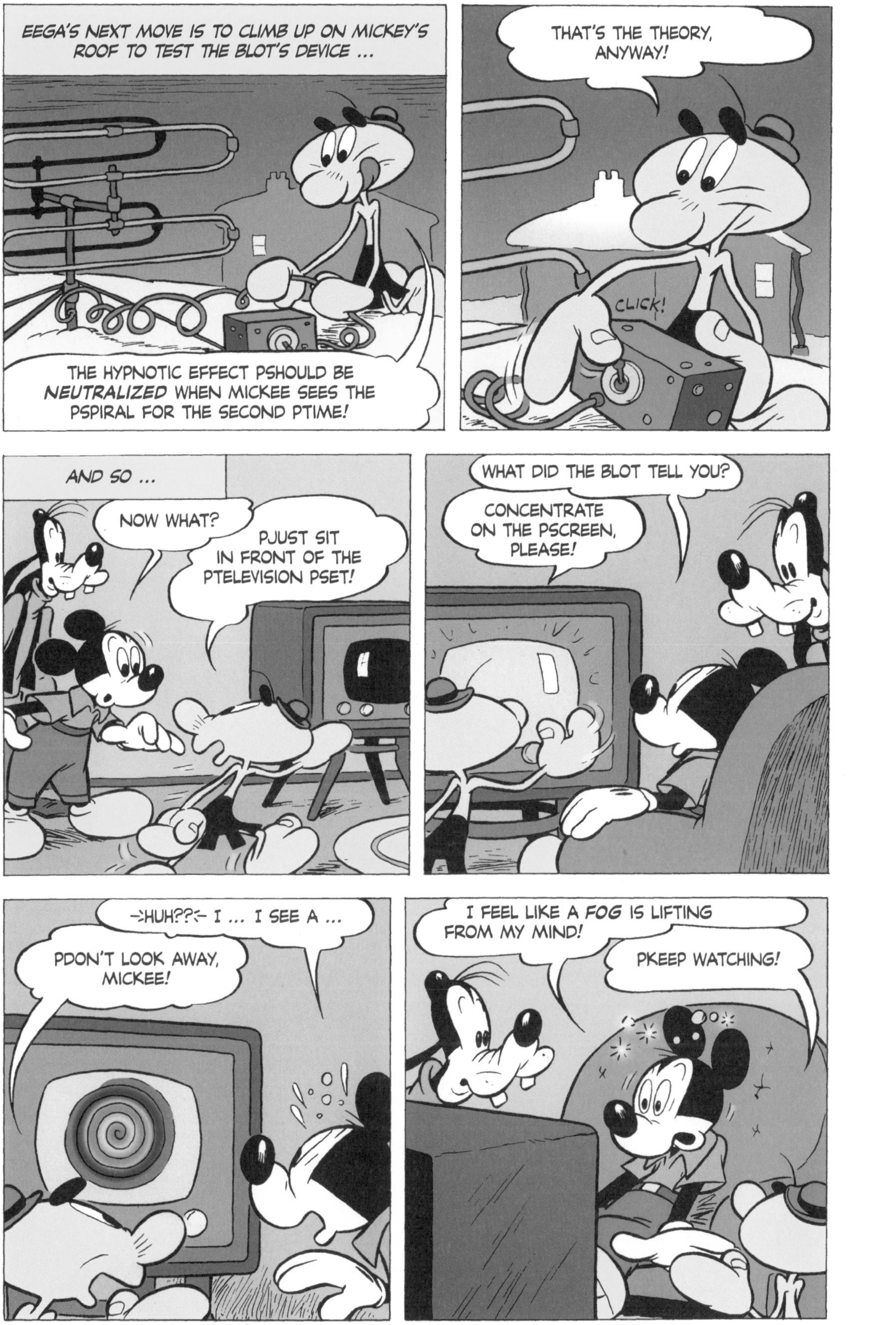
EEGA'S NEXT MOVE IS TO CLIMB UP ON MICKEY'S ROOF TO TEST THE BLOT'S DEVICE ...
THE HYPNOTIC EFFECT PSHOULD BE NEUTRALIZED WHEN MICKEE SEES THE PSPIRAL FOR THE SECOND PTIME!
THAT'S THE THEORY, ANYWAY!
CLICK!
AND SO ...
NOW WHAT?
PJUST SIT IN FRONT OF THE PTELEVISION PSET!
WHAT DID THE BLOT TELL YOU?
CONCENTRATE ON THE PSCREEN, PLEASE!
HUH?? I ... I SEE A ...
PDON'T LOOK AWAY, MICKEE!
I FEEL LIKE A FOG IS LIFTING FROM MY MIND!
PKEEP WATCHING!

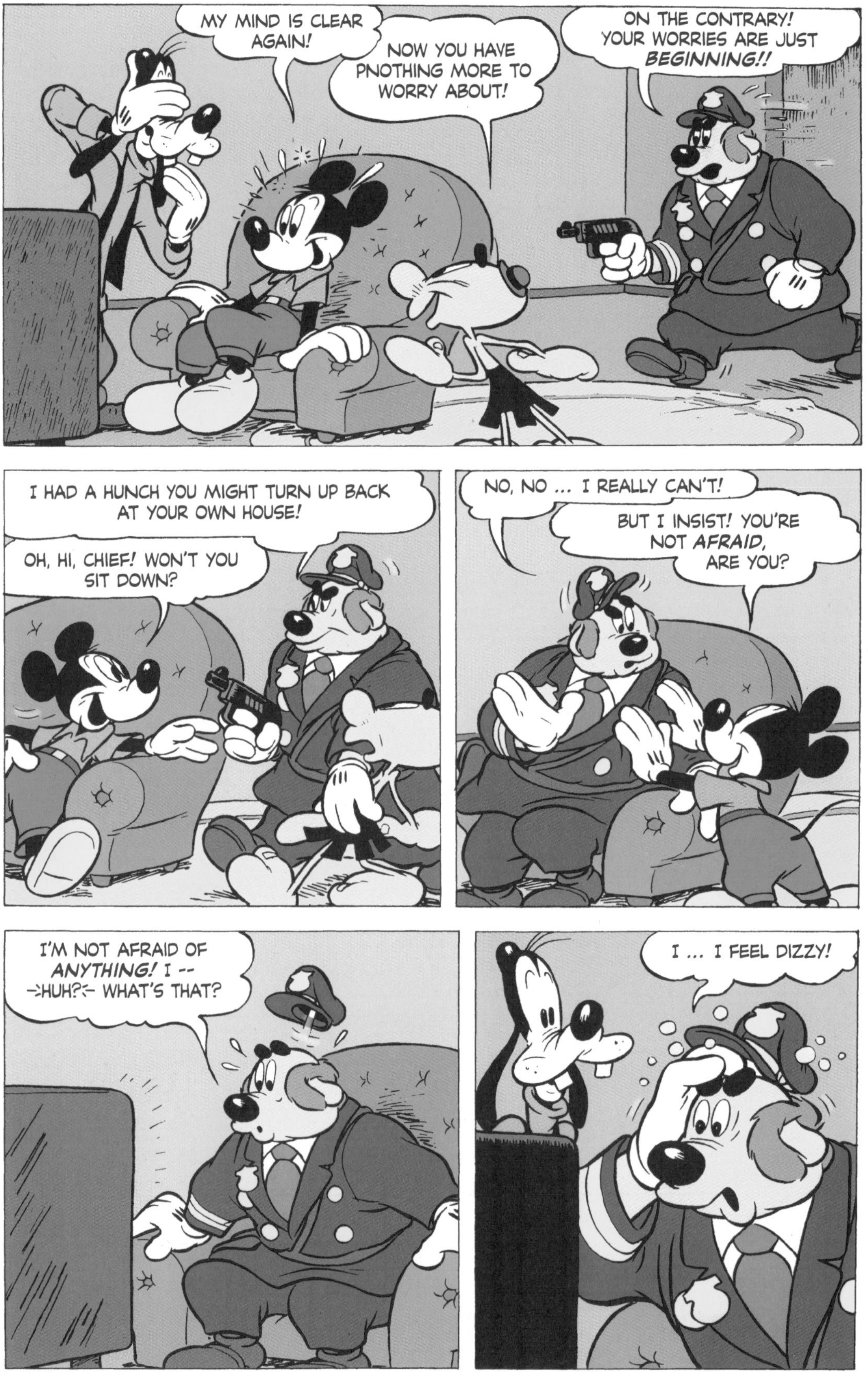
MY MIND IS CLEAR AGAIN!
NOW YOU HAVE PNOTHING MORE TO WORRY ABOUT!
ON THE CONTRARY! YOUR WORRIES ARE JUST BEGINNING!!
I HAD A HUNCH YOU MIGHT TURN UP BACK AT YOUR OWN HOUSE!
OH, HI, CHIEF! WON'T YOU SIT DOWN?
NO, NO ... I REALLY CAN'T!
BUT I INSIST! YOU'RE NOT AFRAID, ARE YOU?
I'M NOT AFRAID OF ANYTHING! I -- HUH? -- WHAT'S THAT?
I ... I FEEL DIZZY!

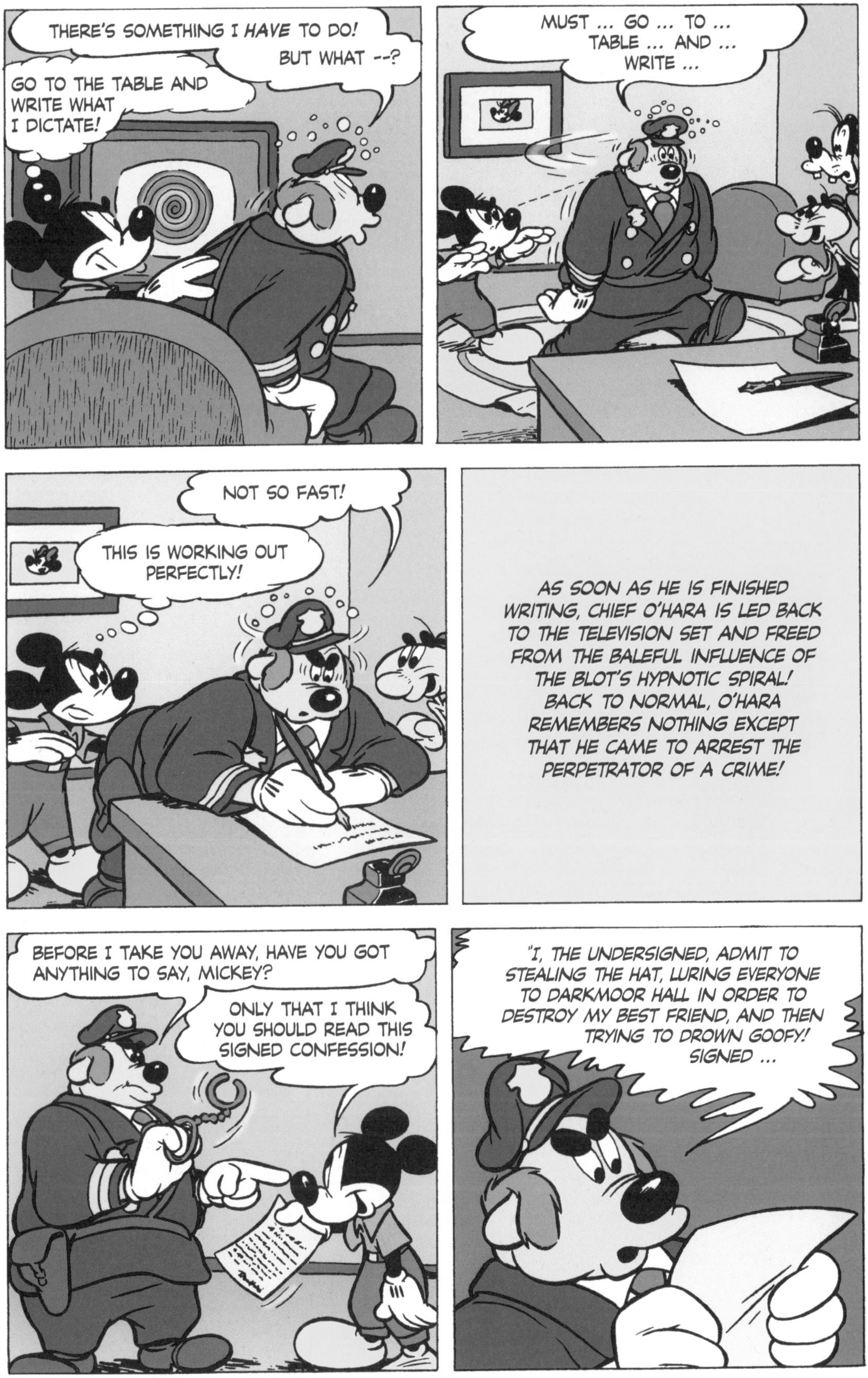

THERE'S SOMETHING I *HAVE* TO DO!
BUT WHAT --?
GO TO THE TABLE AND WRITE WHAT I DICTATE!
MUST ... GO ... TO ... TABLE ... AND ... WRITE ...
NOT SO FAST!
THIS IS WORKING OUT PERFECTLY!
AS SOON AS HE IS FINISHED WRITING, CHIEF O'HARA IS LED BACK TO THE TELEVISION SET AND FREED FROM THE BALEFUL INFLUENCE OF THE BLOT'S HYPNOTIC SPIRAL! BACK TO NORMAL, O'HARA REMEMBERS NOTHING EXCEPT THAT HE CAME TO ARREST THE PERPETRATOR OF A CRIME!
BEFORE I TAKE YOU AWAY, HAVE YOU GOT ANYTHING TO SAY, MICKEY?
ONLY THAT I THINK YOU SHOULD READ THIS SIGNED CONFESSION!
"I, THE UNDERSIGNED, ADMIT TO STEALING THE HAT, LURING EVERYONE TO DARKMOOR HALL IN ORDER TO DESTROY MY BEST FRIEND, AND THEN TRYING TO DROWN GOOFY! SIGNED ...

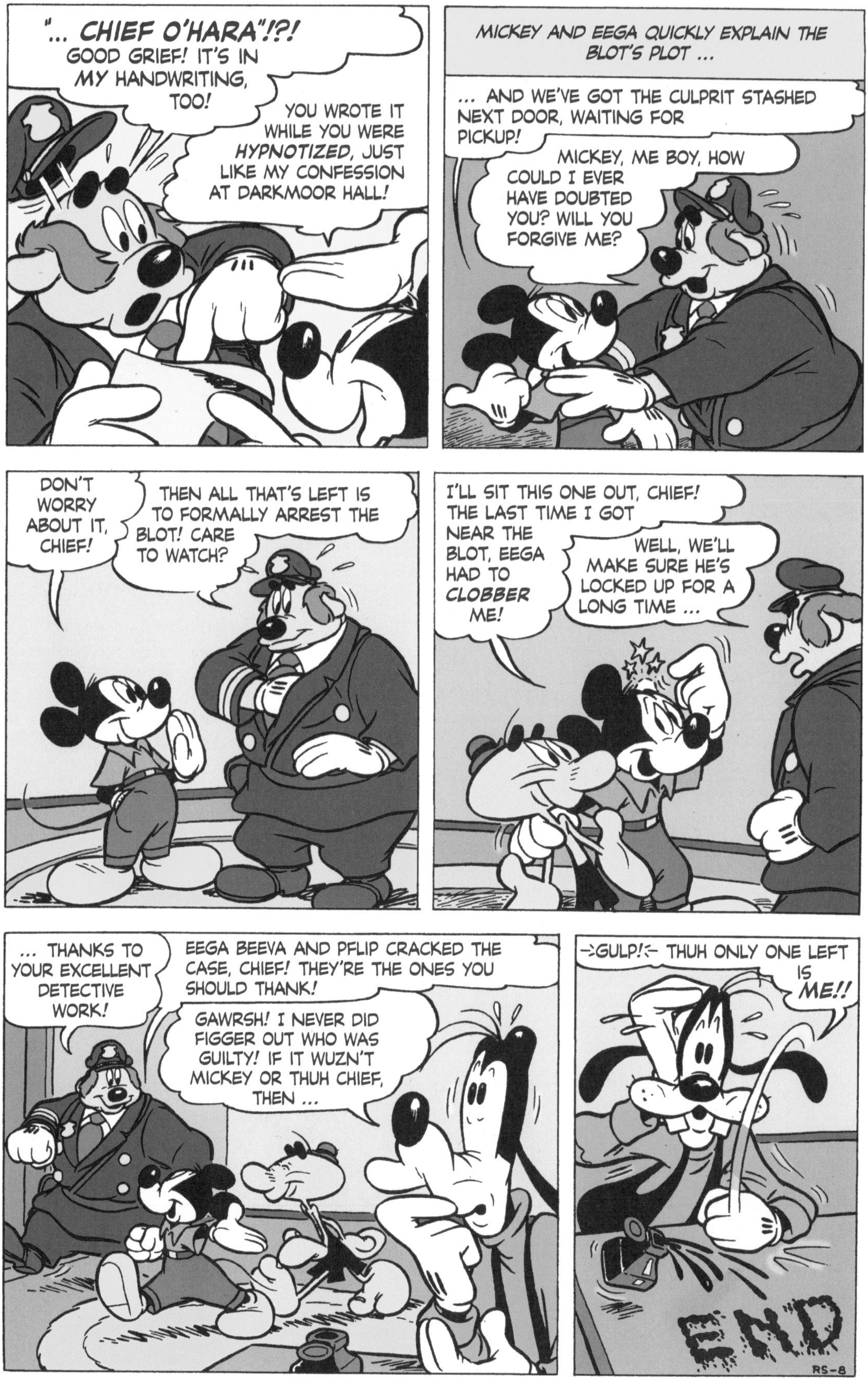
"... CHIEF O'HARA"!?! GOOD GRIEF! IT'S IN MY HANDWRITING, TOO!
YOU WROTE IT WHILE YOU WERE HYPNOTIZED, JUST LIKE MY CONFESSION AT DARKMOOR HALL!
MICKEY AND EEGA QUICKLY EXPLAIN THE BLOT'S PLOT ...
... AND WE'VE GOT THE CULPRIT STASHED NEXT DOOR, WAITING FOR PICKUP!
MICKEY, ME BOY, HOW COULD I EVER HAVE DOUBTED YOU? WILL YOU FORGIVE ME?
DON'T WORRY ABOUT IT, CHIEF!
THEN ALL THAT'S LEFT IS TO FORMALLY ARREST THE BLOT! CARE TO WATCH?
I'LL SIT THIS ONE OUT, CHIEF! THE LAST TIME I GOT NEAR THE BLOT, EEGA HAD TO CLOBBER ME!
WELL, WE'LL MAKE SURE HE'S LOCKED UP FOR A LONG TIME ...
... THANKS TO YOUR EXCELLENT DETECTIVE WORK!
EEGA BEEVA AND PFLIP CRACKED THE CASE, CHIEF! THEY'RE THE ONES YOU SHOULD THANK!
GAWRSH! I NEVER DID FIGGER OUT WHO WAS GUILTY! IF IT WUZN'T MICKEY OR THUH CHIEF, THEN ...
-GULP!- THUH ONLY ONE LEFT IS ME!!
END
RS-8

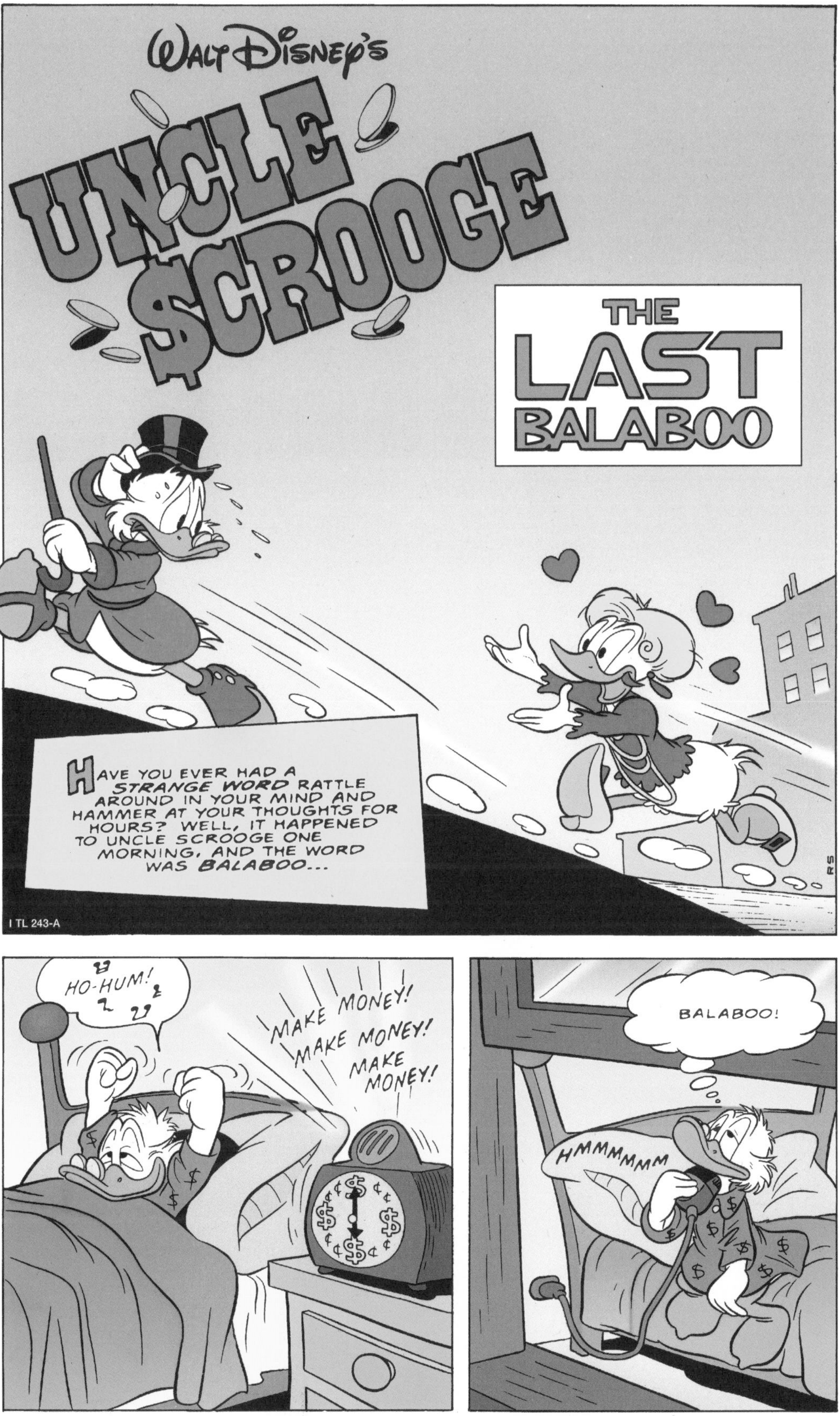
WALT DISNEY'S
UNCLE $CROOGE
THE LAST BALABOO
HAVE YOU EVER HAD A STRANGE WORD RATTLE AROUND IN YOUR MIND AND HAMMER AT YOUR THOUGHTS FOR HOURS? WELL, IT HAPPENED TO UNCLE SCROOGE ONE MORNING, AND THE WORD WAS BALABOO...
I TL 243-A
HO-HUM!
MAKE MONEY! MAKE MONEY! MAKE MONEY!
BALABOO!
HMMMMMM

STORY AND ART BY ROMANO SCARPA
TRANSLATION AND DIALOGUE BY ALBERTO BECATTINI AND BYRON ERICKSON

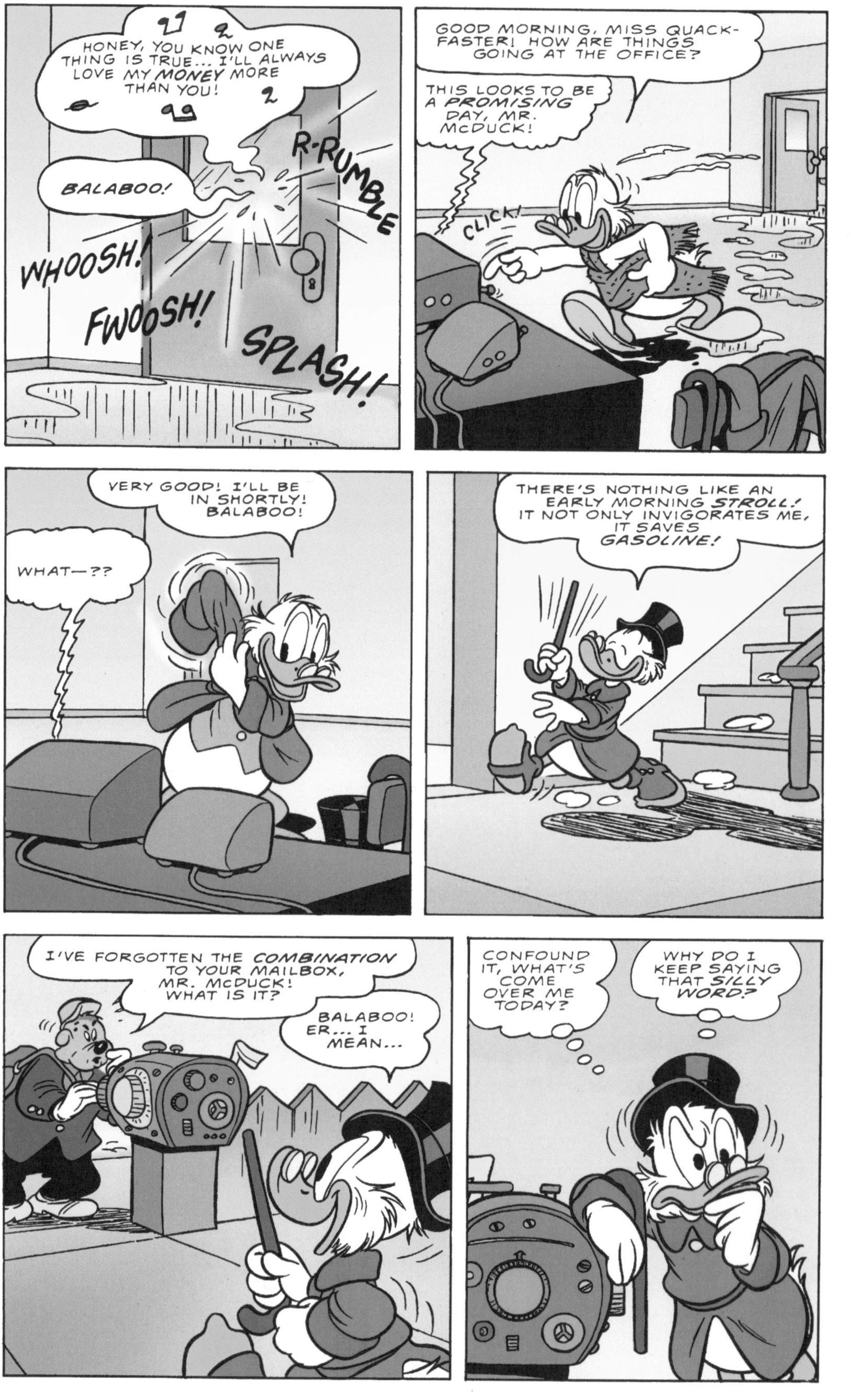
HONEY, YOU KNOW ONE THING IS TRUE... I'LL ALWAYS LOVE MY *MONEY* MORE THAN YOU!
BALABOO!
R-RUMBLE
WHOOSH!
FWOOSH!
SPLASH!
GOOD MORNING, MISS QUACKFASTER! HOW ARE THINGS GOING AT THE OFFICE?
THIS LOOKS TO BE A *PROMISING* DAY, MR. McDUCK!
CLICK!
VERY GOOD! I'LL BE IN SHORTLY! BALABOO!
WHAT—??
THERE'S NOTHING LIKE AN EARLY MORNING *STROLL!* IT NOT ONLY INVIGORATES ME, IT SAVES *GASOLINE!*
I'VE FORGOTTEN THE *COMBINATION* TO YOUR MAILBOX, MR. McDUCK! WHAT IS IT?
BALABOO! ER... I MEAN...
CONFOUND IT, WHAT'S COME OVER ME TODAY?
WHY DO I KEEP SAYING THAT *SILLY WORD?*

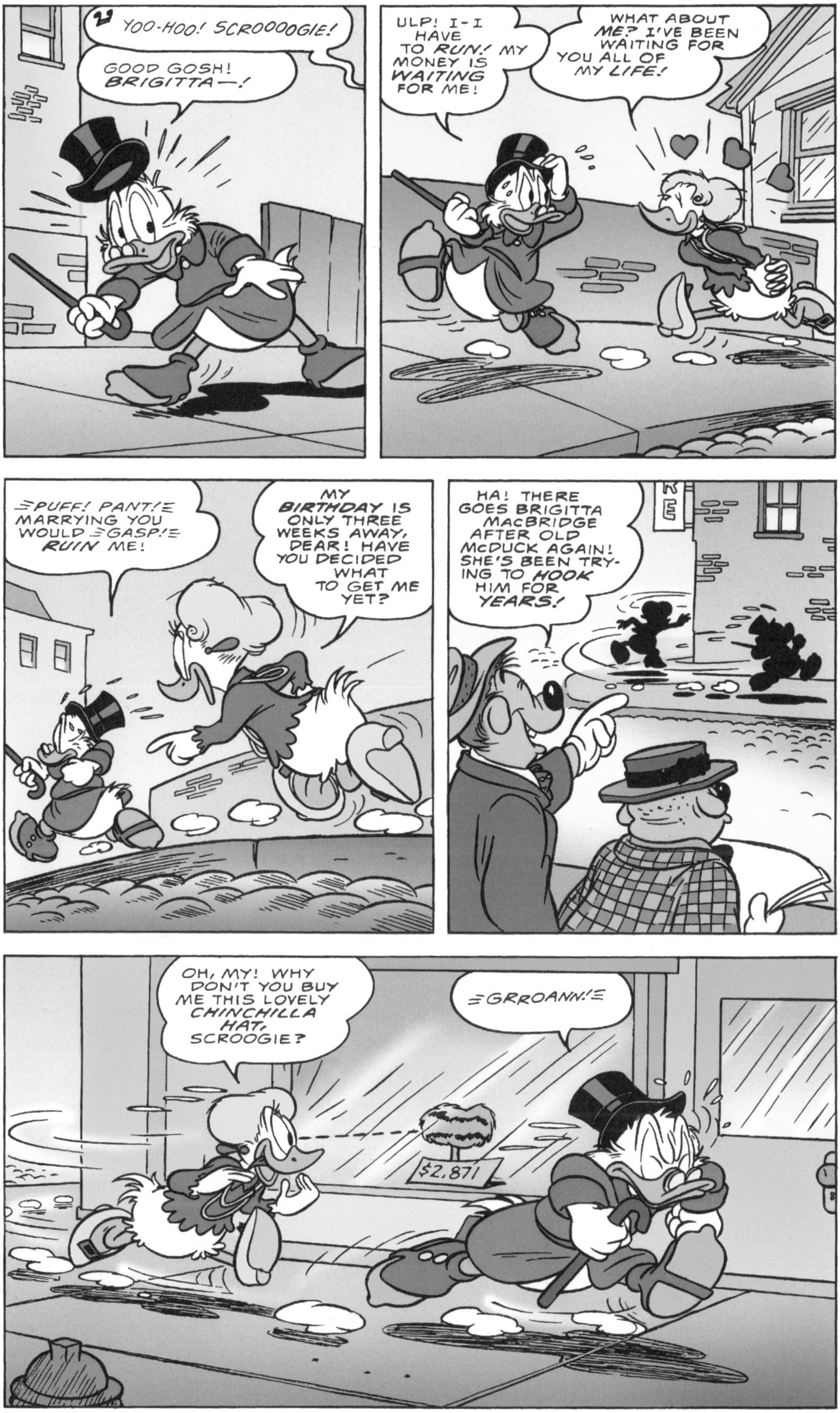

YOO-HOO! SCROOOOGIE!
GOOD GOSH! BRIGITTA—!
ULP! I-I HAVE TO RUN! MY MONEY IS WAITING FOR ME!
WHAT ABOUT ME? I'VE BEEN WAITING FOR YOU ALL OF MY LIFE!
PUFF! PANT! MARRYING YOU WOULD GASP! RUIN ME!
MY BIRTHDAY IS ONLY THREE WEEKS AWAY, DEAR! HAVE YOU DECIDED WHAT TO GET ME YET?
HA! THERE GOES BRIGITTA MacBRIDGE AFTER OLD McDUCK AGAIN! SHE'S BEEN TRYING TO HOOK HIM FOR YEARS!
OH, MY! WHY DON'T YOU BUY ME THIS LOVELY CHINCHILLA HAT, SCROOGIE?
GRRROANN!
$2,871

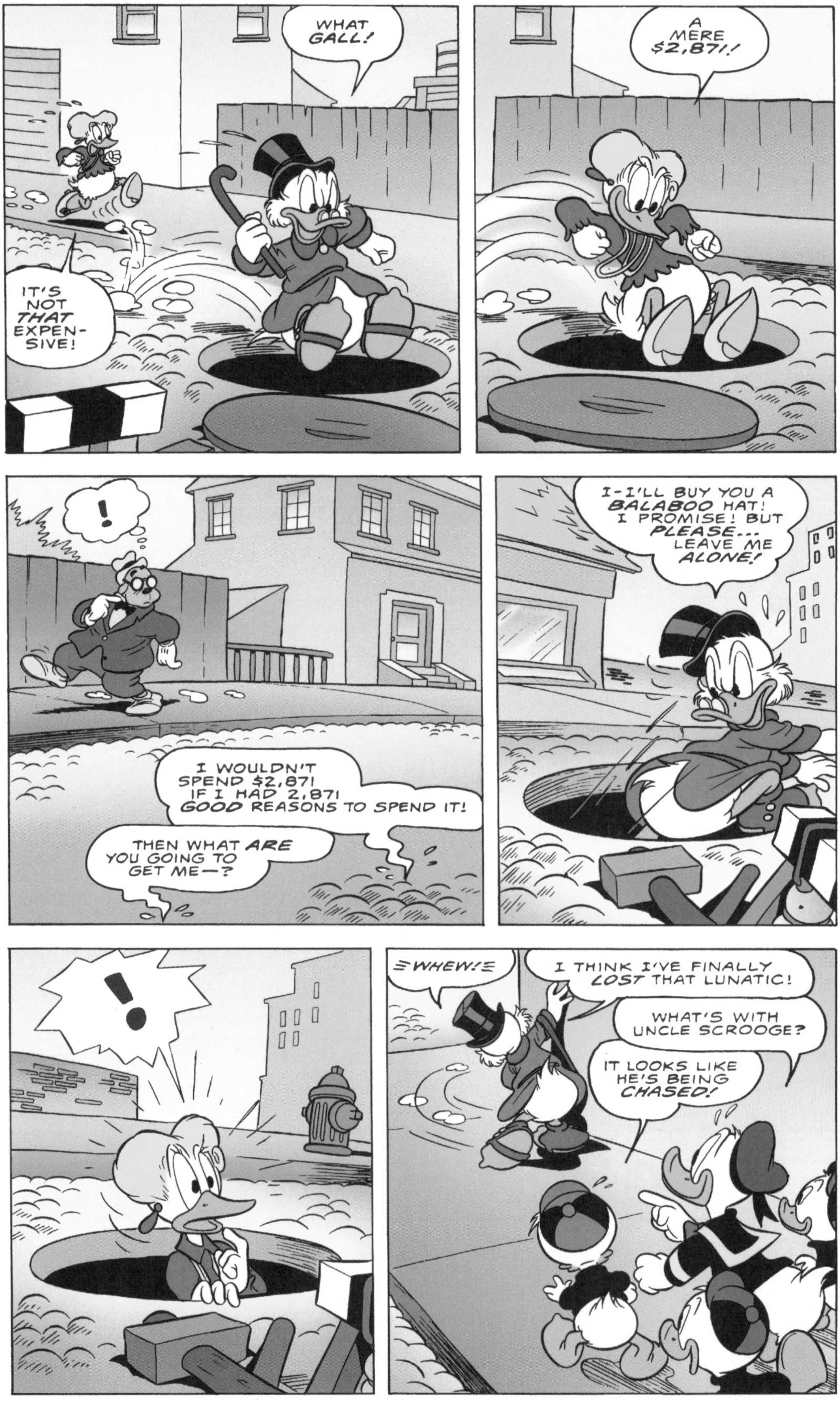

WHAT GALL!
IT'S NOT THAT EXPENSIVE!
A MERE $2,871!
!
I WOULDN'T SPEND $2,871 IF I HAD 2,871 GOOD REASONS TO SPEND IT!
THEN WHAT ARE YOU GOING TO GET ME—?
I-I'LL BUY YOU A BALABOO HAT! I PROMISE! BUT PLEASE... LEAVE ME ALONE!
!
WHEW!
I THINK I'VE FINALLY LOST THAT LUNATIC!
WHAT'S WITH UNCLE SCROOGE?
IT LOOKS LIKE HE'S BEING CHASED!

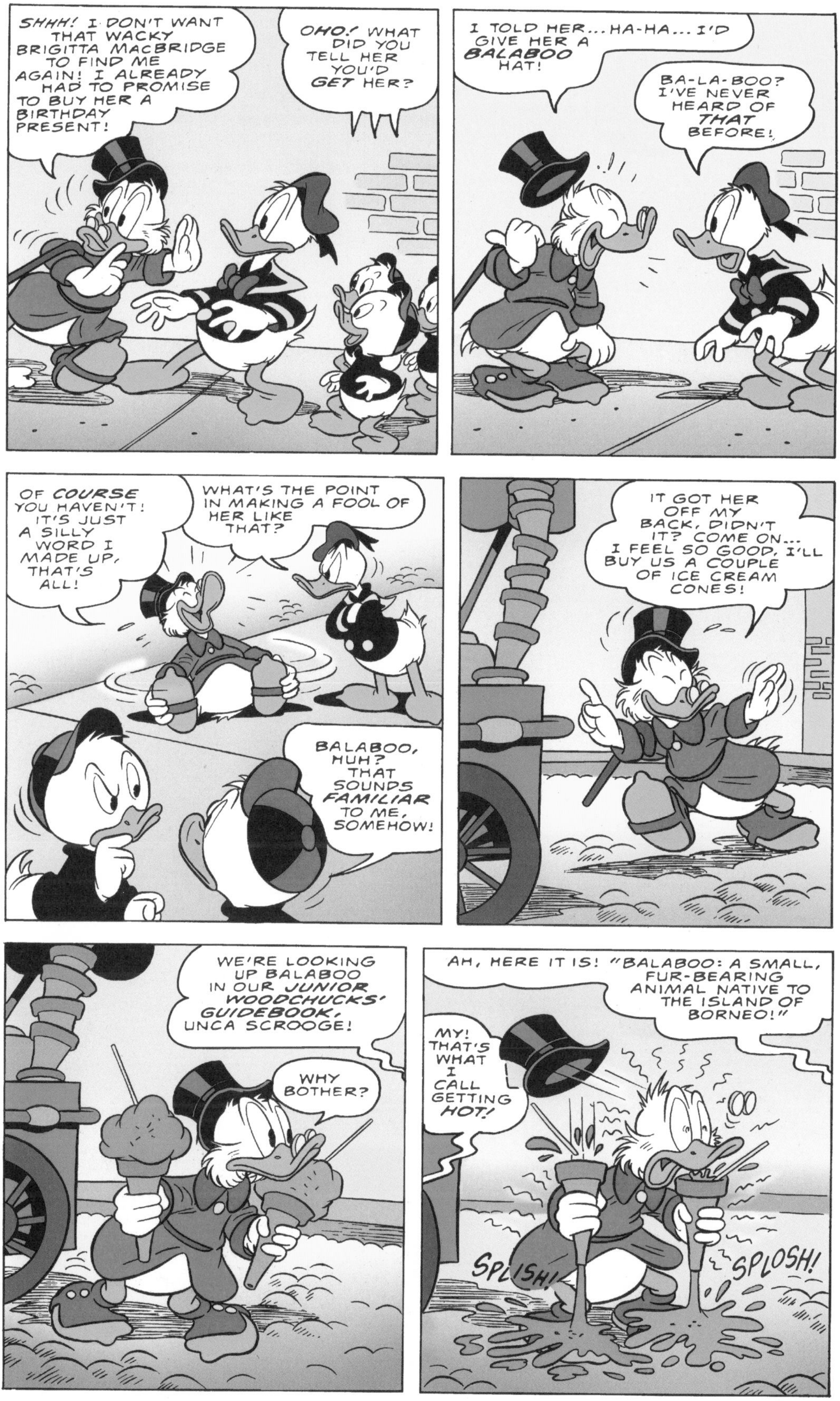
SHHH! I DON'T WANT THAT WACKY BRIGITTA MACBRIDGE TO FIND ME AGAIN! I ALREADY HAD TO PROMISE TO BUY HER A BIRTHDAY PRESENT!
OHO! WHAT DID YOU TELL HER YOU'D GET HER?
I TOLD HER... HA-HA... I'D GIVE HER A BALABOO HAT!
BA-LA-BOO? I'VE NEVER HEARD OF THAT BEFORE!
OF COURSE YOU HAVEN'T! IT'S JUST A SILLY WORD I MADE UP, THAT'S ALL!
WHAT'S THE POINT IN MAKING A FOOL OF HER LIKE THAT?
BALABOO, HUH? THAT SOUNDS FAMILIAR TO ME, SOMEHOW!
IT GOT HER OFF MY BACK, DIDN'T IT? COME ON... I FEEL SO GOOD, I'LL BUY US A COUPLE OF ICE CREAM CONES!
WE'RE LOOKING UP BALABOO IN OUR JUNIOR WOODCHUCKS' GUIDEBOOK, UNCA SCROOGE!
WHY BOTHER?
AH, HERE IT IS! "BALABOO: A SMALL, FUR-BEARING ANIMAL NATIVE TO THE ISLAND OF BORNEO!"
MY! THAT'S WHAT I CALL GETTING HOT!
SPLISH!
SPLOSH!

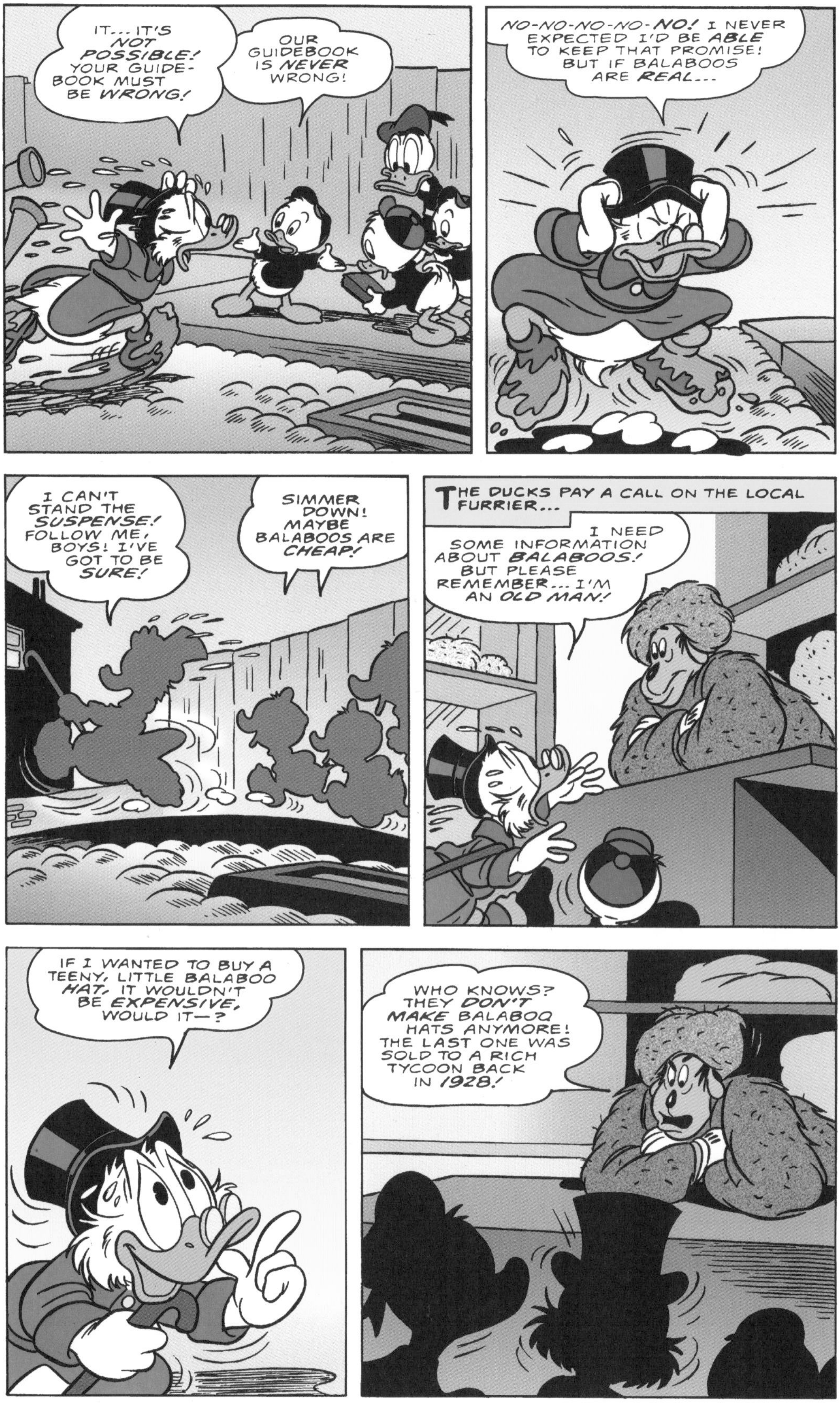
IT... IT'S NOT POSSIBLE! YOUR GUIDEBOOK MUST BE WRONG!
OUR GUIDEBOOK IS NEVER WRONG!
NO-NO-NO-NO-NO! I NEVER EXPECTED I'D BE ABLE TO KEEP THAT PROMISE! BUT IF BALABOOS ARE REAL...
I CAN'T STAND THE SUSPENSE! FOLLOW ME, BOYS! I'VE GOT TO BE SURE!
SIMMER DOWN! MAYBE BALABOOS ARE CHEAP!
THE DUCKS PAY A CALL ON THE LOCAL FURRIER...
I NEED SOME INFORMATION ABOUT BALABOOS! BUT PLEASE REMEMBER... I'M AN OLD MAN!
IF I WANTED TO BUY A TEENY, LITTLE BALABOO HAT, IT WOULDN'T BE EXPENSIVE, WOULD IT—?
WHO KNOWS? THEY DON'T MAKE BALABOO HATS ANYMORE! THE LAST ONE WAS SOLD TO A RICH TYCOON BACK IN 1928!

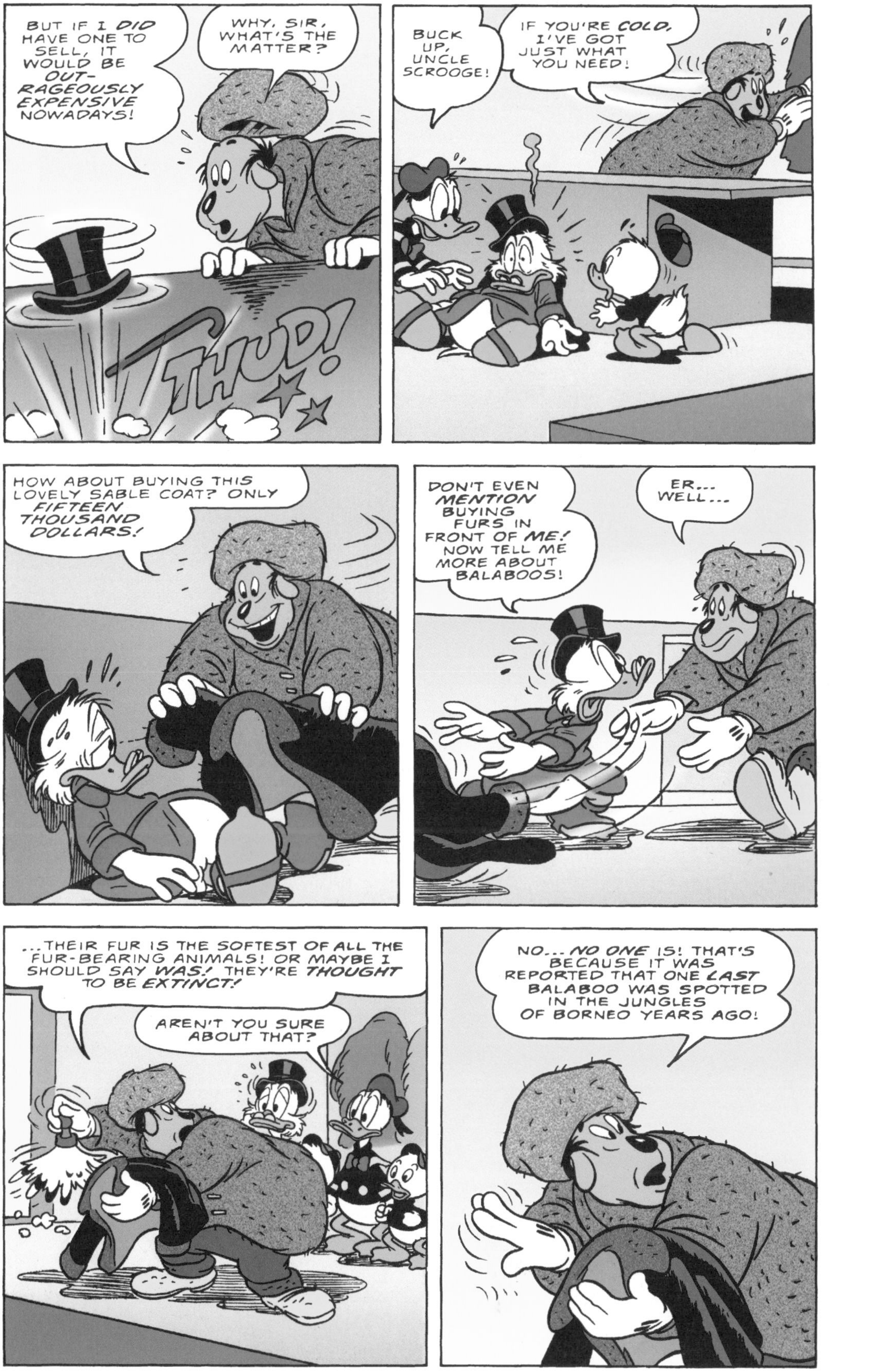
BUT IF I DID HAVE ONE TO SELL, IT WOULD BE OUT-RAGEOUSLY EXPENSIVE NOWADAYS!
WHY, SIR, WHAT'S THE MATTER?
THUD!
BUCK UP, UNCLE SCROOGE!
IF YOU'RE COLD, I'VE GOT JUST WHAT YOU NEED!
HOW ABOUT BUYING THIS LOVELY SABLE COAT? ONLY FIFTEEN THOUSAND DOLLARS!
DON'T EVEN MENTION BUYING FURS IN FRONT OF ME! NOW TELL ME MORE ABOUT BALABOOS!
ER... WELL...
...THEIR FUR IS THE SOFTEST OF ALL THE FUR-BEARING ANIMALS! OR MAYBE I SHOULD SAY WAS! THEY'RE THOUGHT TO BE EXTINCT!
AREN'T YOU SURE ABOUT THAT?
NO... NO ONE IS! THAT'S BECAUSE IT WAS REPORTED THAT ONE LAST BALABOO WAS SPOTTED IN THE JUNGLES OF BORNEO YEARS AGO!

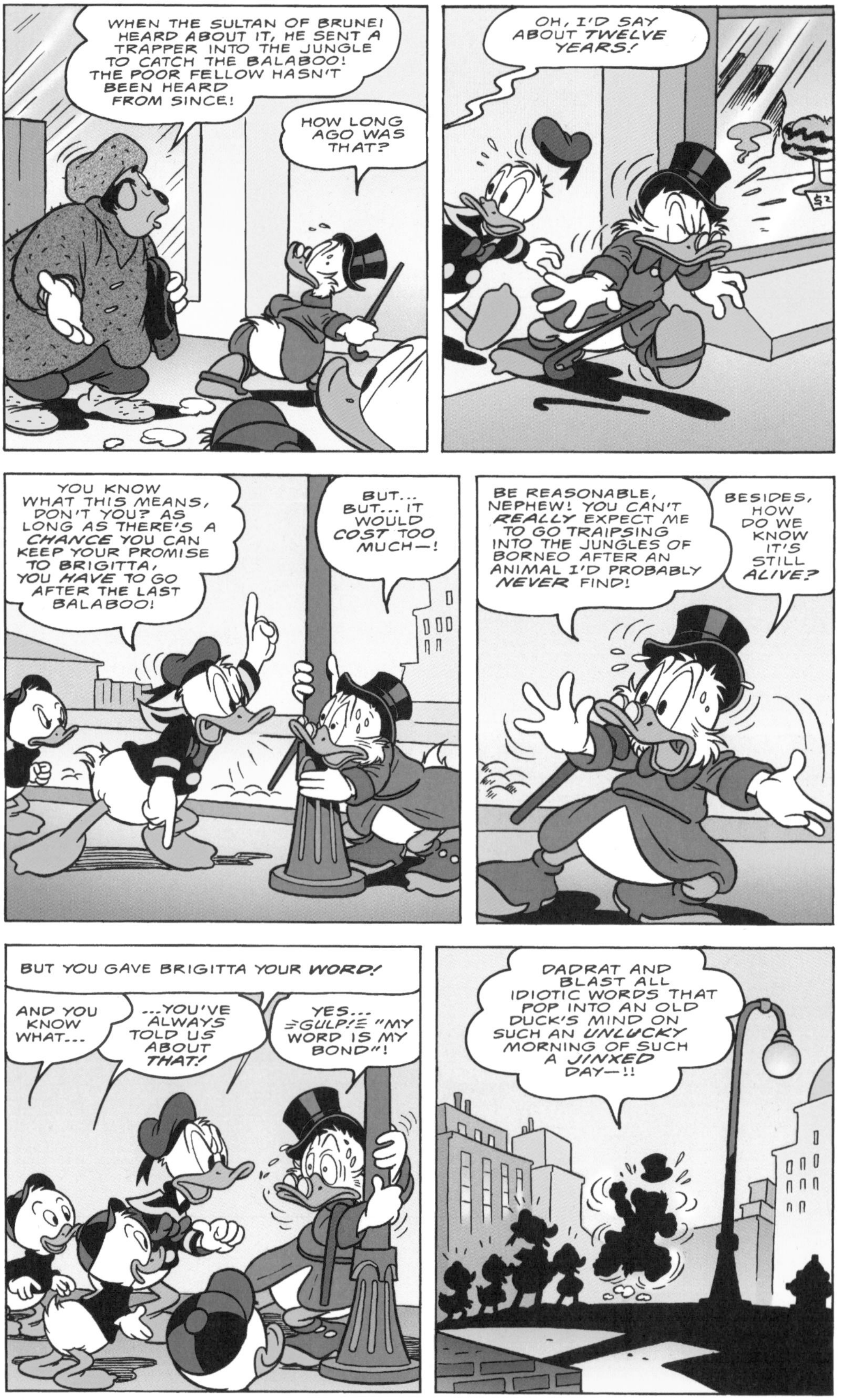
WHEN THE SULTAN OF BRUNEI HEARD ABOUT IT, HE SENT A TRAPPER INTO THE JUNGLE TO CATCH THE BALABOO! THE POOR FELLOW HASN'T BEEN HEARD FROM SINCE!
HOW LONG AGO WAS THAT?
OH, I'D SAY ABOUT TWELVE YEARS!
YOU KNOW WHAT THIS MEANS, DON'T YOU? AS LONG AS THERE'S A CHANCE YOU CAN KEEP YOUR PROMISE TO BRIGITTA, YOU HAVE TO GO AFTER THE LAST BALABOO!
BUT... BUT... IT WOULD COST TOO MUCH—!
BE REASONABLE, NEPHEW! YOU CAN'T REALLY EXPECT ME TO GO TRAIPSING INTO THE JUNGLES OF BORNEO AFTER AN ANIMAL I'D PROBABLY NEVER FIND!
BESIDES, HOW DO WE KNOW IT'S STILL ALIVE?
BUT YOU GAVE BRIGITTA YOUR WORD!
AND YOU KNOW WHAT...
...YOU'VE ALWAYS TOLD US ABOUT THAT!
YES... GULP! "MY WORD IS MY BOND"!
DADRAT AND BLAST ALL IDIOTIC WORDS THAT POP INTO AN OLD DUCK'S MIND ON SUCH AN UNLUCKY MORNING OF SUCH A JINXED DAY—!!

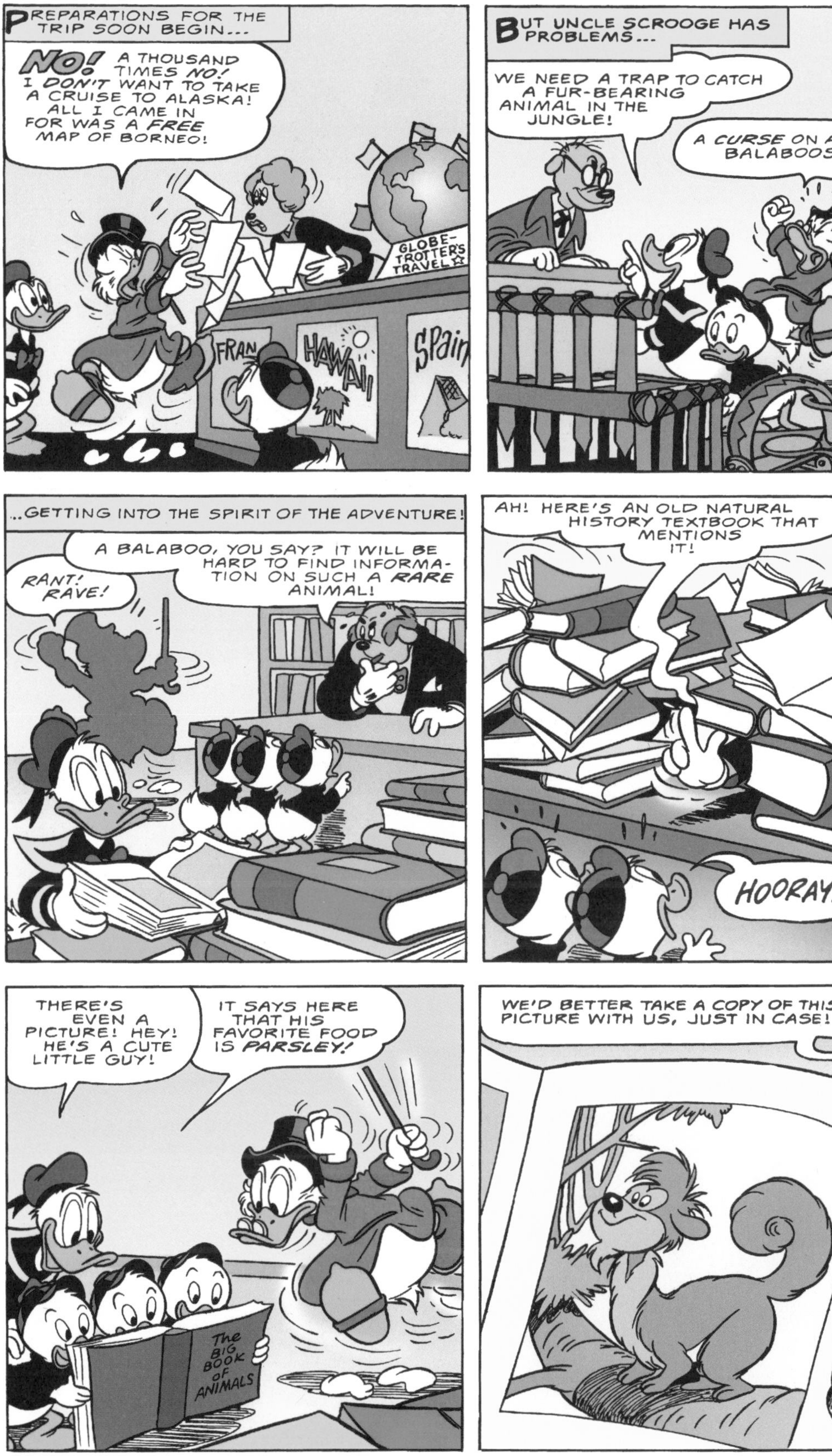
PREPARATIONS FOR THE TRIP SOON BEGIN...
NO! A THOUSAND TIMES NO! I DON'T WANT TO TAKE A CRUISE TO ALASKA! ALL I CAME IN FOR WAS A FREE MAP OF BORNEO!
GLOBE-TROTTER'S TRAVEL
FRAN
HAWAII
SPAIN
BUT UNCLE SCROOGE HAS PROBLEMS...
WE NEED A TRAP TO CATCH A FUR-BEARING ANIMAL IN THE JUNGLE!
A CURSE ON ALL BALABOOS!!
...GETTING INTO THE SPIRIT OF THE ADVENTURE!
RANT! RAVE!
A BALABOO, YOU SAY? IT WILL BE HARD TO FIND INFORMATION ON SUCH A RARE ANIMAL!
AH! HERE'S AN OLD NATURAL HISTORY TEXTBOOK THAT MENTIONS IT!
HOORAY!
THERE'S EVEN A PICTURE! HEY! HE'S A CUTE LITTLE GUY!
IT SAYS HERE THAT HIS FAVORITE FOOD IS PARSLEY!
The BIG BOOK of ANIMALS
WE'D BETTER TAKE A COPY OF THIS PICTURE WITH US, JUST IN CASE!

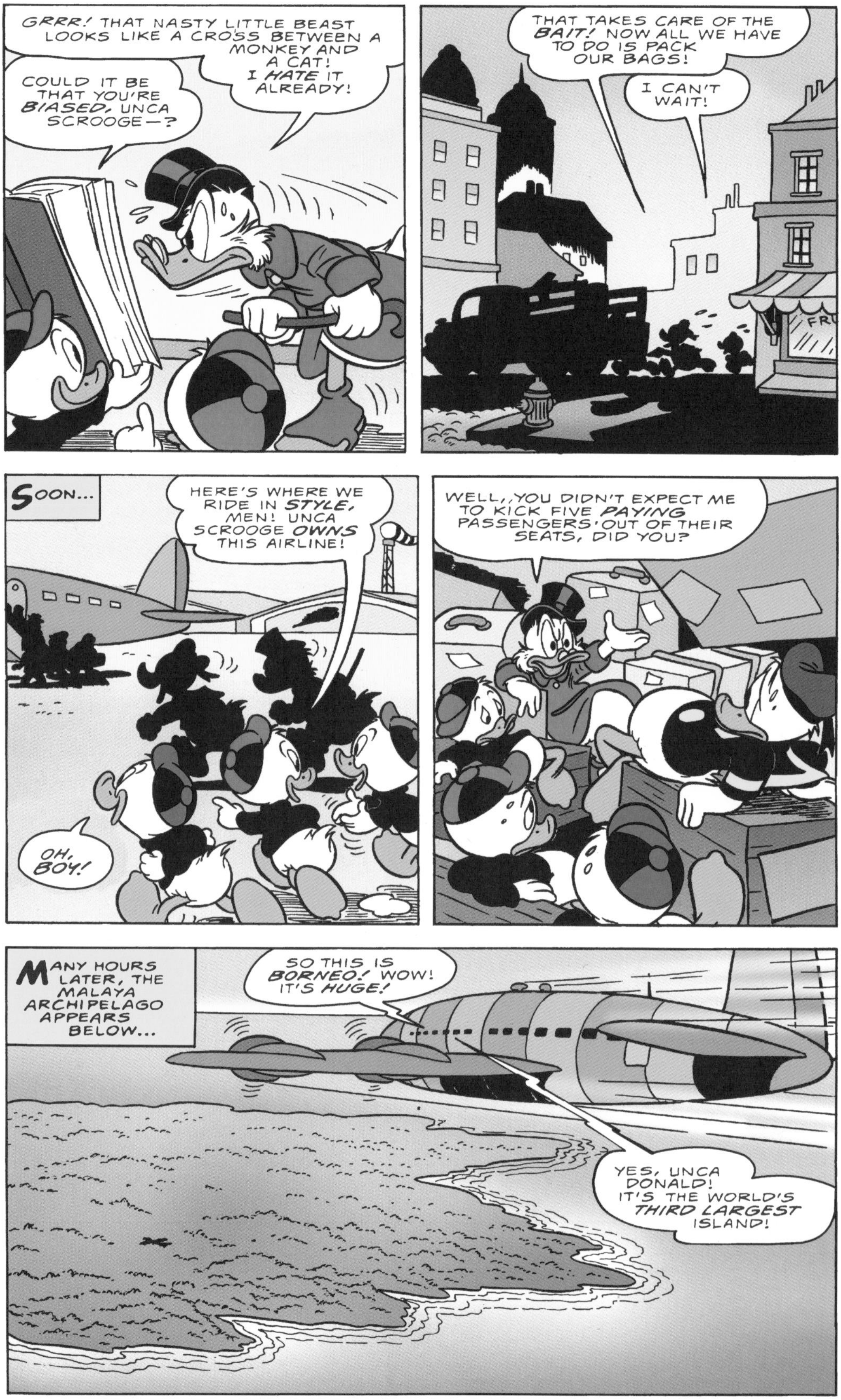
GRRR! THAT NASTY LITTLE BEAST LOOKS LIKE A CROSS BETWEEN A MONKEY AND A CAT! I HATE IT ALREADY!
COULD IT BE THAT YOU'RE BIASED, UNCA SCROOGE—?
THAT TAKES CARE OF THE BAIT! NOW ALL WE HAVE TO DO IS PACK OUR BAGS!
I CAN'T WAIT!
SOON...
HERE'S WHERE WE RIDE IN STYLE, MEN! UNCA SCROOGE OWNS THIS AIRLINE!
OH, BOY!
WELL, YOU DIDN'T EXPECT ME TO KICK FIVE PAYING PASSENGERS OUT OF THEIR SEATS, DID YOU?
MANY HOURS LATER, THE MALAYA ARCHIPELAGO APPEARS BELOW...
SO THIS IS BORNEO! WOW! IT'S HUGE!
YES, UNCA DONALD! IT'S THE WORLD'S THIRD LARGEST ISLAND!

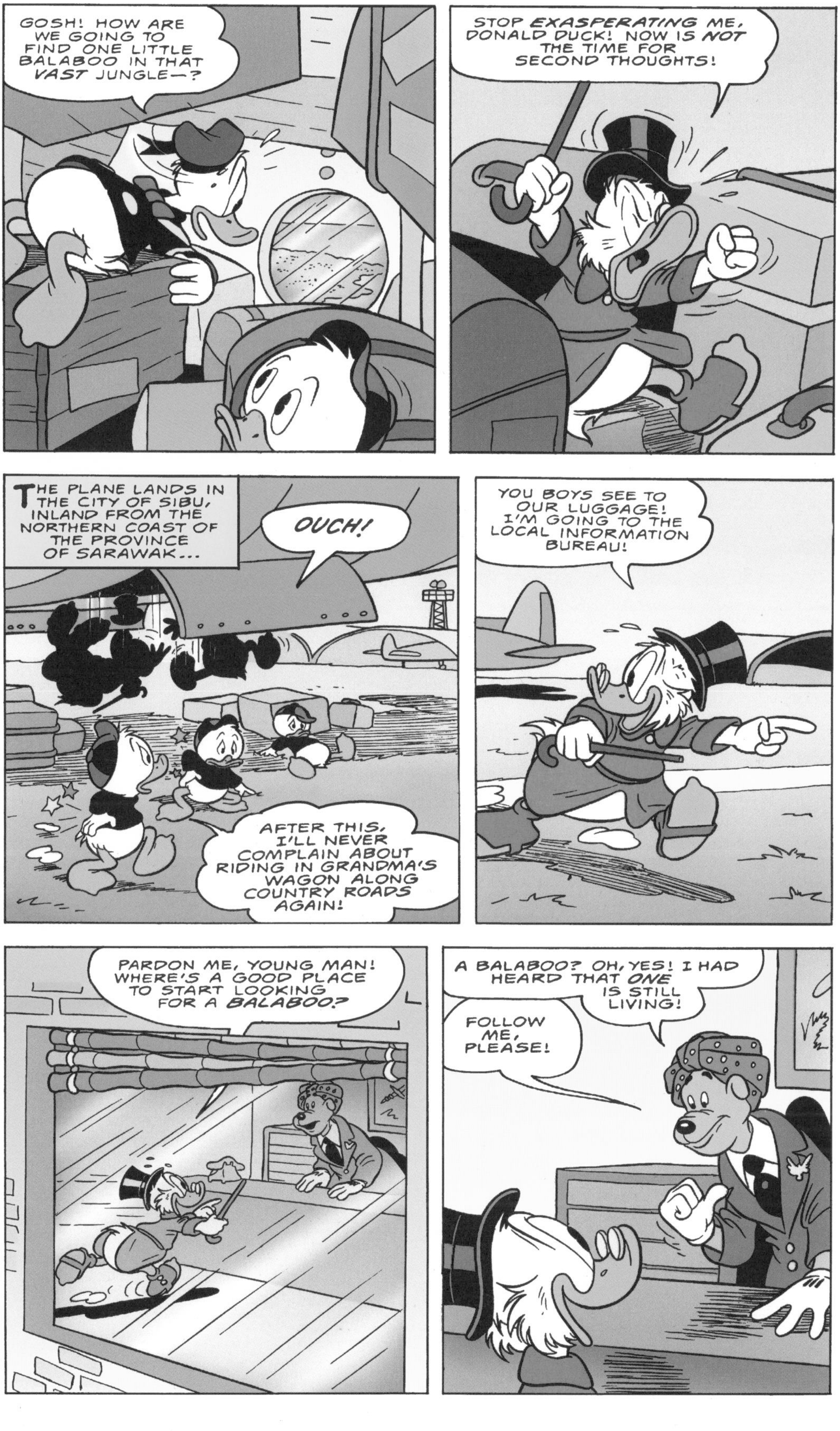
GOSH! HOW ARE WE GOING TO FIND ONE LITTLE BALABOO IN THAT VAST JUNGLE—?
STOP EXASPERATING ME, DONALD DUCK! NOW IS NOT THE TIME FOR SECOND THOUGHTS!
THE PLANE LANDS IN THE CITY OF SIBU, INLAND FROM THE NORTHERN COAST OF THE PROVINCE OF SARAWAK...
OUCH!
AFTER THIS, I'LL NEVER COMPLAIN ABOUT RIDING IN GRANDMA'S WAGON ALONG COUNTRY ROADS AGAIN!
YOU BOYS SEE TO OUR LUGGAGE! I'M GOING TO THE LOCAL INFORMATION BUREAU!
PARDON ME, YOUNG MAN! WHERE'S A GOOD PLACE TO START LOOKING FOR A BALABOO?
A BALABOO? OH, YES! I HAD HEARD THAT ONE IS STILL LIVING!
FOLLOW ME, PLEASE!

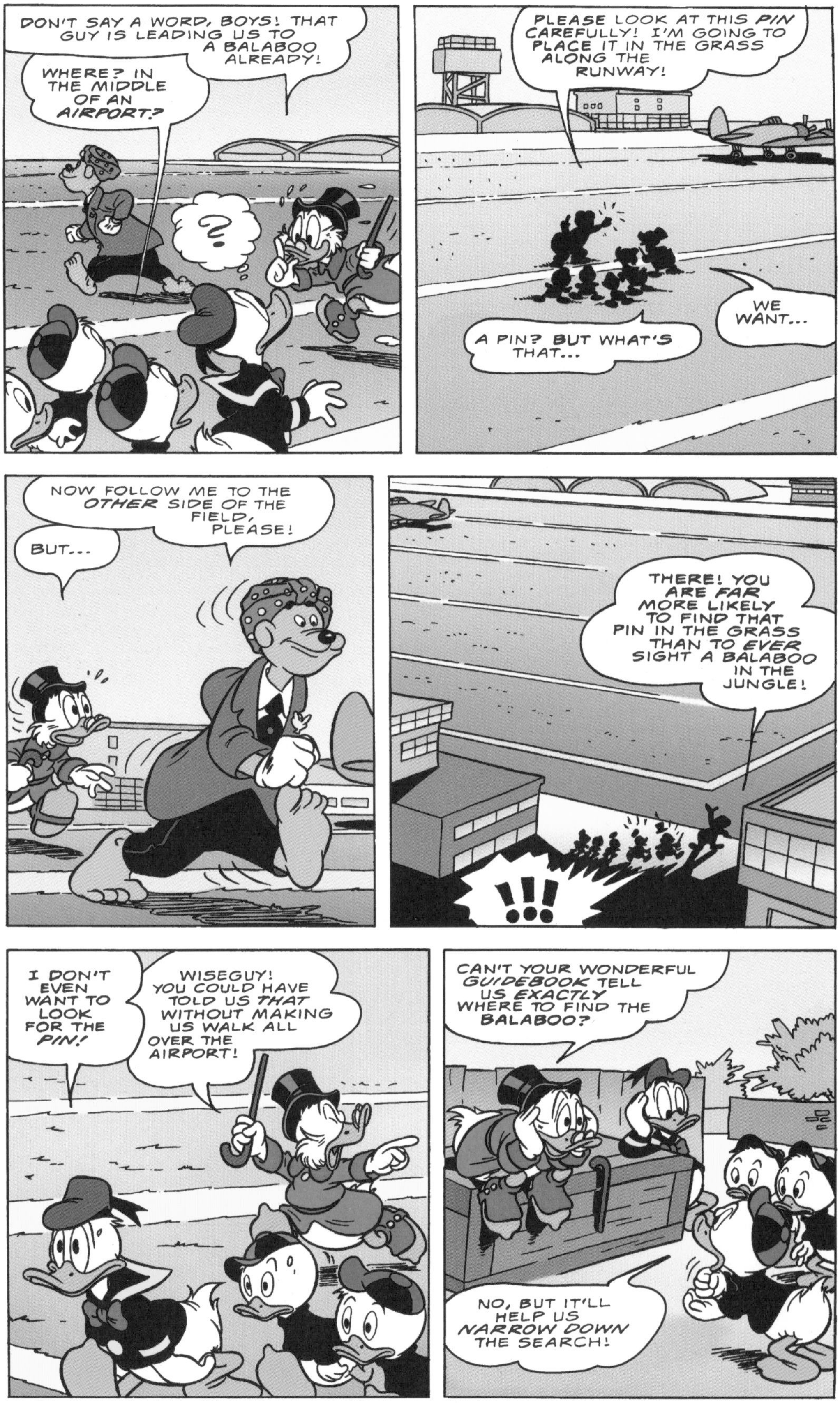
DON'T SAY A WORD, BOYS! THAT GUY IS LEADING US TO A BALABOO ALREADY!
WHERE? IN THE MIDDLE OF AN AIRPORT?
?
PLEASE LOOK AT THIS PIN CAREFULLY! I'M GOING TO PLACE IT IN THE GRASS ALONG THE RUNWAY!
A PIN? BUT WHAT'S THAT...
WE WANT...
NOW FOLLOW ME TO THE OTHER SIDE OF THE FIELD, PLEASE!
BUT...
THERE! YOU ARE FAR MORE LIKELY TO FIND THAT PIN IN THE GRASS THAN TO EVER SIGHT A BALABOO IN THE JUNGLE!
!!!
I DON'T EVEN WANT TO LOOK FOR THE PIN!
WISEGUY! YOU COULD HAVE TOLD US THAT WITHOUT MAKING US WALK ALL OVER THE AIRPORT!
CAN'T YOUR WONDERFUL GUIDEBOOK TELL US EXACTLY WHERE TO FIND THE BALABOO?
NO, BUT IT'LL HELP US NARROW DOWN THE SEARCH!

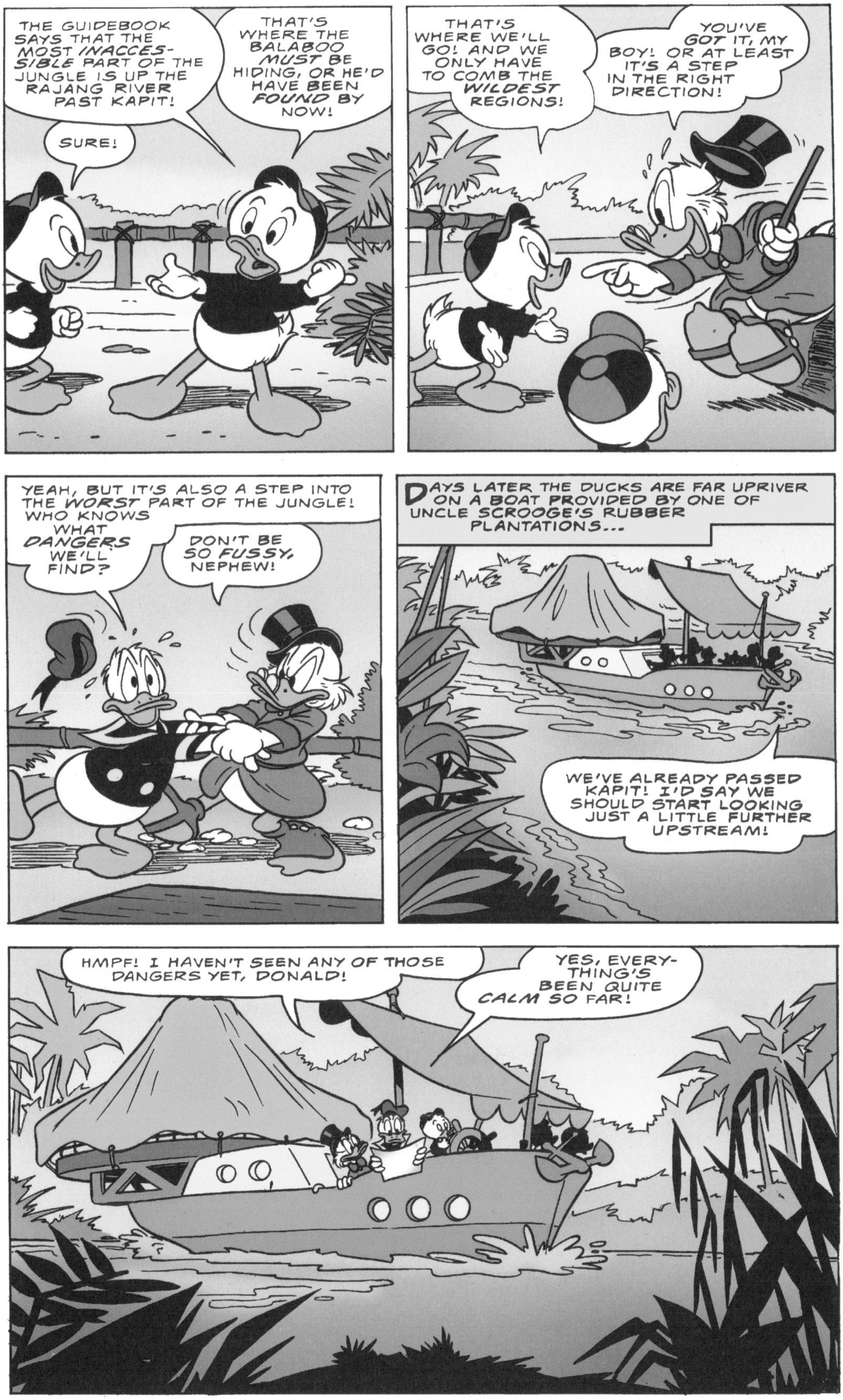
THE GUIDEBOOK SAYS THAT THE MOST INACCESSIBLE PART OF THE JUNGLE IS UP THE RAJANG RIVER PAST KAPIT!
THAT'S WHERE THE BALABOO MUST BE HIDING, OR HE'D HAVE BEEN FOUND BY NOW!
SURE!
THAT'S WHERE WE'LL GO! AND WE ONLY HAVE TO COMB THE WILDEST REGIONS!
YOU'VE GOT IT, MY BOY! OR AT LEAST IT'S A STEP IN THE RIGHT DIRECTION!
YEAH, BUT IT'S ALSO A STEP INTO THE WORST PART OF THE JUNGLE! WHO KNOWS WHAT DANGERS WE'LL FIND?
DON'T BE SO FUSSY, NEPHEW!
DAYS LATER THE DUCKS ARE FAR UPRIVER ON A BOAT PROVIDED BY ONE OF UNCLE SCROOGE'S RUBBER PLANTATIONS...
WE'VE ALREADY PASSED KAPIT! I'D SAY WE SHOULD START LOOKING JUST A LITTLE FURTHER UPSTREAM!
HMPF! I HAVEN'T SEEN ANY OF THOSE DANGERS YET, DONALD!
YES, EVERYTHING'S BEEN QUITE CALM SO FAR!

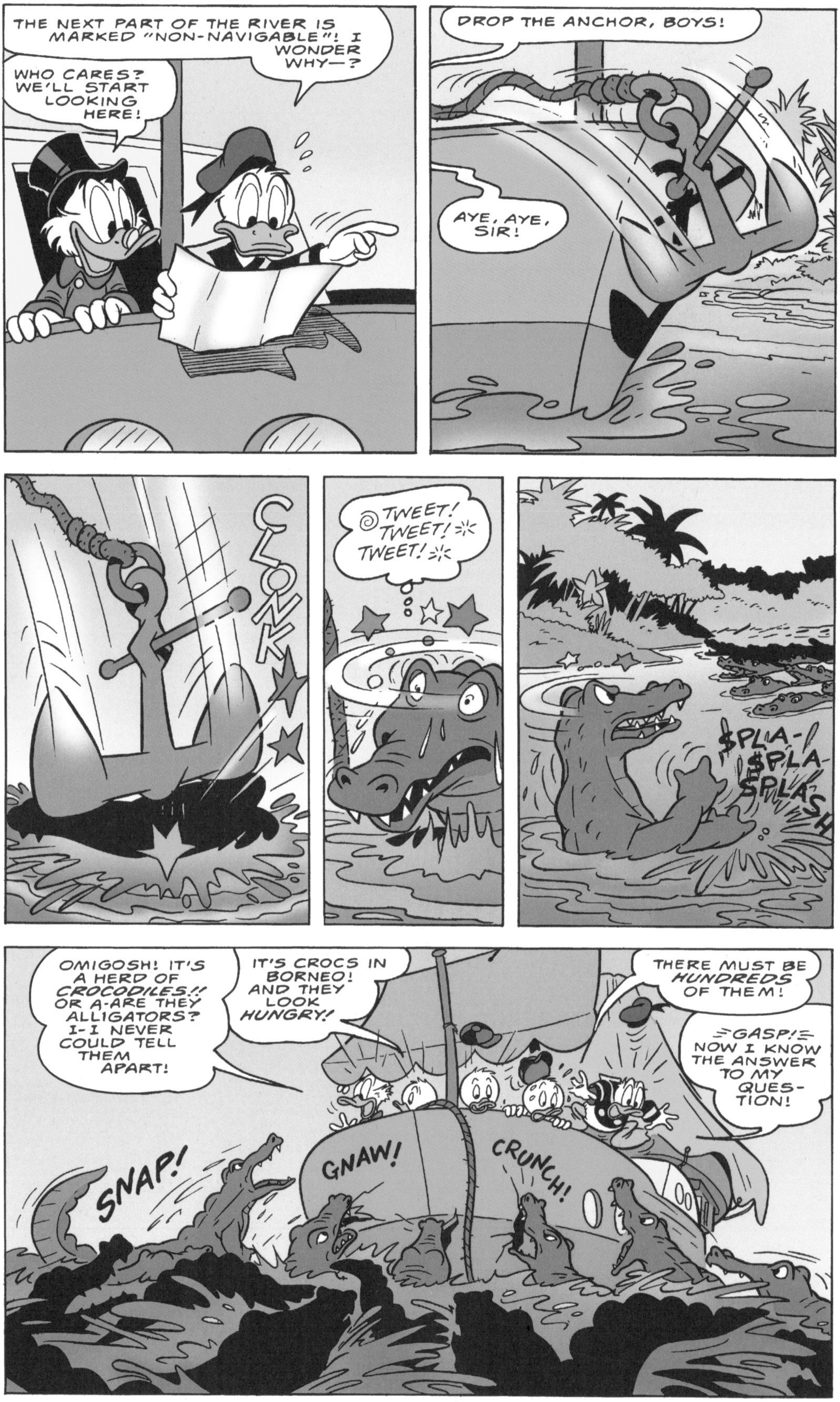
THE NEXT PART OF THE RIVER IS MARKED "NON-NAVIGABLE"! I WONDER WHY—?
WHO CARES? WE'LL START LOOKING HERE!
DROP THE ANCHOR, BOYS!
AYE, AYE, SIR!
CLONK
TWEET! TWEET! TWEET!
SPLA- SPLA- SPLASH
OMIGOSH! IT'S A HERD OF CROCODILES!! OR A-ARE THEY ALLIGATORS? I-I NEVER COULD TELL THEM APART!
IT'S CROCS IN BORNEO! AND THEY LOOK HUNGRY!
THERE MUST BE HUNDREDS OF THEM!
GASP! NOW I KNOW THE ANSWER TO MY QUES-TION!
SNAP!
GNAW!
CRUNCH!

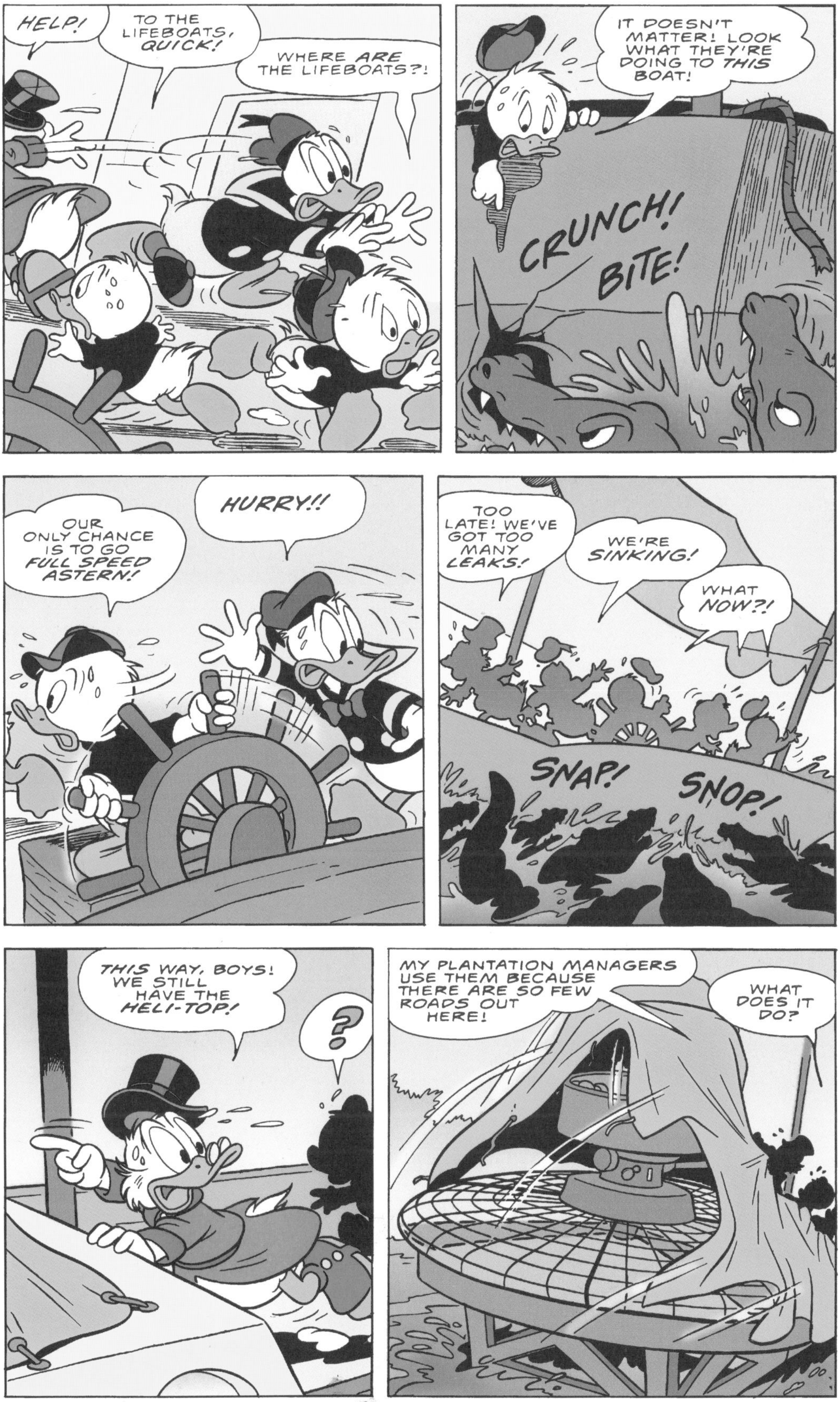
HELP!
TO THE LIFEBOATS, QUICK!
WHERE ARE THE LIFEBOATS?!
IT DOESN'T MATTER! LOOK WHAT THEY'RE DOING TO THIS BOAT!
CRUNCH!
BITE!
OUR ONLY CHANCE IS TO GO FULL SPEED ASTERN!
HURRY!!
TOO LATE! WE'VE GOT TOO MANY LEAKS!
WE'RE SINKING!
WHAT NOW?!
SNAP!
SNOP!
THIS WAY, BOYS! WE STILL HAVE THE HELI-TOP!
?
MY PLANTATION MANAGERS USE THEM BECAUSE THERE ARE SO FEW ROADS OUT HERE!
WHAT DOES IT DO?

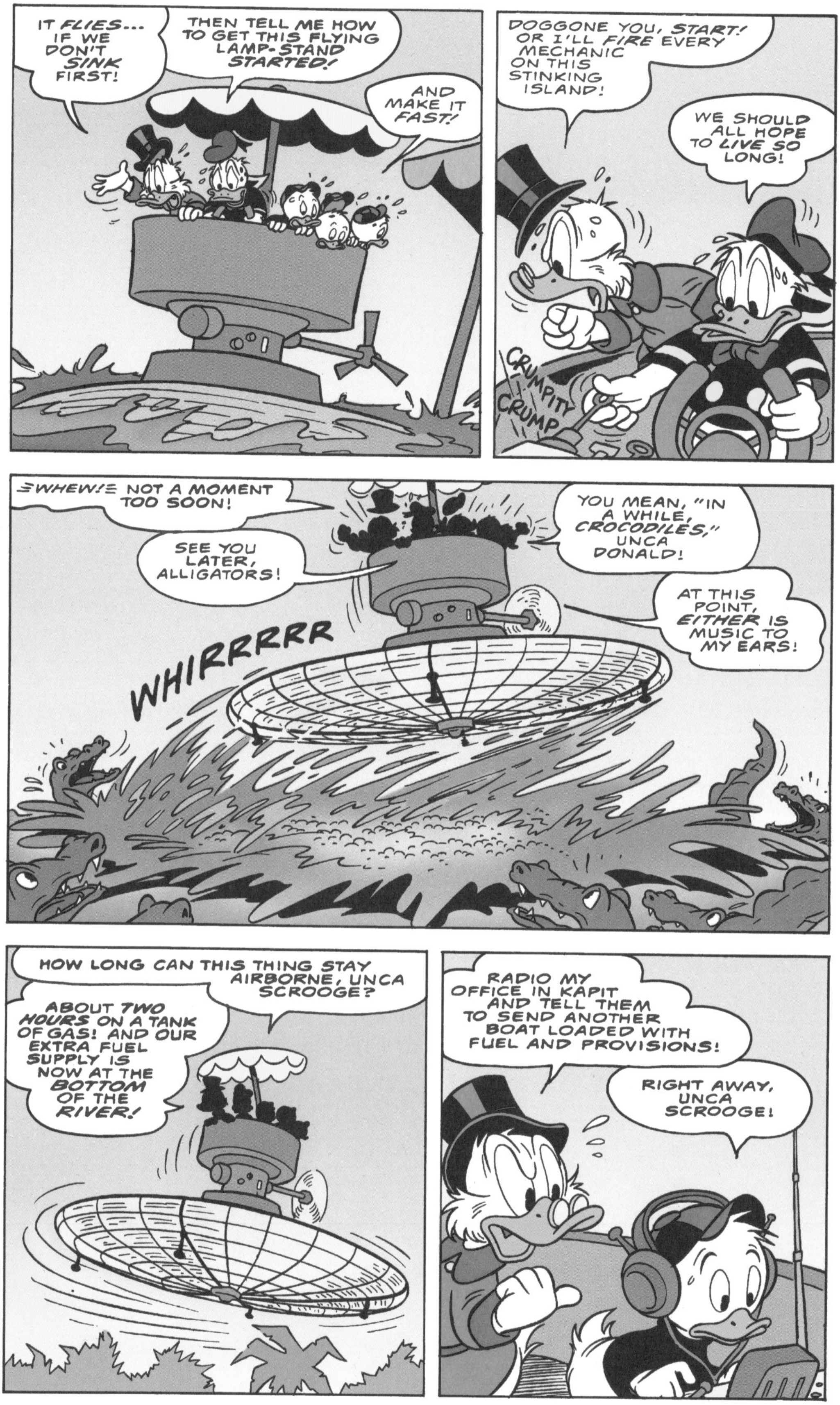
IT FLIES... IF WE DON'T SINK FIRST!
THEN TELL ME HOW TO GET THIS FLYING LAMP-STAND STARTED!
AND MAKE IT FAST!
DOGGONE YOU, START! OR I'LL FIRE EVERY MECHANIC ON THIS STINKING ISLAND!
WE SHOULD ALL HOPE TO LIVE SO LONG!
CRUMPITY CRUMPITY CRUMP
≡WHEW!≡ NOT A MOMENT TOO SOON!
SEE YOU LATER, ALLIGATORS!
YOU MEAN, "IN A WHILE, CROCODILES," UNCA DONALD!
AT THIS POINT, EITHER IS MUSIC TO MY EARS!
WHIRRRRR
HOW LONG CAN THIS THING STAY AIRBORNE, UNCA SCROOGE?
ABOUT TWO HOURS ON A TANK OF GAS! AND OUR EXTRA FUEL SUPPLY IS NOW AT THE BOTTOM OF THE RIVER!
RADIO MY OFFICE IN KAPIT AND TELL THEM TO SEND ANOTHER BOAT LOADED WITH FUEL AND PROVISIONS!
RIGHT AWAY, UNCA SCROOGE!

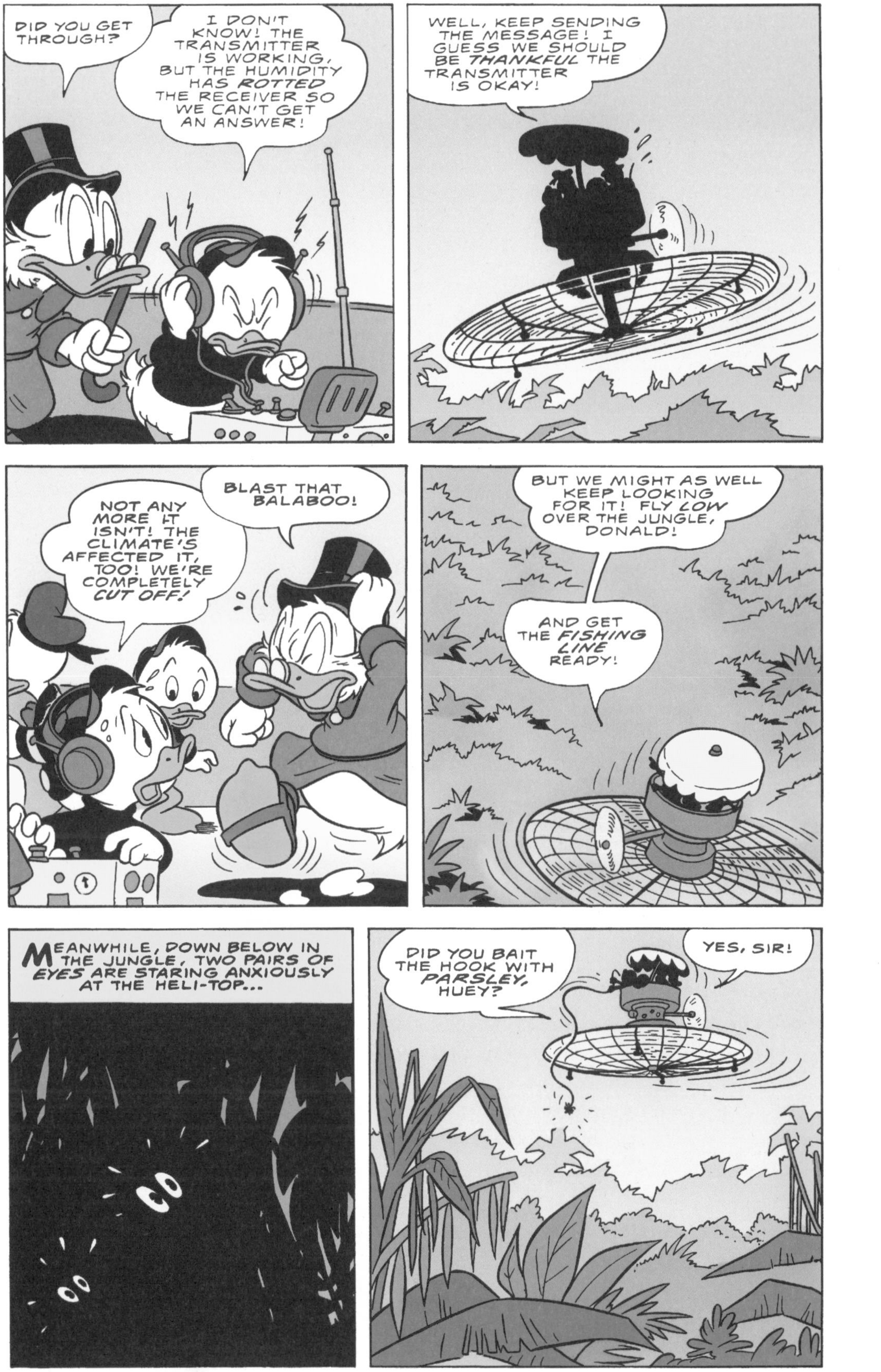
DID YOU GET THROUGH?
I DON'T KNOW! THE TRANSMITTER IS WORKING, BUT THE HUMIDITY HAS ROTTED THE RECEIVER SO WE CAN'T GET AN ANSWER!
WELL, KEEP SENDING THE MESSAGE! I GUESS WE SHOULD BE THANKFUL THE TRANSMITTER IS OKAY!
NOT ANY MORE IT ISN'T! THE CLIMATE'S AFFECTED IT, TOO! WE'RE COMPLETELY CUT OFF!
BLAST THAT BALABOO!
BUT WE MIGHT AS WELL KEEP LOOKING FOR IT! FLY LOW OVER THE JUNGLE, DONALD!
AND GET THE FISHING LINE READY!
MEANWHILE, DOWN BELOW IN THE JUNGLE, TWO PAIRS OF EYES ARE STARING ANXIOUSLY AT THE HELI-TOP...
DID YOU BAIT THE HOOK WITH PARSLEY, HUEY?
YES, SIR!

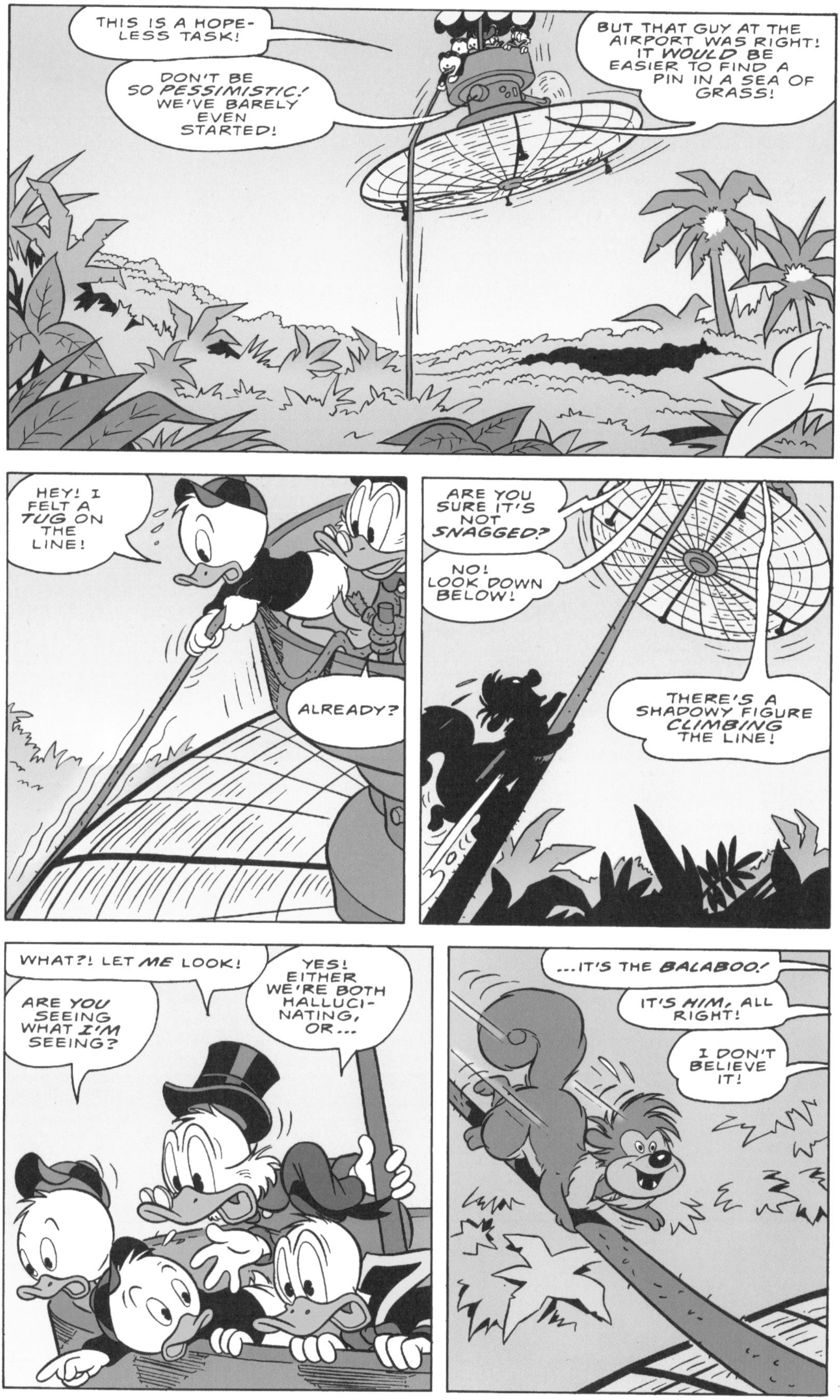
THIS IS A HOPE-LESS TASK!
DON'T BE SO PESSIMISTIC! WE'VE BARELY EVEN STARTED!
BUT THAT GUY AT THE AIRPORT WAS RIGHT! IT WOULD BE EASIER TO FIND A PIN IN A SEA OF GRASS!
HEY! I FELT A TUG ON THE LINE!
ALREADY?
ARE YOU SURE IT'S NOT SNAGGED?
NO! LOOK DOWN BELOW!
THERE'S A SHADOWY FIGURE CLIMBING THE LINE!
WHAT?! LET ME LOOK!
ARE YOU SEEING WHAT I'M SEEING?
YES! EITHER WE'RE BOTH HALLUCI-NATING, OR...
...IT'S THE BALABOO!
IT'S HIM, ALL RIGHT!
I DON'T BELIEVE IT!

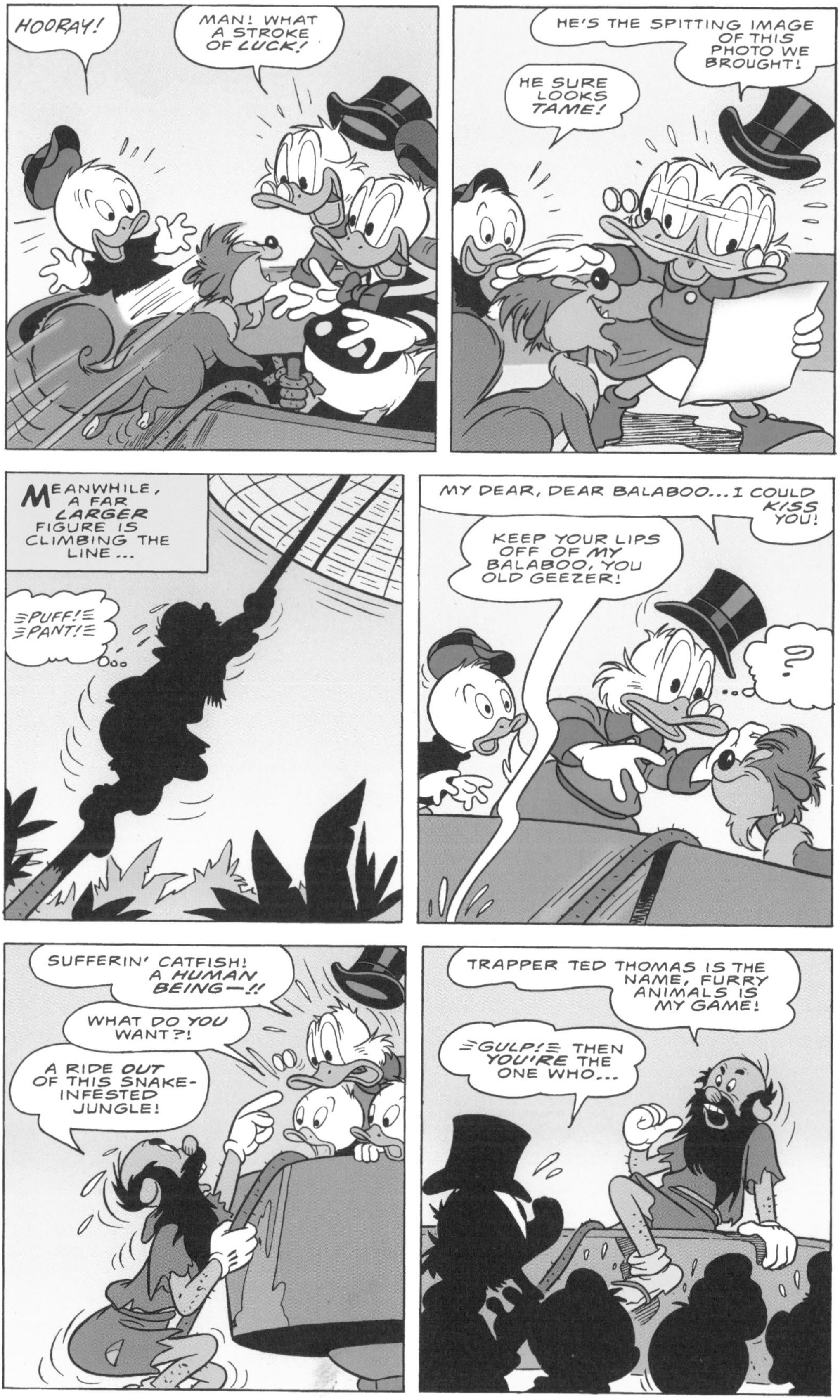
HOORAY!
MAN! WHAT A STROKE OF LUCK!
HE'S THE SPITTING IMAGE OF THIS PHOTO WE BROUGHT!
HE SURE LOOKS TAME!
MEANWHILE, A FAR LARGER FIGURE IS CLIMBING THE LINE...
PUFF! PANT!
MY DEAR, DEAR BALABOO... I COULD KISS YOU!
KEEP YOUR LIPS OFF OF MY BALABOO, YOU OLD GEEZER!
?
SUFFERIN' CATFISH! A HUMAN BEING—!!
WHAT DO YOU WANT?!
A RIDE OUT OF THIS SNAKE-INFESTED JUNGLE!
TRAPPER TED THOMAS IS THE NAME, FURRY ANIMALS IS MY GAME!
GULP! THEN YOU'RE THE ONE WHO...

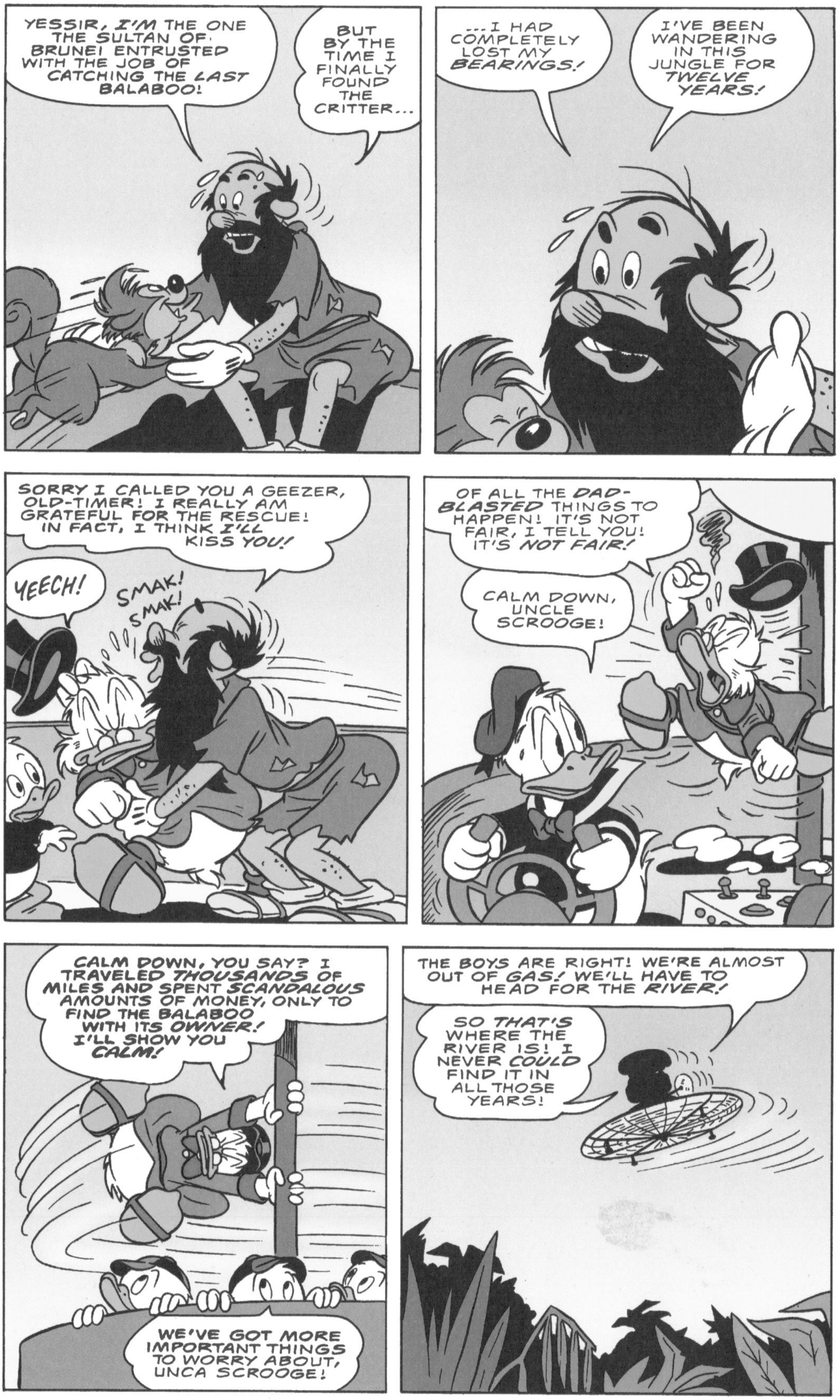

YESSIR, I'M THE ONE THE SULTAN OF BRUNEI ENTRUSTED WITH THE JOB OF CATCHING THE LAST BALABOO!
BUT BY THE TIME I FINALLY FOUND THE CRITTER...
...I HAD COMPLETELY LOST MY BEARINGS!
I'VE BEEN WANDERING IN THIS JUNGLE FOR TWELVE YEARS!
SORRY I CALLED YOU A GEEZER, OLD-TIMER! I REALLY AM GRATEFUL FOR THE RESCUE! IN FACT, I THINK I'LL KISS YOU!
YEECH!
SMAK! SMAK!
OF ALL THE DAD-BLASTED THINGS TO HAPPEN! IT'S NOT FAIR, I TELL YOU! IT'S NOT FAIR!
CALM DOWN, UNCLE SCROOGE!
CALM DOWN, YOU SAY? I TRAVELED THOUSANDS OF MILES AND SPENT SCANDALOUS AMOUNTS OF MONEY, ONLY TO FIND THE BALABOO WITH ITS OWNER! I'LL SHOW YOU CALM!
WE'VE GOT MORE IMPORTANT THINGS TO WORRY ABOUT, UNCA SCROOGE!
THE BOYS ARE RIGHT! WE'RE ALMOST OUT OF GAS! WE'LL HAVE TO HEAD FOR THE RIVER!
SO THAT'S WHERE THE RIVER IS! I NEVER COULD FIND IT IN ALL THOSE YEARS!

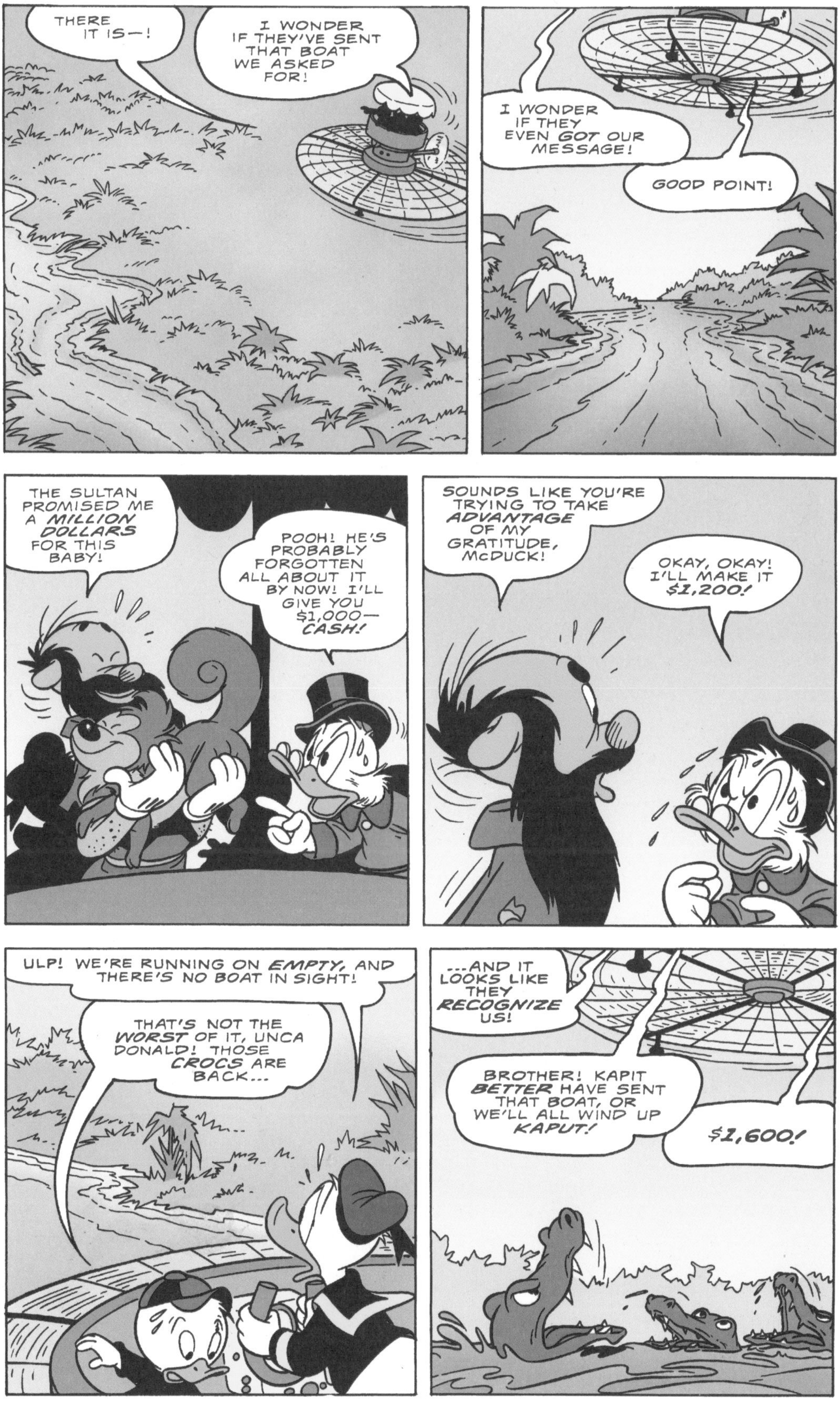
THERE IT IS—!
I WONDER IF THEY'VE SENT THAT BOAT WE ASKED FOR!
I WONDER IF THEY EVEN GOT OUR MESSAGE!
GOOD POINT!
THE SULTAN PROMISED ME A MILLION DOLLARS FOR THIS BABY!
POOH! HE'S PROBABLY FORGOTTEN ALL ABOUT IT BY NOW! I'LL GIVE YOU $1,000— CASH!
SOUNDS LIKE YOU'RE TRYING TO TAKE ADVANTAGE OF MY GRATITUDE, McDUCK!
OKAY, OKAY! I'LL MAKE IT $1,200!
ULP! WE'RE RUNNING ON EMPTY, AND THERE'S NO BOAT IN SIGHT!
THAT'S NOT THE WORST OF IT, UNCA DONALD! THOSE CROCS ARE BACK...
...AND IT LOOKS LIKE THEY RECOGNIZE US!
BROTHER! KAPIT BETTER HAVE SENT THAT BOAT, OR WE'LL ALL WIND UP KAPUT!
$1,600!

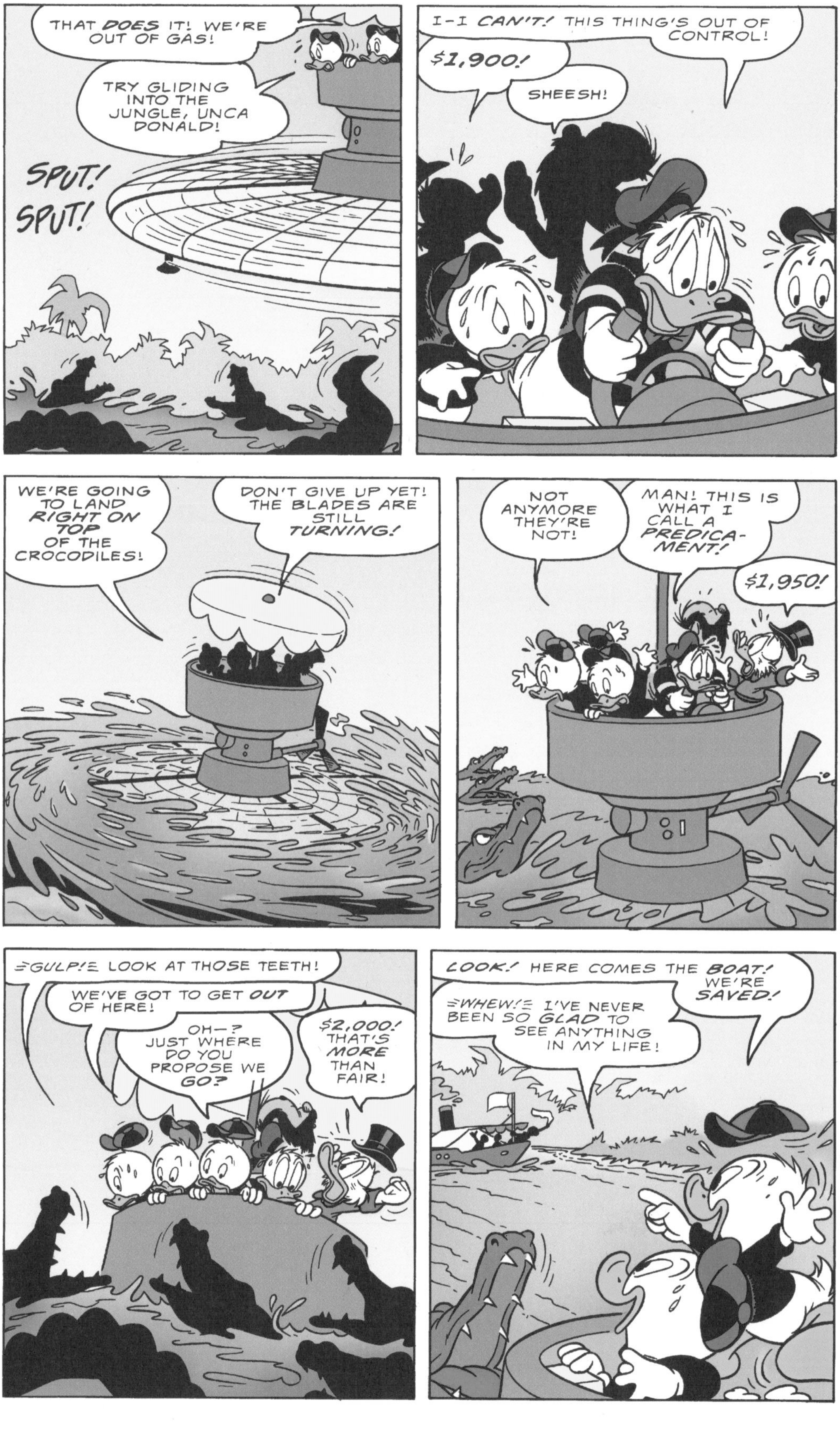
THAT DOES IT! WE'RE OUT OF GAS!
TRY GLIDING INTO THE JUNGLE, UNCA DONALD!
SPUT! SPUT!
I-I CAN'T! THIS THING'S OUT OF CONTROL!
$1,900!
SHEESH!
WE'RE GOING TO LAND RIGHT ON TOP OF THE CROCODILES!
DON'T GIVE UP YET! THE BLADES ARE STILL TURNING!
NOT ANYMORE THEY'RE NOT!
MAN! THIS IS WHAT I CALL A PREDICA-MENT!
$1,950!
GULP! LOOK AT THOSE TEETH!
WE'VE GOT TO GET OUT OF HERE!
OH—? JUST WHERE DO YOU PROPOSE WE GO?
$2,000! THAT'S MORE THAN FAIR!
LOOK! HERE COMES THE BOAT! WE'RE SAVED!
WHEW! I'VE NEVER BEEN SO GLAD TO SEE ANYTHING IN MY LIFE!

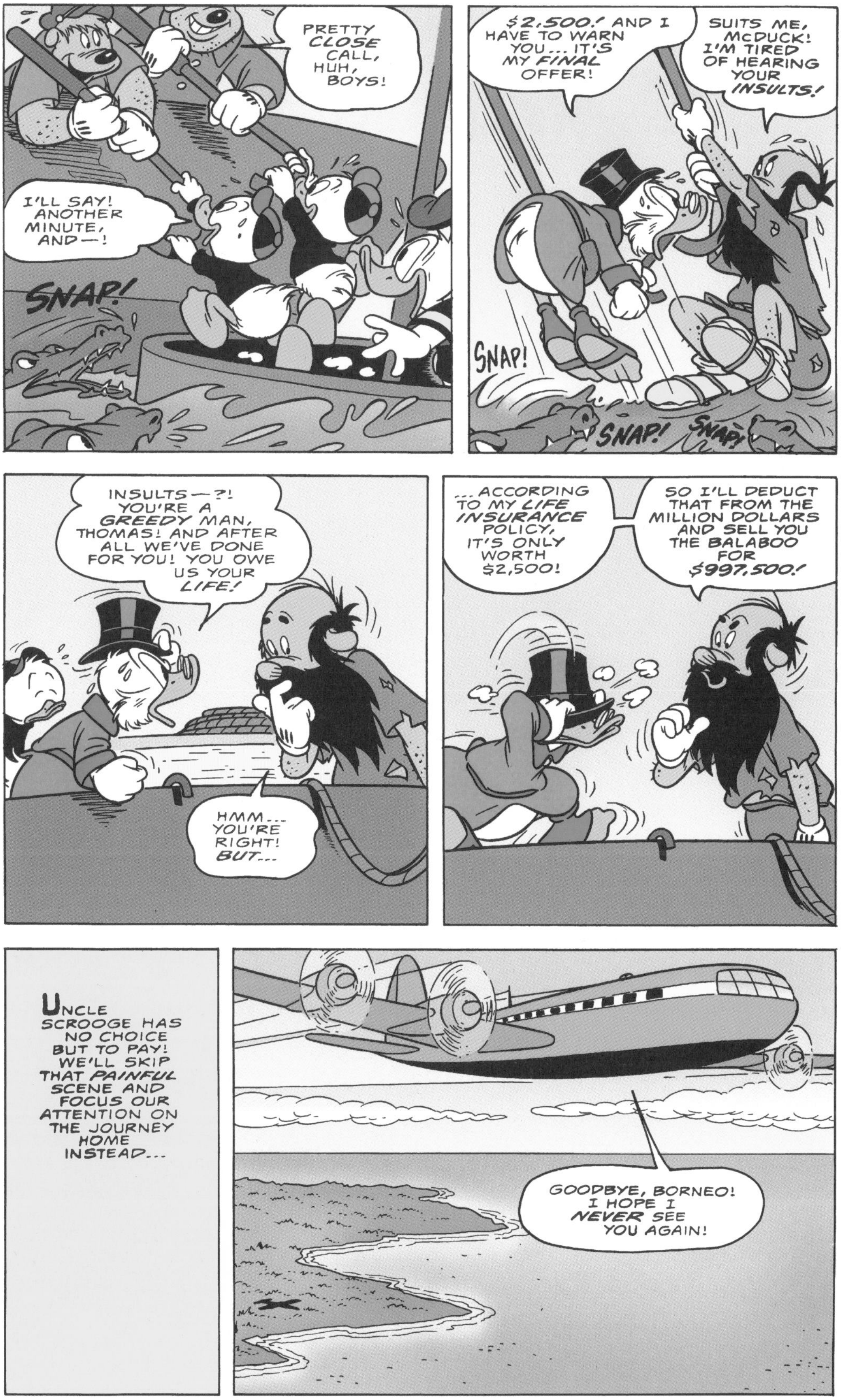

PRETTY CLOSE CALL, HUH, BOYS!
I'LL SAY! ANOTHER MINUTE, AND—!
SNAP!
$2,500! AND I HAVE TO WARN YOU... IT'S MY FINAL OFFER!
SUITS ME, McDUCK! I'M TIRED OF HEARING YOUR INSULTS!
SNAP!
SNAP!
SNAP!
INSULTS—?! YOU'RE A GREEDY MAN, THOMAS! AND AFTER ALL WE'VE DONE FOR YOU! YOU OWE US YOUR LIFE!
HMM... YOU'RE RIGHT! BUT...
...ACCORDING TO MY LIFE INSURANCE POLICY, IT'S ONLY WORTH $2,500!
SO I'LL DEDUCT THAT FROM THE MILLION DOLLARS AND SELL YOU THE BALABOO FOR $997,500!
UNCLE SCROOGE HAS NO CHOICE BUT TO PAY! WE'LL SKIP THAT PAINFUL SCENE AND FOCUS OUR ATTENTION ON THE JOURNEY HOME INSTEAD...
GOODBYE, BORNEO! I HOPE I NEVER SEE YOU AGAIN!

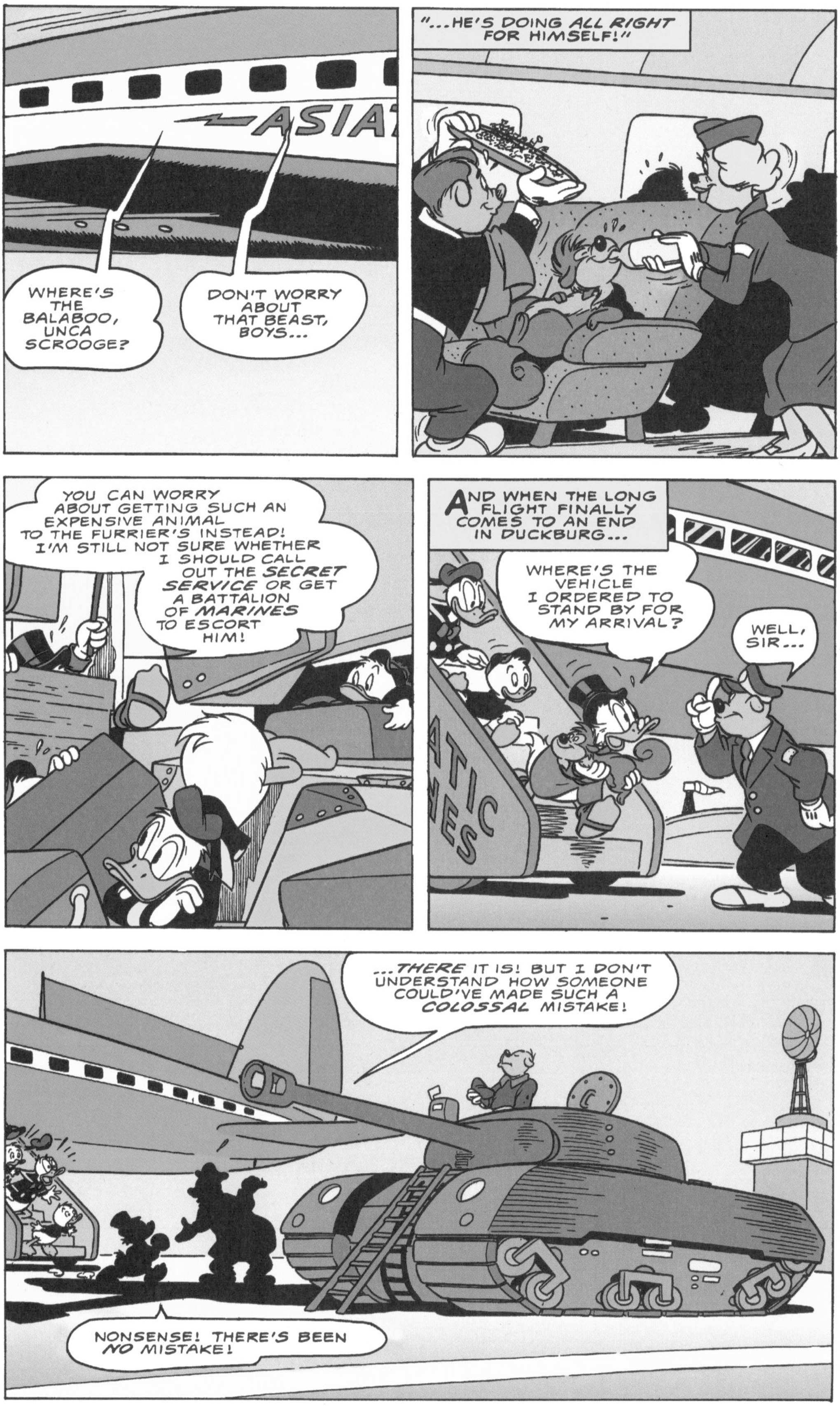
WHERE'S THE BALABOO, UNCA SCROOGE?
DON'T WORRY ABOUT THAT BEAST, BOYS...
"...HE'S DOING ALL RIGHT FOR HIMSELF!"
YOU CAN WORRY ABOUT GETTING SUCH AN EXPENSIVE ANIMAL TO THE FURRIER'S INSTEAD! I'M STILL NOT SURE WHETHER I SHOULD CALL OUT THE SECRET SERVICE OR GET A BATTALION OF MARINES TO ESCORT HIM!
AND WHEN THE LONG FLIGHT FINALLY COMES TO AN END IN DUCKBURG...
WHERE'S THE VEHICLE I ORDERED TO STAND BY FOR MY ARRIVAL?
WELL, SIR...
...THERE IT IS! BUT I DON'T UNDERSTAND HOW SOMEONE COULD'VE MADE SUCH A COLOSSAL MISTAKE!
NONSENSE! THERE'S BEEN NO MISTAKE!

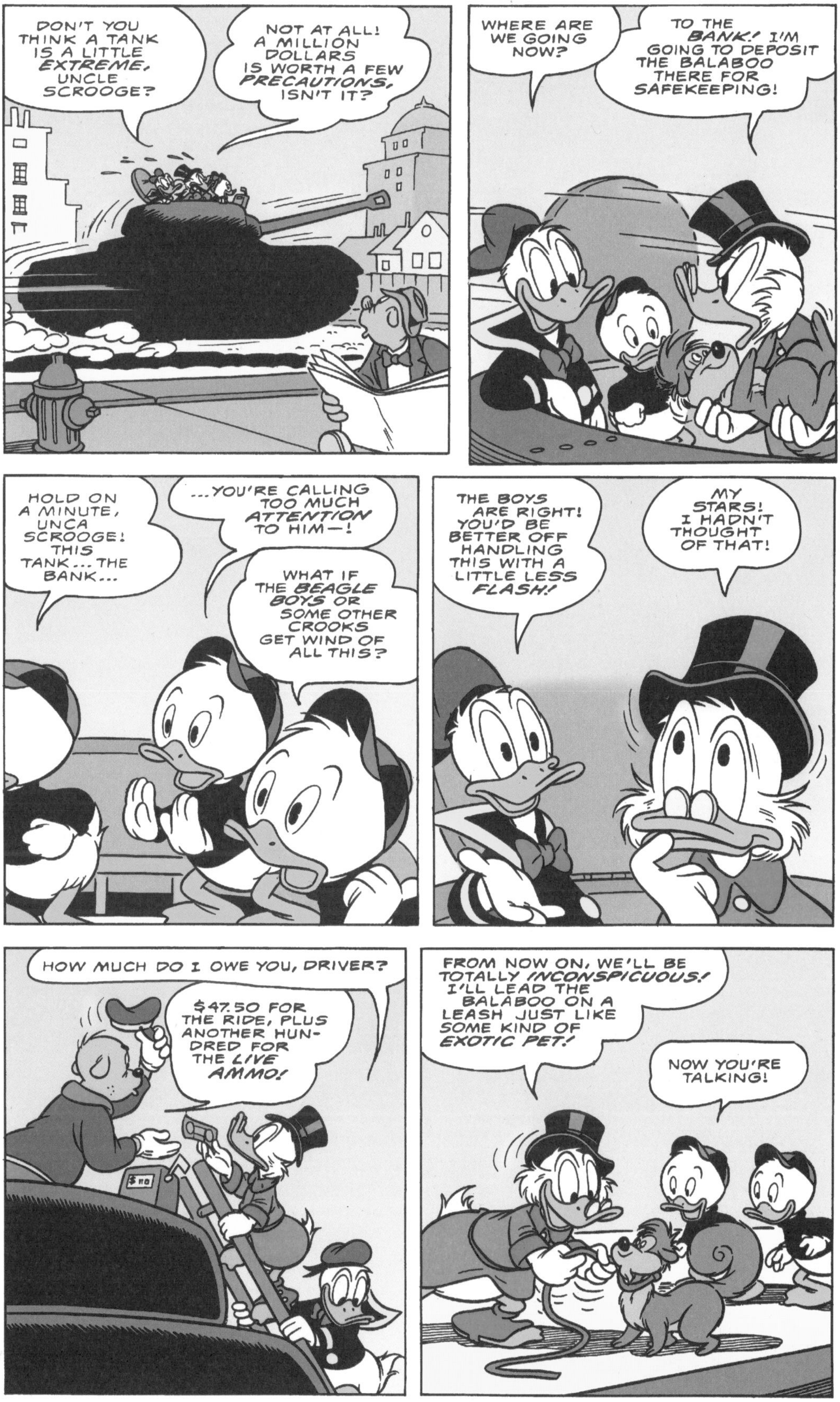
DON'T YOU THINK A TANK IS A LITTLE *EXTREME,* UNCLE SCROOGE?
NOT AT ALL! A MILLION DOLLARS IS WORTH A FEW *PRECAUTIONS,* ISN'T IT?
WHERE ARE WE GOING NOW?
TO THE *BANK!* I'M GOING TO DEPOSIT THE BALABOO THERE FOR SAFEKEEPING!
HOLD ON A MINUTE, UNCA SCROOGE! THIS TANK... THE BANK...
...YOU'RE CALLING TOO MUCH *ATTENTION* TO HIM—!
WHAT IF THE *BEAGLE BOYS* OR SOME OTHER CROOKS GET WIND OF ALL THIS?
THE BOYS ARE RIGHT! YOU'D BE BETTER OFF HANDLING THIS WITH A LITTLE LESS *FLASH!*
MY STARS! I HADN'T THOUGHT OF THAT!
HOW MUCH DO I OWE YOU, DRIVER?
$47.50 FOR THE RIDE, PLUS ANOTHER HUNDRED FOR THE *LIVE AMMO!*
FROM NOW ON, WE'LL BE TOTALLY *INCONSPICUOUS!* I'LL LEAD THE BALABOO ON A LEASH JUST LIKE SOME KIND OF *EXOTIC PET!*
NOW YOU'RE TALKING!

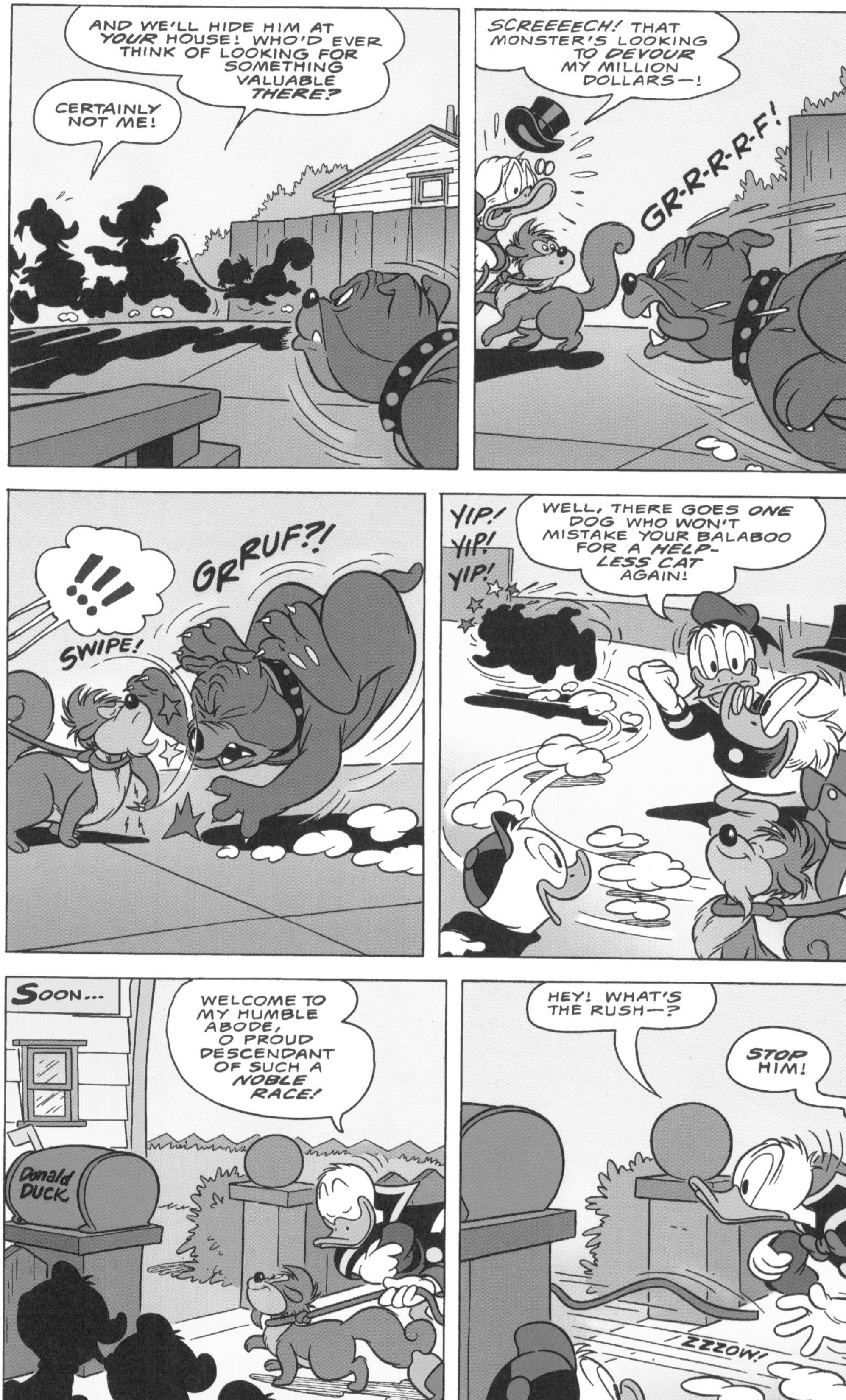
AND WE'LL HIDE HIM AT YOUR HOUSE! WHO'D EVER THINK OF LOOKING FOR SOMETHING VALUABLE THERE?
CERTAINLY NOT ME!
SCREEEECH! THAT MONSTER'S LOOKING TO DEVOUR MY MILLION DOLLARS—!
GR-R-R-R-F!
!!!
GRRUF?!
SWIPE!
YIP!
YIP!
YIP!
WELL, THERE GOES ONE DOG WHO WON'T MISTAKE YOUR BALABOO FOR A HELP-LESS CAT AGAIN!
SOON...
WELCOME TO MY HUMBLE ABODE, O PROUD DESCENDANT OF SUCH A NOBLE RACE!
Donald DUCK
HEY! WHAT'S THE RUSH—?
STOP HIM!
ZZZOW!

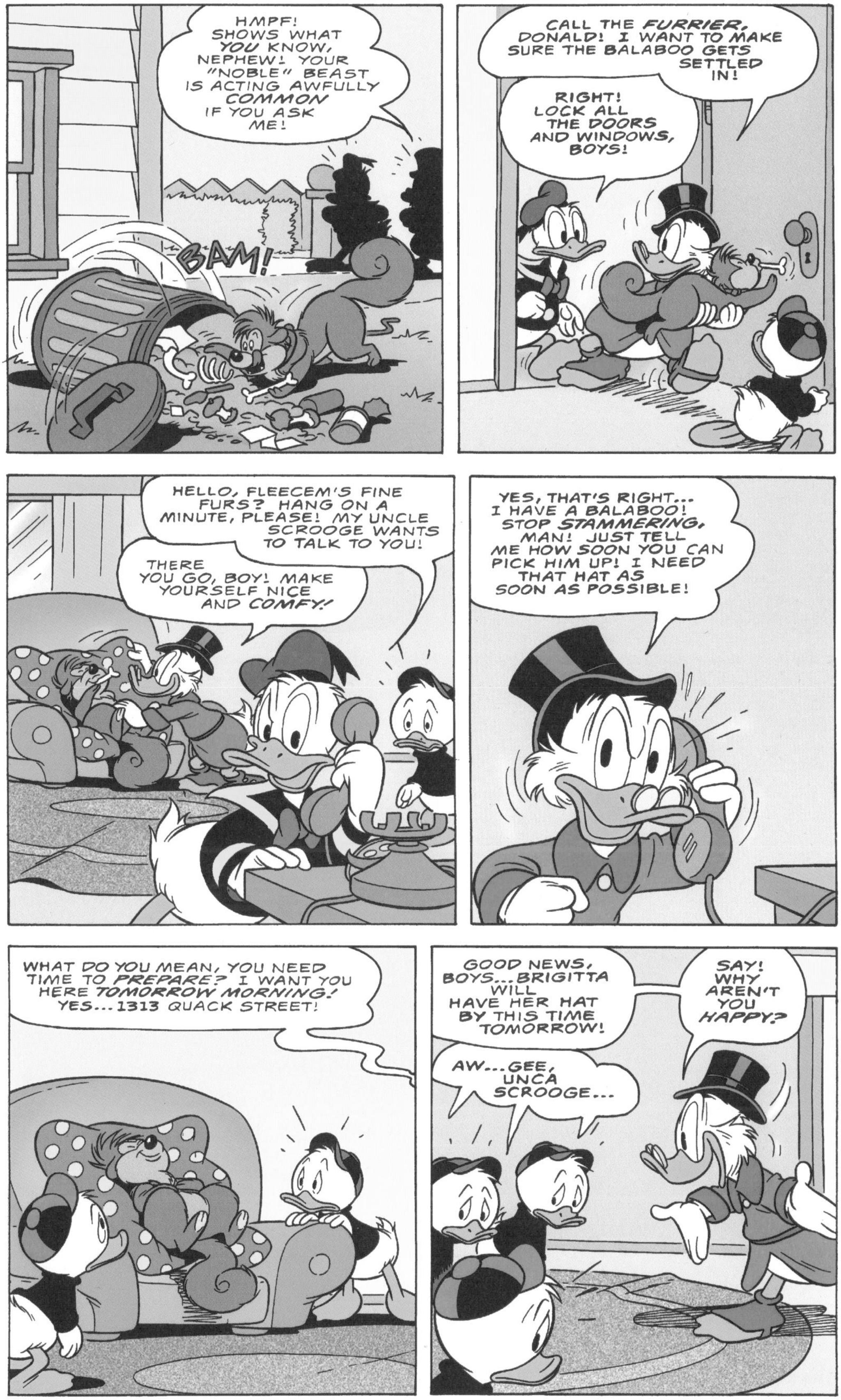

HMPF! SHOWS WHAT YOU KNOW, NEPHEW! YOUR "NOBLE" BEAST IS ACTING AWFULLY COMMON IF YOU ASK ME!
BAM!
CALL THE FURRIER, DONALD! I WANT TO MAKE SURE THE BALABOO GETS SETTLED IN!
RIGHT! LOCK ALL THE DOORS AND WINDOWS, BOYS!
HELLO, FLEECEM'S FINE FURS? HANG ON A MINUTE, PLEASE! MY UNCLE SCROOGE WANTS TO TALK TO YOU!
THERE YOU GO, BOY! MAKE YOURSELF NICE AND COMFY!
YES, THAT'S RIGHT... I HAVE A BALABOO! STOP STAMMERING, MAN! JUST TELL ME HOW SOON YOU CAN PICK HIM UP! I NEED THAT HAT AS SOON AS POSSIBLE!
WHAT DO YOU MEAN, YOU NEED TIME TO PREPARE? I WANT YOU HERE TOMORROW MORNING! YES... 1313 QUACK STREET!
GOOD NEWS, BOYS... BRIGITTA WILL HAVE HER HAT BY THIS TIME TOMORROW!
SAY! WHY AREN'T YOU HAPPY?
AW... GEE, UNCA SCROOGE...

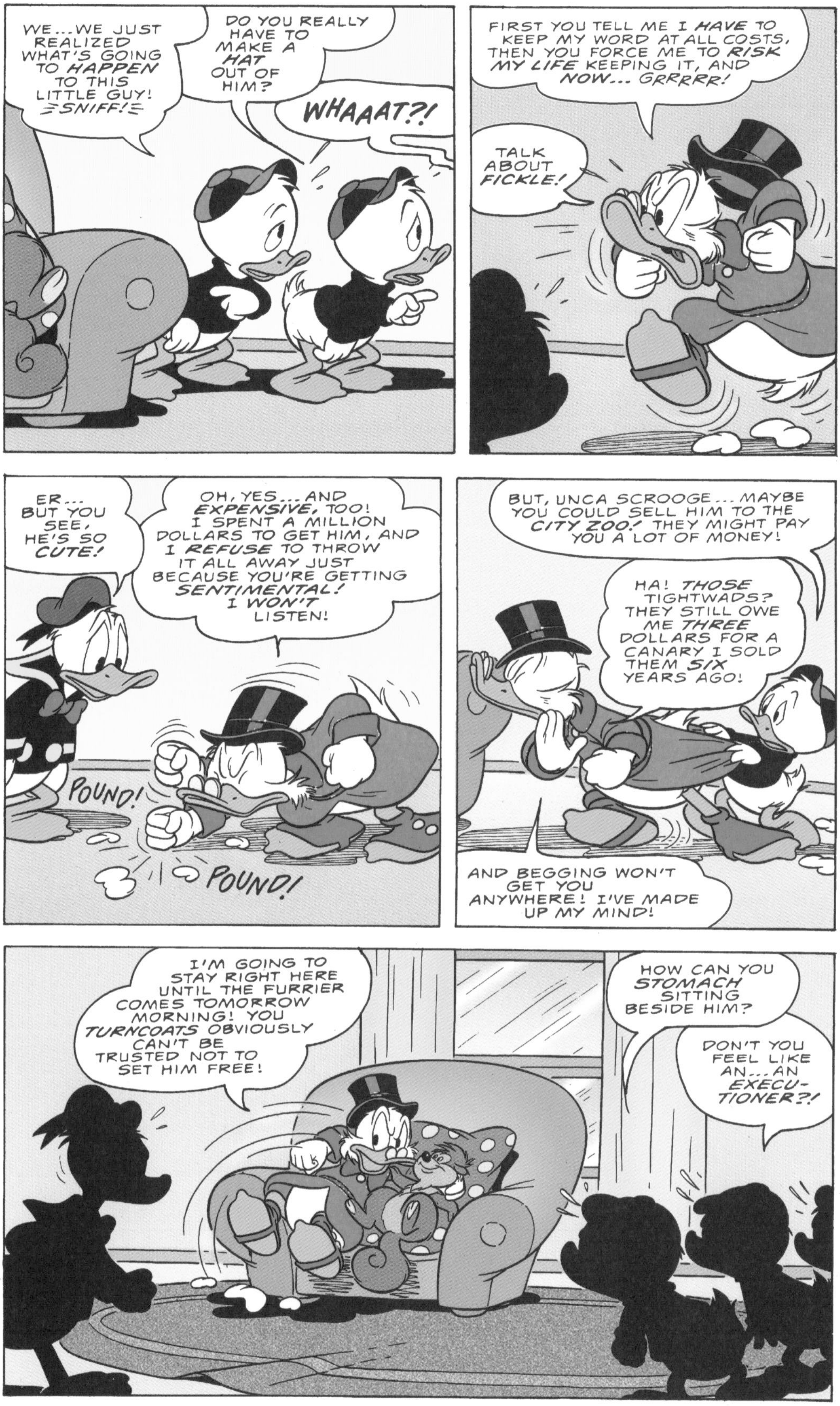
WE...WE JUST REALIZED WHAT'S GOING TO HAPPEN TO THIS LITTLE GUY! SNIFF!
DO YOU REALLY HAVE TO MAKE A HAT OUT OF HIM?
WHAAAT?!
FIRST YOU TELL ME I HAVE TO KEEP MY WORD AT ALL COSTS, THEN YOU FORCE ME TO RISK MY LIFE KEEPING IT, AND NOW... GRRRRR!
TALK ABOUT FICKLE!
ER... BUT YOU SEE, HE'S SO CUTE!
OH, YES... AND EXPENSIVE, TOO! I SPENT A MILLION DOLLARS TO GET HIM, AND I REFUSE TO THROW IT ALL AWAY JUST BECAUSE YOU'RE GETTING SENTIMENTAL! I WON'T LISTEN!
POUND!
POUND!
BUT, UNCA SCROOGE... MAYBE YOU COULD SELL HIM TO THE CITY ZOO! THEY MIGHT PAY YOU A LOT OF MONEY!
HA! THOSE TIGHTWADS? THEY STILL OWE ME THREE DOLLARS FOR A CANARY I SOLD THEM SIX YEARS AGO!
AND BEGGING WON'T GET YOU ANYWHERE! I'VE MADE UP MY MIND!
I'M GOING TO STAY RIGHT HERE UNTIL THE FURRIER COMES TOMORROW MORNING! YOU TURNCOATS OBVIOUSLY CAN'T BE TRUSTED NOT TO SET HIM FREE!
HOW CAN YOU STOMACH SITTING BESIDE HIM?
DON'T YOU FEEL LIKE AN... AN EXECU-TIONER?!

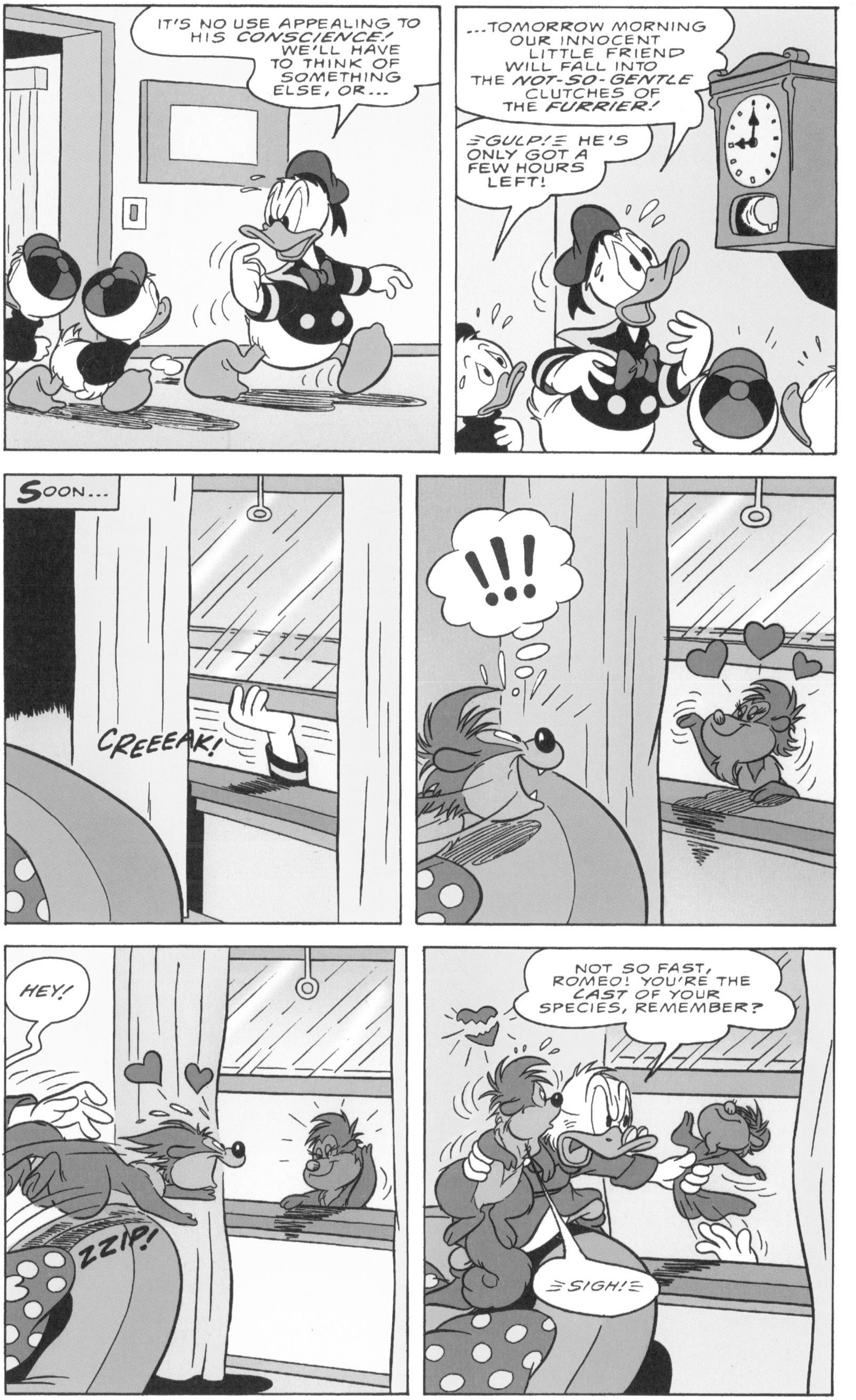

IT'S NO USE APPEALING TO HIS CONSCIENCE! WE'LL HAVE TO THINK OF SOMETHING ELSE, OR...
...TOMORROW MORNING OUR INNOCENT LITTLE FRIEND WILL FALL INTO THE NOT-SO-GENTLE CLUTCHES OF THE FURRIER!
GULP! HE'S ONLY GOT A FEW HOURS LEFT!
SOON...
CREEEAK!
!!!
HEY!
ZZIP!
NOT SO FAST, ROMEO! YOU'RE THE LAST OF YOUR SPECIES, REMEMBER?
SIGH!

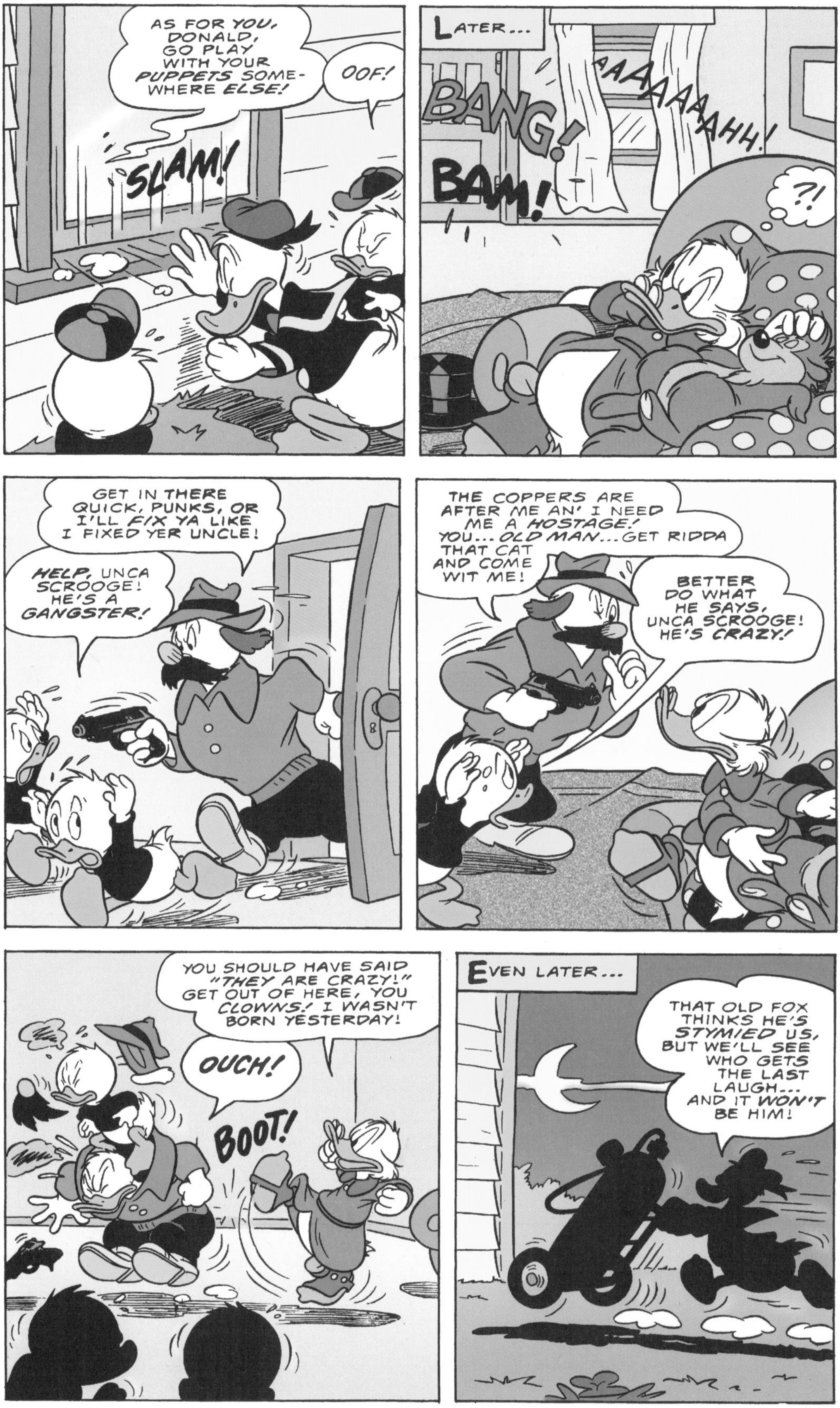
AS FOR YOU, DONALD, GO PLAY WITH YOUR PUPPETS SOMEWHERE ELSE!
OOF!
SLAM!
LATER...
BANG!
BAM!
AAAAAAAHH!
?!
GET IN THERE QUICK, PUNKS, OR I'LL FIX YA LIKE I FIXED YER UNCLE!
HELP, UNCA SCROOGE! HE'S A GANGSTER!
THE COPPERS ARE AFTER ME AN' I NEED ME A HOSTAGE! YOU... OLD MAN... GET RIDDA THAT CAT AND COME WIT ME!
BETTER DO WHAT HE SAYS, UNCA SCROOGE! HE'S CRAZY!
YOU SHOULD HAVE SAID "THEY ARE CRAZY!" GET OUT OF HERE, YOU CLOWNS! I WASN'T BORN YESTERDAY!
OUCH!
BOOT!
EVEN LATER...
THAT OLD FOX THINKS HE'S STYMIED US, BUT WE'LL SEE WHO GETS THE LAST LAUGH... AND IT WON'T BE HIM!

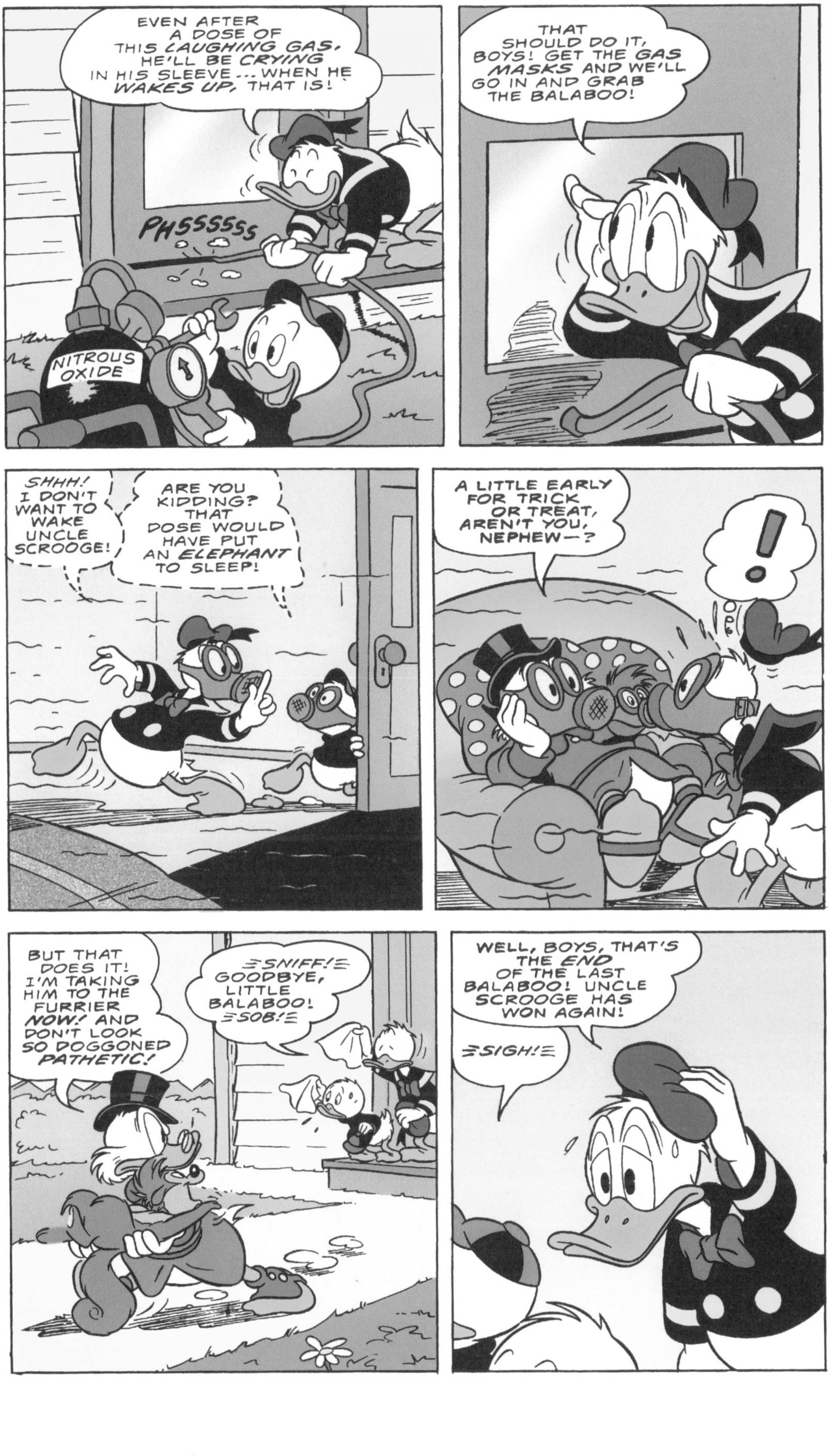
EVEN AFTER A DOSE OF THIS LAUGHING GAS, HE'LL BE CRYING IN HIS SLEEVE... WHEN HE WAKES UP, THAT IS!
PHSSSSSS
NITROUS OXIDE
THAT SHOULD DO IT, BOYS! GET THE GAS MASKS AND WE'LL GO IN AND GRAB THE BALABOO!
SHHH! I DON'T WANT TO WAKE UNCLE SCROOGE!
ARE YOU KIDDING? THAT DOSE WOULD HAVE PUT AN ELEPHANT TO SLEEP!
A LITTLE EARLY FOR TRICK OR TREAT, AREN'T YOU, NEPHEW—?
!
BUT THAT DOES IT! I'M TAKING HIM TO THE FURRIER NOW! AND DON'T LOOK SO DOGGONED PATHETIC!
SNIFF! GOODBYE, LITTLE BALABOO! SOB!
WELL, BOYS, THAT'S THE END OF THE LAST BALABOO! UNCLE SCROOGE HAS WON AGAIN!
SIGH!

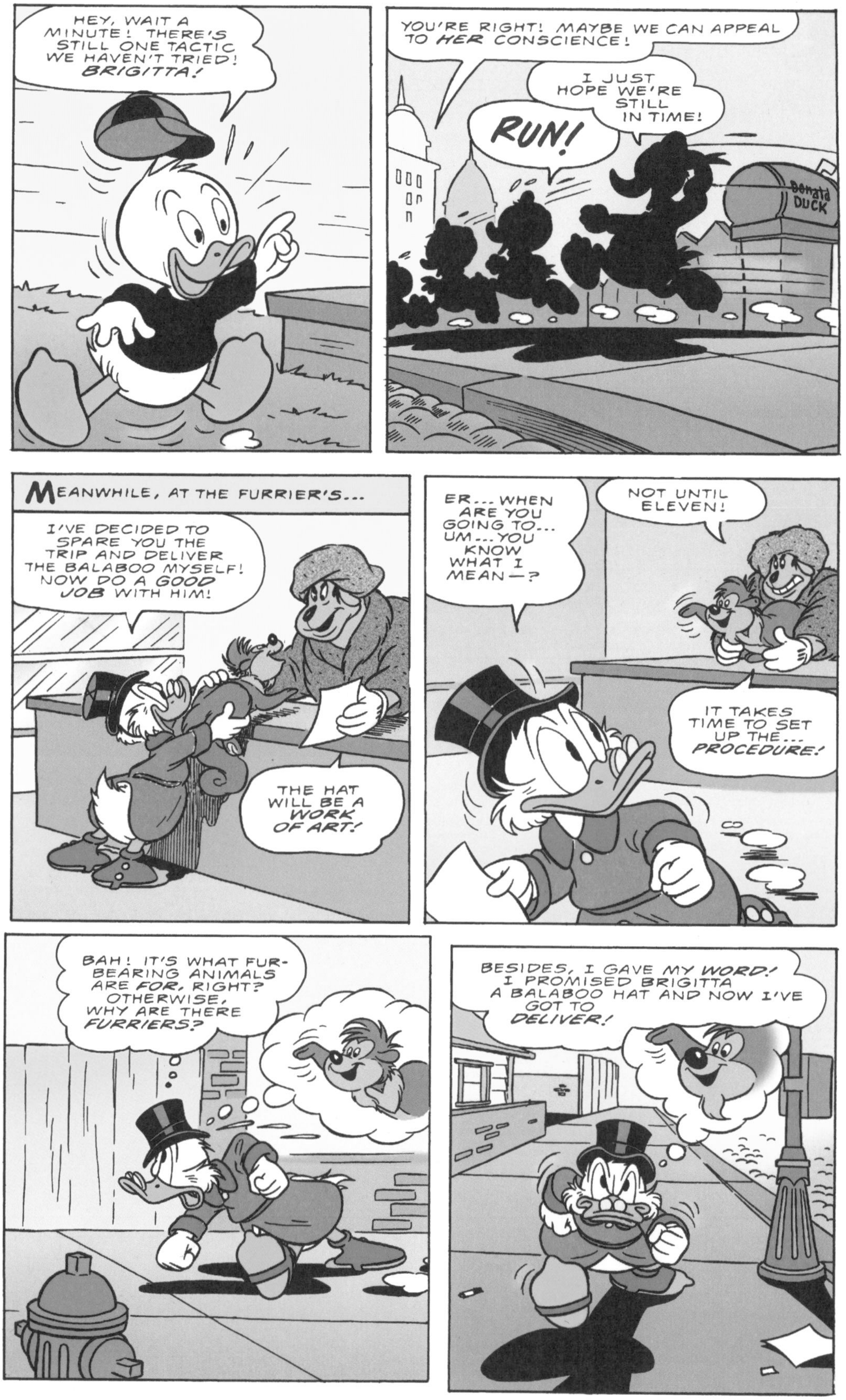
HEY, WAIT A MINUTE! THERE'S STILL ONE TACTIC WE HAVEN'T TRIED! BRIGITTA!
YOU'RE RIGHT! MAYBE WE CAN APPEAL TO HER CONSCIENCE!
I JUST HOPE WE'RE STILL IN TIME!
RUN!
Donald DUCK
MEANWHILE, AT THE FURRIER'S...
I'VE DECIDED TO SPARE YOU THE TRIP AND DELIVER THE BALABOO MYSELF! NOW DO A GOOD JOB WITH HIM!
THE HAT WILL BE A WORK OF ART!
ER... WHEN ARE YOU GOING TO... UM... YOU KNOW WHAT I MEAN—?
NOT UNTIL ELEVEN!
IT TAKES TIME TO SET UP THE... PROCEDURE!
BAH! IT'S WHAT FUR-BEARING ANIMALS ARE FOR, RIGHT? OTHERWISE, WHY ARE THERE FURRIERS?
BESIDES, I GAVE MY WORD! I PROMISED BRIGITTA A BALABOO HAT AND NOW I'VE GOT TO DELIVER!

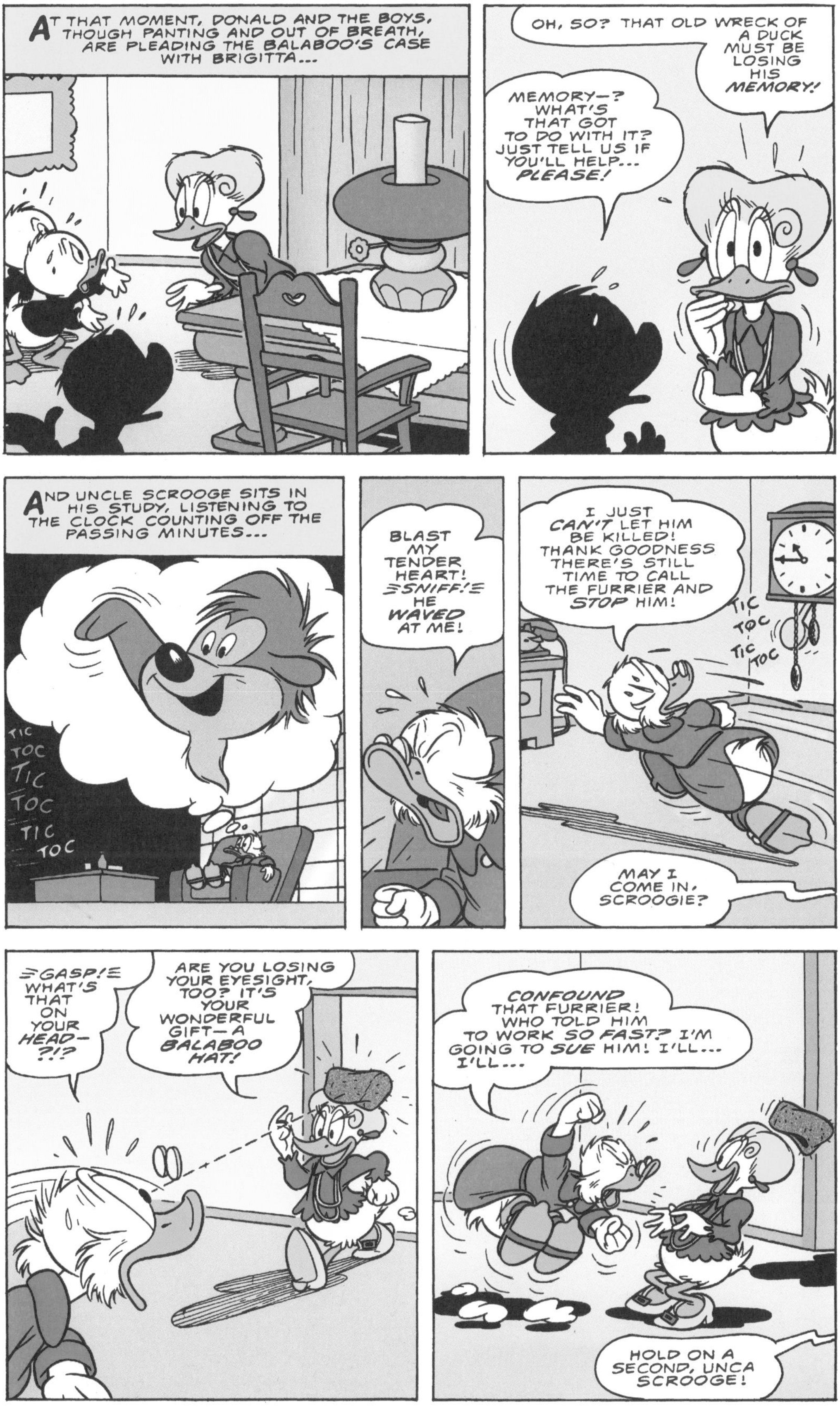
AT THAT MOMENT, DONALD AND THE BOYS, THOUGH PANTING AND OUT OF BREATH, ARE PLEADING THE BALABOO'S CASE WITH BRIGITTA...
MEMORY—? WHAT'S THAT GOT TO DO WITH IT? JUST TELL US IF YOU'LL HELP... PLEASE!
OH, SO? THAT OLD WRECK OF A DUCK MUST BE LOSING HIS MEMORY!
AND UNCLE SCROOGE SITS IN HIS STUDY, LISTENING TO THE CLOCK COUNTING OFF THE PASSING MINUTES...
TIC TOC TIC TOC TIC TOC
BLAST MY TENDER HEART! SNIFF! HE WAVED AT ME!
I JUST CAN'T LET HIM BE KILLED! THANK GOODNESS THERE'S STILL TIME TO CALL THE FURRIER AND STOP HIM!
TIC TOC TIC TOC
MAY I COME IN, SCROOGIE?
GASP! WHAT'S THAT ON YOUR HEAD—?!?
ARE YOU LOSING YOUR EYESIGHT, TOO? IT'S YOUR WONDERFUL GIFT—A BALABOO HAT!
CONFOUND THAT FURRIER! WHO TOLD HIM TO WORK SO FAST? I'M GOING TO SUE HIM! I'LL... I'LL...
HOLD ON A SECOND, UNCA SCROOGE!

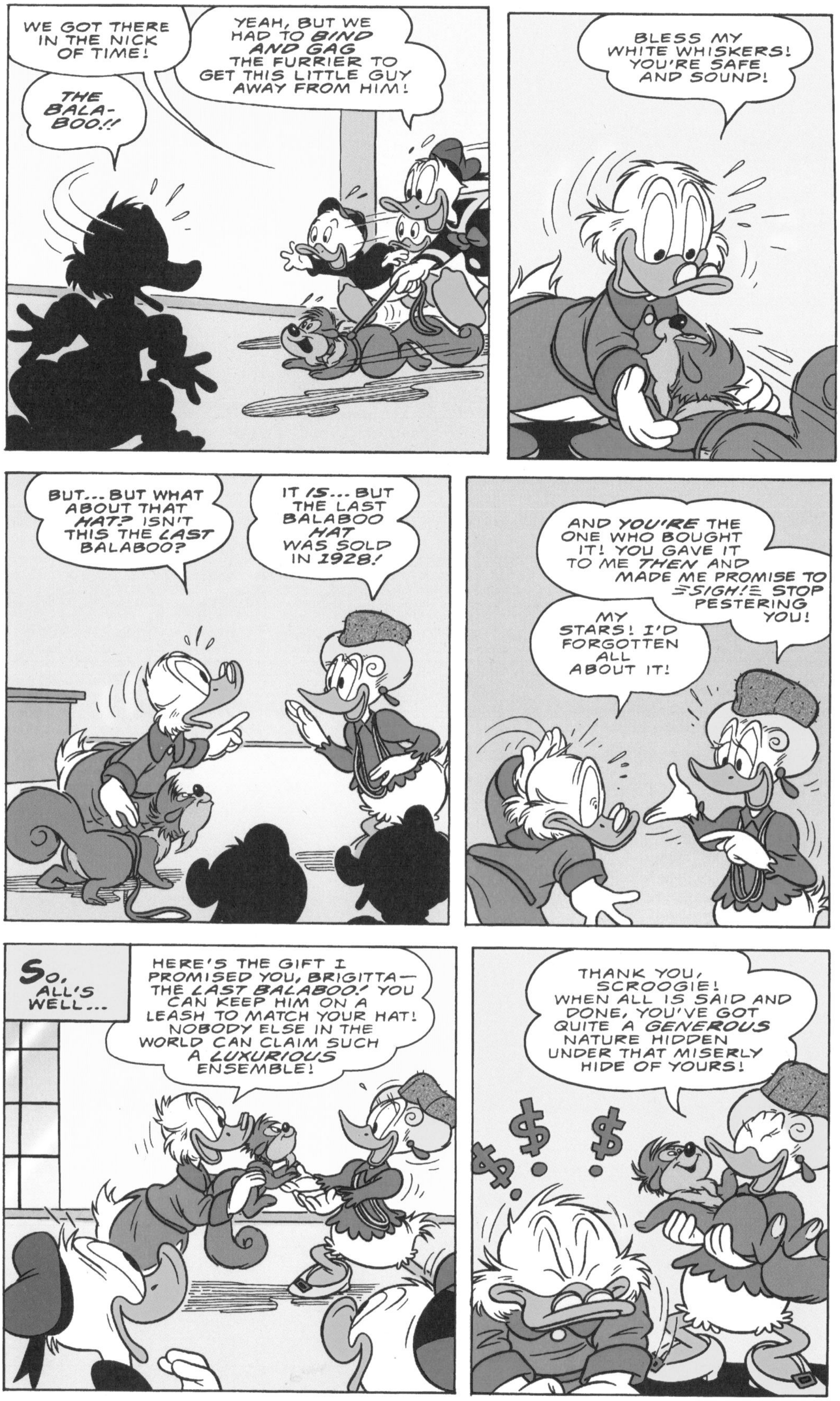
WE GOT THERE IN THE NICK OF TIME!
YEAH, BUT WE HAD TO BIND AND GAG THE FURRIER TO GET THIS LITTLE GUY AWAY FROM HIM!
THE BALA-BOO!!
BLESS MY WHITE WHISKERS! YOU'RE SAFE AND SOUND!
BUT... BUT WHAT ABOUT THAT HAT? ISN'T THIS THE LAST BALABOO?
IT IS... BUT THE LAST BALABOO HAT WAS SOLD IN 1928!
AND YOU'RE THE ONE WHO BOUGHT IT! YOU GAVE IT TO ME THEN AND MADE ME PROMISE TO =SIGH!= STOP PESTERING YOU!
MY STARS! I'D FORGOTTEN ALL ABOUT IT!
SO, ALL'S WELL...
HERE'S THE GIFT I PROMISED YOU, BRIGITTA— THE LAST BALABOO! YOU CAN KEEP HIM ON A LEASH TO MATCH YOUR HAT! NOBODY ELSE IN THE WORLD CAN CLAIM SUCH A LUXURIOUS ENSEMBLE!
THANK YOU, SCROOGIE! WHEN ALL IS SAID AND DONE, YOU'VE GOT QUITE A GENEROUS NATURE HIDDEN UNDER THAT MISERLY HIDE OF YOURS!

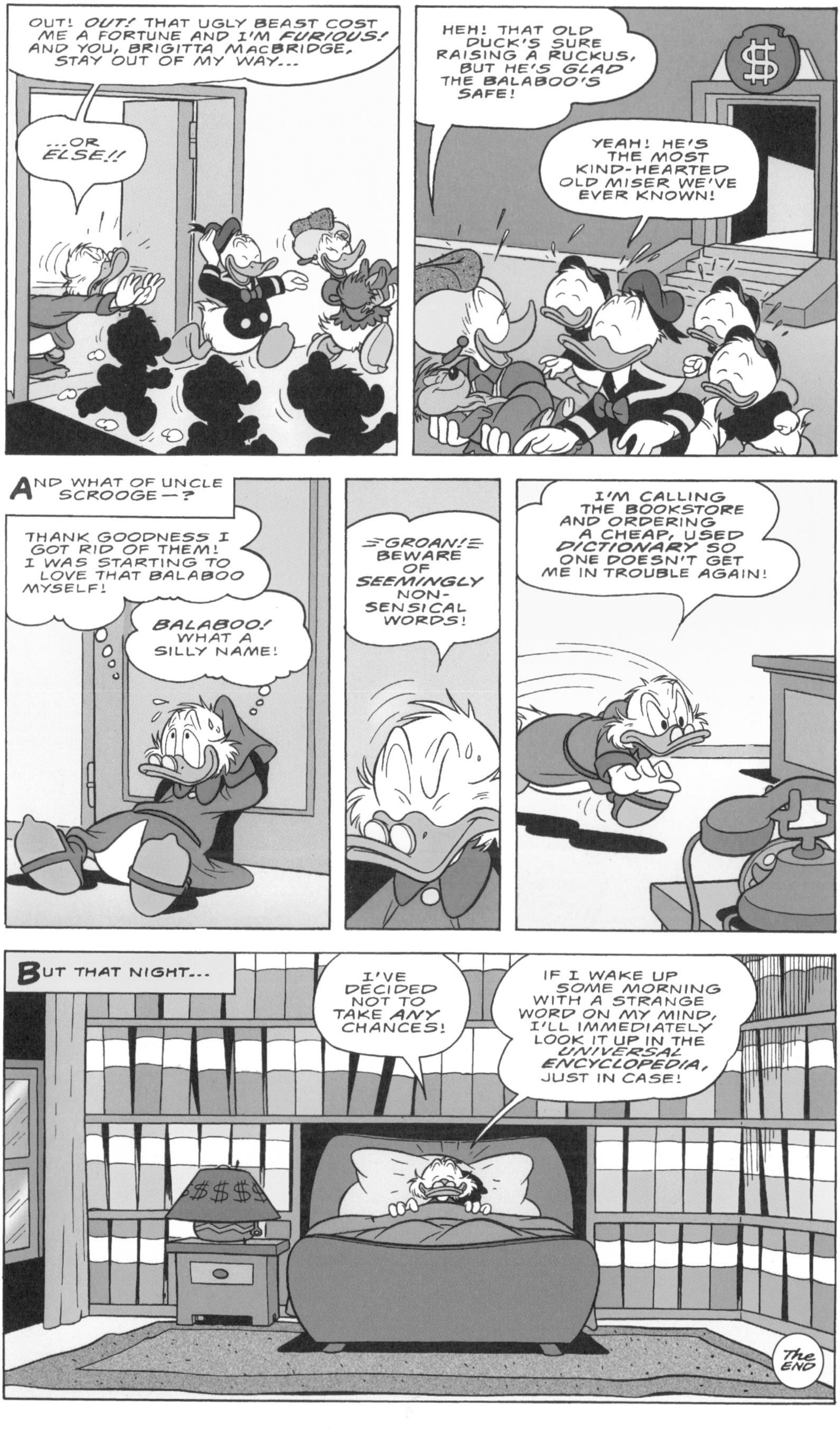
OUT! OUT! THAT UGLY BEAST COST ME A FORTUNE AND I'M FURIOUS! AND YOU, BRIGITTA MacBRIDGE, STAY OUT OF MY WAY...
...OR ELSE!!
HEH! THAT OLD DUCK'S SURE RAISING A RUCKUS, BUT HE'S GLAD THE BALABOO'S SAFE!
YEAH! HE'S THE MOST KIND-HEARTED OLD MISER WE'VE EVER KNOWN!
AND WHAT OF UNCLE SCROOGE—?
THANK GOODNESS I GOT RID OF THEM! I WAS STARTING TO LOVE THAT BALABOO MYSELF!
BALABOO! WHAT A SILLY NAME!
GROAN! BEWARE OF SEEMINGLY NON-SENSICAL WORDS!
I'M CALLING THE BOOKSTORE AND ORDERING A CHEAP, USED DICTIONARY SO ONE DOESN'T GET ME IN TROUBLE AGAIN!
BUT THAT NIGHT...
I'VE DECIDED NOT TO TAKE ANY CHANCES!
IF I WAKE UP SOME MORNING WITH A STRANGE WORD ON MY MIND, I'LL IMMEDIATELY LOOK IT UP IN THE UNIVERSAL ENCYCLOPEDIA, JUST IN CASE!
The END

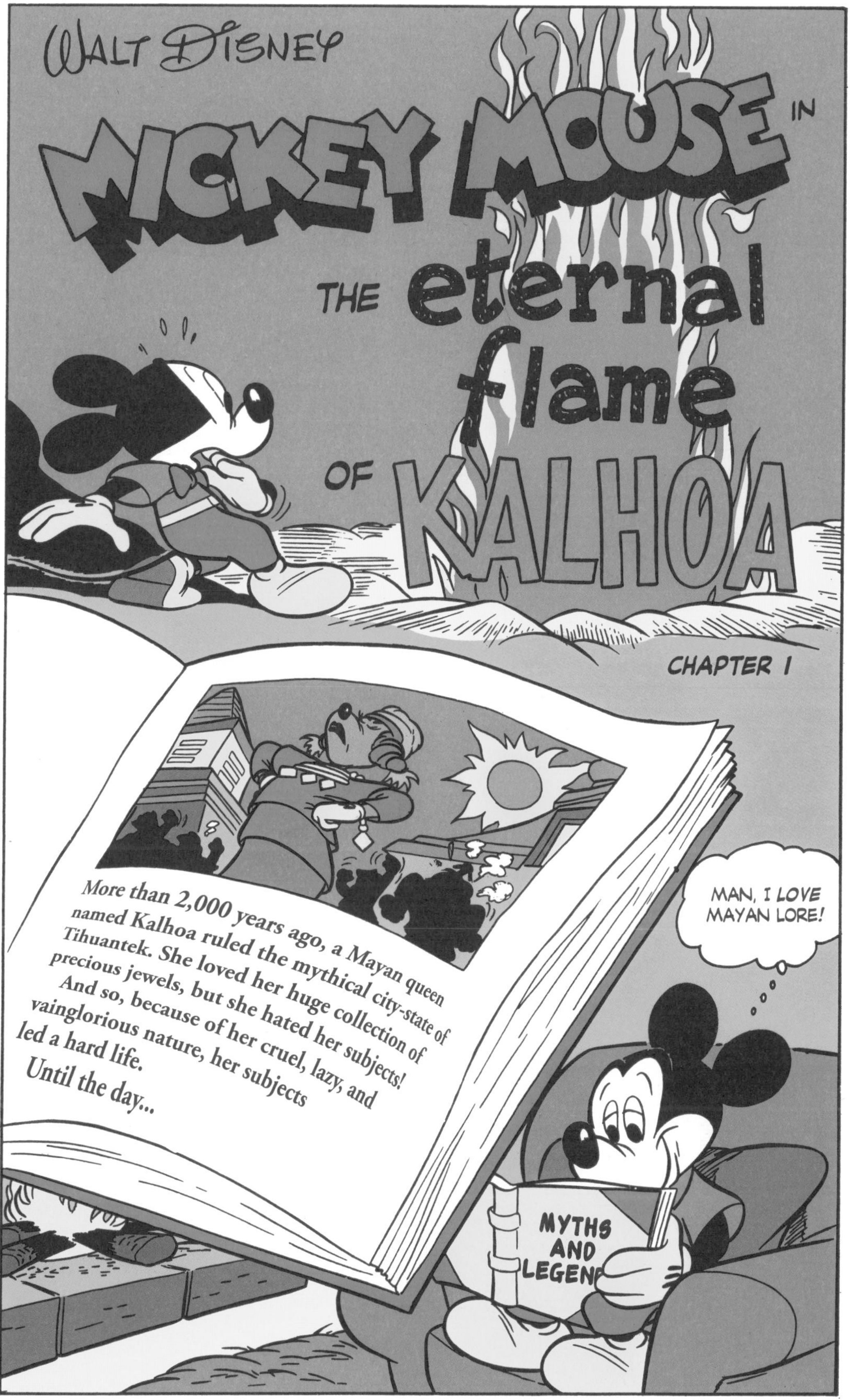
WALT DISNEY
MICKEY MOUSE IN
THE eternal flame OF KALHOA
CHAPTER 1
More than 2,000 years ago, a Mayan queen named Kalhoa ruled the mythical city-state of Tihuantek. She loved her huge collection of precious jewels, but she hated her subjects! And so, because of her cruel, lazy, and vainglorious nature, her subjects led a hard life. Until the day...
MAN, I LOVE MAYAN LORE!
MYTHS AND LEGEN

STORY AND ART BY ROMANO SCARPA
TRANSLATION AND DIALOGUE BY JONATHAN GRAY WITH DAVID GERSTEIN

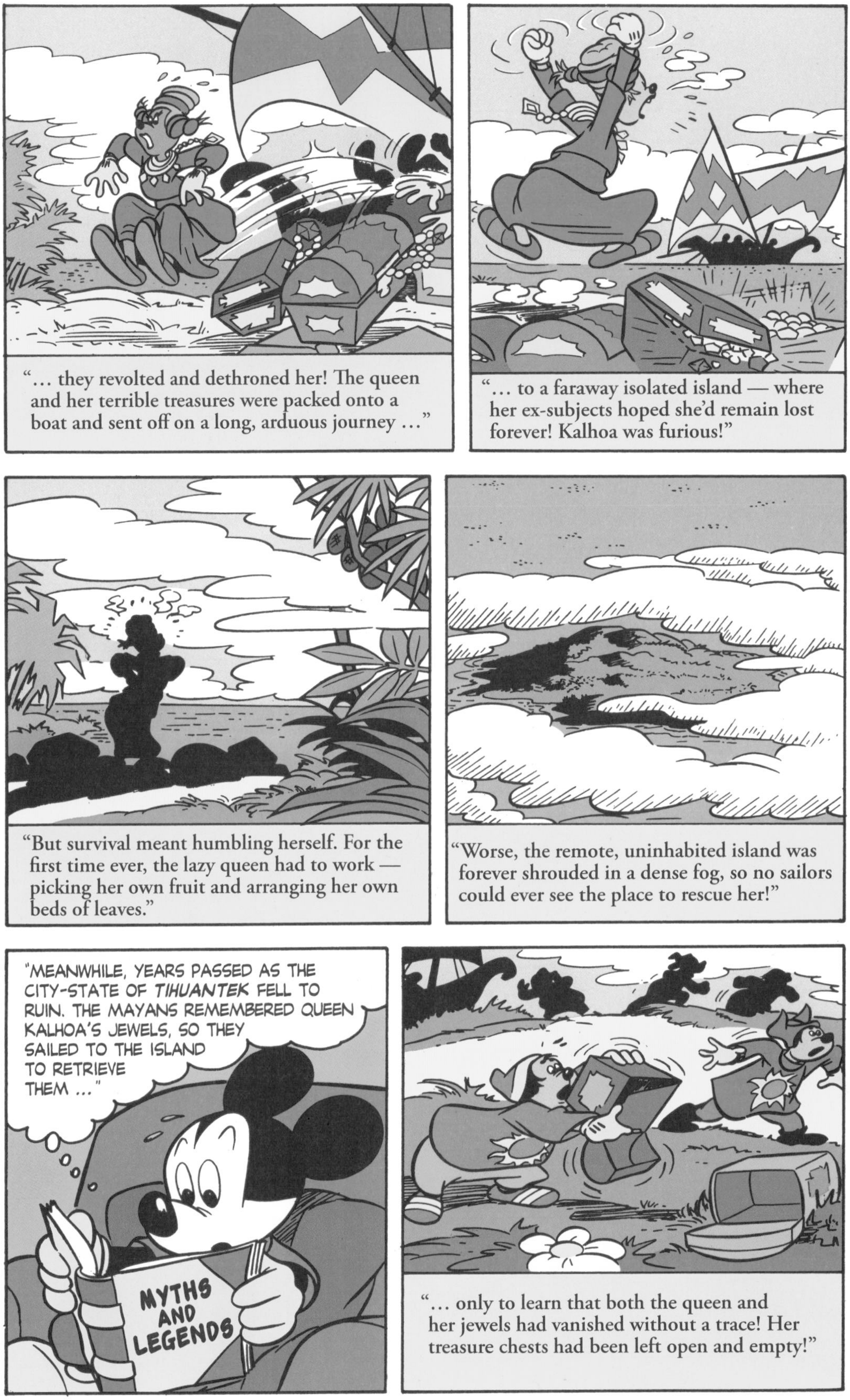
"… they revolted and dethroned her! The queen and her terrible treasures were packed onto a boat and sent off on a long, arduous journey …"
"… to a faraway isolated island — where her ex-subjects hoped she'd remain lost forever! Kalhoa was furious!"
"But survival meant humbling herself. For the first time ever, the lazy queen had to work — picking her own fruit and arranging her own beds of leaves."
"Worse, the remote, uninhabited island was forever shrouded in a dense fog, so no sailors could ever see the place to rescue her!"
"MEANWHILE, YEARS PASSED AS THE CITY-STATE OF TIHUANTEK FELL TO RUIN. THE MAYANS REMEMBERED QUEEN KALHOA'S JEWELS, SO THEY SAILED TO THE ISLAND TO RETRIEVE THEM …"
MYTHS AND LEGENDS
"… only to learn that both the queen and her jewels had vanished without a trace! Her treasure chests had been left open and empty!"

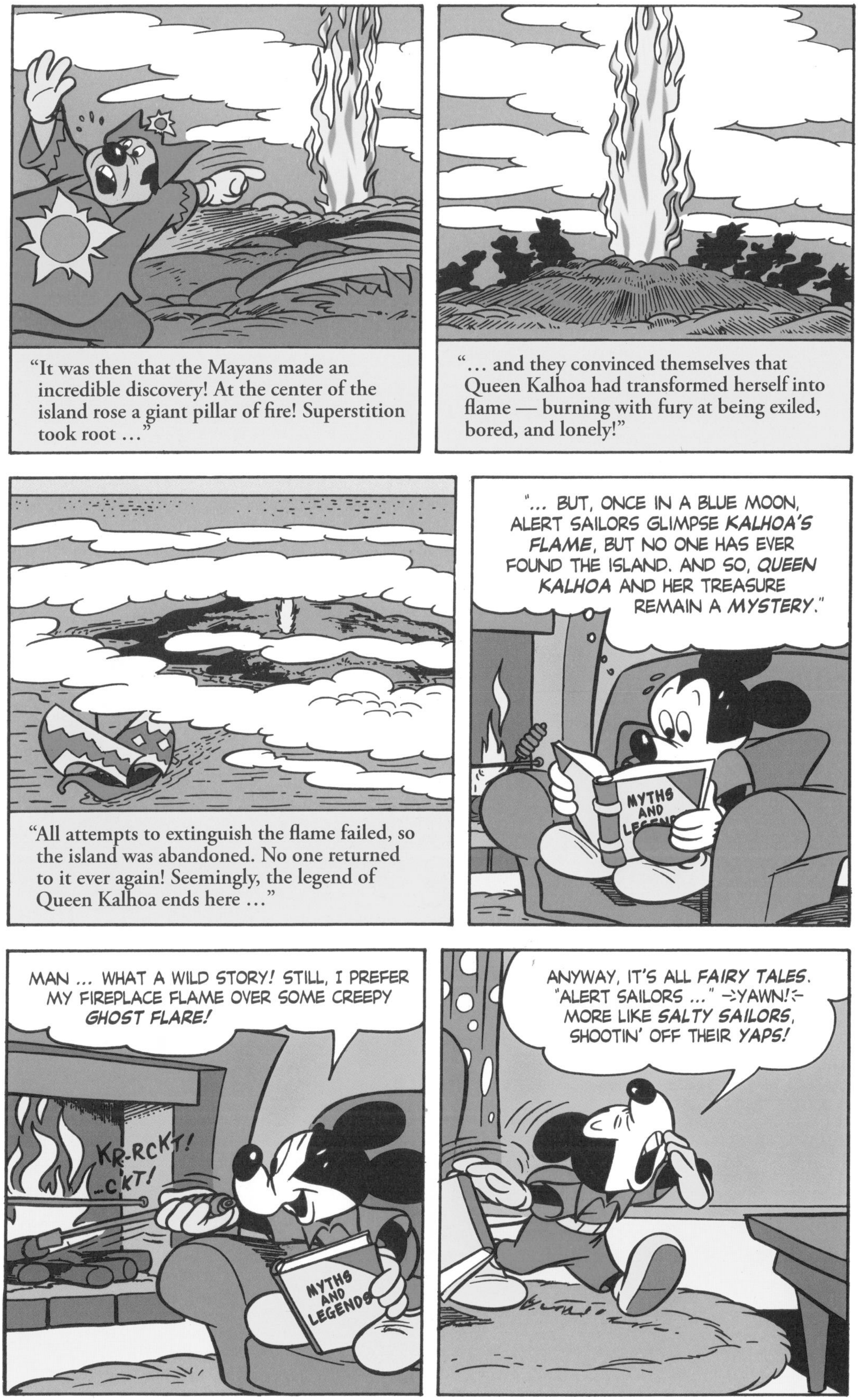
"It was then that the Mayans made an incredible discovery! At the center of the island rose a giant pillar of fire! Superstition took root …"
"… and they convinced themselves that Queen Kalhoa had transformed herself into flame — burning with fury at being exiled, bored, and lonely!"
"All attempts to extinguish the flame failed, so the island was abandoned. No one returned to it ever again! Seemingly, the legend of Queen Kalhoa ends here …"
"… BUT, ONCE IN A BLUE MOON, ALERT SAILORS GLIMPSE KALHOA'S FLAME, BUT NO ONE HAS EVER FOUND THE ISLAND. AND SO, QUEEN KALHOA AND HER TREASURE REMAIN A MYSTERY."
MYTHS AND LEGENDS
MAN … WHAT A WILD STORY! STILL, I PREFER MY FIREPLACE FLAME OVER SOME CREEPY GHOST FLARE!
KR-RCKT! …C'KT!
MYTHS AND LEGENDS
ANYWAY, IT'S ALL FAIRY TALES. "ALERT SAILORS …" ->YAWN!<- MORE LIKE SALTY SAILORS, SHOOTIN' OFF THEIR YAPS!

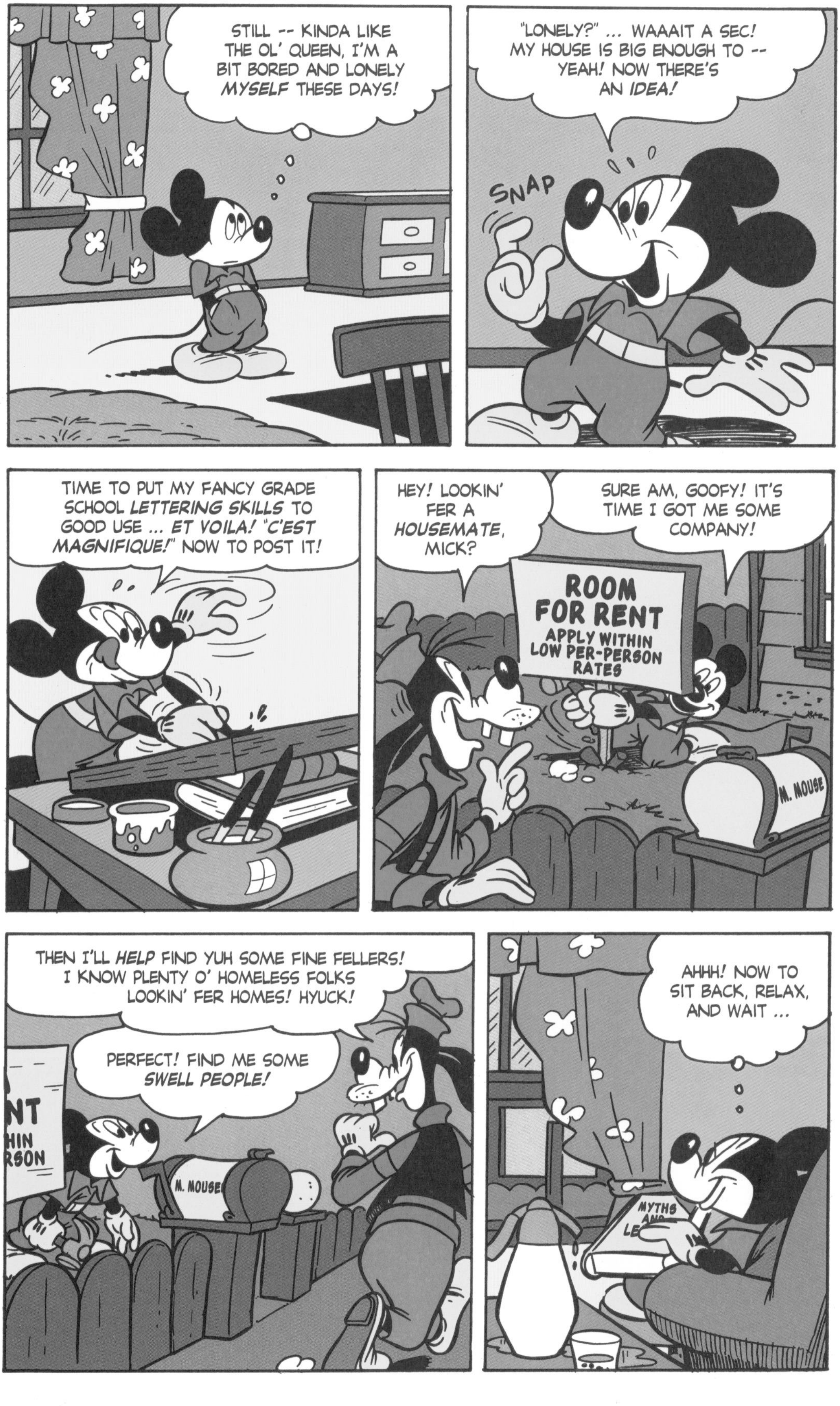
STILL -- KINDA LIKE THE OL' QUEEN, I'M A BIT BORED AND LONELY *MYSELF* THESE DAYS!
"LONELY?" ... WAAAIT A SEC! MY HOUSE IS BIG ENOUGH TO -- YEAH! NOW THERE'S AN *IDEA!*
SNAP
TIME TO PUT MY FANCY GRADE SCHOOL *LETTERING SKILLS* TO GOOD USE ... *ET VOILA!* *"C'EST MAGNIFIQUE!"* NOW TO POST IT!
HEY! LOOKIN' FER A *HOUSEMATE*, MICK?
SURE AM, GOOFY! IT'S TIME I GOT ME SOME COMPANY!
ROOM FOR RENT
APPLY WITHIN
LOW PER-PERSON RATES
M. MOUSE
THEN I'LL *HELP* FIND YUH SOME FINE FELLERS! I KNOW PLENTY O' HOMELESS FOLKS LOOKIN' FER HOMES! HYUCK!
PERFECT! FIND ME SOME *SWELL PEOPLE!*
M. MOUSE
AHHH! NOW TO SIT BACK, RELAX, AND WAIT ...

ROOM
RENT
APPLY WITHIN
LOW PER-PERSON
RATES

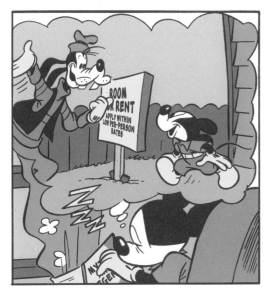

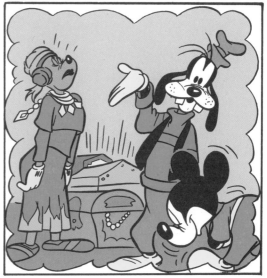

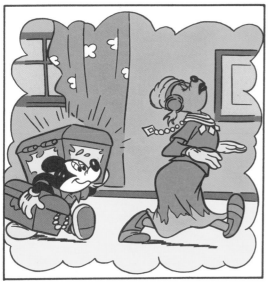

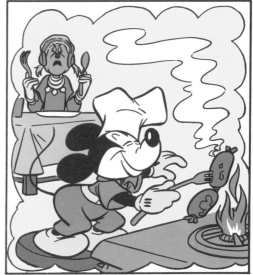

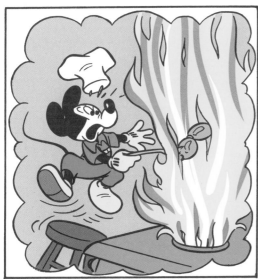

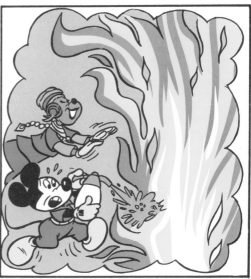

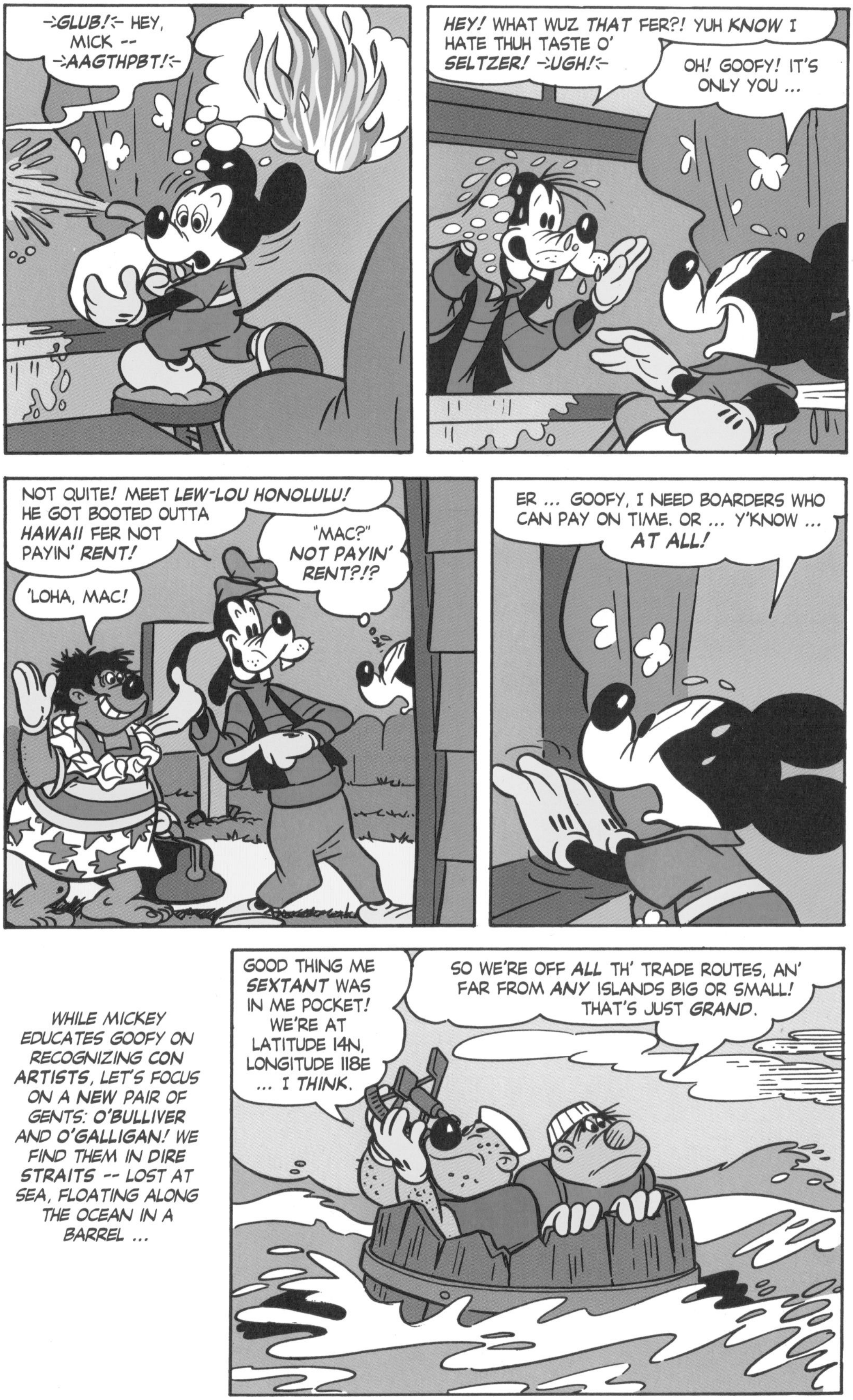
–GLUB!– HEY, MICK -- –AAGTHPBT!–
HEY! WHAT WUZ THAT FER?! YUH KNOW I HATE THUH TASTE O' SELTZER! –UGH!–
OH! GOOFY! IT'S ONLY YOU ...
NOT QUITE! MEET LEW-LOU HONOLULU! HE GOT BOOTED OUTTA HAWAII FER NOT PAYIN' RENT!
'LOHA, MAC!
"MAC?" NOT PAYIN' RENT?!?
ER ... GOOFY, I NEED BOARDERS WHO CAN PAY ON TIME. OR ... Y'KNOW ... AT ALL!
WHILE MICKEY EDUCATES GOOFY ON RECOGNIZING CON ARTISTS, LET'S FOCUS ON A NEW PAIR OF GENTS: O'BULLIVER AND O'GALLIGAN! WE FIND THEM IN DIRE STRAITS -- LOST AT SEA, FLOATING ALONG THE OCEAN IN A BARREL ...
GOOD THING ME SEXTANT WAS IN ME POCKET! WE'RE AT LATITUDE 14N, LONGITUDE 118E ... I THINK.
SO WE'RE OFF ALL TH' TRADE ROUTES, AN' FAR FROM ANY ISLANDS BIG OR SMALL! THAT'S JUST GRAND.

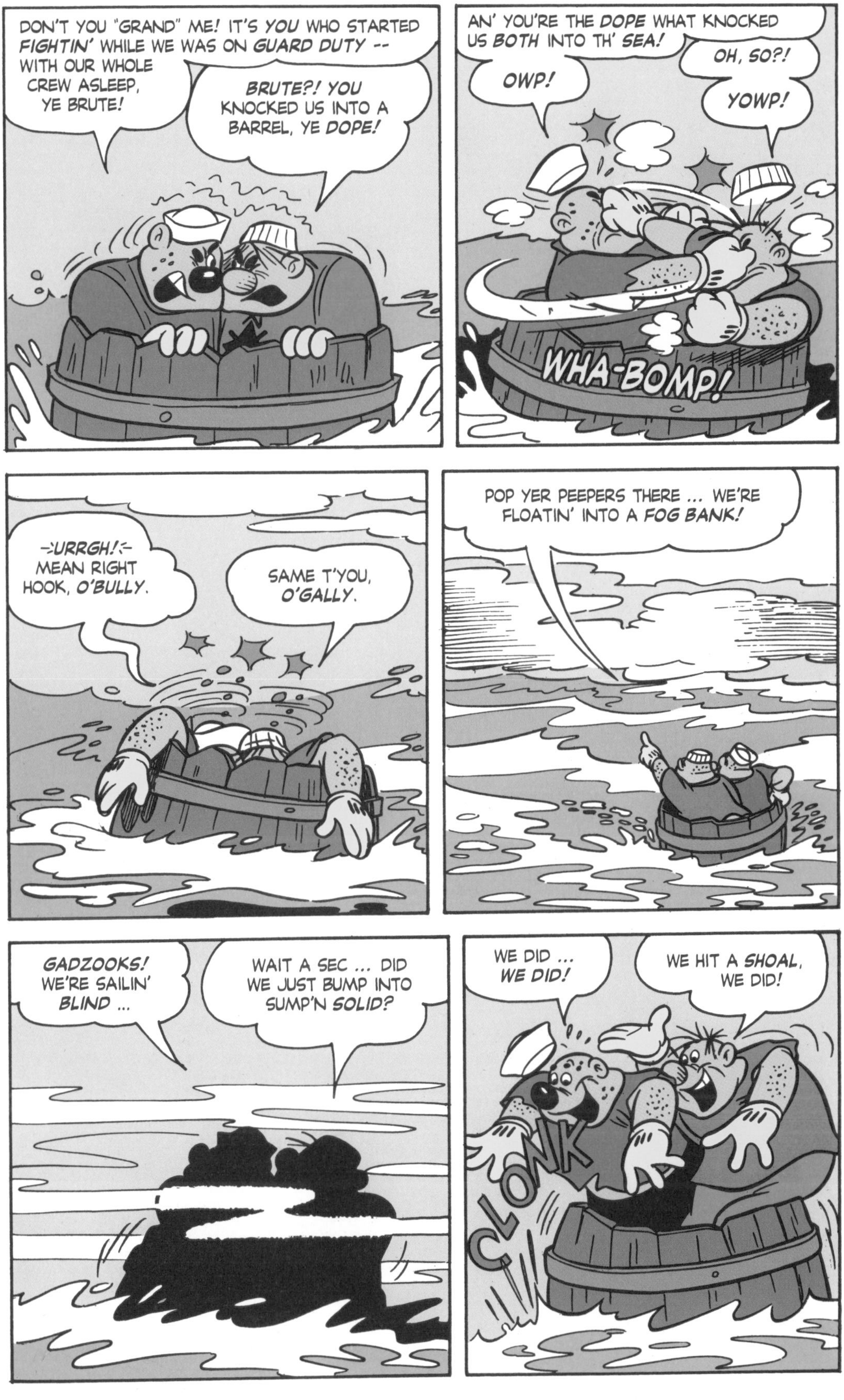
DON'T YOU "GRAND" ME! IT'S YOU WHO STARTED FIGHTIN' WHILE WE WAS ON GUARD DUTY -- WITH OUR WHOLE CREW ASLEEP, YE BRUTE!
BRUTE?! YOU KNOCKED US INTO A BARREL, YE DOPE!
AN' YOU'RE THE DOPE WHAT KNOCKED US BOTH INTO TH' SEA!
OH, SO?!
OWP!
YOWP!
WHA-BOMP!
URRGH! MEAN RIGHT HOOK, O'BULLY.
SAME T'YOU, O'GALLY.
POP YER PEEPERS THERE ... WE'RE FLOATIN' INTO A FOG BANK!
GADZOOKS! WE'RE SAILIN' BLIND ...
WAIT A SEC ... DID WE JUST BUMP INTO SUMP'N SOLID?
WE DID ... WE DID!
WE HIT A SHOAL, WE DID!
CLONK

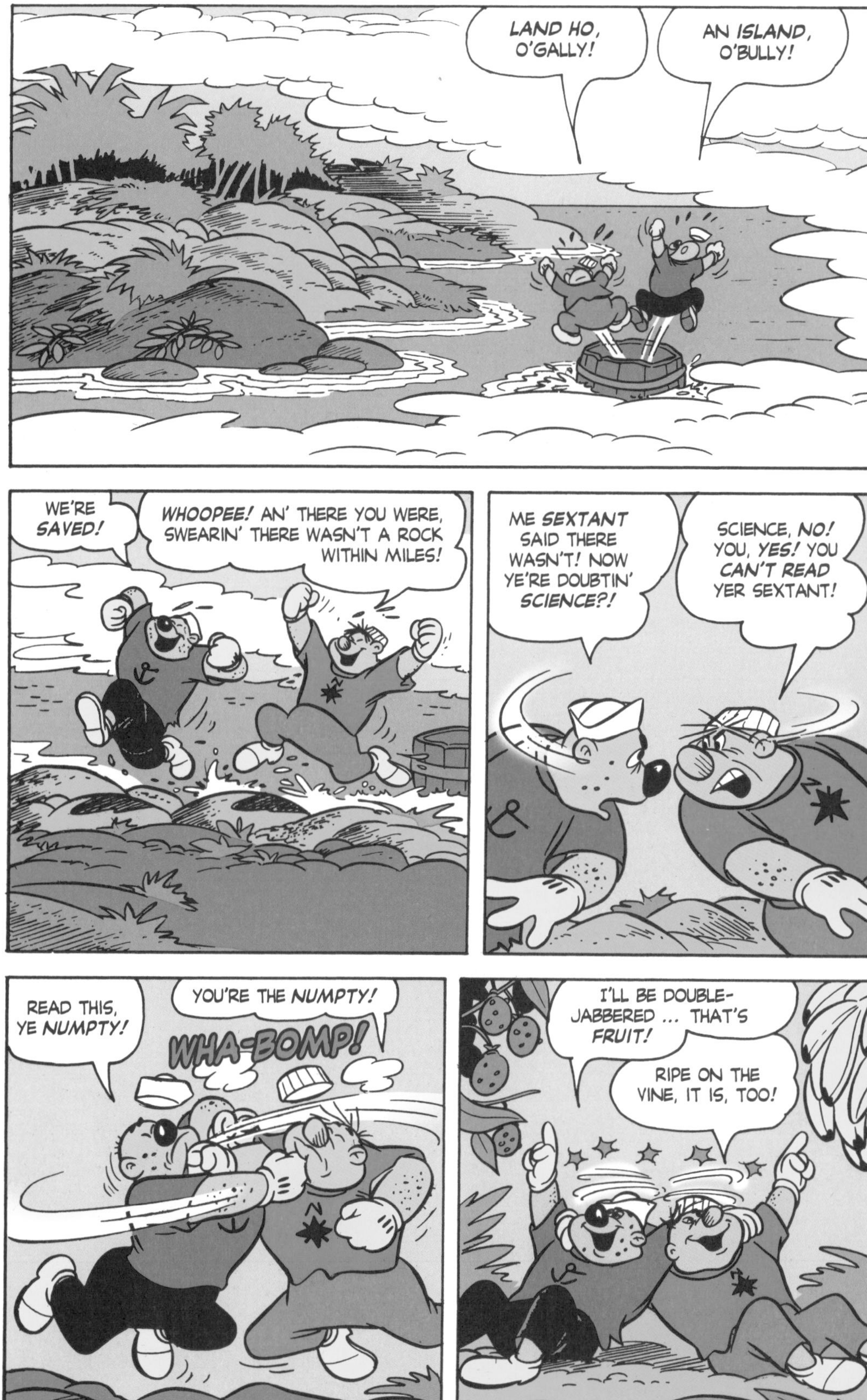
LAND HO, O'GALLY!
AN ISLAND, O'BULLY!
WE'RE SAVED!
WHOOPEE! AN' THERE YOU WERE, SWEARIN' THERE WASN'T A ROCK WITHIN MILES!
ME SEXTANT SAID THERE WASN'T! NOW YE'RE DOUBTIN' SCIENCE?!
SCIENCE, NO! YOU, YES! YOU CAN'T READ YER SEXTANT!
READ THIS, YE NUMPTY!
YOU'RE THE NUMPTY!
WHA-BOMP!
I'LL BE DOUBLE-JABBERED ... THAT'S FRUIT!
RIPE ON THE VINE, IT IS, TOO!

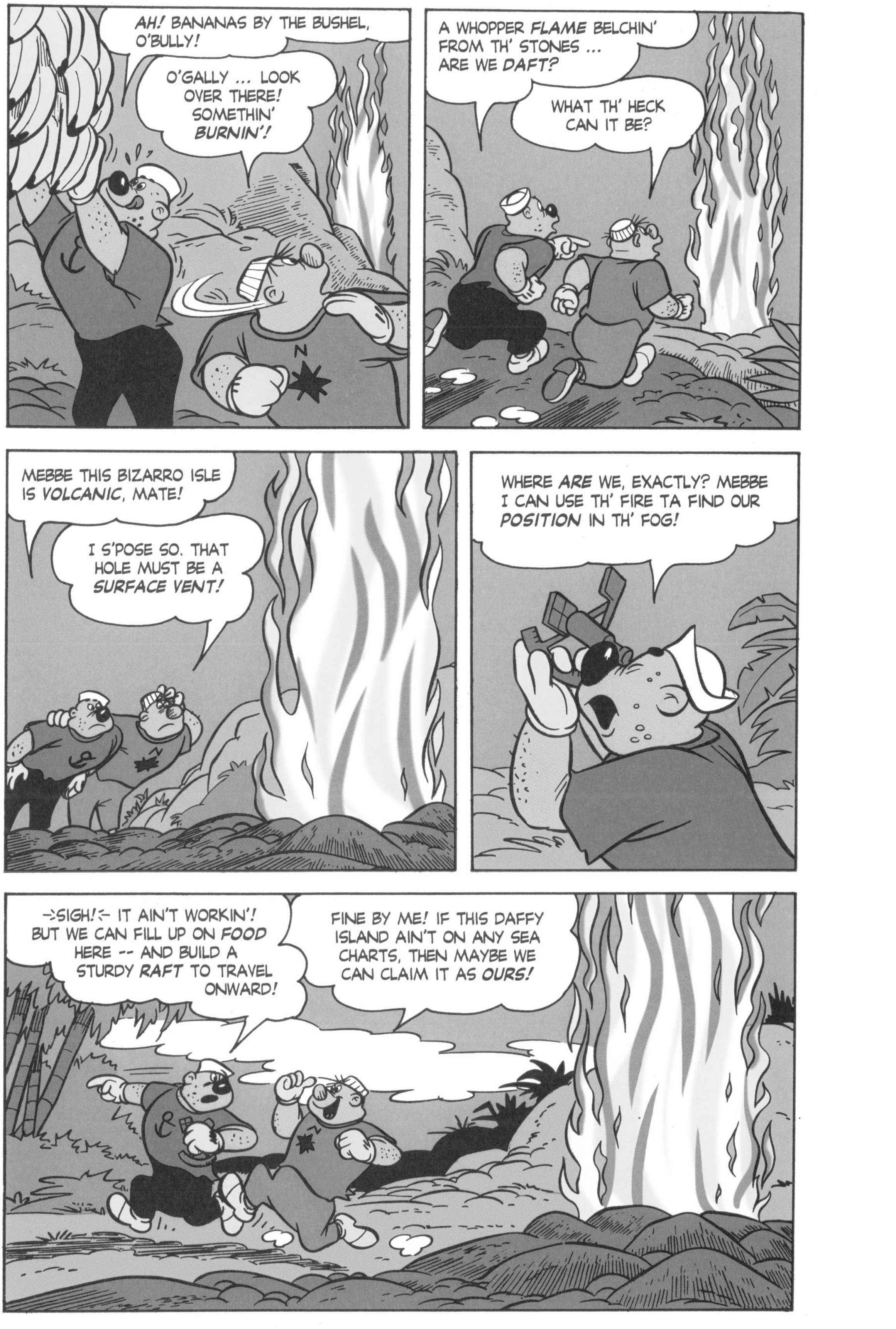

AH! BANANAS BY THE BUSHEL, O'BULLY!
O'GALLY ... LOOK OVER THERE! SOMETHIN' BURNIN'!
A WHOPPER FLAME BELCHIN' FROM TH' STONES ... ARE WE DAFT?
WHAT TH' HECK CAN IT BE?
MEBBE THIS BIZARRO ISLE IS VOLCANIC, MATE!
I S'POSE SO. THAT HOLE MUST BE A SURFACE VENT!
WHERE ARE WE, EXACTLY? MEBBE I CAN USE TH' FIRE TA FIND OUR POSITION IN TH' FOG!
-SIGH!- IT AIN'T WORKIN'! BUT WE CAN FILL UP ON FOOD HERE -- AND BUILD A STURDY RAFT TO TRAVEL ONWARD!
FINE BY ME! IF THIS DAFFY ISLAND AIN'T ON ANY SEA CHARTS, THEN MAYBE WE CAN CLAIM IT AS OURS!

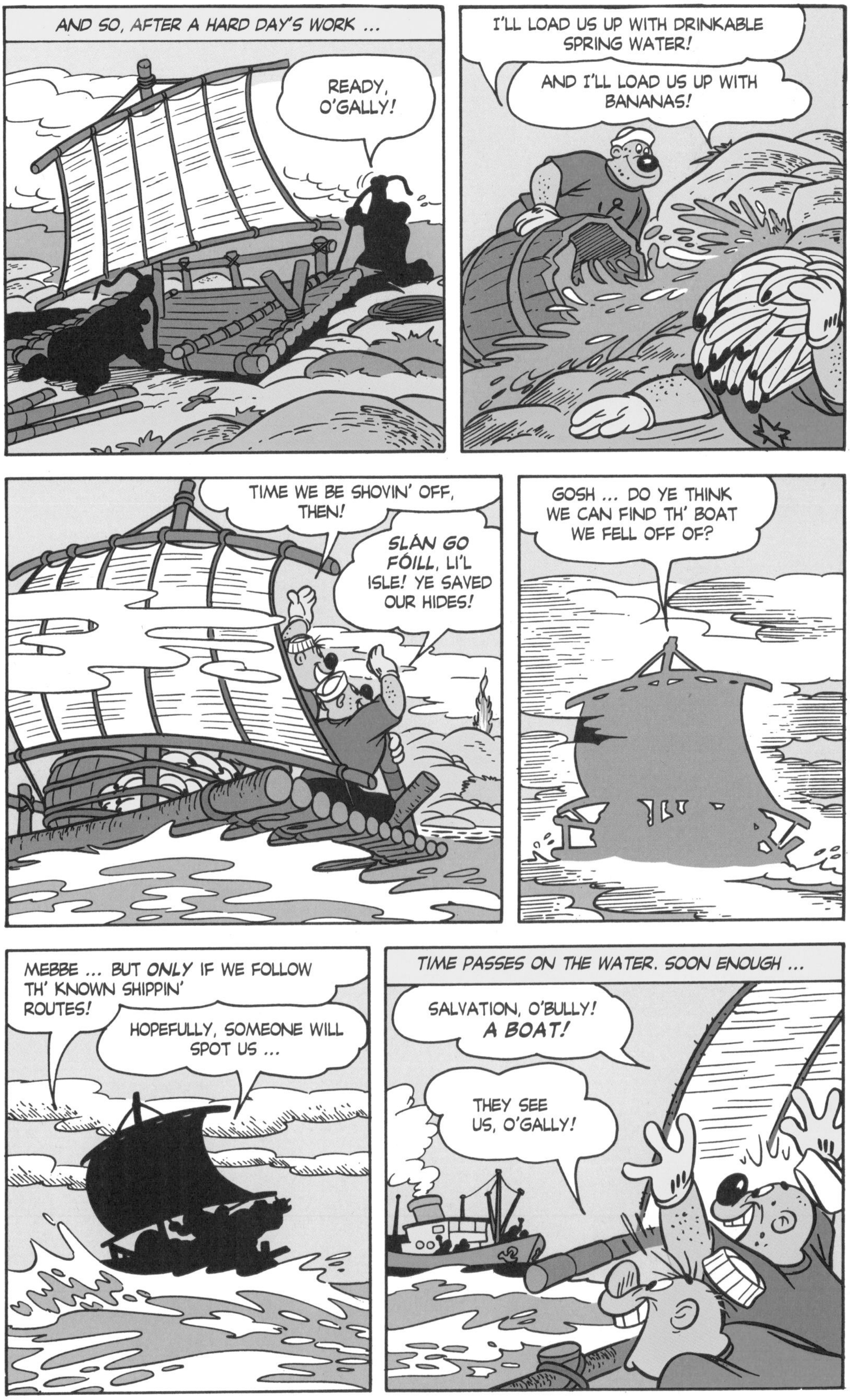
AND SO, AFTER A HARD DAY'S WORK ...
READY, O'GALLY!
I'LL LOAD US UP WITH DRINKABLE SPRING WATER!
AND I'LL LOAD US UP WITH BANANAS!
TIME WE BE SHOVIN' OFF, THEN!
SLÁN GO FÓILL, LI'L ISLE! YE SAVED OUR HIDES!
GOSH ... DO YE THINK WE CAN FIND TH' BOAT WE FELL OFF OF?
MEBBE ... BUT ONLY IF WE FOLLOW TH' KNOWN SHIPPIN' ROUTES!
HOPEFULLY, SOMEONE WILL SPOT US ...
TIME PASSES ON THE WATER. SOON ENOUGH ...
SALVATION, O'BULLY! A BOAT!
THEY SEE US, O'GALLY!

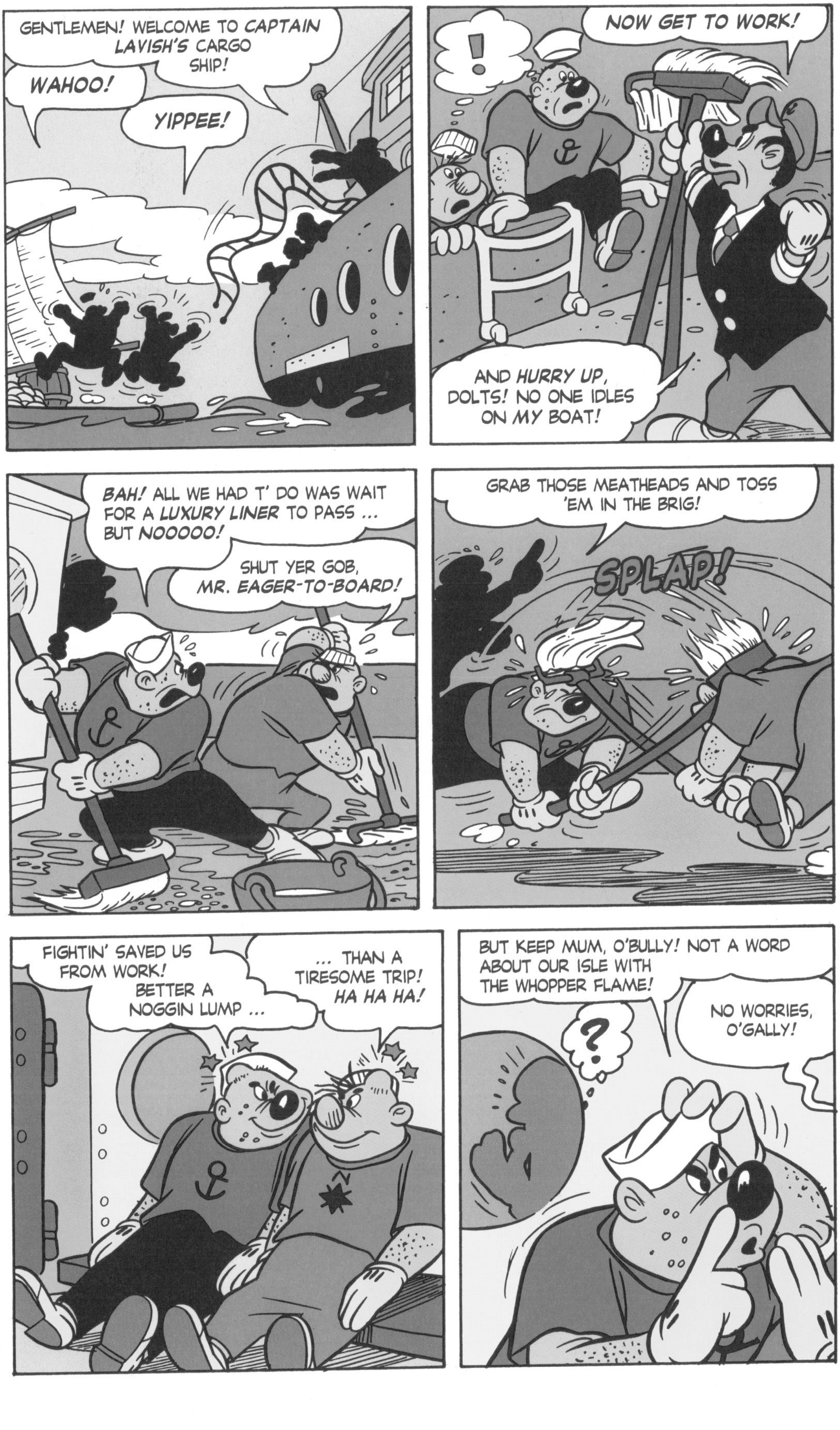
GENTLEMEN! WELCOME TO CAPTAIN LAVISH'S CARGO SHIP!
WAHOO!
YIPPEE!
!
NOW GET TO WORK!
AND HURRY UP, DOLTS! NO ONE IDLES ON MY BOAT!
BAH! ALL WE HAD T' DO WAS WAIT FOR A LUXURY LINER TO PASS ... BUT NOOOOO!
SHUT YER GOB, MR. EAGER-TO-BOARD!
GRAB THOSE MEATHEADS AND TOSS 'EM IN THE BRIG!
SPLAP!
FIGHTIN' SAVED US FROM WORK!
BETTER A NOGGIN LUMP ...
... THAN A TIRESOME TRIP! HA HA HA!
BUT KEEP MUM, O'BULLY! NOT A WORD ABOUT OUR ISLE WITH THE WHOPPER FLAME!
?
NO WORRIES, O'GALLY!

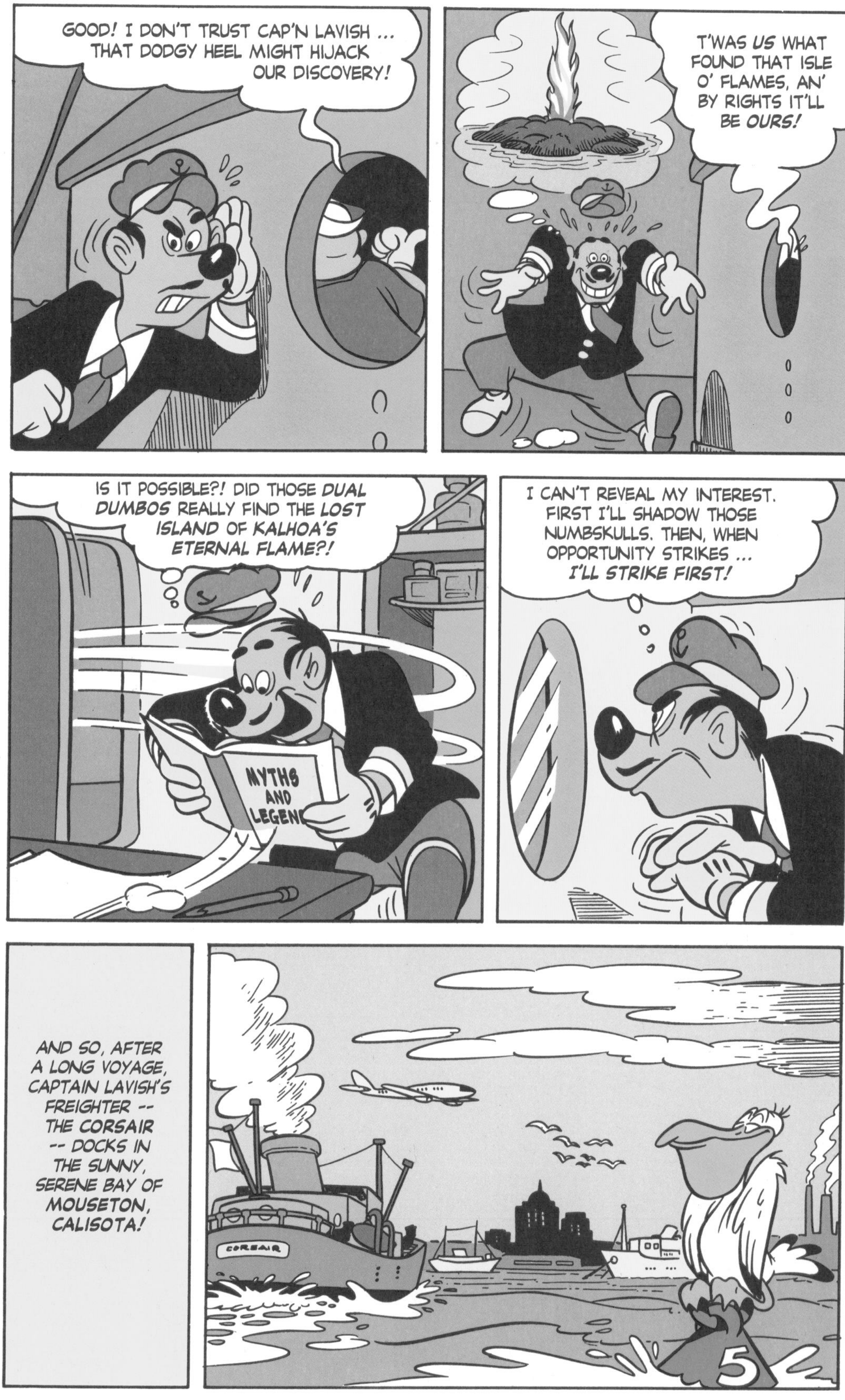
GOOD! I DON'T TRUST CAP'N LAVISH ... THAT DODGY HEEL MIGHT HIJACK OUR DISCOVERY!
T'WAS US WHAT FOUND THAT ISLE O' FLAMES, AN' BY RIGHTS IT'LL BE OURS!
IS IT POSSIBLE?! DID THOSE DUAL DUMBOS REALLY FIND THE LOST ISLAND OF KALHOA'S ETERNAL FLAME?!
MYTHS AND LEGEN
I CAN'T REVEAL MY INTEREST. FIRST I'LL SHADOW THOSE NUMBSKULLS. THEN, WHEN OPPORTUNITY STRIKES ... I'LL STRIKE FIRST!
AND SO, AFTER A LONG VOYAGE, CAPTAIN LAVISH'S FREIGHTER -- THE CORSAIR -- DOCKS IN THE SUNNY, SERENE BAY OF MOUSETON, CALISOTA!
CORSAIR
5

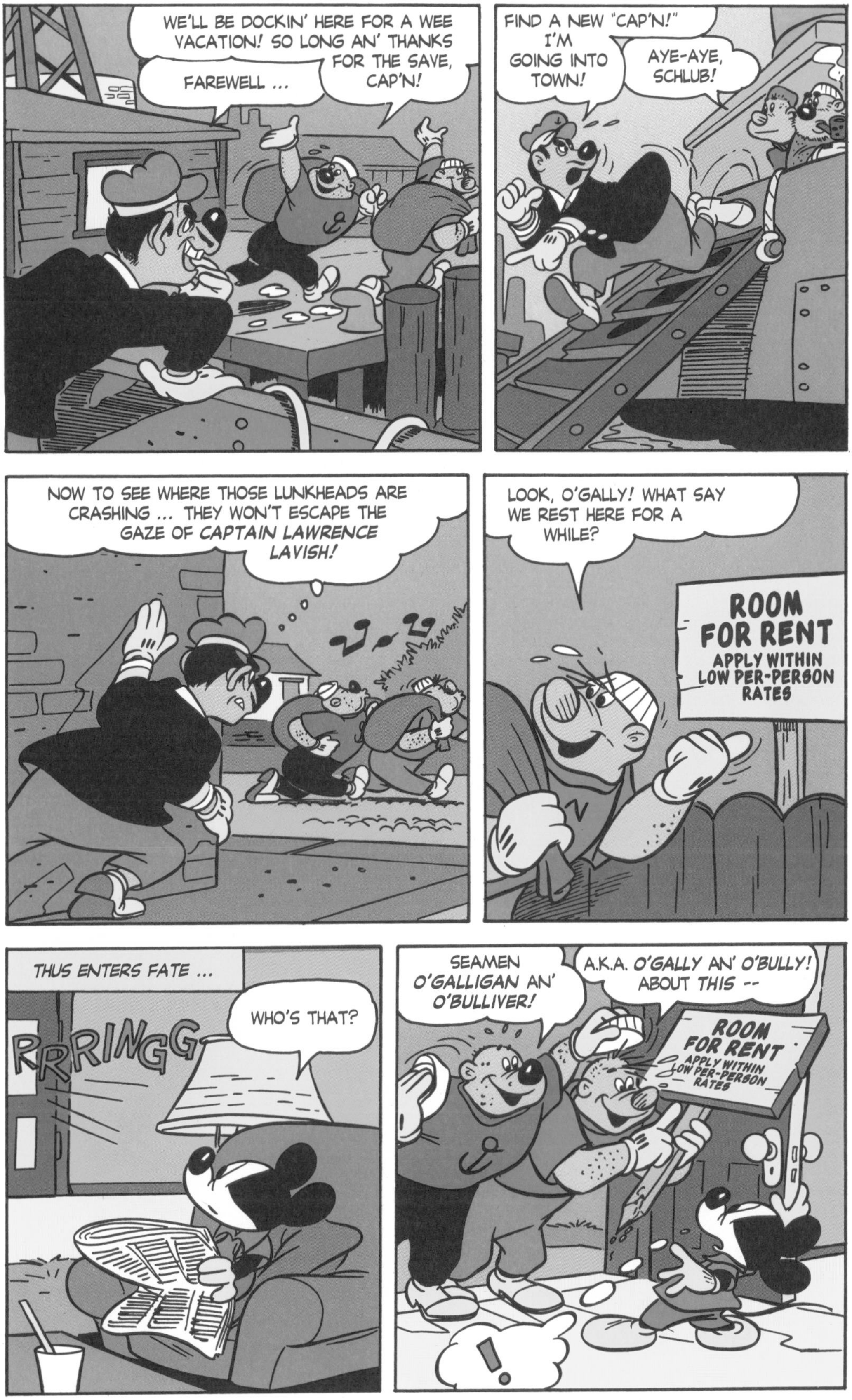

WE'LL BE DOCKIN' HERE FOR A WEE VACATION! SO LONG AN' THANKS FOR THE SAVE, CAP'N!
FAREWELL ...
FIND A NEW "CAP'N!" I'M GOING INTO TOWN!
AYE-AYE, SCHLUB!
NOW TO SEE WHERE THOSE LUNKHEADS ARE CRASHING ... THEY WON'T ESCAPE THE GAZE OF *CAPTAIN LAWRENCE LAVISH!*
LOOK, O'GALLY! WHAT SAY WE REST HERE FOR A WHILE?
ROOM FOR RENT
APPLY WITHIN
LOW PER-PERSON RATES
THUS ENTERS FATE ...
RRRINGG
WHO'S THAT?
SEAMEN O'GALLIGAN AN' O'BULLIVER!
A.K.A. O'GALLY AN' O'BULLY! ABOUT THIS --
ROOM FOR RENT
APPLY WITHIN
LOW PER-PERSON RATES
!

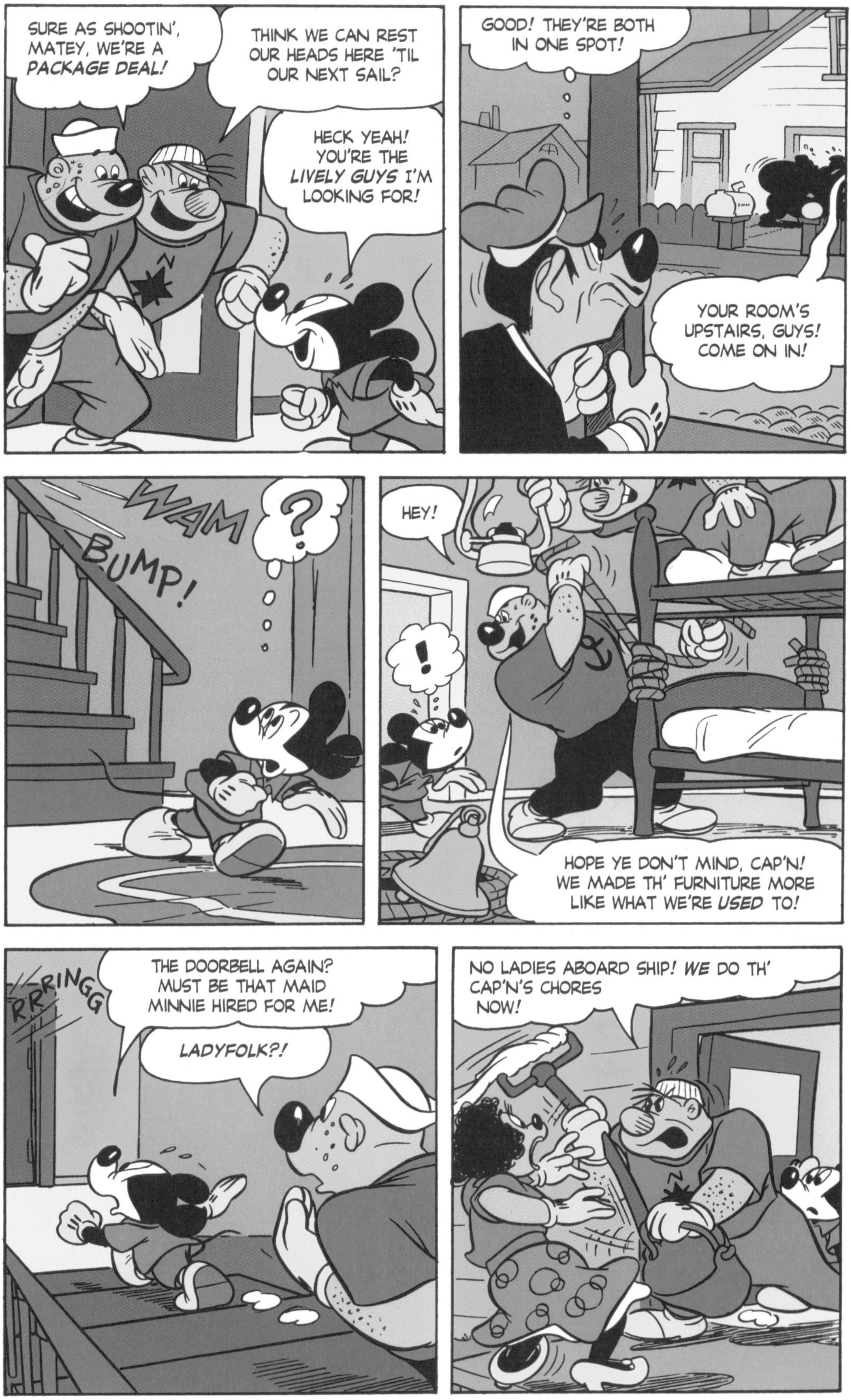
SURE AS SHOOTIN', MATEY, WE'RE A *PACKAGE DEAL!*
THINK WE CAN REST OUR HEADS HERE 'TIL OUR NEXT SAIL?
HECK YEAH! YOU'RE THE *LIVELY GUYS* I'M LOOKING FOR!
GOOD! THEY'RE BOTH IN ONE SPOT!
YOUR ROOM'S UPSTAIRS, GUYS! COME ON IN!
WAM
BUMP!
?
HEY!
!
HOPE YE DON'T MIND, CAP'N! WE MADE TH' FURNITURE MORE LIKE WHAT WE'RE *USED* TO!
RRRINGG
THE DOORBELL AGAIN? MUST BE THAT MAID MINNIE HIRED FOR ME!
LADYFOLK?!
NO LADIES ABOARD SHIP! *WE* DO TH' CAP'N'S CHORES NOW!

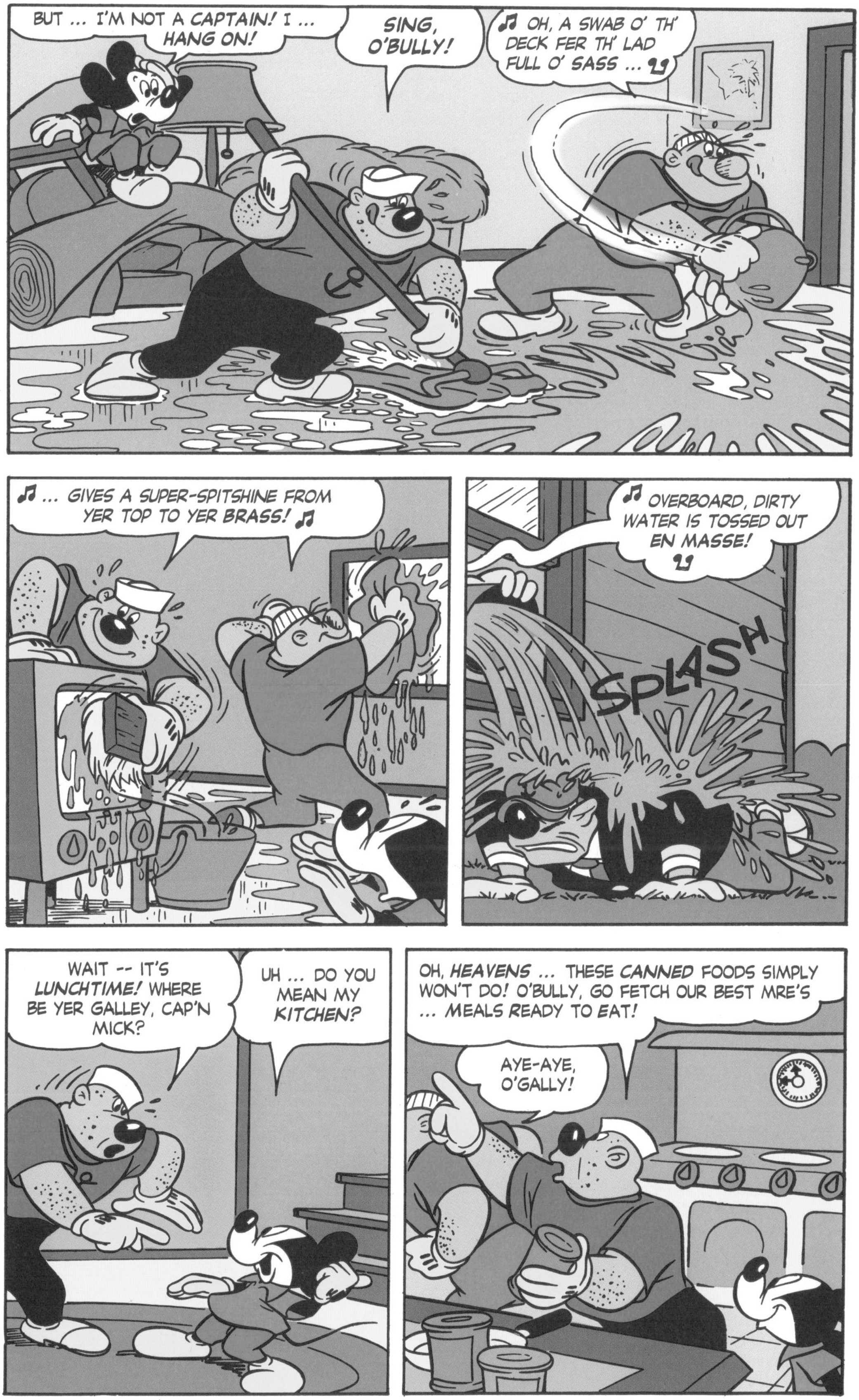
BUT ... I'M NOT A CAPTAIN! I ... HANG ON!
SING, O'BULLY!
♫ OH, A SWAB O' TH' DECK FER TH' LAD FULL O' SASS ...
♫ ... GIVES A SUPER-SPITSHINE FROM YER TOP TO YER BRASS! ♫
♫ OVERBOARD, DIRTY WATER IS TOSSED OUT EN MASSE!
SPLASH
WAIT -- IT'S LUNCHTIME! WHERE BE YER GALLEY, CAP'N MICK?
UH ... DO YOU MEAN MY KITCHEN?
OH, HEAVENS ... THESE CANNED FOODS SIMPLY WON'T DO! O'BULLY, GO FETCH OUR BEST MRE'S ... MEALS READY TO EAT!
AYE-AYE, O'GALLY!

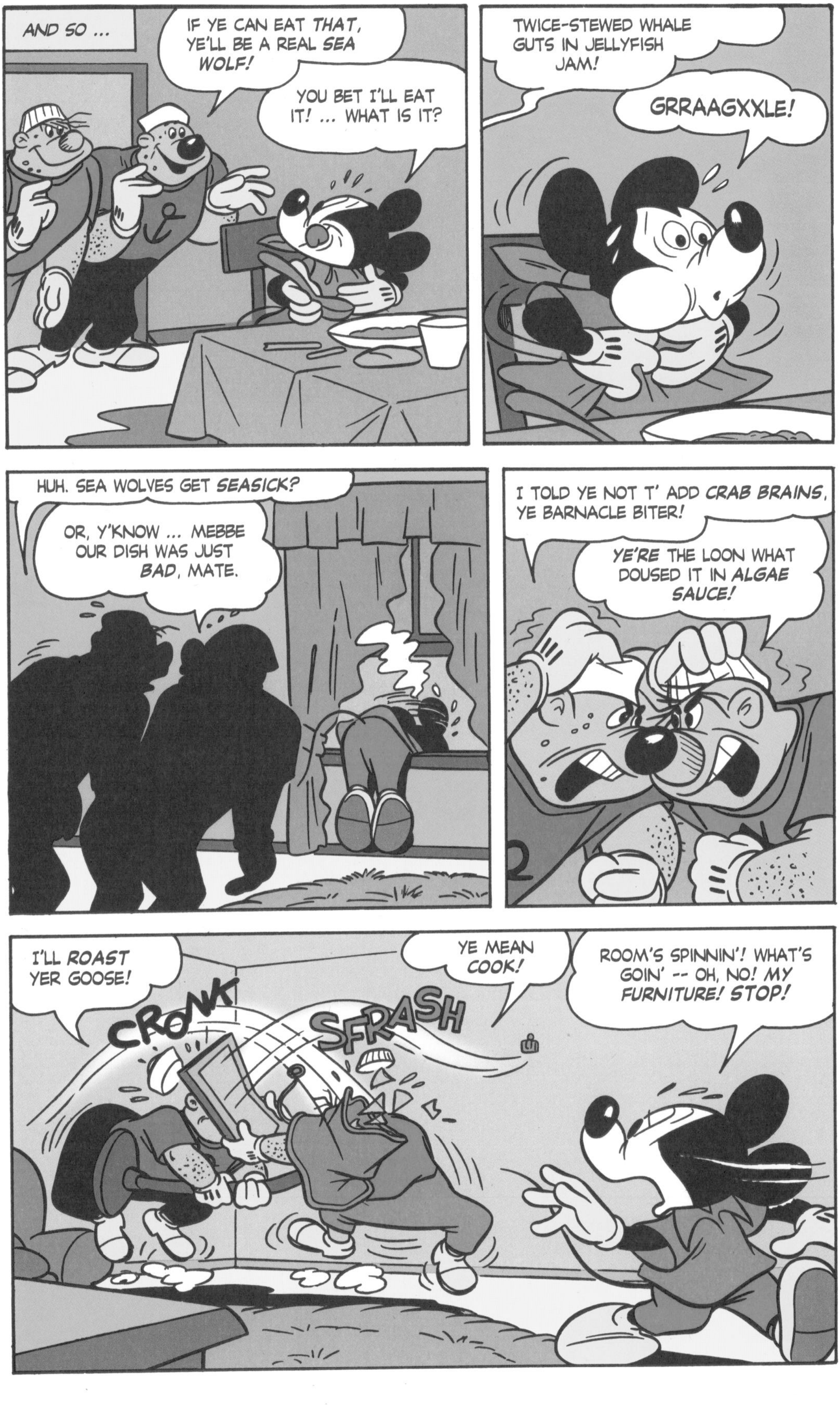
AND SO ...
IF YE CAN EAT THAT, YE'LL BE A REAL SEA WOLF!
YOU BET I'LL EAT IT! ... WHAT IS IT?
TWICE-STEWED WHALE GUTS IN JELLYFISH JAM!
GRRAAGXXLE!
HUH. SEA WOLVES GET SEASICK?
OR, Y'KNOW ... MEBBE OUR DISH WAS JUST BAD, MATE.
I TOLD YE NOT T' ADD CRAB BRAINS, YE BARNACLE BITER!
YE'RE THE LOON WHAT DOUSED IT IN ALGAE SAUCE!
I'LL ROAST YER GOOSE!
YE MEAN COOK!
ROOM'S SPINNIN'! WHAT'S GOIN' -- OH, NO! MY FURNITURE! STOP!
CRONK
SFRASH

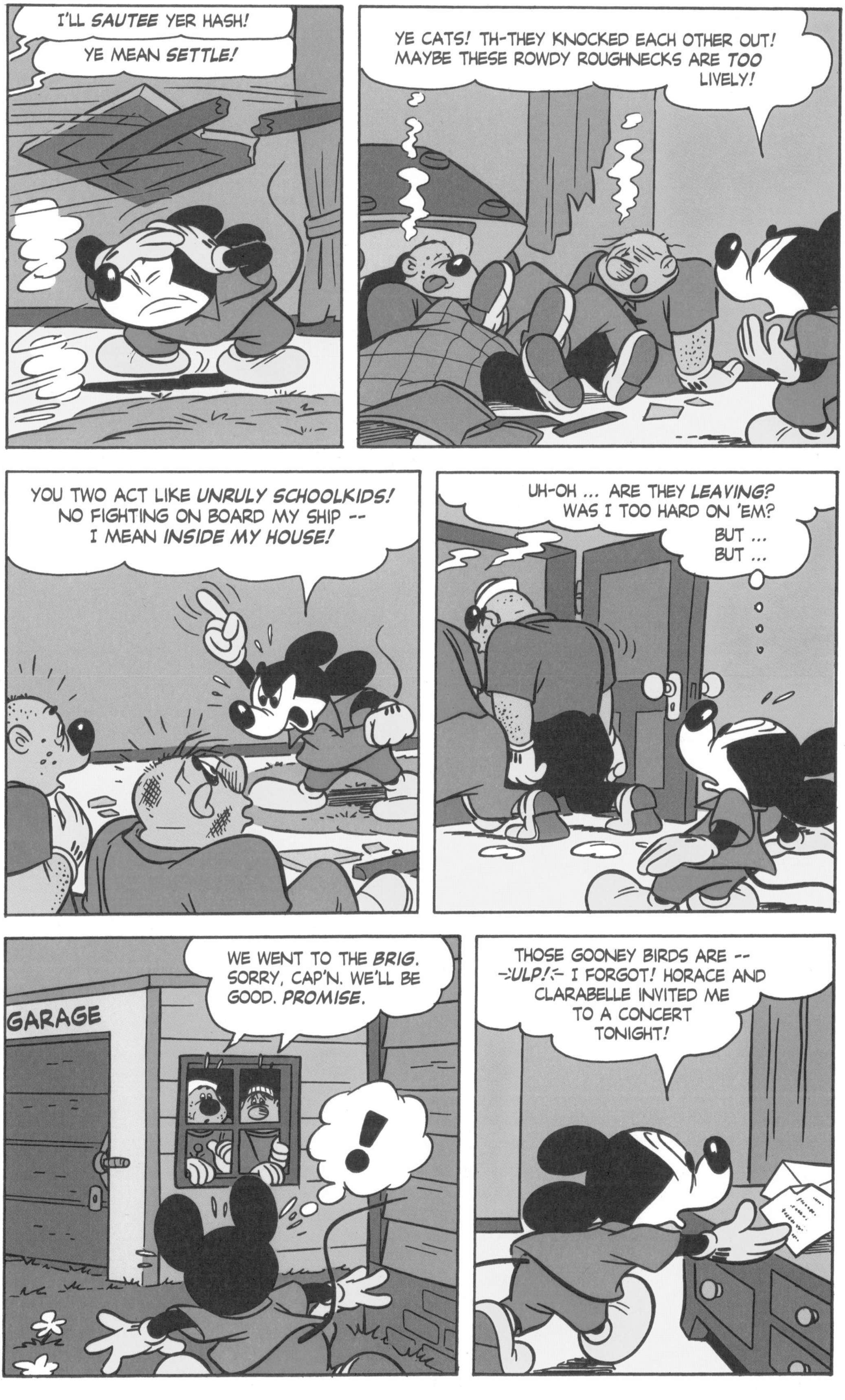
I'LL SAUTEE YER HASH!
YE MEAN SETTLE!
YE CATS! TH-THEY KNOCKED EACH OTHER OUT! MAYBE THESE ROWDY ROUGHNECKS ARE TOO LIVELY!
YOU TWO ACT LIKE UNRULY SCHOOLKIDS! NO FIGHTING ON BOARD MY SHIP -- I MEAN INSIDE MY HOUSE!
UH-OH ... ARE THEY LEAVING? WAS I TOO HARD ON 'EM?
BUT ... BUT ...
WE WENT TO THE BRIG. SORRY, CAP'N. WE'LL BE GOOD. PROMISE.
GARAGE
!
THOSE GOONEY BIRDS ARE -- -ULP!- I FORGOT! HORACE AND CLARABELLE INVITED ME TO A CONCERT TONIGHT!

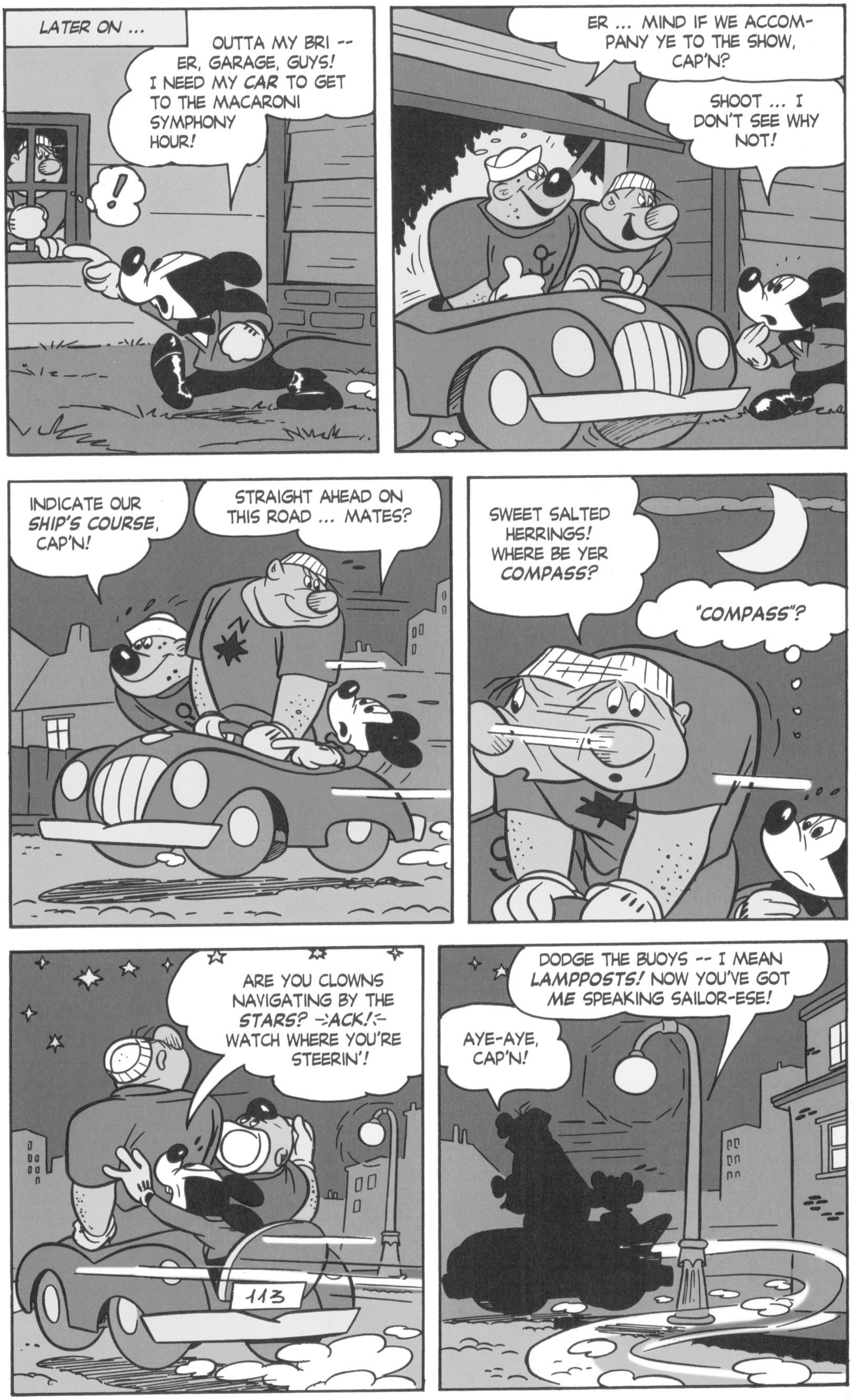
LATER ON ...
OUTTA MY BRI -- ER, GARAGE, GUYS! I NEED MY CAR TO GET TO THE MACARONI SYMPHONY HOUR!
!
ER ... MIND IF WE ACCOMPANY YE TO THE SHOW, CAP'N?
SHOOT ... I DON'T SEE WHY NOT!
INDICATE OUR SHIP'S COURSE, CAP'N!
STRAIGHT AHEAD ON THIS ROAD ... MATES?
SWEET SALTED HERRINGS! WHERE BE YER COMPASS?
"COMPASS"?
ARE YOU CLOWNS NAVIGATING BY THE STARS? -ACK!- WATCH WHERE YOU'RE STEERIN'!
113
DODGE THE BUOYS -- I MEAN LAMPPOSTS! NOW YOU'VE GOT ME SPEAKING SAILOR-ESE!
AYE-AYE, CAP'N!

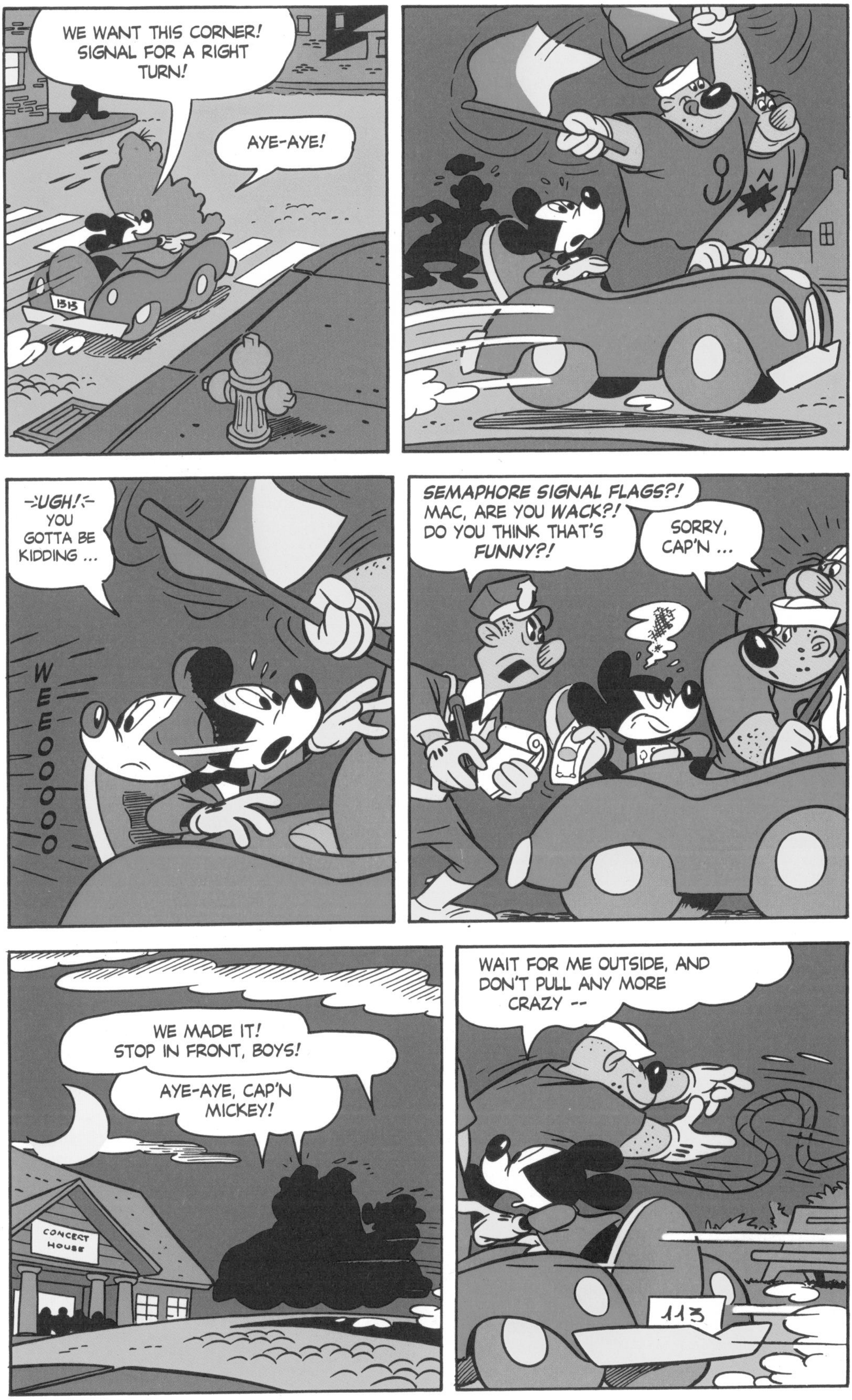
WE WANT THIS CORNER! SIGNAL FOR A RIGHT TURN!
AYE-AYE!
1313
—UGH!— YOU GOTTA BE KIDDING ...
WEEOOOOOO
SEMAPHORE SIGNAL FLAGS?! MAC, ARE YOU WACK?! DO YOU THINK THAT'S FUNNY?!
SORRY, CAP'N ...
WE MADE IT! STOP IN FRONT, BOYS!
AYE-AYE, CAP'N MICKEY!
CONCERT HOUSE
WAIT FOR ME OUTSIDE, AND DON'T PULL ANY MORE CRAZY --
113

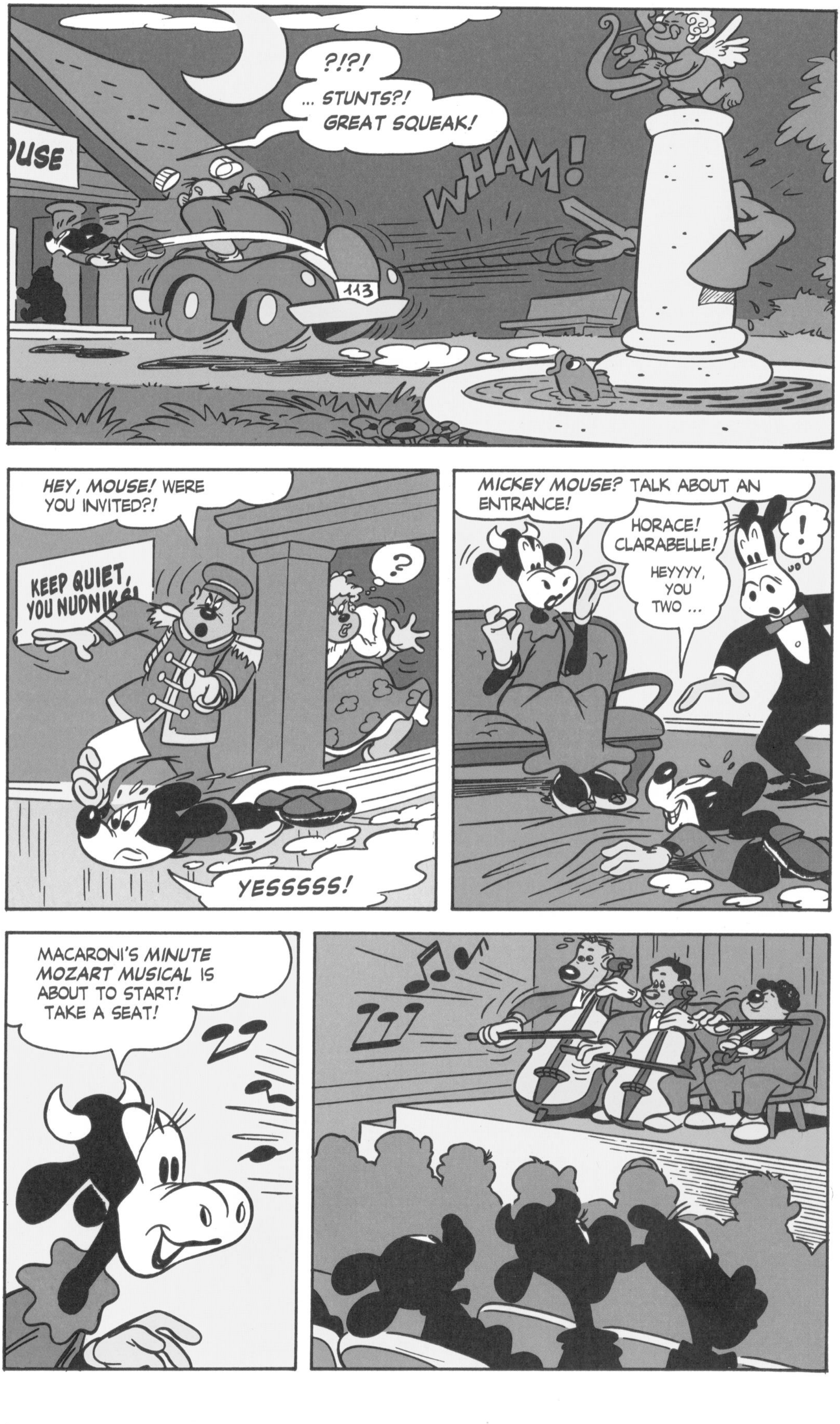
?!?!
... STUNTS?! GREAT SQUEAK!
WHAM!
113
HEY, MOUSE! WERE YOU INVITED?!
KEEP QUIET, YOU NUDNIKS!
?
YESSSSS!
MICKEY MOUSE? TALK ABOUT AN ENTRANCE!
HORACE! CLARABELLE!
HEYYYY, YOU TWO ...
!
MACARONI'S MINUTE MOZART MUSICAL IS ABOUT TO START! TAKE A SEAT!

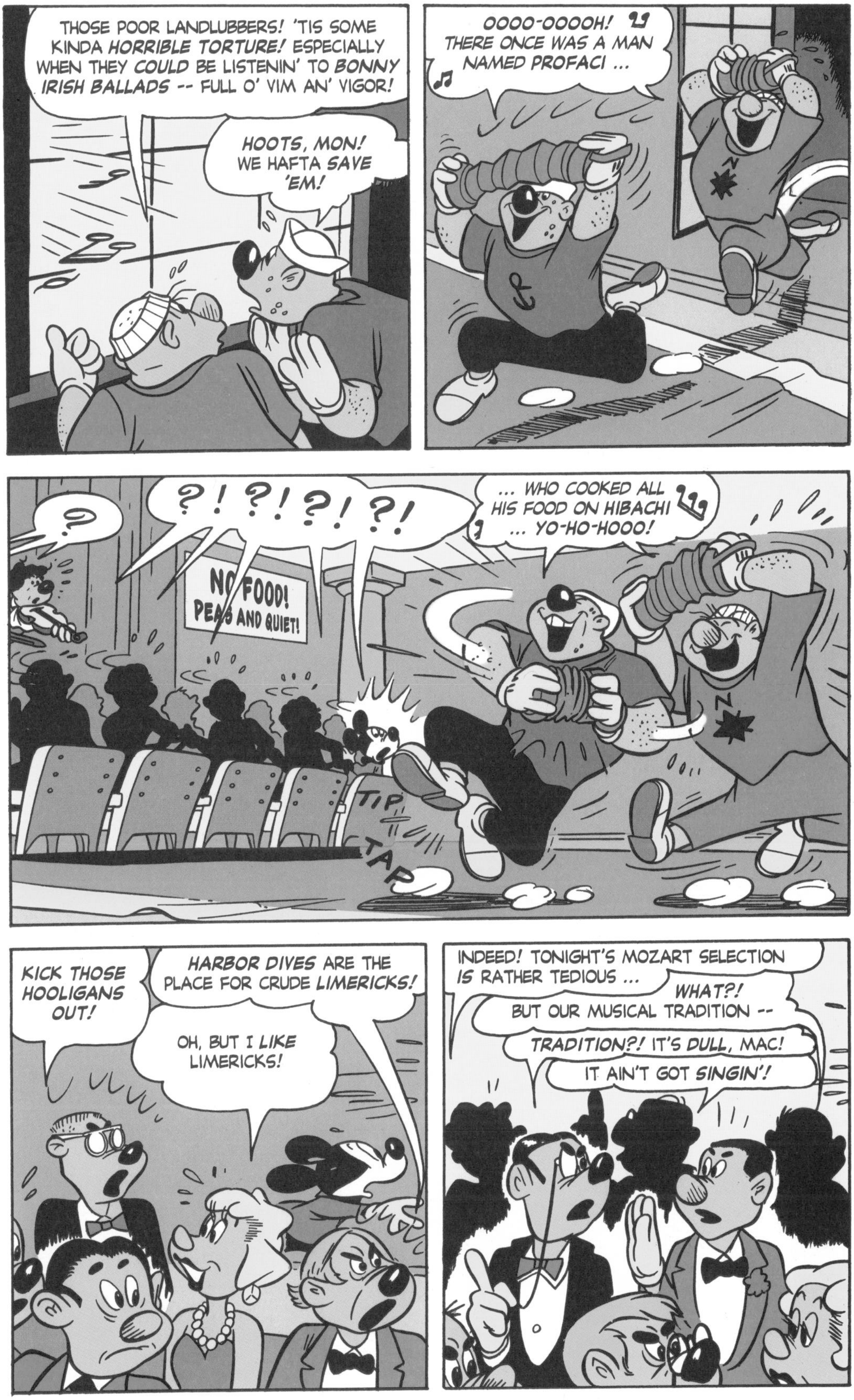
THOSE POOR LANDLUBBERS! 'TIS SOME KINDA HORRIBLE TORTURE! ESPECIALLY WHEN THEY COULD BE LISTENIN' TO BONNY IRISH BALLADS -- FULL O' VIM AN' VIGOR!
HOOTS, MON! WE HAFTA SAVE 'EM!
OOOO-OOOOH! THERE ONCE WAS A MAN NAMED PROFACI ...
?
?!?!?!?!
... WHO COOKED ALL HIS FOOD ON HIBACHI ... YO-HO-HOOO!
NO FOOD! PEAS AND QUIET!
TIP
TAP
KICK THOSE HOOLIGANS OUT!
HARBOR DIVES ARE THE PLACE FOR CRUDE LIMERICKS!
OH, BUT I LIKE LIMERICKS!
INDEED! TONIGHT'S MOZART SELECTION IS RATHER TEDIOUS ...
WHAT?! BUT OUR MUSICAL TRADITION --
TRADITION?! IT'S DULL, MAC!
IT AIN'T GOT SINGIN'!

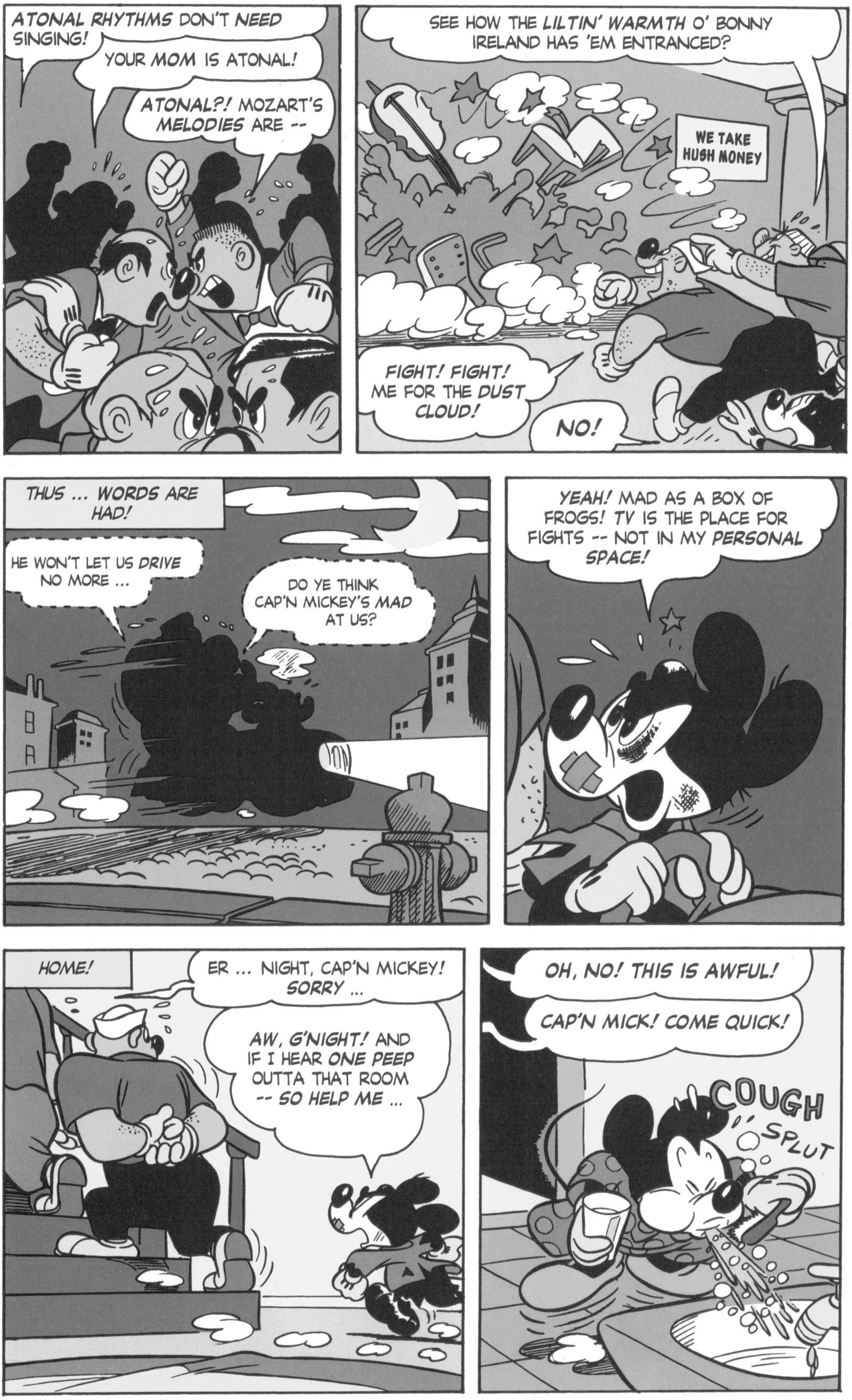
ATONAL RHYTHMS DON'T NEED SINGING!
YOUR MOM IS ATONAL!
ATONAL?! MOZART'S MELODIES ARE --
SEE HOW THE LILTIN' WARMTH O' BONNY IRELAND HAS 'EM ENTRANCED?
WE TAKE HUSH MONEY
FIGHT! FIGHT! ME FOR THE DUST CLOUD!
NO!
THUS ... WORDS ARE HAD!
HE WON'T LET US DRIVE NO MORE ...
DO YE THINK CAP'N MICKEY'S MAD AT US?
YEAH! MAD AS A BOX OF FROGS! TV IS THE PLACE FOR FIGHTS -- NOT IN MY PERSONAL SPACE!
HOME!
ER ... NIGHT, CAP'N MICKEY! SORRY ...
AW, G'NIGHT! AND IF I HEAR ONE PEEP OUTTA THAT ROOM -- SO HELP ME ...
OH, NO! THIS IS AWFUL!
CAP'N MICK! COME QUICK!
COUGH
SPLUT

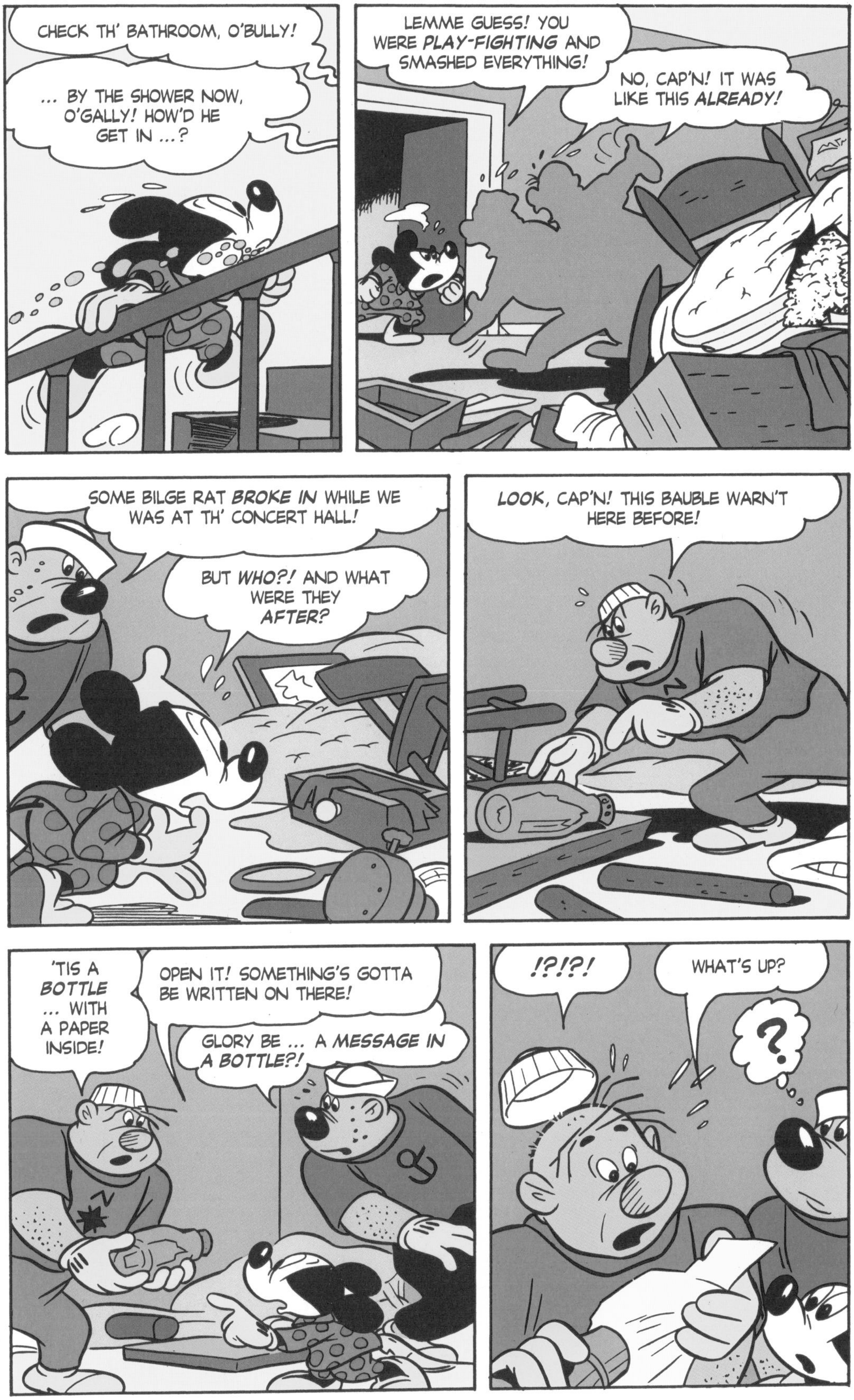
CHECK TH' BATHROOM, O'BULLY!
... BY THE SHOWER NOW, O'GALLY! HOW'D HE GET IN ...?
LEMME GUESS! YOU WERE *PLAY-FIGHTING* AND SMASHED EVERYTHING!
NO, CAP'N! IT WAS LIKE THIS *ALREADY!*
SOME BILGE RAT *BROKE IN* WHILE WE WAS AT TH' CONCERT HALL!
BUT *WHO?!* AND WHAT WERE THEY *AFTER?*
LOOK, CAP'N! THIS BAUBLE WARN'T HERE BEFORE!
'TIS A *BOTTLE* ... WITH A PAPER INSIDE!
OPEN IT! SOMETHING'S GOTTA BE WRITTEN ON THERE!
GLORY BE ... A *MESSAGE IN A BOTTLE?!*
!?!?!
WHAT'S UP?
?

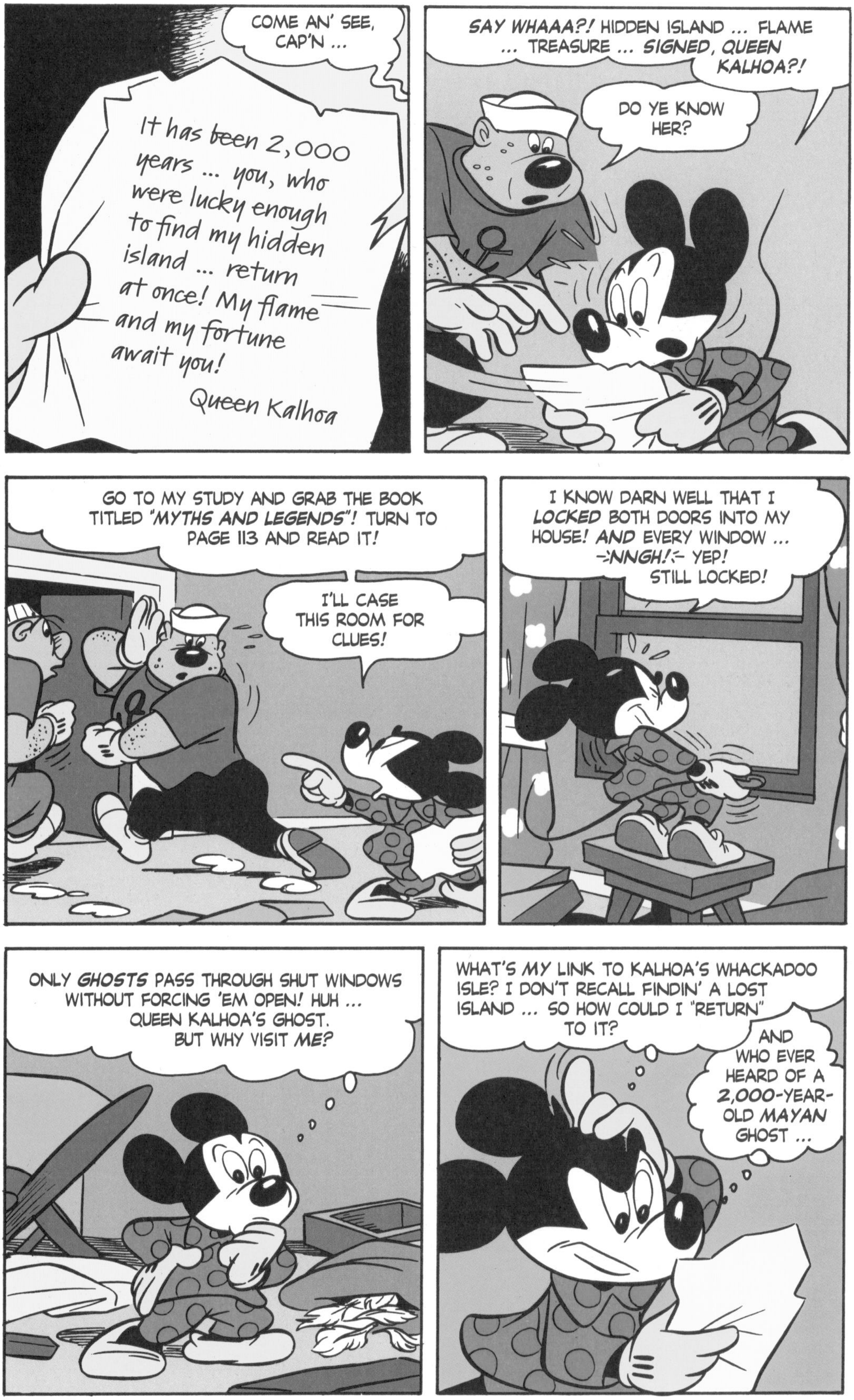

COME AN' SEE, CAP'N ...
It has been 2,000 years ... you, who were lucky enough to find my hidden island ... return at once! My flame and my fortune await you!
Queen Kalhoa
SAY WHAAA?! HIDDEN ISLAND ... FLAME ... TREASURE ... *SIGNED, QUEEN KALHOA?!*
DO YE KNOW HER?
GO TO MY STUDY AND GRAB THE BOOK TITLED "*MYTHS AND LEGENDS*"! TURN TO PAGE 113 AND READ IT!
I'LL CASE THIS ROOM FOR CLUES!
I KNOW DARN WELL THAT I *LOCKED* BOTH DOORS INTO MY HOUSE! *AND* EVERY WINDOW ...
NNGH! YEP! STILL LOCKED!
ONLY *GHOSTS* PASS THROUGH SHUT WINDOWS WITHOUT FORCING 'EM OPEN! HUH ... QUEEN KALHOA'S GHOST. BUT WHY VISIT *ME?*
WHAT'S *MY* LINK TO KALHOA'S WHACKADOO ISLE? I DON'T RECALL FINDIN' A LOST ISLAND ... SO HOW COULD I "RETURN" TO IT?
AND WHO EVER HEARD OF A *2,000*-YEAR-OLD *MAYAN* GHOST ...

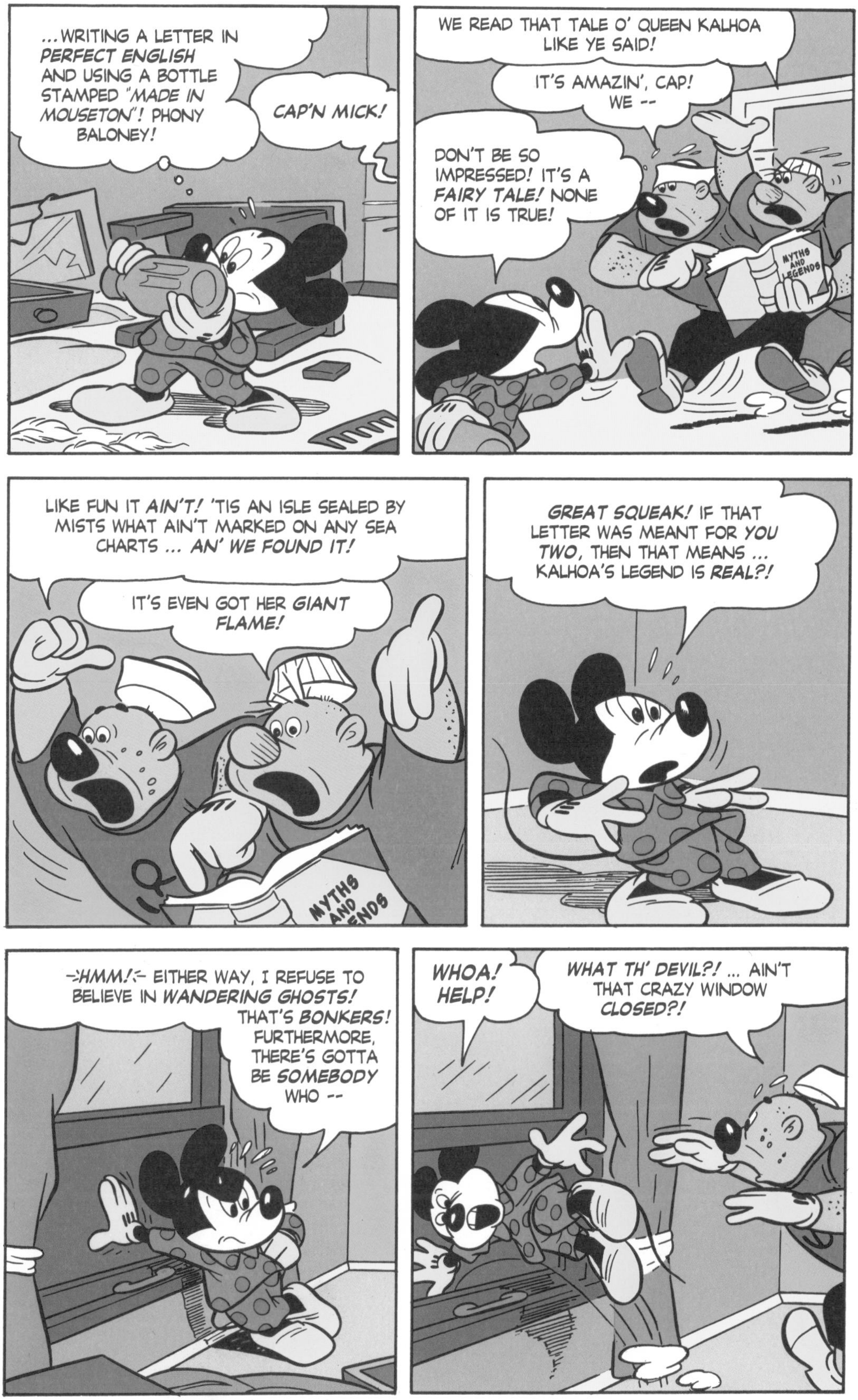
...WRITING A LETTER IN PERFECT ENGLISH AND USING A BOTTLE STAMPED "MADE IN MOUSETON"! PHONY BALONEY!
CAP'N MICK!
WE READ THAT TALE O' QUEEN KALHOA LIKE YE SAID!
IT'S AMAZIN', CAP! WE --
DON'T BE SO IMPRESSED! IT'S A FAIRY TALE! NONE OF IT IS TRUE!
MYTHS AND LEGENDS
LIKE FUN IT AIN'T! 'TIS AN ISLE SEALED BY MISTS WHAT AIN'T MARKED ON ANY SEA CHARTS ... AN' WE FOUND IT!
IT'S EVEN GOT HER GIANT FLAME!
GREAT SQUEAK! IF THAT LETTER WAS MEANT FOR YOU TWO, THEN THAT MEANS ... KALHOA'S LEGEND IS REAL?!
-HMM!- EITHER WAY, I REFUSE TO BELIEVE IN WANDERING GHOSTS!
THAT'S BONKERS! FURTHERMORE, THERE'S GOTTA BE SOMEBODY WHO --
WHOA! HELP!
WHAT TH' DEVIL?! ... AIN'T THAT CRAZY WINDOW CLOSED?!

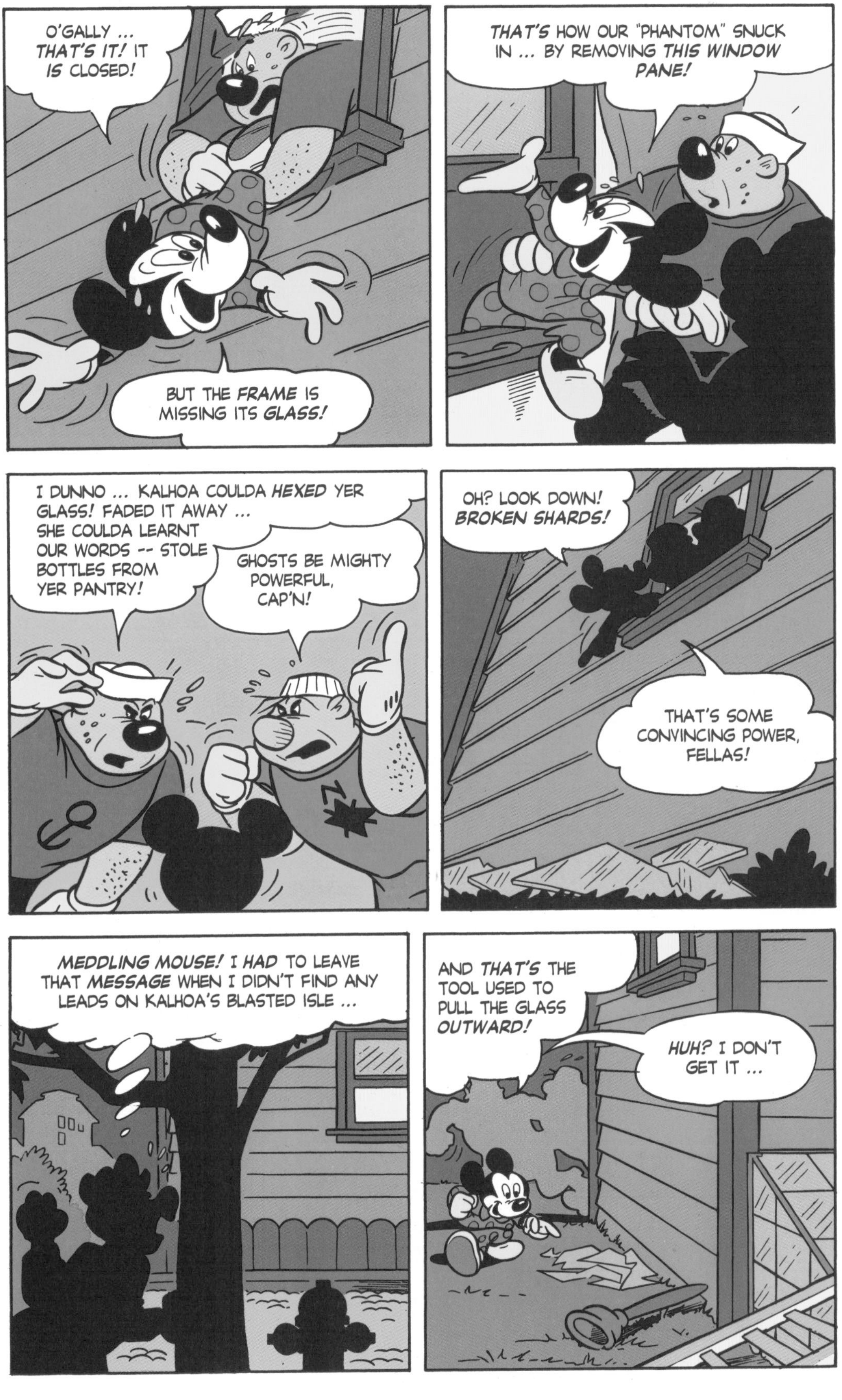
O'GALLY ... THAT'S IT! IT IS CLOSED!
BUT THE FRAME IS MISSING ITS GLASS!
THAT'S HOW OUR "PHANTOM" SNUCK IN ... BY REMOVING THIS WINDOW PANE!
I DUNNO ... KALHOA COULDA HEXED YER GLASS! FADED IT AWAY ... SHE COULDA LEARNT OUR WORDS -- STOLE BOTTLES FROM YER PANTRY!
GHOSTS BE MIGHTY POWERFUL, CAP'N!
OH? LOOK DOWN! BROKEN SHARDS!
THAT'S SOME CONVINCING POWER, FELLAS!
MEDDLING MOUSE! I HAD TO LEAVE THAT MESSAGE WHEN I DIDN'T FIND ANY LEADS ON KALHOA'S BLASTED ISLE ...
AND THAT'S THE TOOL USED TO PULL THE GLASS OUTWARD!
HUH? I DON'T GET IT ...

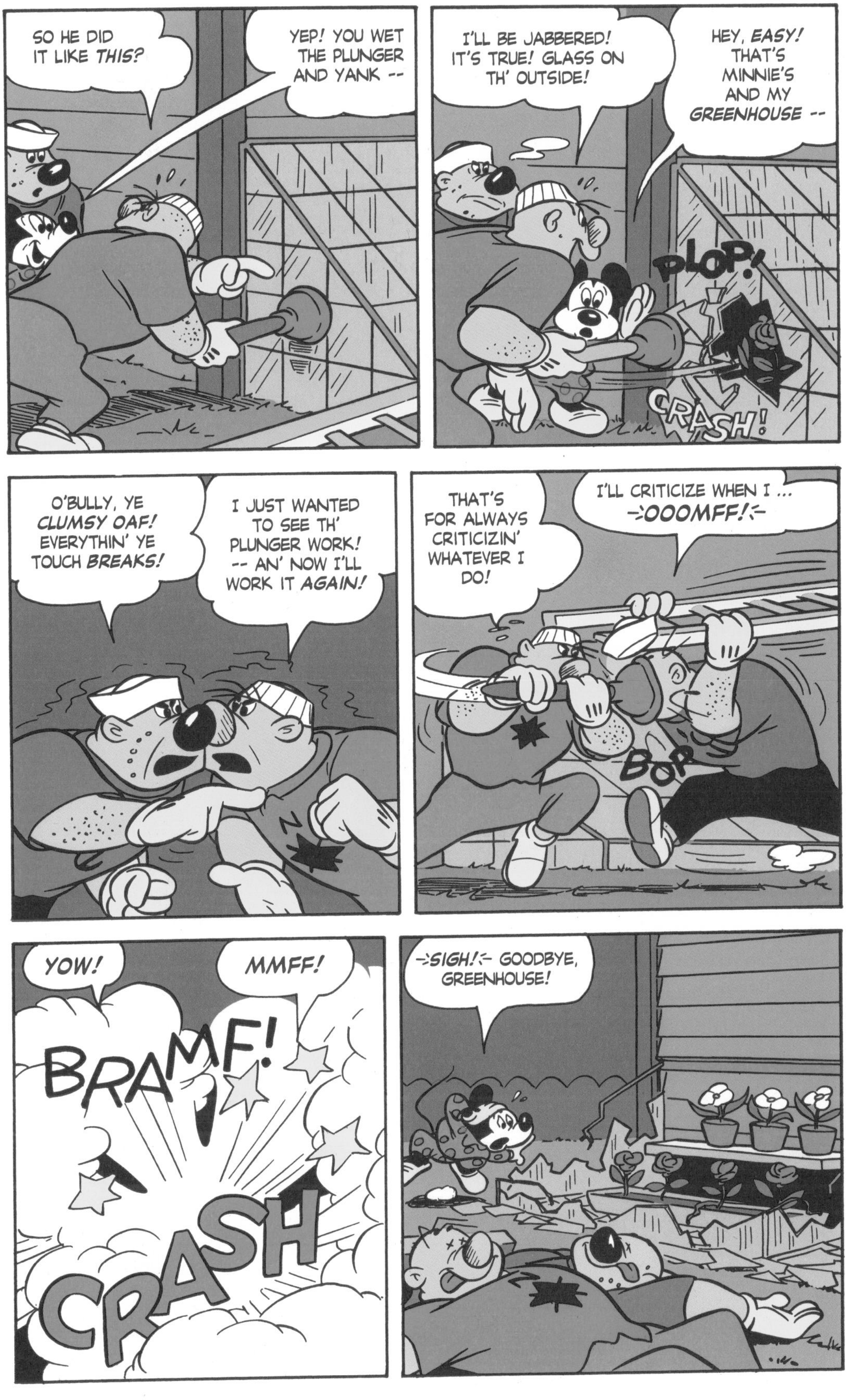

SO HE DID IT LIKE *THIS?*
YEP! YOU WET THE PLUNGER AND YANK --
I'LL BE JABBERED! IT'S TRUE! GLASS ON TH' OUTSIDE!
HEY, *EASY!* THAT'S MINNIE'S AND MY *GREENHOUSE* --
PLOP!
CRASH!
O'BULLY, YE *CLUMSY OAF!* EVERYTHIN' YE TOUCH *BREAKS!*
I JUST WANTED TO SEE TH' PLUNGER WORK! -- AN' NOW I'LL WORK IT *AGAIN!*
THAT'S FOR ALWAYS CRITICIZIN' WHATEVER I DO!
I'LL CRITICIZE WHEN I ... *OOOMFF!*
BOP
YOW!
MMFF!
BRAMF!
CRASH
SIGH! GOODBYE, GREENHOUSE!

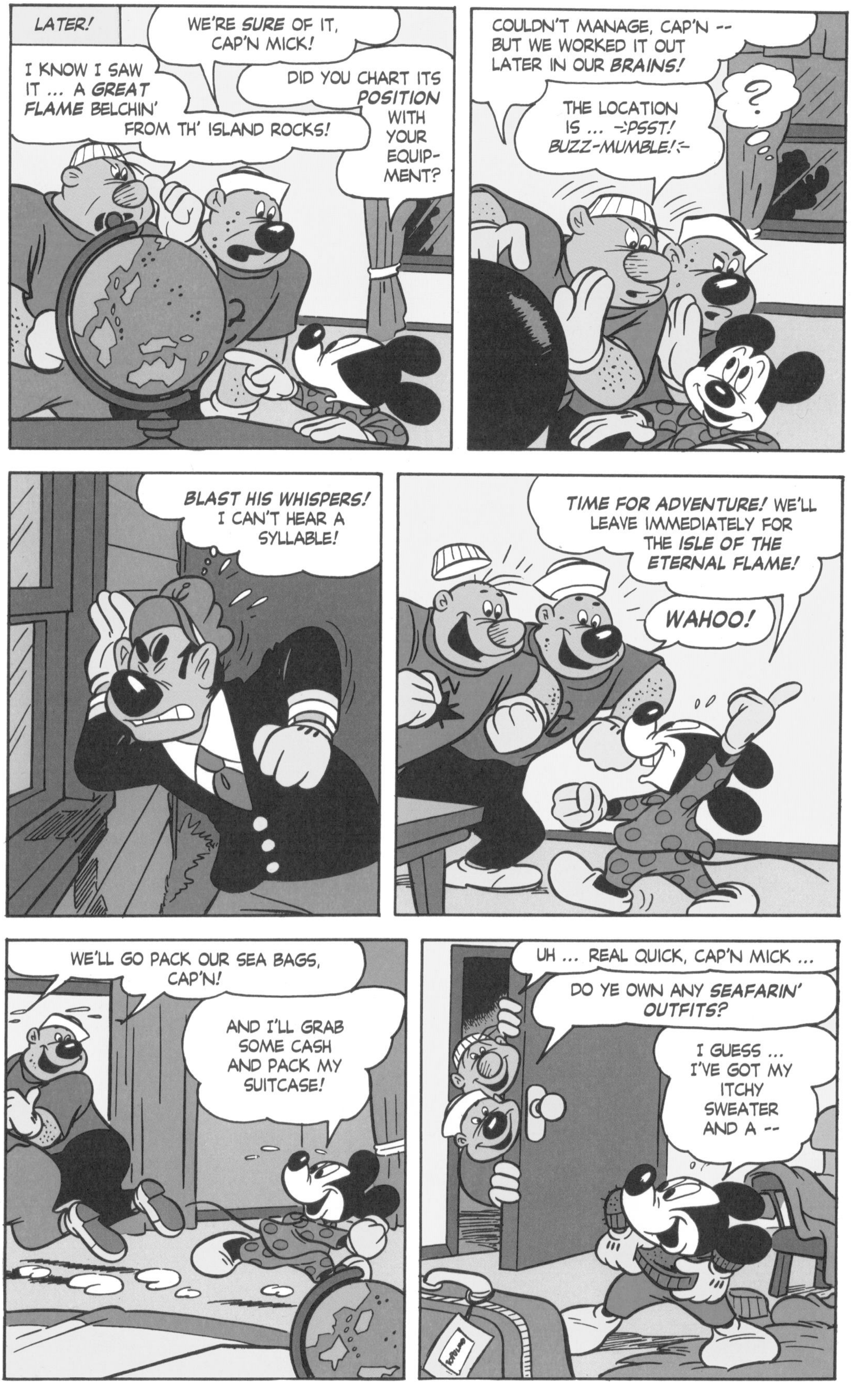
LATER!
I KNOW I SAW IT ... A GREAT FLAME BELCHIN' FROM TH' ISLAND ROCKS!
WE'RE SURE OF IT, CAP'N MICK!
DID YOU CHART ITS POSITION WITH YOUR EQUIP-MENT?
COULDN'T MANAGE, CAP'N -- BUT WE WORKED IT OUT LATER IN OUR BRAINS!
THE LOCATION IS ... PSST! BUZZ-MUMBLE!
?
BLAST HIS WHISPERS! I CAN'T HEAR A SYLLABLE!
TIME FOR ADVENTURE! WE'LL LEAVE IMMEDIATELY FOR THE ISLE OF THE ETERNAL FLAME!
WAHOO!
WE'LL GO PACK OUR SEA BAGS, CAP'N!
AND I'LL GRAB SOME CASH AND PACK MY SUITCASE!
UH ... REAL QUICK, CAP'N MICK ...
DO YE OWN ANY SEAFARIN' OUTFITS?
I GUESS ... I'VE GOT MY ITCHY SWEATER AND A --

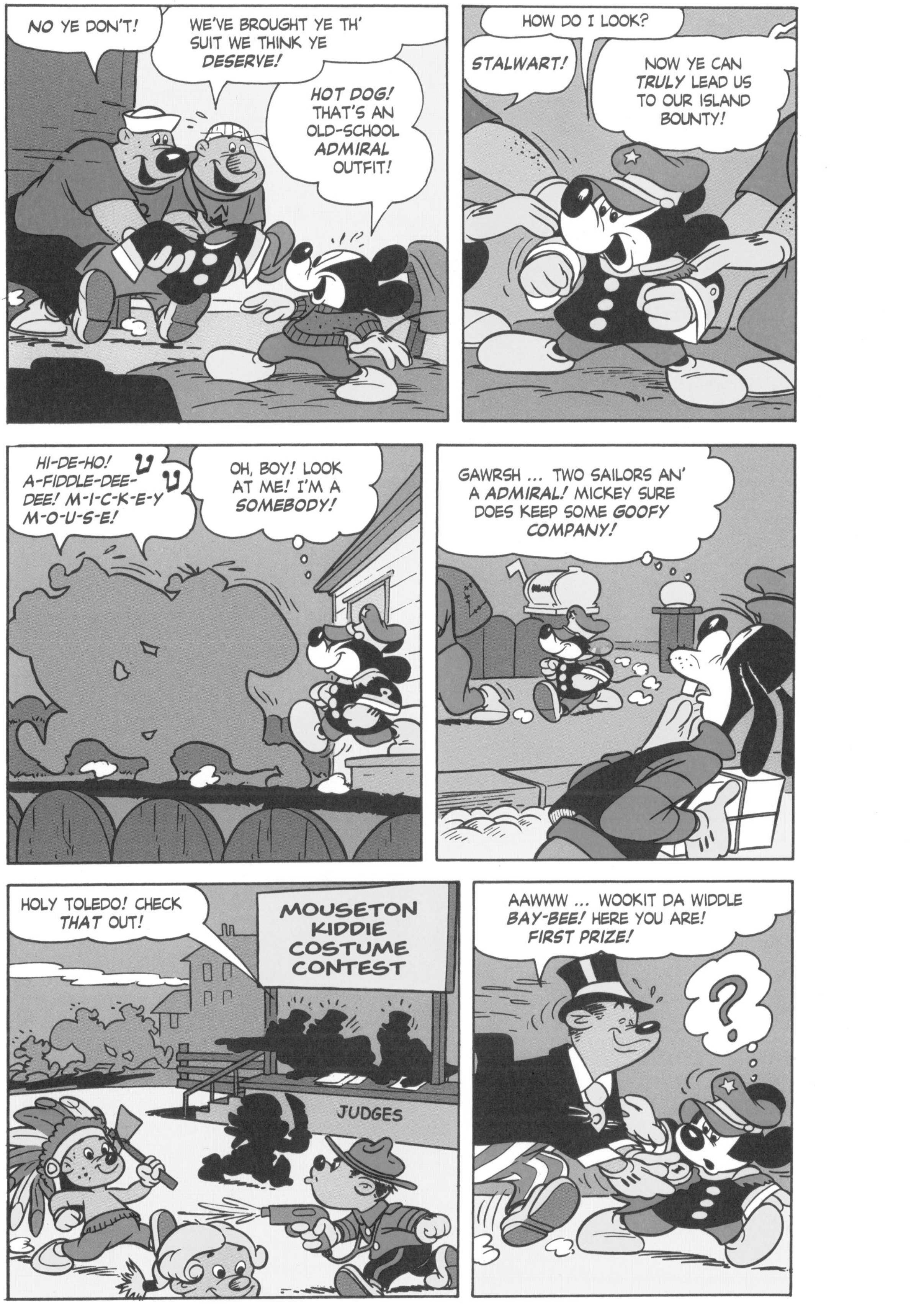
NO YE DON'T!
WE'VE BROUGHT YE TH' SUIT WE THINK YE DESERVE!
HOT DOG! THAT'S AN OLD-SCHOOL ADMIRAL OUTFIT!
HOW DO I LOOK?
STALWART!
NOW YE CAN TRULY LEAD US TO OUR ISLAND BOUNTY!
HI-DE-HO! A-FIDDLE-DEE-DEE! M-I-C-K-E-Y M-O-U-S-E!
OH, BOY! LOOK AT ME! I'M A SOMEBODY!
GAWRSH ... TWO SAILORS AN' A ADMIRAL! MICKEY SURE DOES KEEP SOME GOOFY COMPANY!
HOLY TOLEDO! CHECK THAT OUT!
MOUSETON KIDDIE COSTUME CONTEST
JUDGES
AAWWW ... WOOKIT DA WIDDLE BAY-BEE! HERE YOU ARE! FIRST PRIZE!
?

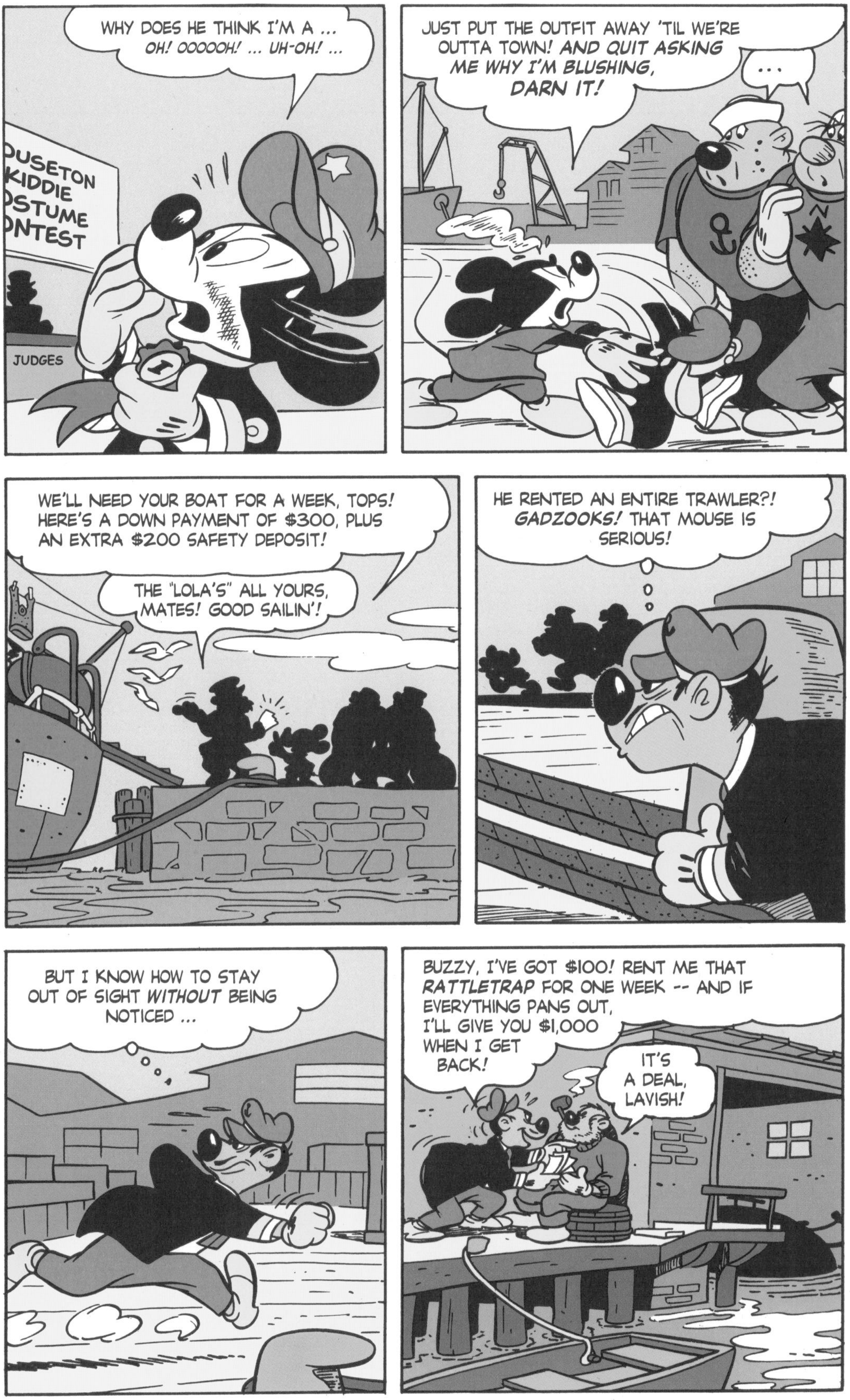

WHY DOES HE THINK I'M A ... OH! OOOOOH! ... UH-OH! ...
USETON KIDDIE STUME NTEST
JUDGES
JUST PUT THE OUTFIT AWAY 'TIL WE'RE OUTTA TOWN! AND QUIT ASKING ME WHY I'M BLUSHING, DARN IT!
...
WE'LL NEED YOUR BOAT FOR A WEEK, TOPS! HERE'S A DOWN PAYMENT OF $300, PLUS AN EXTRA $200 SAFETY DEPOSIT!
THE "LOLA'S" ALL YOURS, MATES! GOOD SAILIN'!
HE RENTED AN ENTIRE TRAWLER?! GADZOOKS! THAT MOUSE IS SERIOUS!
BUT I KNOW HOW TO STAY OUT OF SIGHT WITHOUT BEING NOTICED ...
BUZZY, I'VE GOT $100! RENT ME THAT RATTLETRAP FOR ONE WEEK -- AND IF EVERYTHING PANS OUT, I'LL GIVE YOU $1,000 WHEN I GET BACK!
IT'S A DEAL, LAVISH!

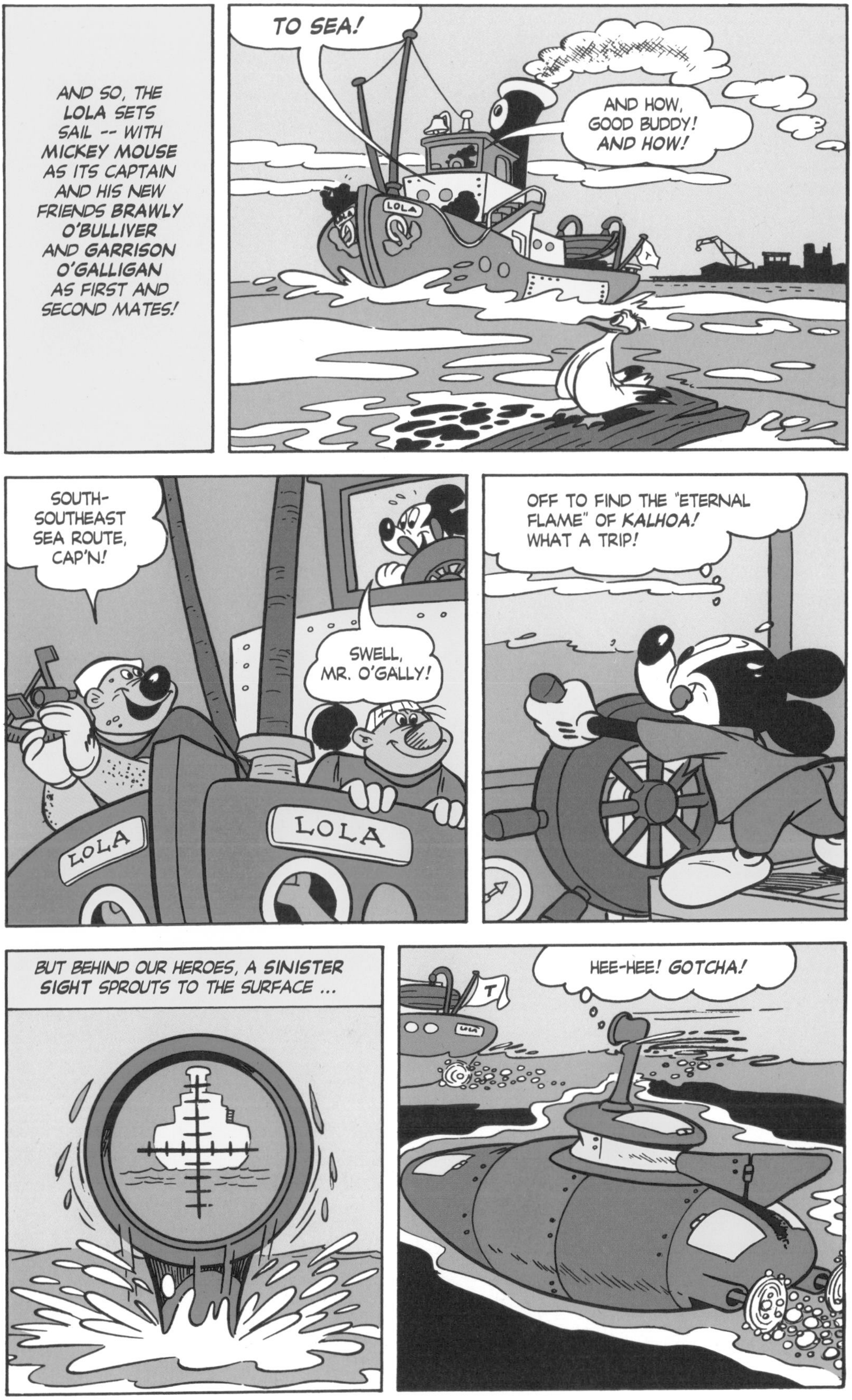
AND SO, THE LOLA SETS SAIL -- WITH MICKEY MOUSE AS ITS CAPTAIN AND HIS NEW FRIENDS BRAWLY O'BULLIVER AND GARRISON O'GALLIGAN AS FIRST AND SECOND MATES!
TO SEA!
AND HOW, GOOD BUDDY! AND HOW!
LOLA
SOUTH-SOUTHEAST SEA ROUTE, CAP'N!
SWELL, MR. O'GALLY!
LOLA
LOLA
OFF TO FIND THE "ETERNAL FLAME" OF KALHOA! WHAT A TRIP!
BUT BEHIND OUR HEROES, A SINISTER SIGHT SPROUTS TO THE SURFACE ...
HEE-HEE! GOTCHA!
T

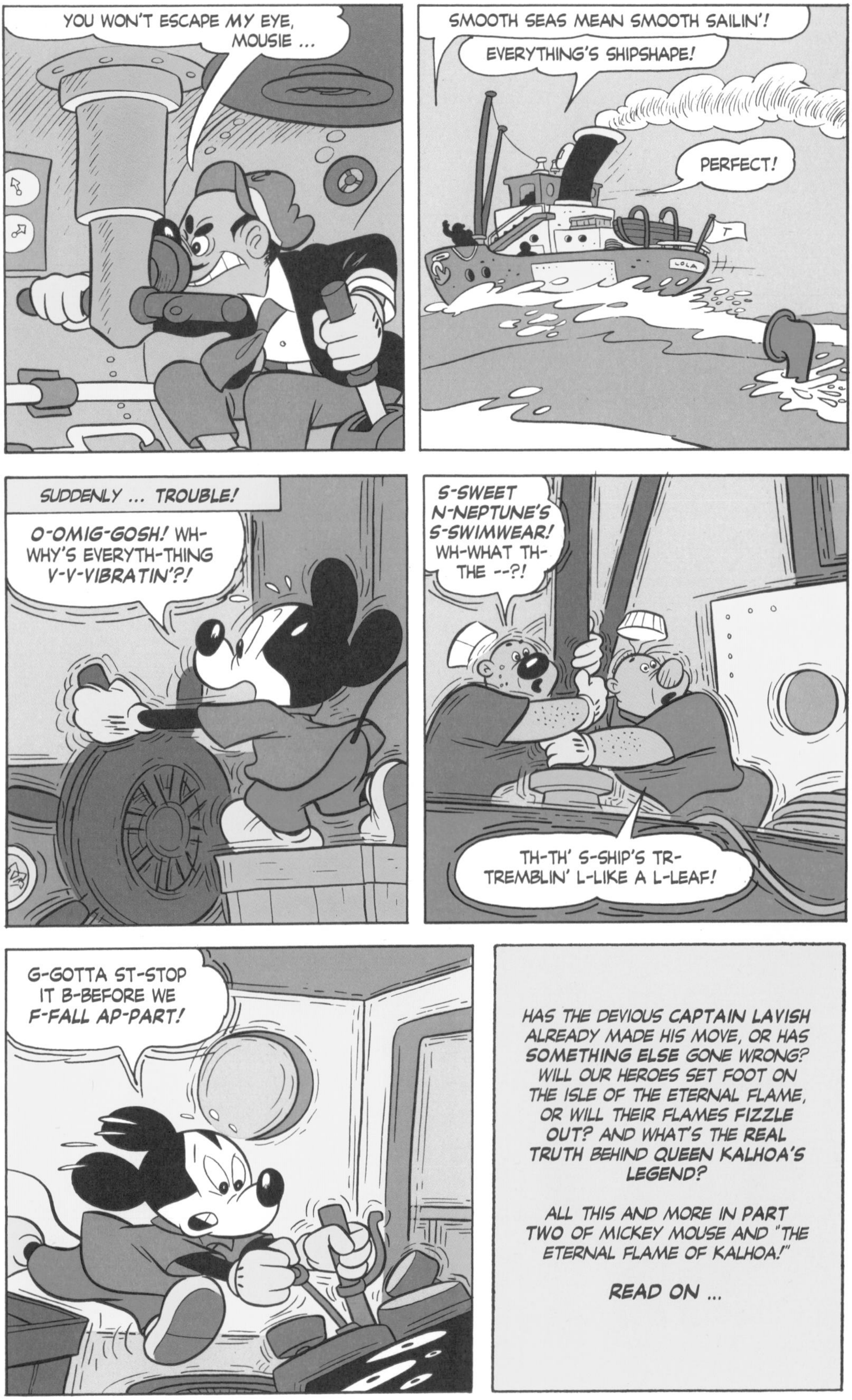
YOU WON'T ESCAPE MY EYE, MOUSIE ...
SMOOTH SEAS MEAN SMOOTH SAILIN'!
EVERYTHING'S SHIPSHAPE!
PERFECT!
LOLA
SUDDENLY ... TROUBLE!
O-OMIG-GOSH! WH-WHY'S EVERYTH-THING V-V-VIBRATIN'?!
S-SWEET N-NEPTUNE'S S-SWIMWEAR! WH-WHAT TH-THE --?!
TH-TH' S-SHIP'S TR-TREMBLIN' L-LIKE A L-LEAF!
G-GOTTA ST-STOP IT B-BEFORE WE F-FALL AP-PART!
HAS THE DEVIOUS CAPTAIN LAVISH ALREADY MADE HIS MOVE, OR HAS SOMETHING ELSE GONE WRONG? WILL OUR HEROES SET FOOT ON THE ISLE OF THE ETERNAL FLAME, OR WILL THEIR FLAMES FIZZLE OUT? AND WHAT'S THE REAL TRUTH BEHIND QUEEN KALHOA'S LEGEND?
ALL THIS AND MORE IN PART TWO OF MICKEY MOUSE AND "THE ETERNAL FLAME OF KALHOA!"
READ ON ...

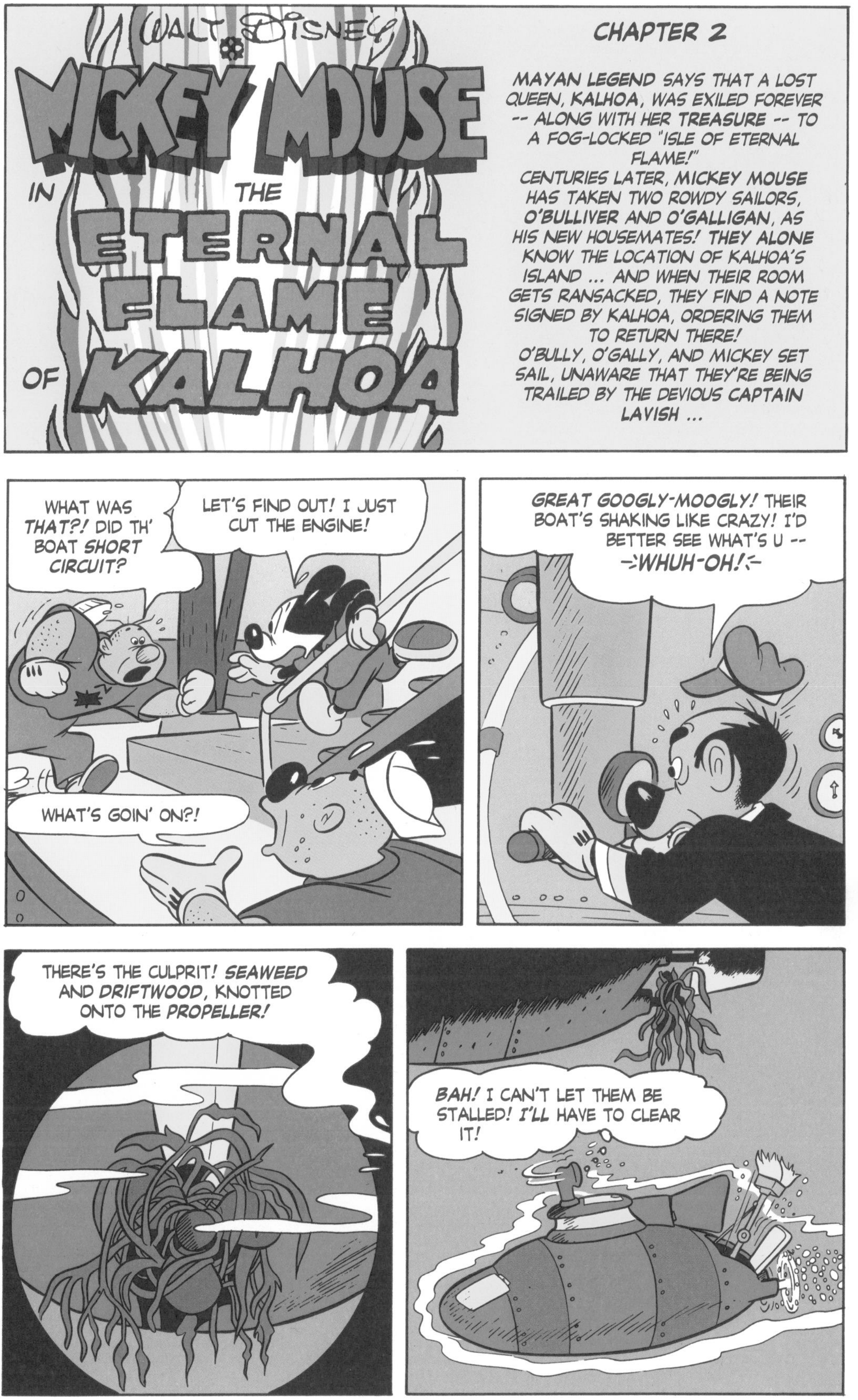
WALT DISNEY
MICKEY MOUSE IN THE ETERNAL FLAME OF KALHOA
CHAPTER 2
MAYAN LEGEND SAYS THAT A LOST QUEEN, KALHOA, WAS EXILED FOREVER -- ALONG WITH HER TREASURE -- TO A FOG-LOCKED "ISLE OF ETERNAL FLAME!" CENTURIES LATER, MICKEY MOUSE HAS TAKEN TWO ROWDY SAILORS, O'BULLIVER AND O'GALLIGAN, AS HIS NEW HOUSEMATES! THEY ALONE KNOW THE LOCATION OF KALHOA'S ISLAND ... AND WHEN THEIR ROOM GETS RANSACKED, THEY FIND A NOTE SIGNED BY KALHOA, ORDERING THEM TO RETURN THERE! O'BULLY, O'GALLY, AND MICKEY SET SAIL, UNAWARE THAT THEY'RE BEING TRAILED BY THE DEVIOUS CAPTAIN LAVISH ...
WHAT WAS THAT?! DID TH' BOAT SHORT CIRCUIT?
LET'S FIND OUT! I JUST CUT THE ENGINE!
WHAT'S GOIN' ON?!
GREAT GOOGLY-MOOGLY! THEIR BOAT'S SHAKING LIKE CRAZY! I'D BETTER SEE WHAT'S U -- WHUH-OH!
THERE'S THE CULPRIT! SEAWEED AND DRIFTWOOD, KNOTTED ONTO THE PROPELLER!
BAH! I CAN'T LET THEM BE STALLED! I'LL HAVE TO CLEAR IT!

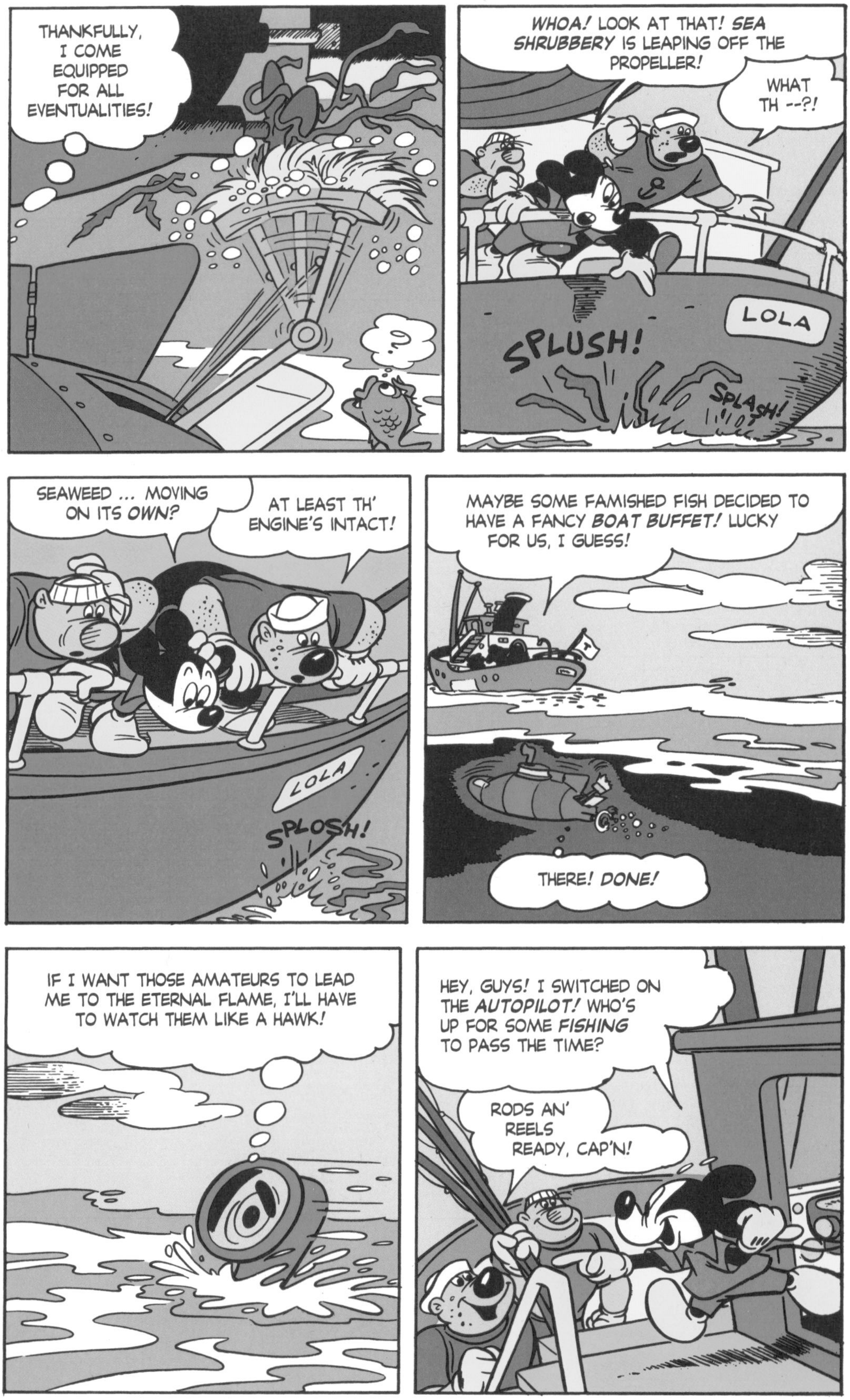
THANKFULLY, I COME EQUIPPED FOR ALL EVENTUALITIES!
?
WHOA! LOOK AT THAT! SEA SHRUBBERY IS LEAPING OFF THE PROPELLER!
WHAT TH --?!
LOLA
SPLUSH!
SPLASH!
SEAWEED ... MOVING ON ITS OWN?
AT LEAST TH' ENGINE'S INTACT!
LOLA
SPLOSH!
MAYBE SOME FAMISHED FISH DECIDED TO HAVE A FANCY BOAT BUFFET! LUCKY FOR US, I GUESS!
THERE! DONE!
IF I WANT THOSE AMATEURS TO LEAD ME TO THE ETERNAL FLAME, I'LL HAVE TO WATCH THEM LIKE A HAWK!
HEY, GUYS! I SWITCHED ON THE AUTOPILOT! WHO'S UP FOR SOME FISHING TO PASS THE TIME?
RODS AN' REELS READY, CAP'N!

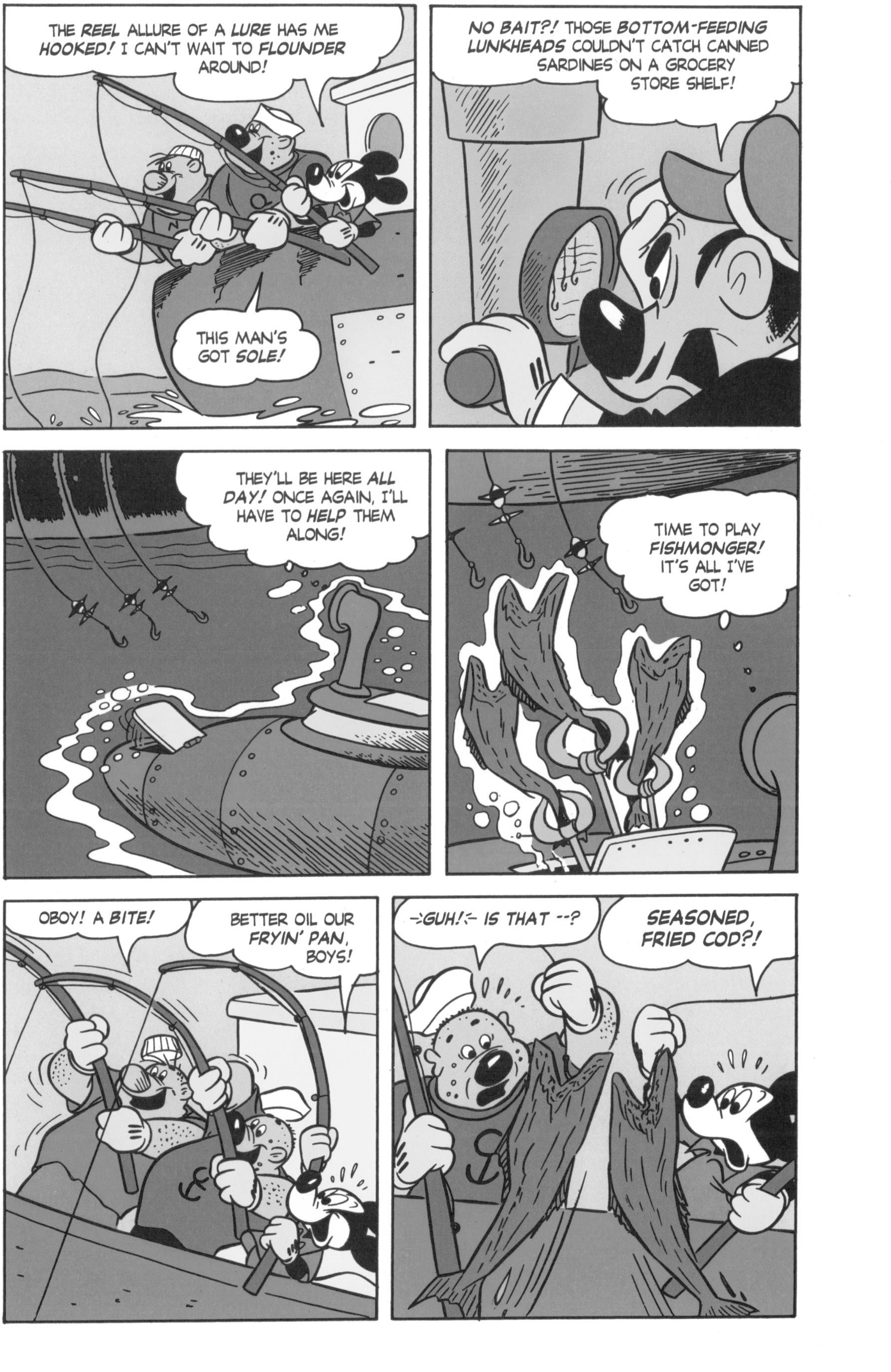

THE REEL ALLURE OF A LURE HAS ME HOOKED! I CAN'T WAIT TO FLOUNDER AROUND!
THIS MAN'S GOT SOLE!
NO BAIT?! THOSE BOTTOM-FEEDING LUNKHEADS COULDN'T CATCH CANNED SARDINES ON A GROCERY STORE SHELF!
THEY'LL BE HERE ALL DAY! ONCE AGAIN, I'LL HAVE TO HELP THEM ALONG!
TIME TO PLAY FISHMONGER! IT'S ALL I'VE GOT!
OBOY! A BITE!
BETTER OIL OUR FRYIN' PAN, BOYS!
-GUH!- IS THAT --?
SEASONED, FRIED COD?!

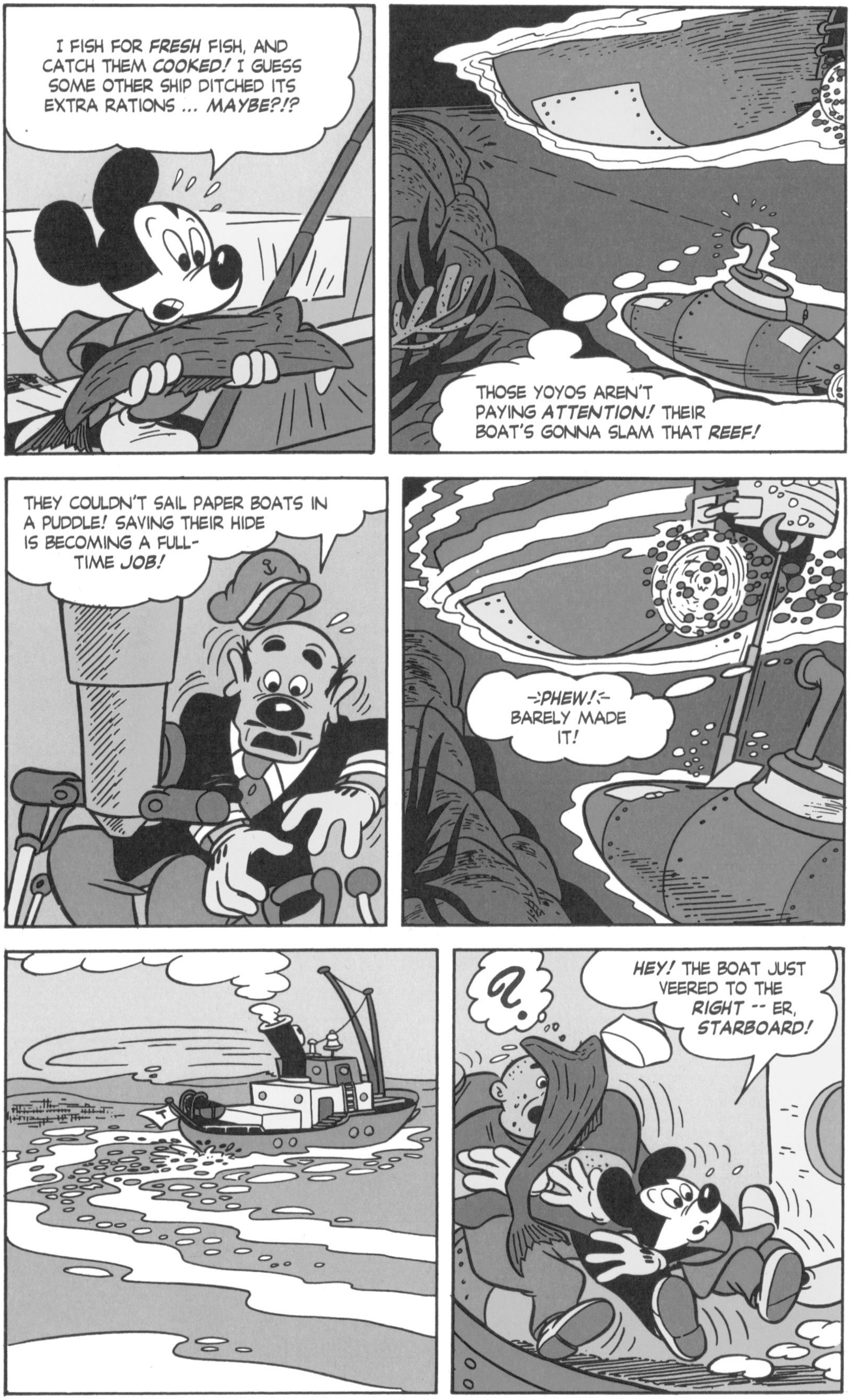
I FISH FOR FRESH FISH, AND CATCH THEM COOKED! I GUESS SOME OTHER SHIP DITCHED ITS EXTRA RATIONS ... MAYBE?!?
THOSE YOYOS AREN'T PAYING ATTENTION! THEIR BOAT'S GONNA SLAM THAT REEF!
THEY COULDN'T SAIL PAPER BOATS IN A PUDDLE! SAVING THEIR HIDE IS BECOMING A FULL-TIME JOB!
-PHEW!- BARELY MADE IT!
HEY! THE BOAT JUST VEERED TO THE RIGHT -- ER, STARBOARD!

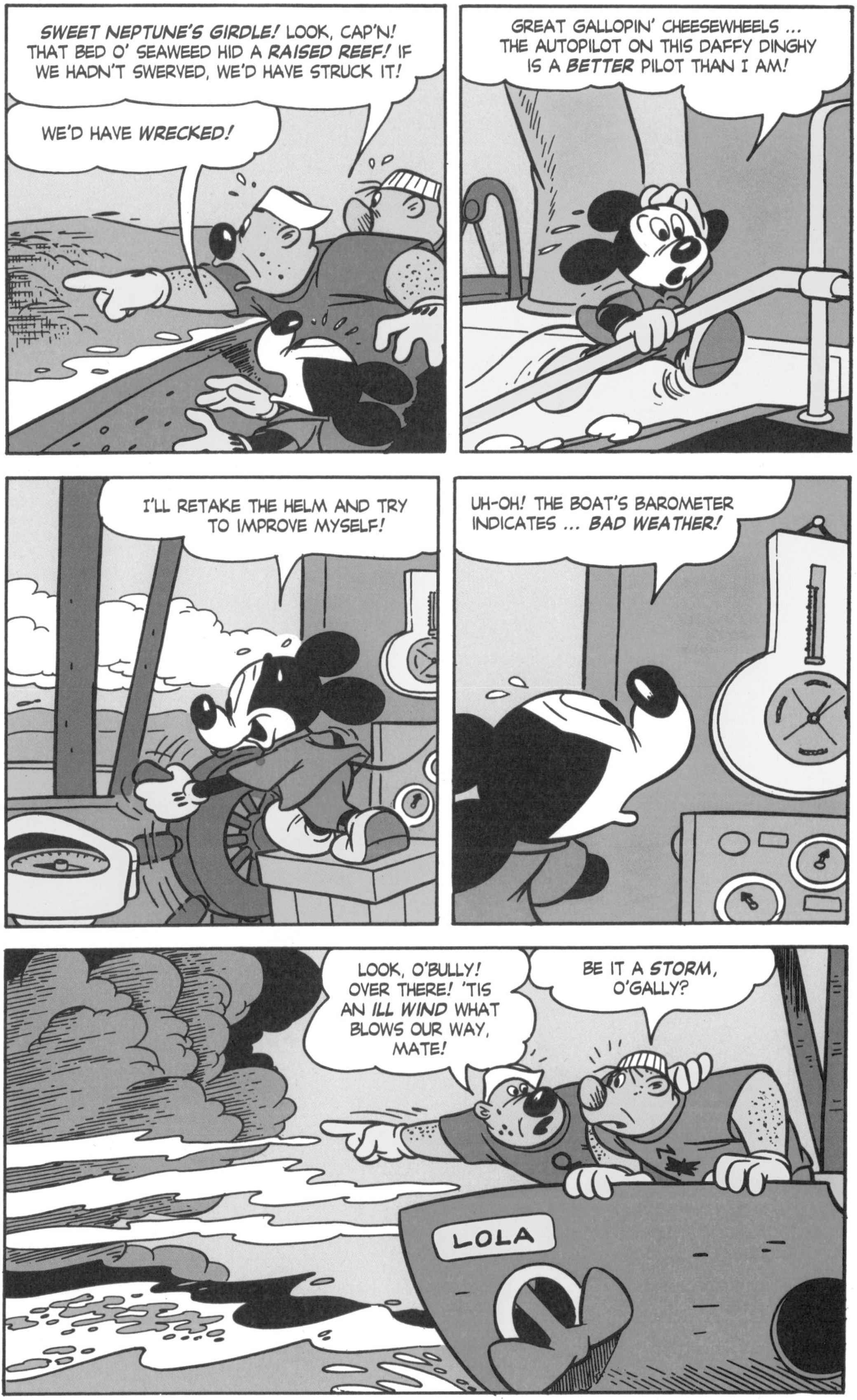

SWEET NEPTUNE'S GIRDLE! LOOK, CAP'N! THAT BED O' SEAWEED HID A RAISED REEF! IF WE HADN'T SWERVED, WE'D HAVE STRUCK IT!
WE'D HAVE WRECKED!
GREAT GALLOPIN' CHEESEWHEELS ... THE AUTOPILOT ON THIS DAFFY DINGHY IS A BETTER PILOT THAN I AM!
I'LL RETAKE THE HELM AND TRY TO IMPROVE MYSELF!
UH-OH! THE BOAT'S BAROMETER INDICATES ... BAD WEATHER!
LOOK, O'BULLY! OVER THERE! 'TIS AN ILL WIND WHAT BLOWS OUR WAY, MATE!
BE IT A STORM, O'GALLY?
LOLA

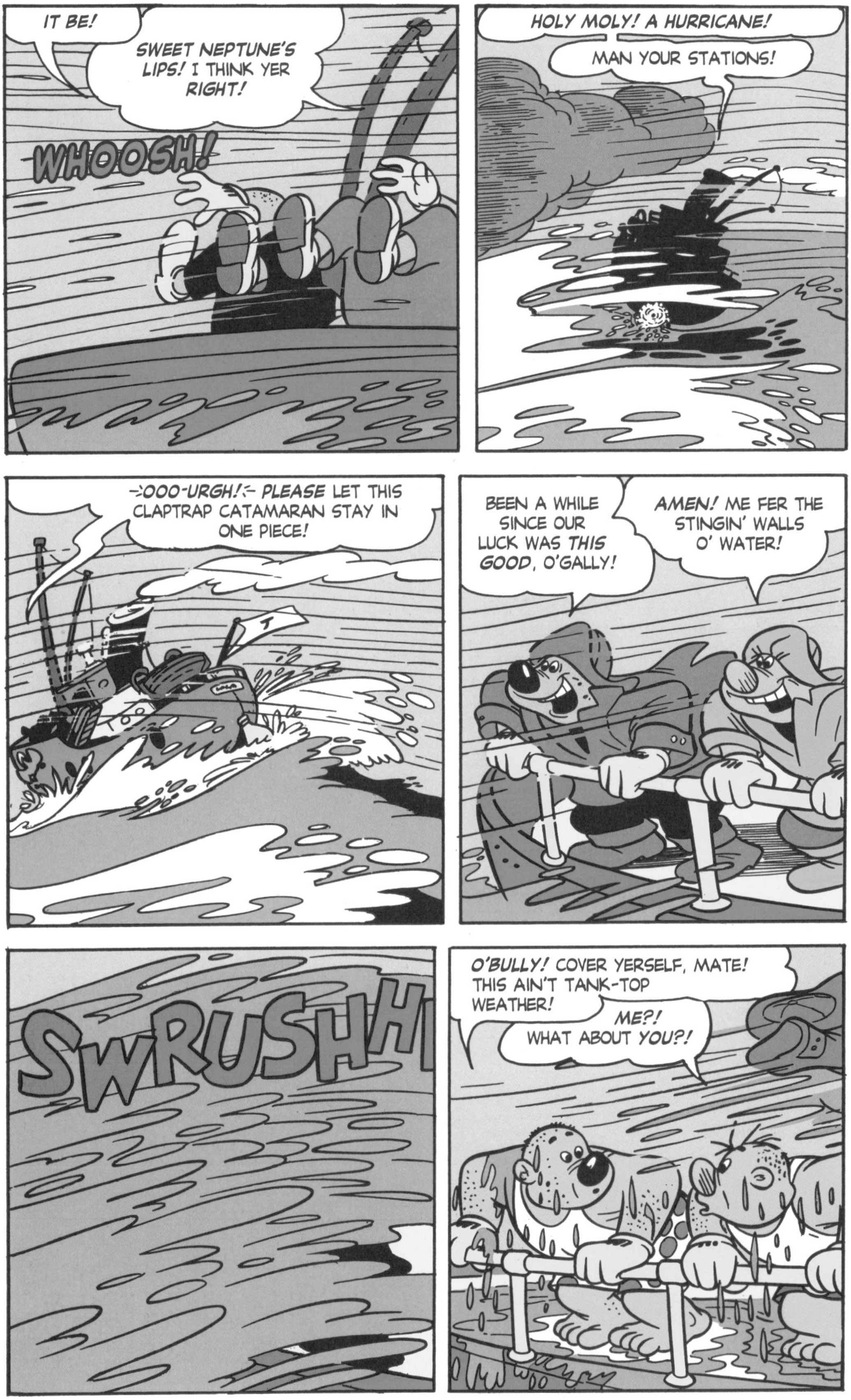

IT BE!
SWEET NEPTUNE'S LIPS! I THINK YER RIGHT!
WHOOSH!
HOLY MOLY! A HURRICANE!
MAN YOUR STATIONS!
-OOO-URGH!- PLEASE LET THIS CLAPTRAP CATAMARAN STAY IN ONE PIECE!
BEEN A WHILE SINCE OUR LUCK WAS THIS GOOD, O'GALLY!
AMEN! ME FER THE STINGIN' WALLS O' WATER!
SWRUSHH
O'BULLY! COVER YERSELF, MATE! THIS AIN'T TANK-TOP WEATHER!
ME?! WHAT ABOUT YOU?!

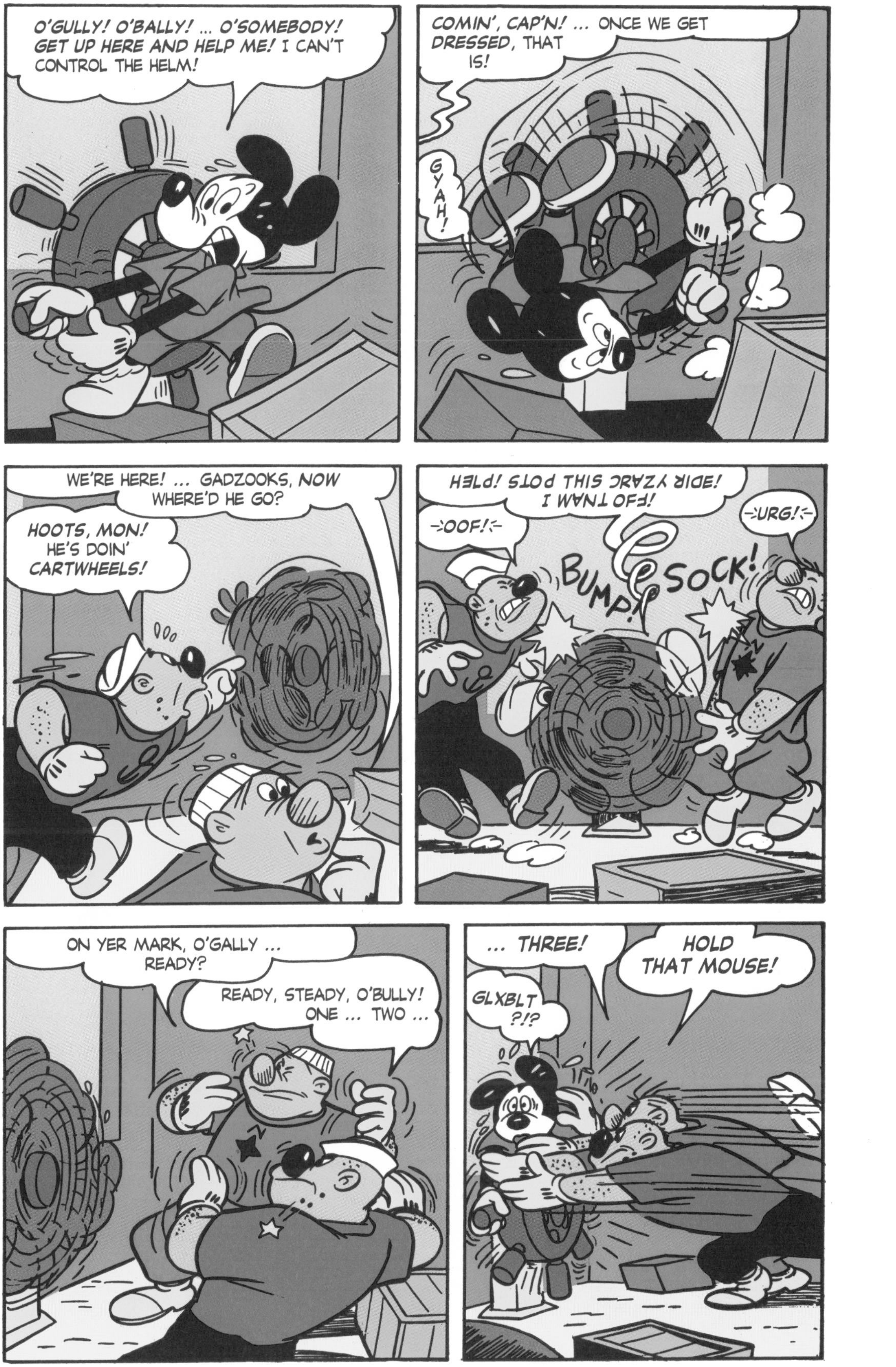
O'GULLY! O'BALLY! ... O'SOMEBODY! GET UP HERE AND HELP ME! I CAN'T CONTROL THE HELM!
COMIN', CAP'N! ... ONCE WE GET DRESSED, THAT IS!
GYAH!
WE'RE HERE! ... GADZOOKS, NOW WHERE'D HE GO?
HOOTS, MON! HE'S DOIN' CARTWHEELS!
HELP! STOP THIS CRAZY RIDE! I WANT OFF!
-OOF!-
-URG!-
BUMP!
SOCK!
ON YER MARK, O'GALLY ... READY?
READY, STEADY, O'BULLY! ONE ... TWO ...
... THREE!
HOLD THAT MOUSE!
GLXBLT ?!?

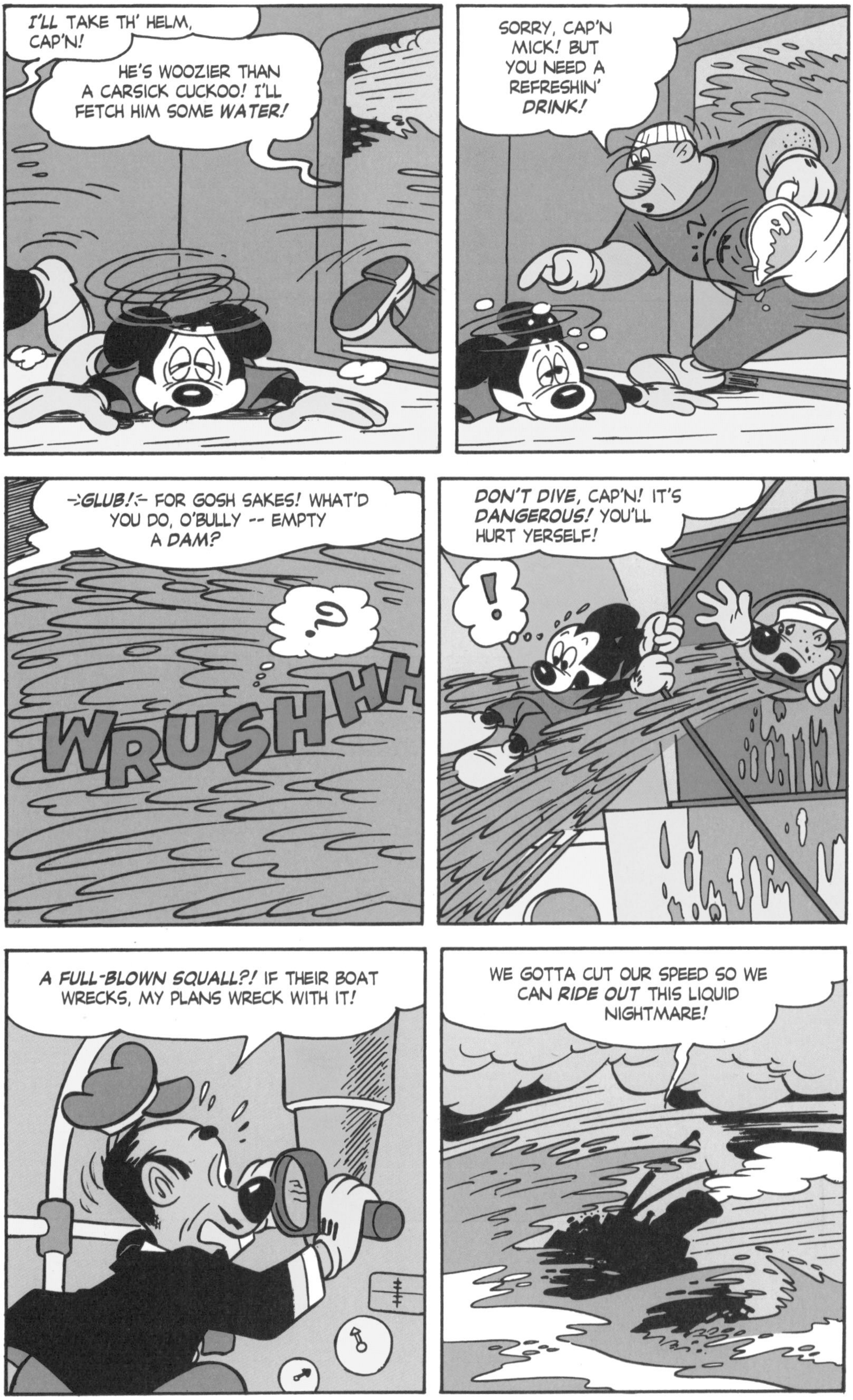

I'LL TAKE TH' HELM, CAP'N!
HE'S WOOZIER THAN A CARSICK CUCKOO! I'LL FETCH HIM SOME WATER!
SORRY, CAP'N MICK! BUT YOU NEED A REFRESHIN' DRINK!
-GLUB!- FOR GOSH SAKES! WHAT'D YOU DO, O'BULLY -- EMPTY A DAM?
?
WRUSHHH
DON'T DIVE, CAP'N! IT'S DANGEROUS! YOU'LL HURT YERSELF!
!
A FULL-BLOWN SQUALL?! IF THEIR BOAT WRECKS, MY PLANS WRECK WITH IT!
WE GOTTA CUT OUR SPEED SO WE CAN RIDE OUT THIS LIQUID NIGHTMARE!

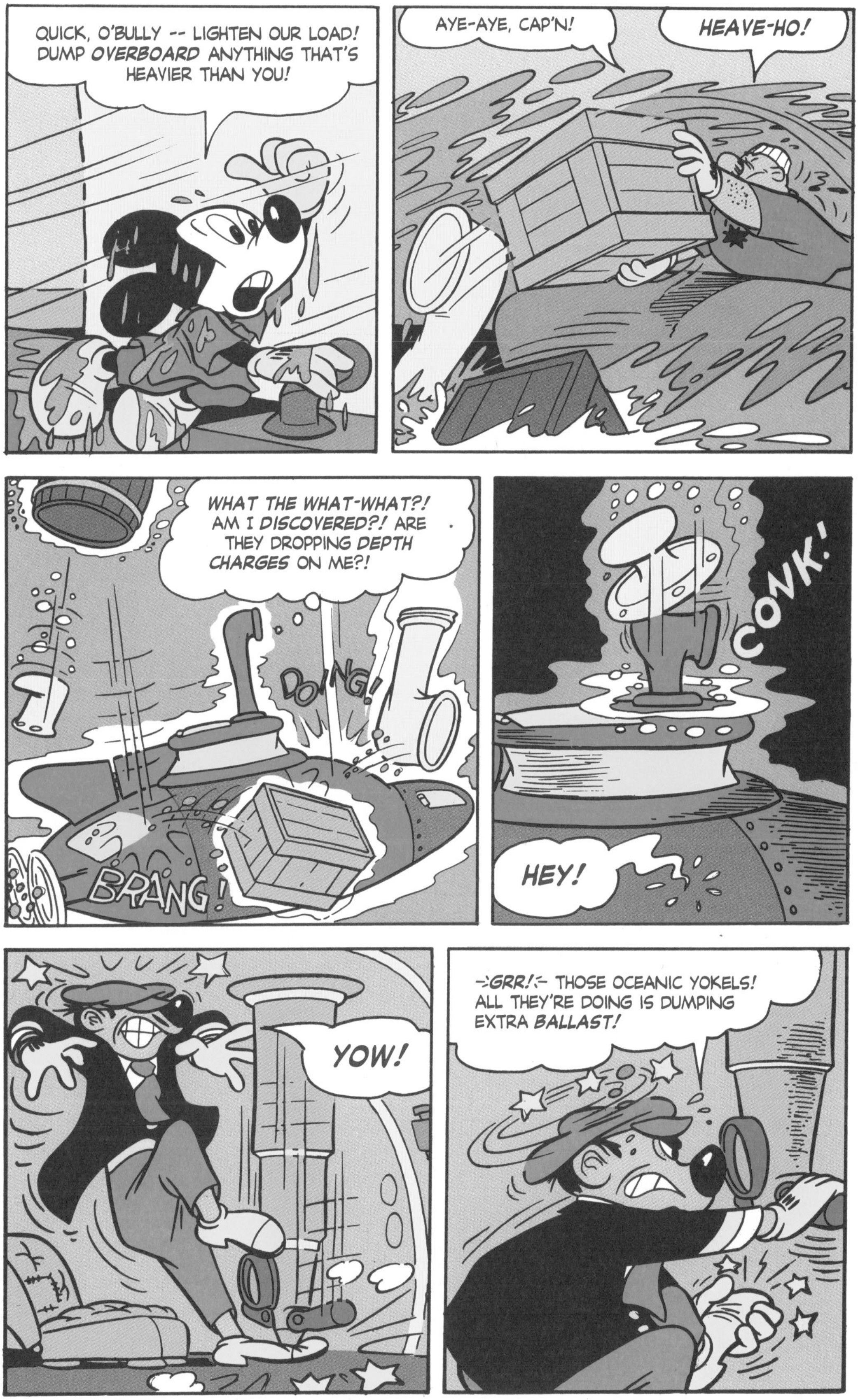
QUICK, O'BULLY -- LIGHTEN OUR LOAD! DUMP OVERBOARD ANYTHING THAT'S HEAVIER THAN YOU!
AYE-AYE, CAP'N!
HEAVE-HO!
WHAT THE WHAT-WHAT?! AM I DISCOVERED?! ARE THEY DROPPING DEPTH CHARGES ON ME?!
DOING!
BRANG!
CONK!
HEY!
YOW!
-GRR!- THOSE OCEANIC YOKELS! ALL THEY'RE DOING IS DUMPING EXTRA BALLAST!

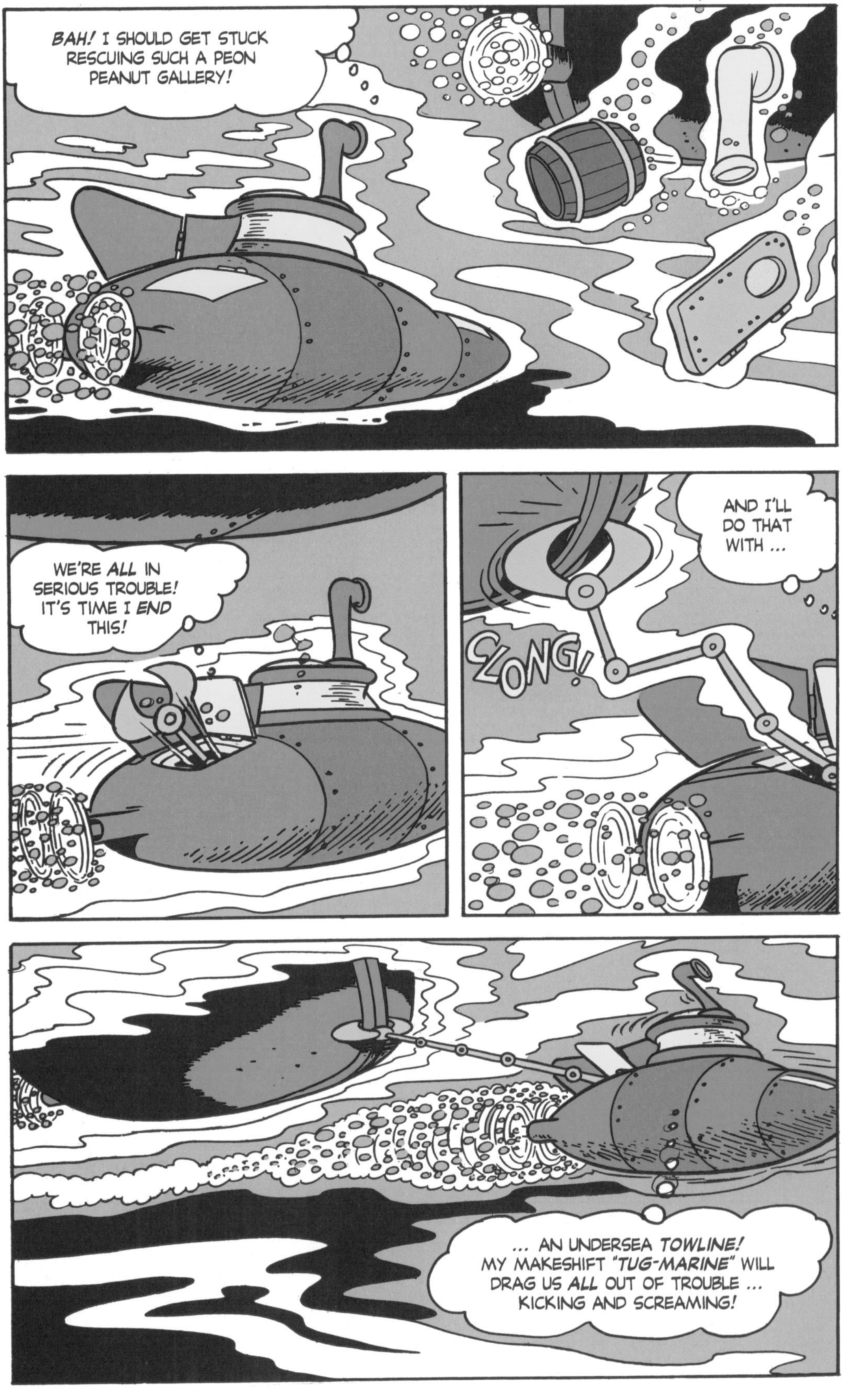
BAH! I SHOULD GET STUCK RESCUING SUCH A PEON PEANUT GALLERY!
WE'RE ALL IN SERIOUS TROUBLE! IT'S TIME I END THIS!
AND I'LL DO THAT WITH ...
CLONG!
... AN UNDERSEA TOWLINE! MY MAKESHIFT "TUG-MARINE" WILL DRAG US ALL OUT OF TROUBLE ... KICKING AND SCREAMING!

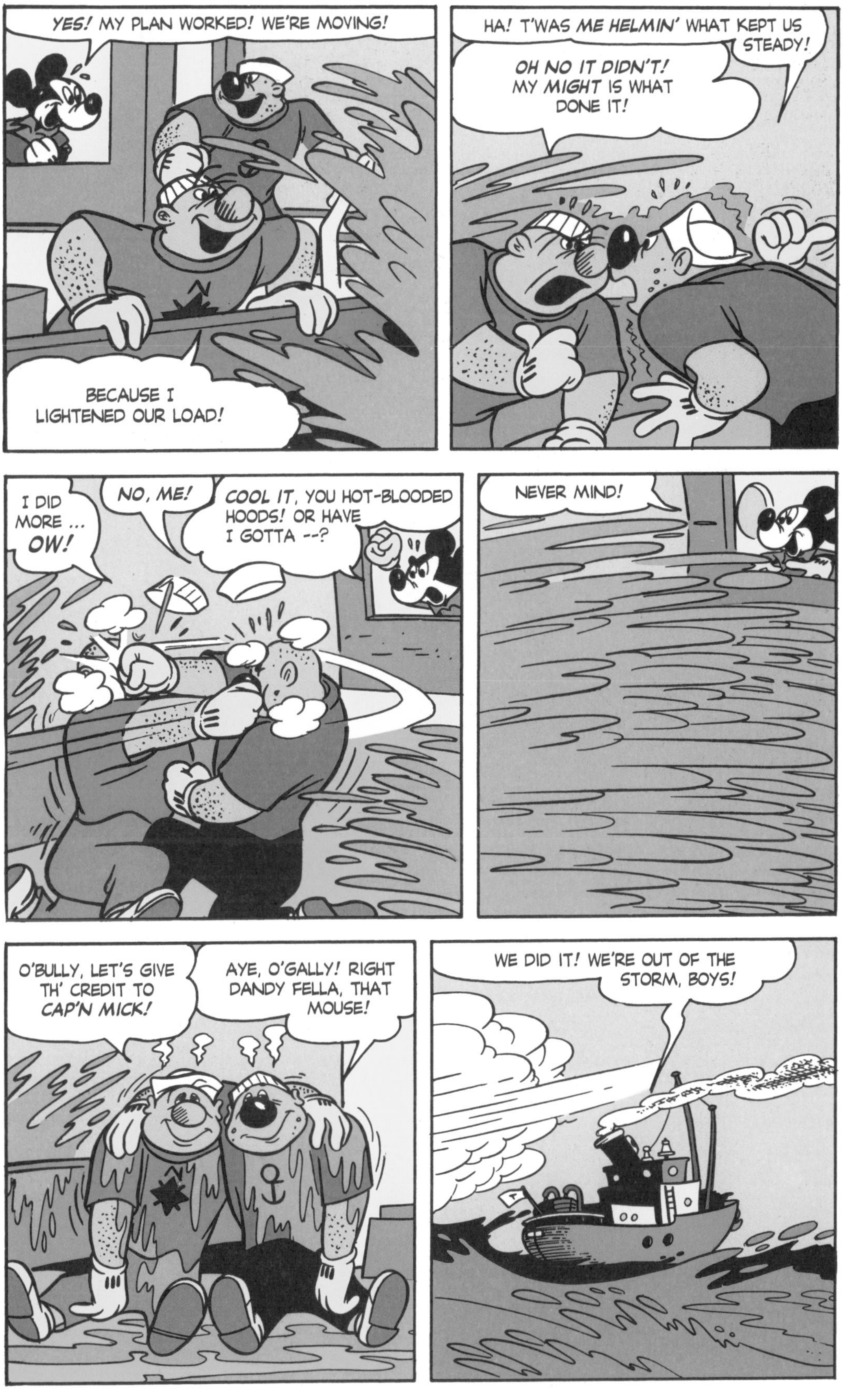
YES! MY PLAN WORKED! WE'RE MOVING!
BECAUSE I LIGHTENED OUR LOAD!
HA! T'WAS ME HELMIN' WHAT KEPT US STEADY!
OH NO IT DIDN'T! MY MIGHT IS WHAT DONE IT!
I DID MORE ... OW!
NO, ME!
COOL IT, YOU HOT-BLOODED HOODS! OR HAVE I GOTTA --?
NEVER MIND!
O'BULLY, LET'S GIVE TH' CREDIT TO CAP'N MICK!
AYE, O'GALLY! RIGHT DANDY FELLA, THAT MOUSE!
WE DID IT! WE'RE OUT OF THE STORM, BOYS!

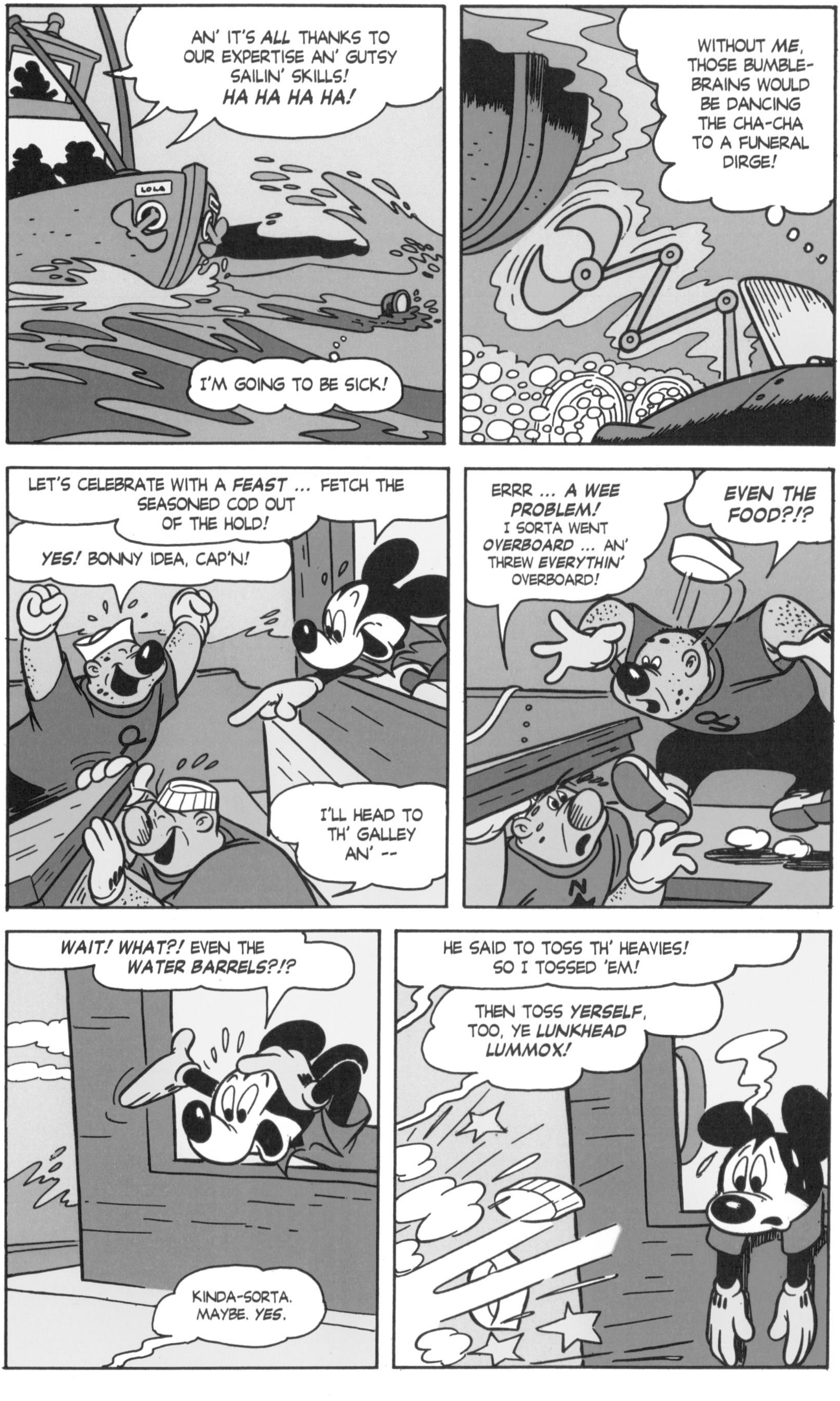
AN' IT'S ALL THANKS TO OUR EXPERTISE AN' GUTSY SAILIN' SKILLS! HA HA HA HA!
I'M GOING TO BE SICK!
WITHOUT ME, THOSE BUMBLE-BRAINS WOULD BE DANCING THE CHA-CHA TO A FUNERAL DIRGE!
LET'S CELEBRATE WITH A FEAST ... FETCH THE SEASONED COD OUT OF THE HOLD!
YES! BONNY IDEA, CAP'N!
I'LL HEAD TO TH' GALLEY AN' --
ERRR ... A WEE PROBLEM! I SORTA WENT OVERBOARD ... AN' THREW EVERYTHIN' OVERBOARD!
EVEN THE FOOD?!?
WAIT! WHAT?! EVEN THE WATER BARRELS?!?
KINDA-SORTA. MAYBE. YES.
HE SAID TO TOSS TH' HEAVIES! SO I TOSSED 'EM!
THEN TOSS YERSELF, TOO, YE LUNKHEAD LUMMOX!

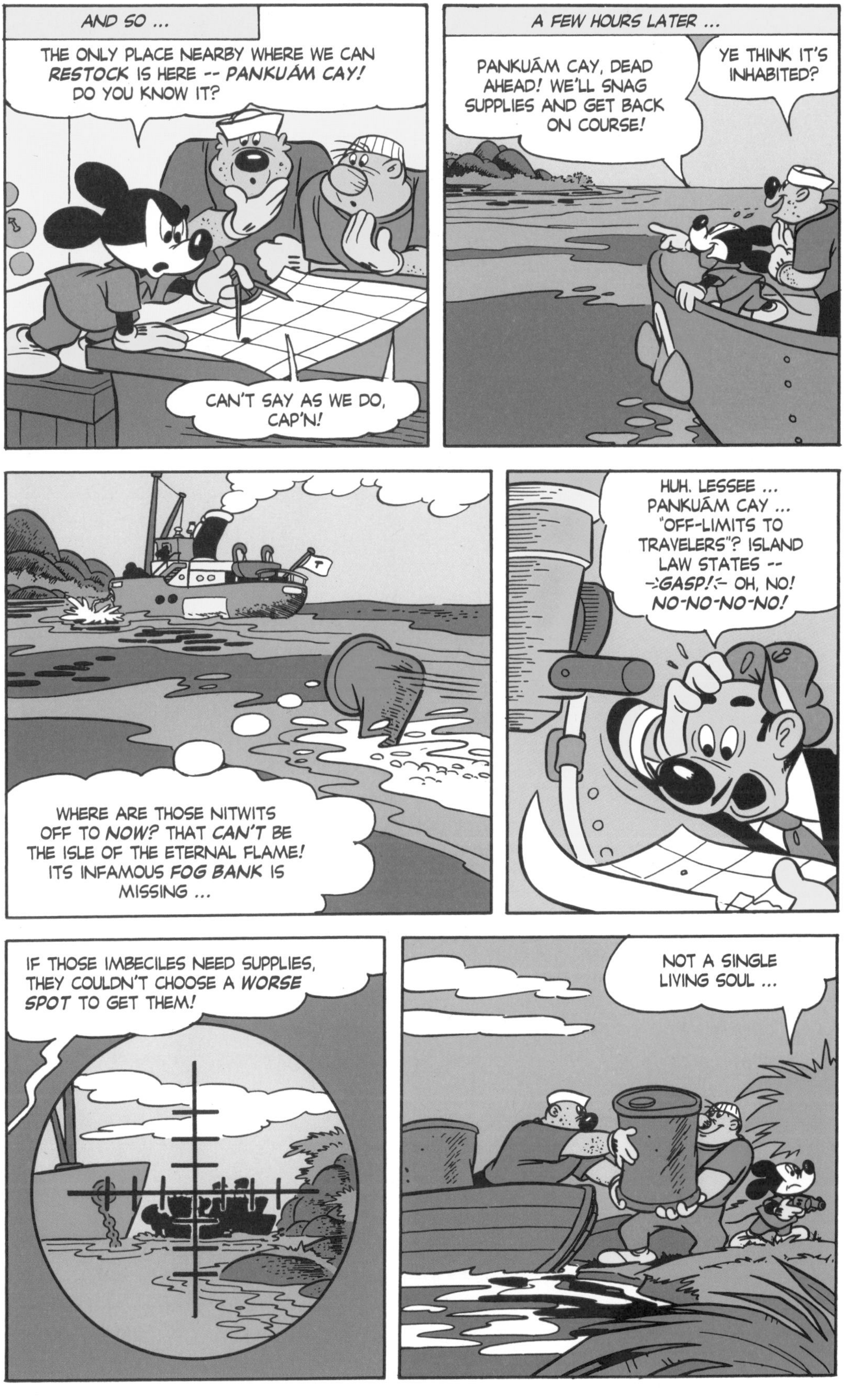
AND SO ...
THE ONLY PLACE NEARBY WHERE WE CAN RESTOCK IS HERE -- PANKUÁM CAY! DO YOU KNOW IT?
CAN'T SAY AS WE DO, CAP'N!
A FEW HOURS LATER ...
PANKUÁM CAY, DEAD AHEAD! WE'LL SNAG SUPPLIES AND GET BACK ON COURSE!
YE THINK IT'S INHABITED?
WHERE ARE THOSE NITWITS OFF TO NOW? THAT CAN'T BE THE ISLE OF THE ETERNAL FLAME! ITS INFAMOUS FOG BANK IS MISSING ...
HUH. LESSEE ... PANKUÁM CAY ... "OFF-LIMITS TO TRAVELERS"? ISLAND LAW STATES -- -GASP!- OH, NO! NO-NO-NO-NO!
IF THOSE IMBECILES NEED SUPPLIES, THEY COULDN'T CHOOSE A WORSE SPOT TO GET THEM!
NOT A SINGLE LIVING SOUL ...

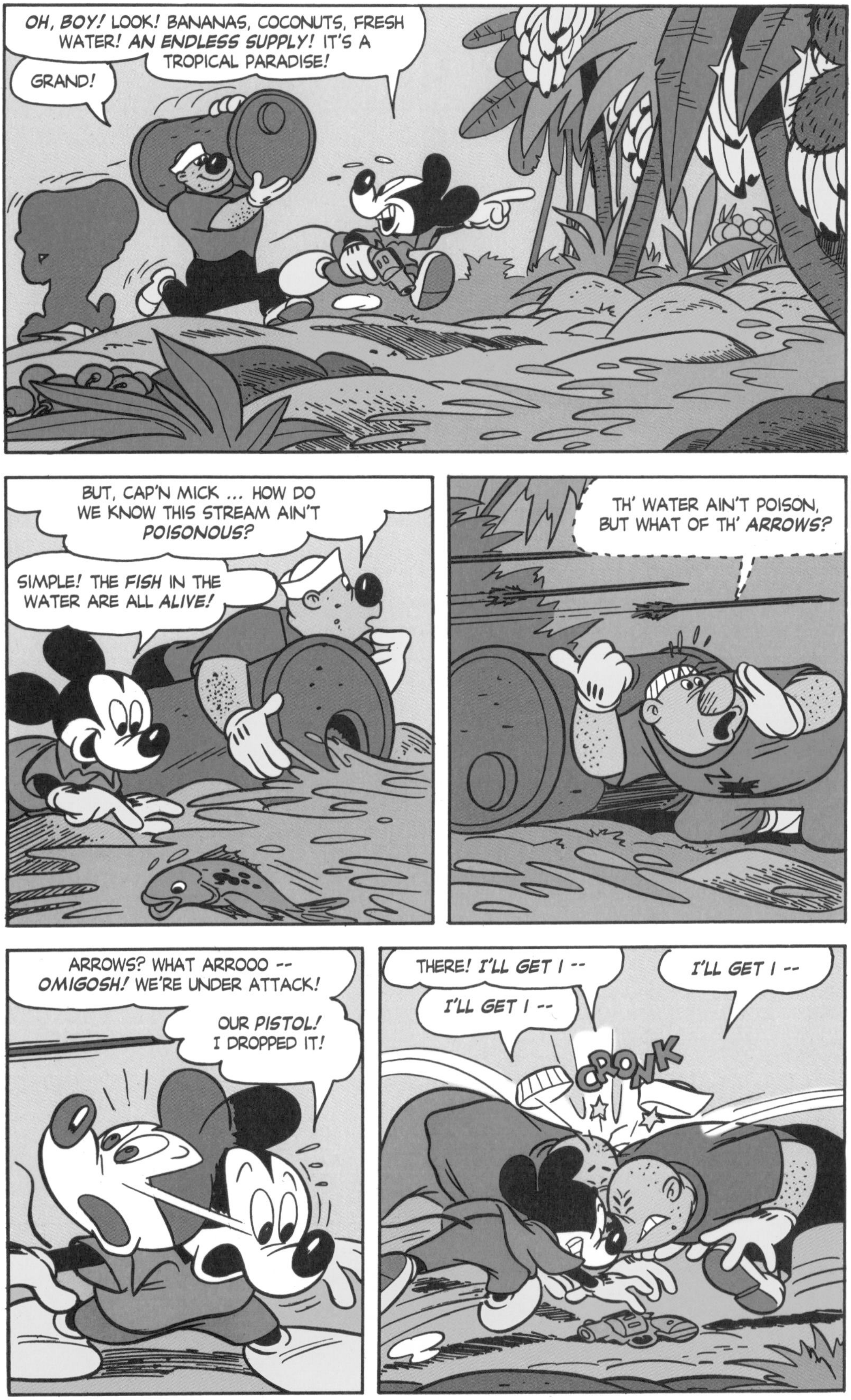
OH, BOY! LOOK! BANANAS, COCONUTS, FRESH WATER! AN ENDLESS SUPPLY! IT'S A TROPICAL PARADISE!
GRAND!
BUT, CAP'N MICK ... HOW DO WE KNOW THIS STREAM AIN'T POISONOUS?
SIMPLE! THE FISH IN THE WATER ARE ALL ALIVE!
TH' WATER AIN'T POISON, BUT WHAT OF TH' ARROWS?
ARROWS? WHAT ARROOO -- OMIGOSH! WE'RE UNDER ATTACK!
OUR PISTOL! I DROPPED IT!
THERE! I'LL GET I --
I'LL GET I --
I'LL GET I --
CRONK

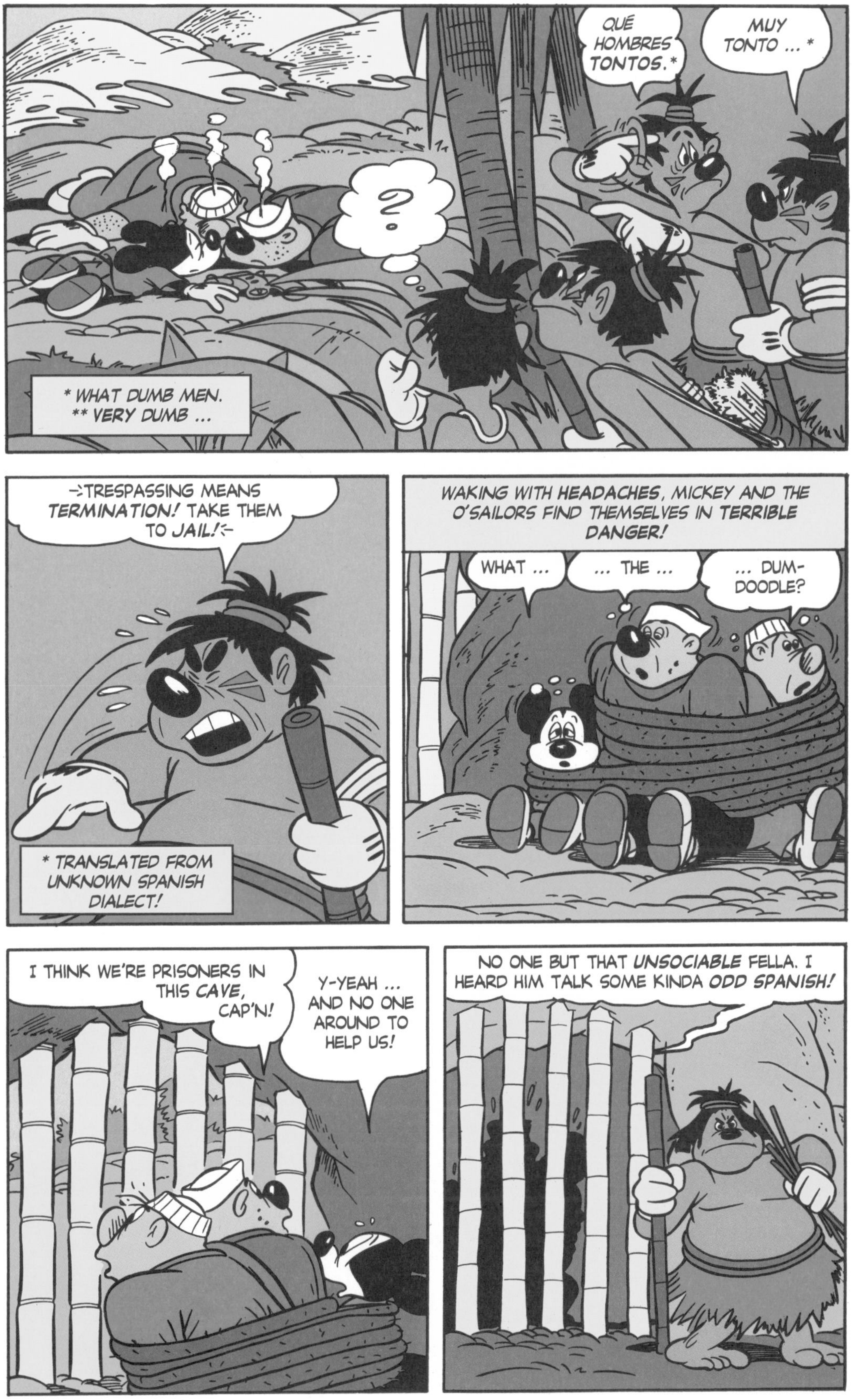
QUÉ HOMBRES TONTOS.*
MUY TONTO ... *
* WHAT DUMB MEN.
** VERY DUMB ...
-TRESPASSING MEANS TERMINATION! TAKE THEM TO JAIL!-
* TRANSLATED FROM UNKNOWN SPANISH DIALECT!
WAKING WITH HEADACHES, MICKEY AND THE O'SAILORS FIND THEMSELVES IN TERRIBLE DANGER!
WHAT ...
... THE ...
... DUM-DOODLE?
I THINK WE'RE PRISONERS IN THIS CAVE, CAP'N!
Y-YEAH ... AND NO ONE AROUND TO HELP US!
NO ONE BUT THAT UNSOCIABLE FELLA. I HEARD HIM TALK SOME KINDA ODD SPANISH!

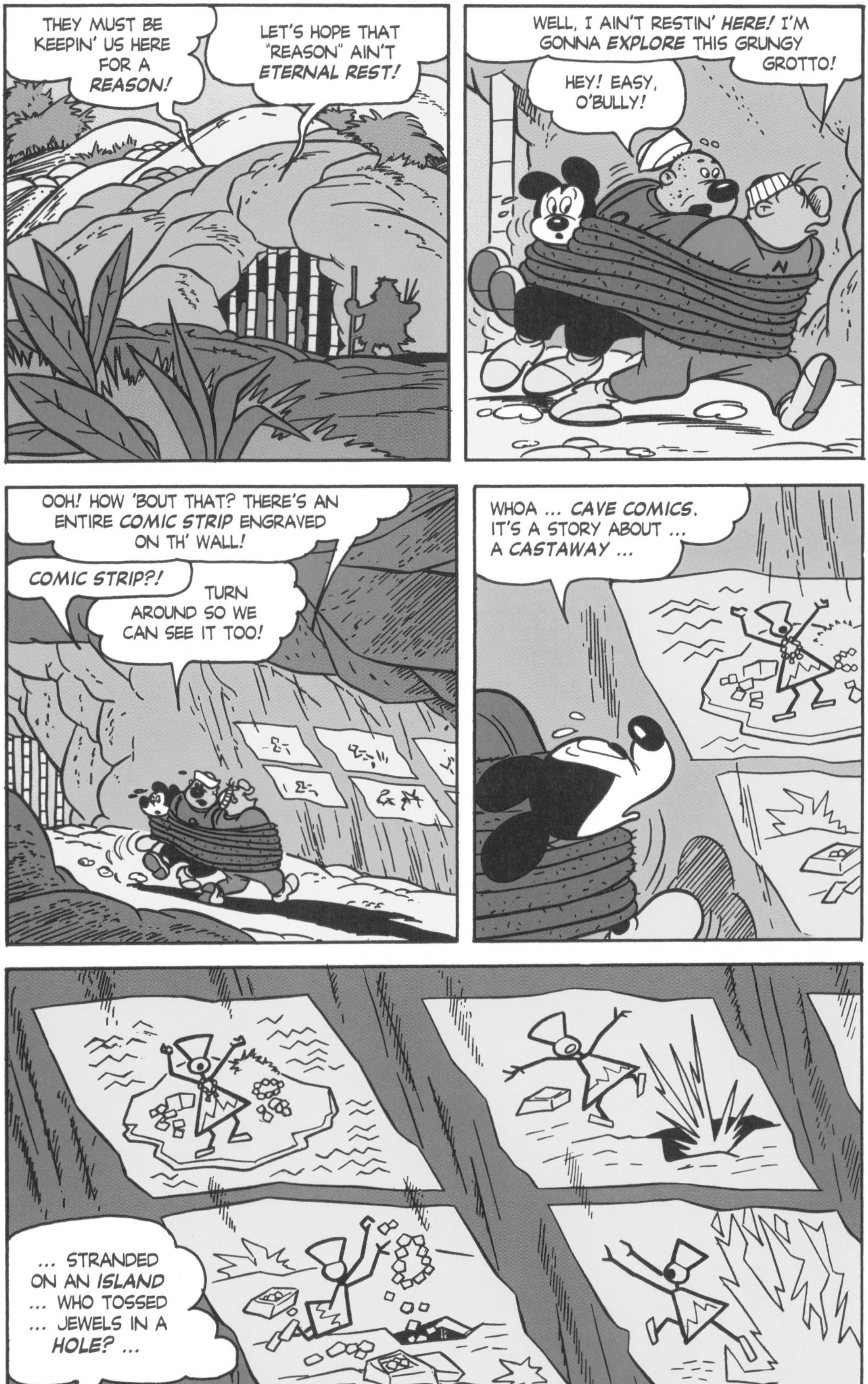
THEY MUST BE KEEPIN' US HERE FOR A *REASON!*
LET'S HOPE THAT "REASON" AIN'T *ETERNAL REST!*
WELL, I AIN'T RESTIN' *HERE!* I'M GONNA *EXPLORE* THIS GRUNGY GROTTO!
HEY! EASY, O'BULLY!
OOH! HOW 'BOUT THAT? THERE'S AN ENTIRE *COMIC STRIP* ENGRAVED ON TH' WALL!
COMIC STRIP?!
TURN AROUND SO WE CAN SEE IT TOO!
WHOA ... *CAVE COMICS.* IT'S A STORY ABOUT ... A *CASTAWAY* ...
... STRANDED ON AN *ISLAND* ... WHO TOSSED ... JEWELS IN A *HOLE?* ...

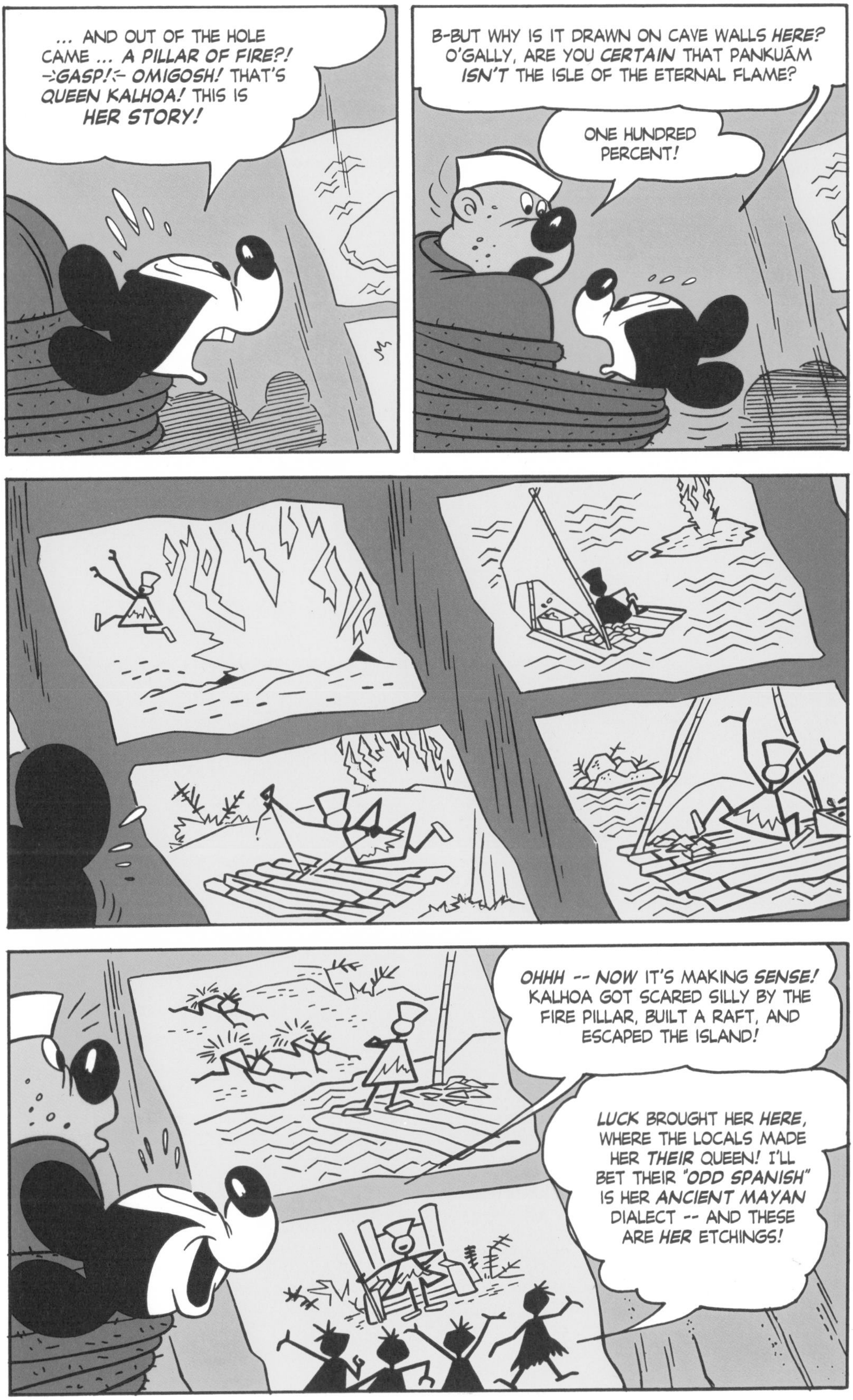
... AND OUT OF THE HOLE CAME ... A PILLAR OF FIRE?! -GASP!- OMIGOSH! THAT'S QUEEN KALHOA! THIS IS HER STORY!
B-BUT WHY IS IT DRAWN ON CAVE WALLS HERE? O'GALLY, ARE YOU CERTAIN THAT PANKUĀM ISN'T THE ISLE OF THE ETERNAL FLAME?
ONE HUNDRED PERCENT!
OHHH -- NOW IT'S MAKING SENSE! KALHOA GOT SCARED SILLY BY THE FIRE PILLAR, BUILT A RAFT, AND ESCAPED THE ISLAND!
LUCK BROUGHT HER HERE, WHERE THE LOCALS MADE HER THEIR QUEEN! I'LL BET THEIR "ODD SPANISH" IS HER ANCIENT MAYAN DIALECT -- AND THESE ARE HER ETCHINGS!

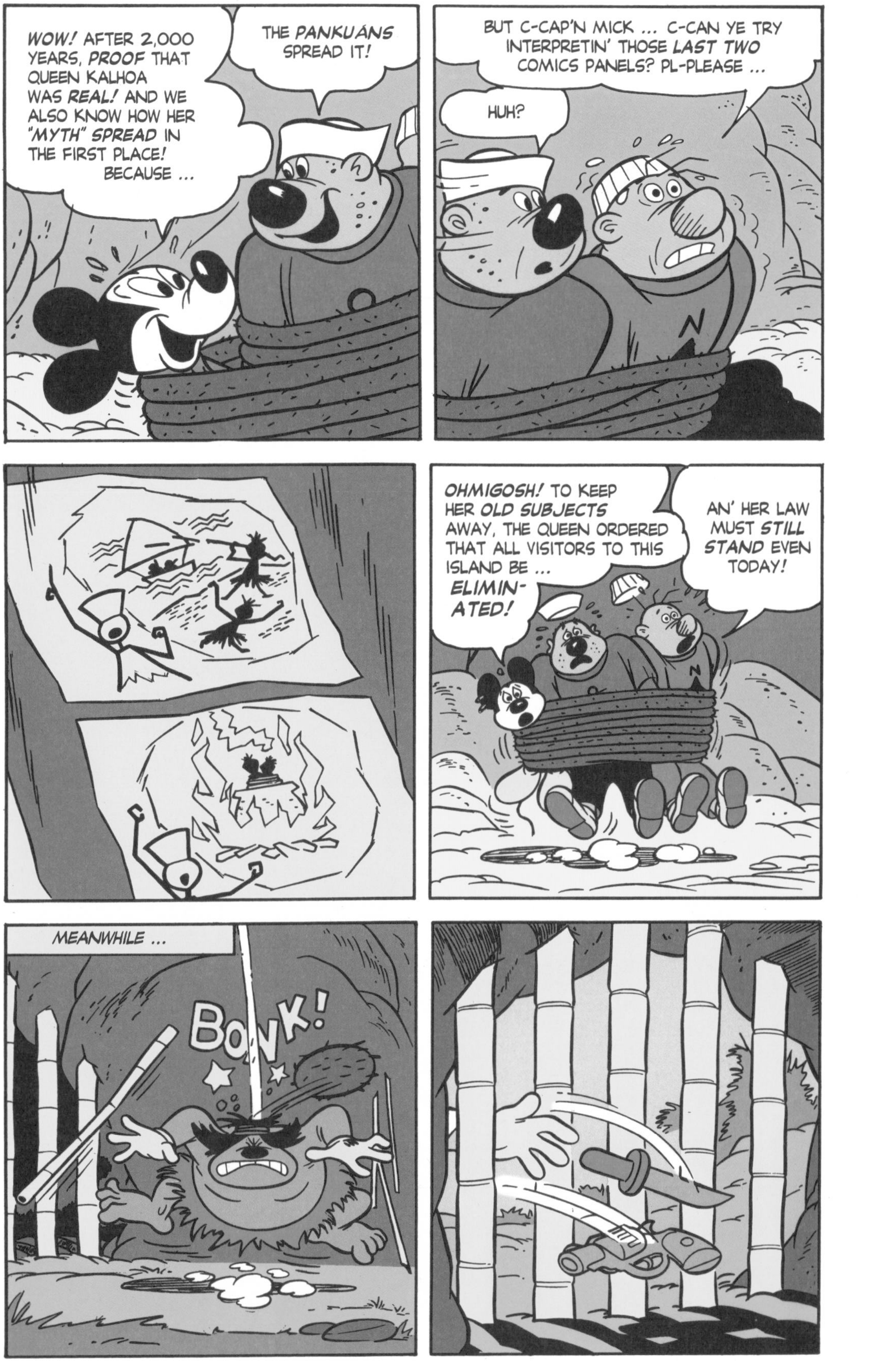

WOW! AFTER 2,000 YEARS, PROOF THAT QUEEN KALHOA WAS REAL! AND WE ALSO KNOW HOW HER "MYTH" SPREAD IN THE FIRST PLACE! BECAUSE ...
THE PANKUANS SPREAD IT!
BUT C-CAP'N MICK ... C-CAN YE TRY INTERPRETIN' THOSE LAST TWO COMICS PANELS? PL-PLEASE ...
HUH?
OHMIGOSH! TO KEEP HER OLD SUBJECTS AWAY, THE QUEEN ORDERED THAT ALL VISITORS TO THIS ISLAND BE ... ELIMIN-ATED!
AN' HER LAW MUST STILL STAND EVEN TODAY!
MEANWHILE ...
BONK!

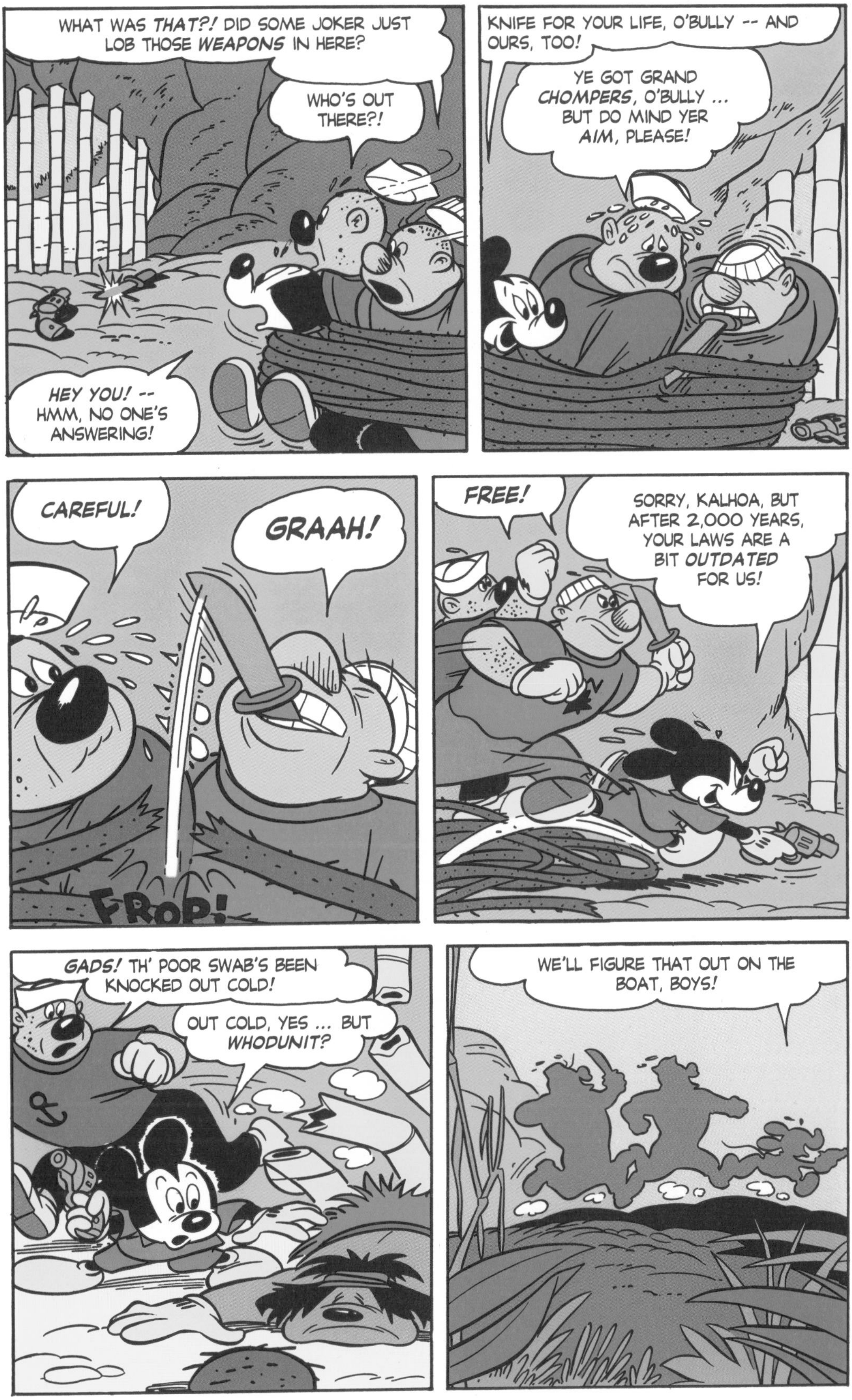
WHAT WAS THAT?! DID SOME JOKER JUST LOB THOSE WEAPONS IN HERE?
WHO'S OUT THERE?!
HEY YOU! -- HMM, NO ONE'S ANSWERING!
KNIFE FOR YOUR LIFE, O'BULLY -- AND OURS, TOO!
YE GOT GRAND CHOMPERS, O'BULLY ... BUT DO MIND YER AIM, PLEASE!
CAREFUL!
GRAAH!
FROP!
FREE!
SORRY, KALHOA, BUT AFTER 2,000 YEARS, YOUR LAWS ARE A BIT OUTDATED FOR US!
GADS! TH' POOR SWAB'S BEEN KNOCKED OUT COLD!
OUT COLD, YES ... BUT WHODUNIT?
WE'LL FIGURE THAT OUT ON THE BOAT, BOYS!

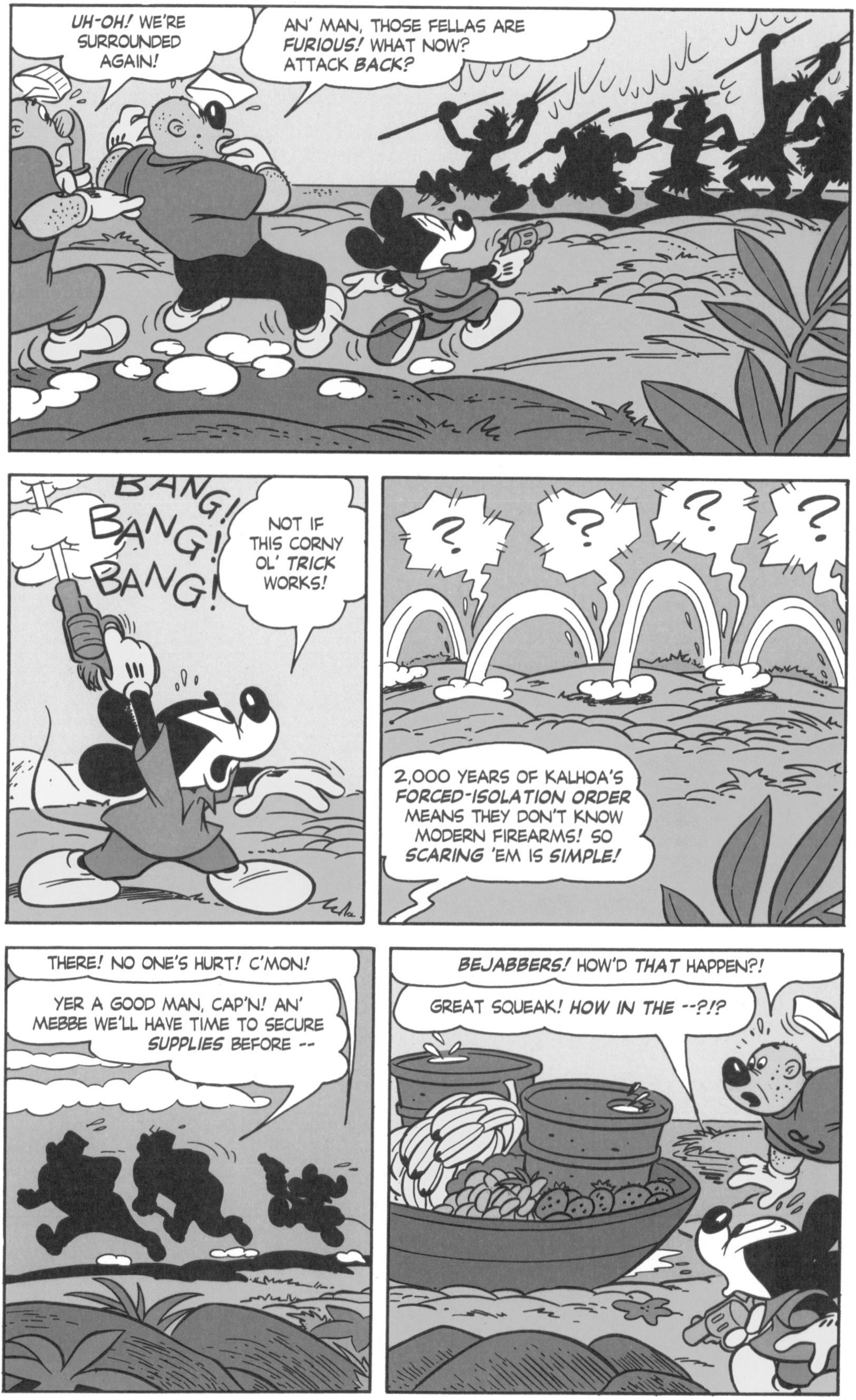
UH-OH! WE'RE SURROUNDED AGAIN!
AN' MAN, THOSE FELLAS ARE FURIOUS! WHAT NOW? ATTACK BACK?
BANG! BANG! BANG!
NOT IF THIS CORNY OL' TRICK WORKS!
? ? ? ?
2,000 YEARS OF KALHOA'S FORCED-ISOLATION ORDER MEANS THEY DON'T KNOW MODERN FIREARMS! SO SCARING 'EM IS SIMPLE!
THERE! NO ONE'S HURT! C'MON!
YER A GOOD MAN, CAP'N! AN' MEBBE WE'LL HAVE TIME TO SECURE SUPPLIES BEFORE --
BEJABBERS! HOW'D THAT HAPPEN?!
GREAT SQUEAK! HOW IN THE --?!?

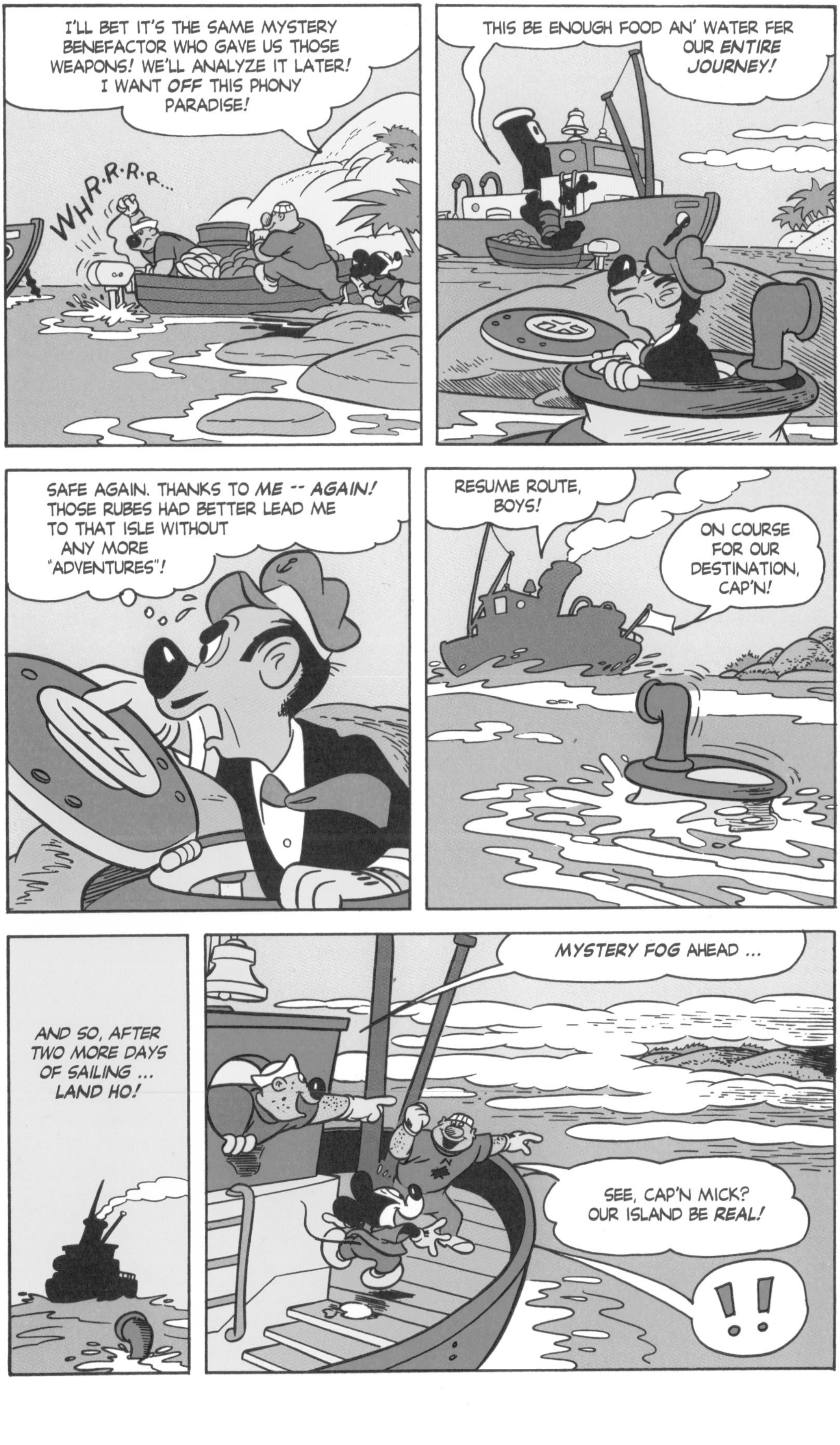
I'LL BET IT'S THE SAME MYSTERY BENEFACTOR WHO GAVE US THOSE WEAPONS! WE'LL ANALYZE IT LATER! I WANT OFF THIS PHONY PARADISE!
WHR-R-R-R...
THIS BE ENOUGH FOOD AN' WATER FER OUR ENTIRE JOURNEY!
SAFE AGAIN. THANKS TO ME -- AGAIN! THOSE RUBES HAD BETTER LEAD ME TO THAT ISLE WITHOUT ANY MORE "ADVENTURES"!
RESUME ROUTE, BOYS!
ON COURSE FOR OUR DESTINATION, CAP'N!
AND SO, AFTER TWO MORE DAYS OF SAILING ... LAND HO!
MYSTERY FOG AHEAD ...
SEE, CAP'N MICK? OUR ISLAND BE REAL!
!!

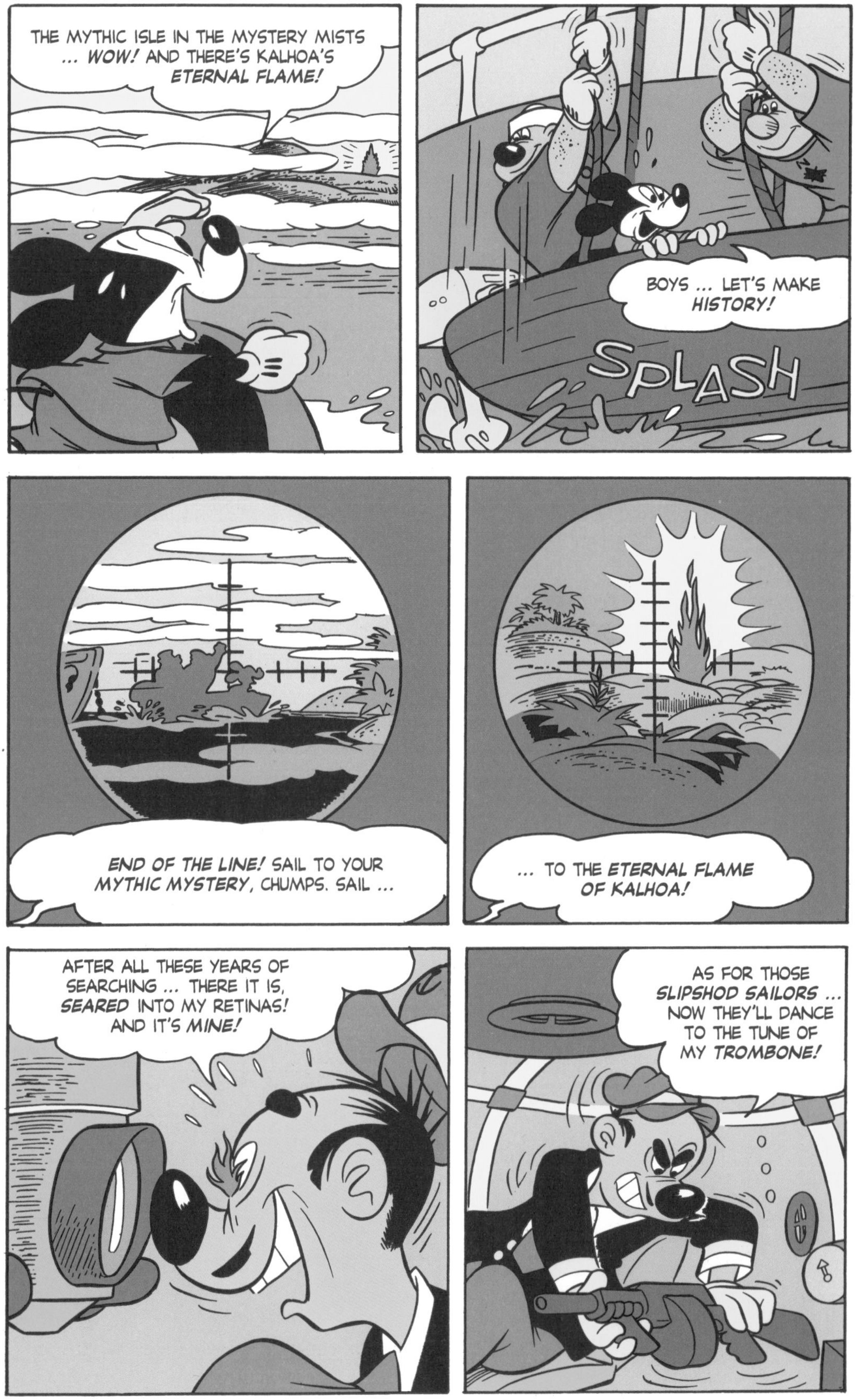
THE MYTHIC ISLE IN THE MYSTERY MISTS ... WOW! AND THERE'S KALHOA'S ETERNAL FLAME!
BOYS ... LET'S MAKE HISTORY!
SPLASH
END OF THE LINE! SAIL TO YOUR MYTHIC MYSTERY, CHUMPS. SAIL ...
... TO THE ETERNAL FLAME OF KALHOA!
AFTER ALL THESE YEARS OF SEARCHING ... THERE IT IS, SEARED INTO MY RETINAS! AND IT'S MINE!
AS FOR THOSE SLIPSHOD SAILORS ... NOW THEY'LL DANCE TO THE TUNE OF MY TROMBONE!

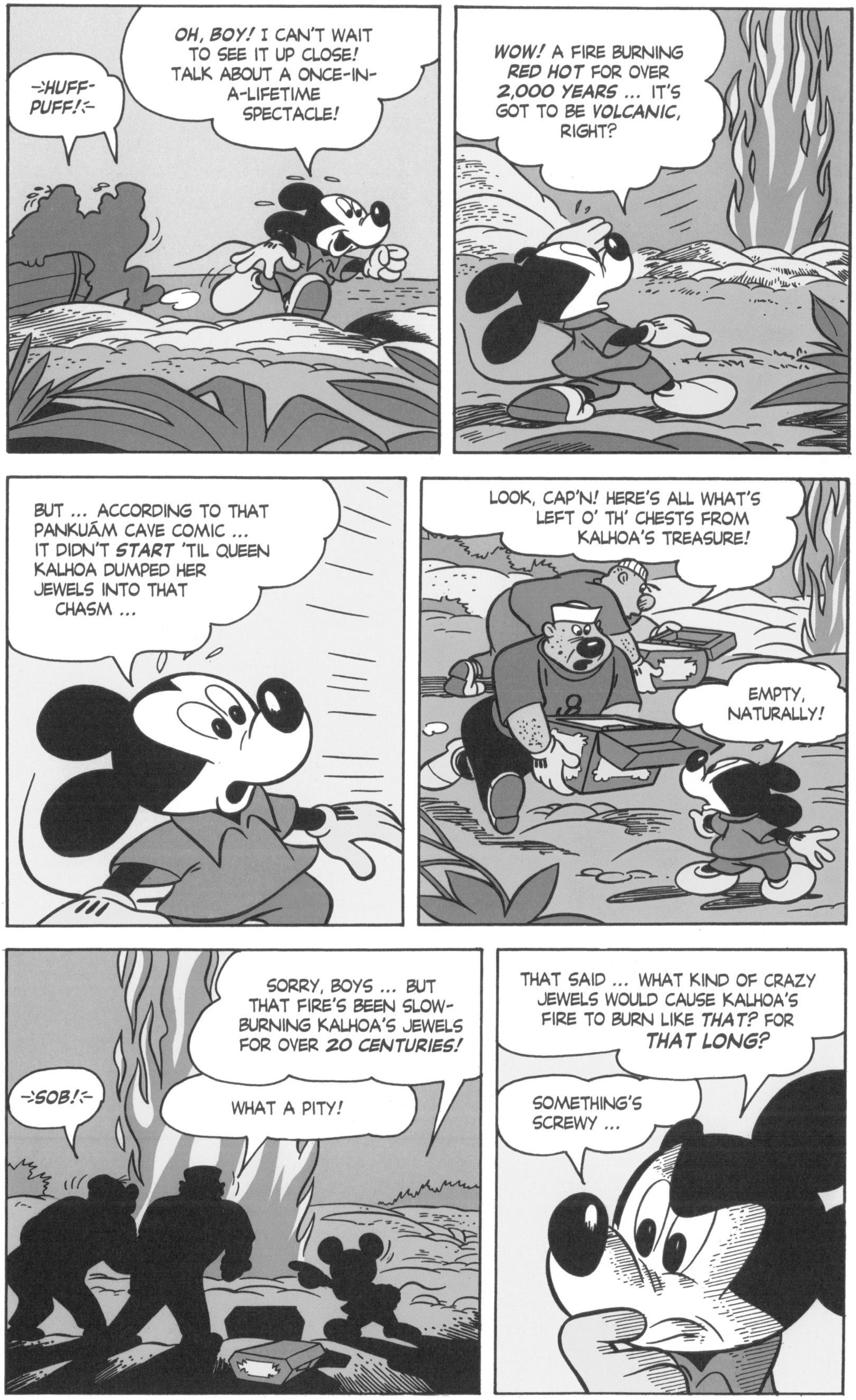
-HUFF- PUFF!-
OH, BOY! I CAN'T WAIT TO SEE IT UP CLOSE! TALK ABOUT A ONCE-IN-A-LIFETIME SPECTACLE!
WOW! A FIRE BURNING RED HOT FOR OVER 2,000 YEARS ... IT'S GOT TO BE VOLCANIC, RIGHT?
BUT ... ACCORDING TO THAT PANKUÁM CAVE COMIC ... IT DIDN'T START 'TIL QUEEN KALHOA DUMPED HER JEWELS INTO THAT CHASM ...
LOOK, CAP'N! HERE'S ALL WHAT'S LEFT O' TH' CHESTS FROM KALHOA'S TREASURE!
EMPTY, NATURALLY!
SORRY, BOYS ... BUT THAT FIRE'S BEEN SLOW-BURNING KALHOA'S JEWELS FOR OVER 20 CENTURIES!
-SOB!-
WHAT A PITY!
THAT SAID ... WHAT KIND OF CRAZY JEWELS WOULD CAUSE KALHOA'S FIRE TO BURN LIKE THAT? FOR THAT LONG?
SOMETHING'S SCREWY ...

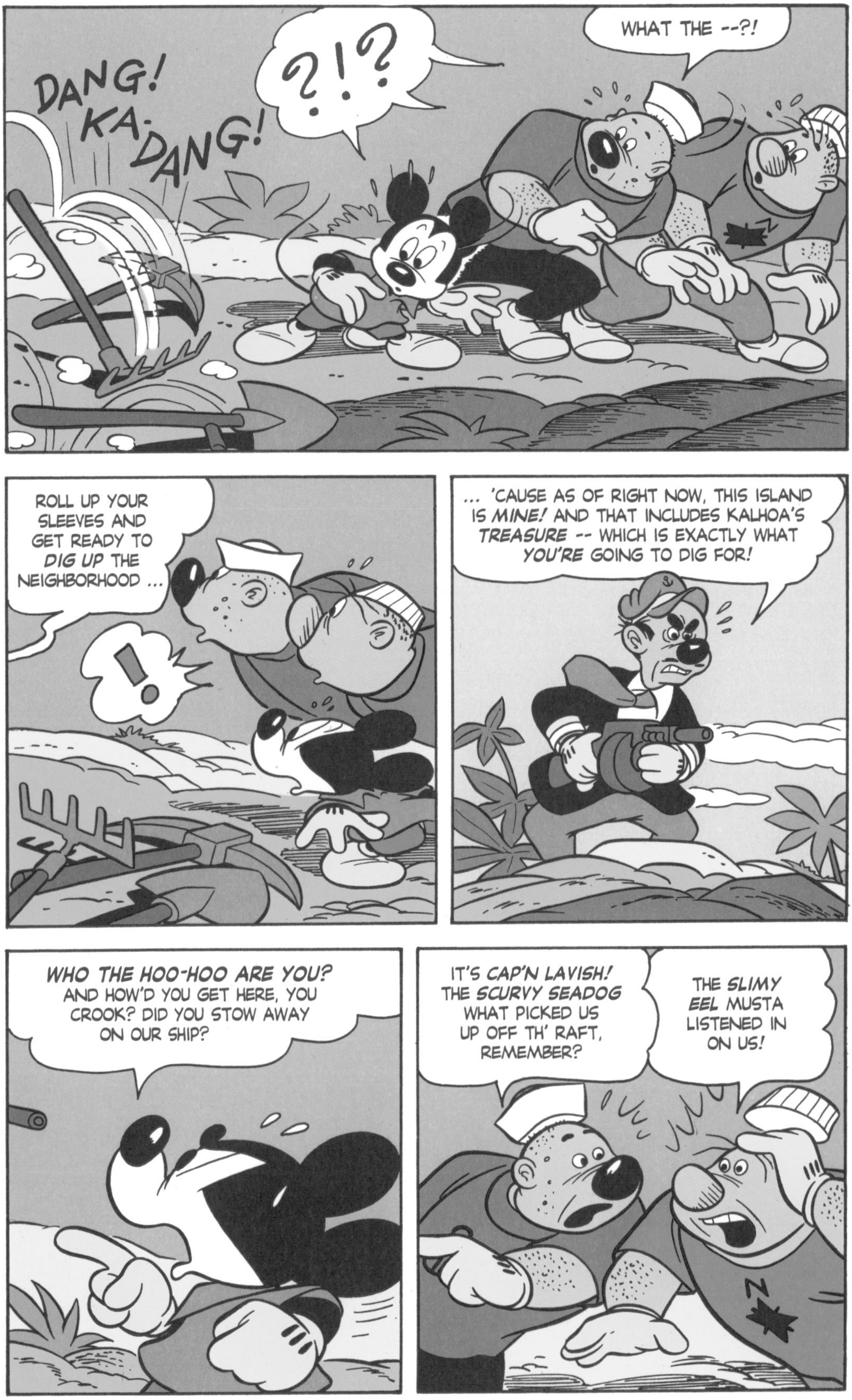
DANG! KA-DANG!
?!?
WHAT THE --?!
ROLL UP YOUR SLEEVES AND GET READY TO DIG UP THE NEIGHBORHOOD ...
!
... 'CAUSE AS OF RIGHT NOW, THIS ISLAND IS MINE! AND THAT INCLUDES KALHOA'S TREASURE -- WHICH IS EXACTLY WHAT YOU'RE GOING TO DIG FOR!
WHO THE HOO-HOO ARE YOU? AND HOW'D YOU GET HERE, YOU CROOK? DID YOU STOW AWAY ON OUR SHIP?
IT'S CAP'N LAVISH! THE SCURVY SEADOG WHAT PICKED US UP OFF TH' RAFT, REMEMBER?
THE SLIMY EEL MUSTA LISTENED IN ON US!

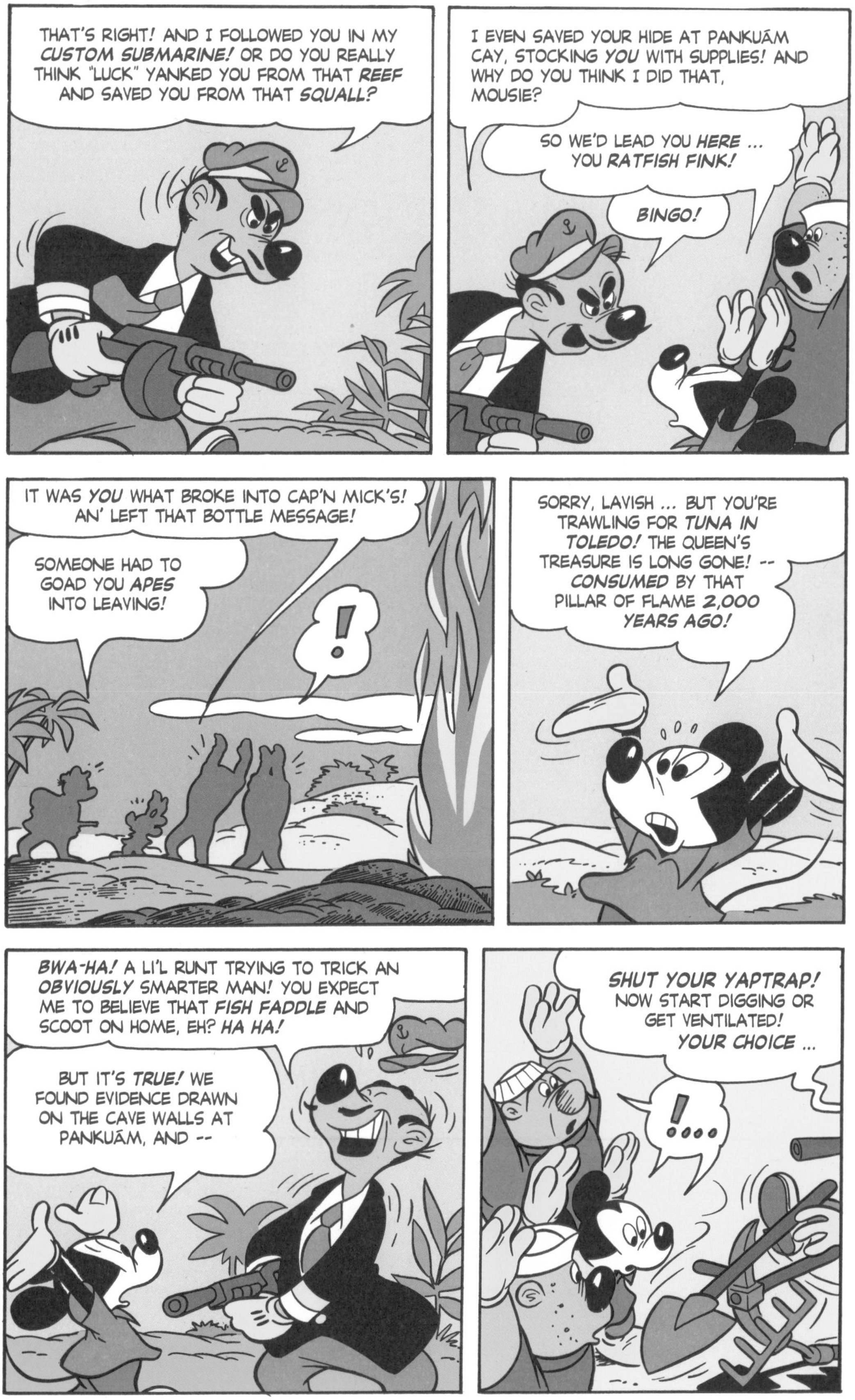
THAT'S RIGHT! AND I FOLLOWED YOU IN MY CUSTOM SUBMARINE! OR DO YOU REALLY THINK "LUCK" YANKED YOU FROM THAT REEF AND SAVED YOU FROM THAT SQUALL?
I EVEN SAVED YOUR HIDE AT PANKUÁM CAY, STOCKING YOU WITH SUPPLIES! AND WHY DO YOU THINK I DID THAT, MOUSIE?
SO WE'D LEAD YOU HERE ... YOU RATFISH FINK!
BINGO!
IT WAS YOU WHAT BROKE INTO CAP'N MICK'S! AN' LEFT THAT BOTTLE MESSAGE!
SOMEONE HAD TO GOAD YOU APES INTO LEAVING!
!
SORRY, LAVISH ... BUT YOU'RE TRAWLING FOR TUNA IN TOLEDO! THE QUEEN'S TREASURE IS LONG GONE! -- CONSUMED BY THAT PILLAR OF FLAME 2,000 YEARS AGO!
BWA-HA! A LI'L RUNT TRYING TO TRICK AN OBVIOUSLY SMARTER MAN! YOU EXPECT ME TO BELIEVE THAT FISH FADDLE AND SCOOT ON HOME, EH? HA HA!
BUT IT'S TRUE! WE FOUND EVIDENCE DRAWN ON THE CAVE WALLS AT PANKUÁM, AND --
SHUT YOUR YAPTRAP! NOW START DIGGING OR GET VENTILATED! YOUR CHOICE ...
!....

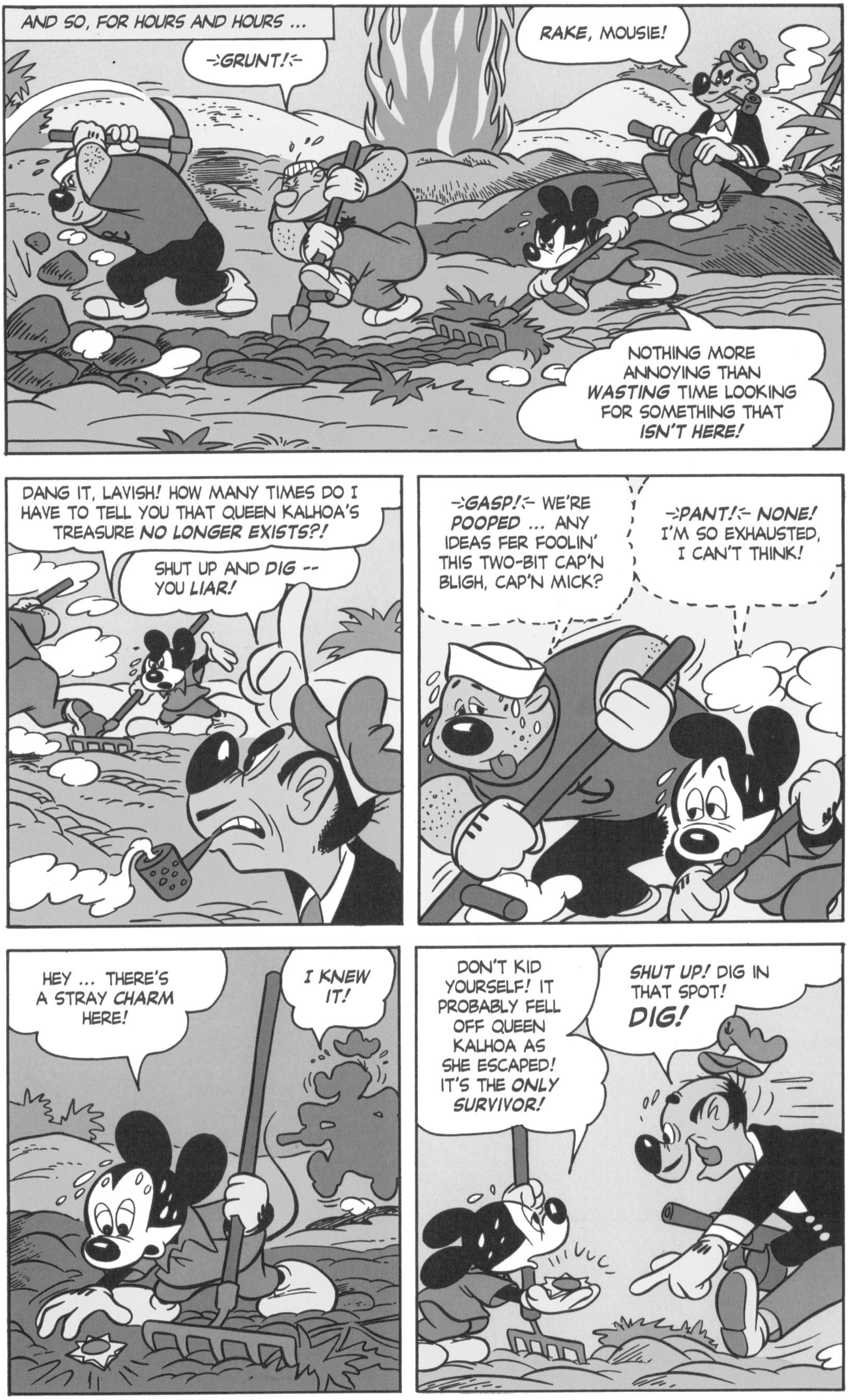

AND SO, FOR HOURS AND HOURS ...
-GRUNT!-
RAKE, MOUSIE!
NOTHING MORE ANNOYING THAN WASTING TIME LOOKING FOR SOMETHING THAT ISN'T HERE!
DANG IT, LAVISH! HOW MANY TIMES DO I HAVE TO TELL YOU THAT QUEEN KALHOA'S TREASURE NO LONGER EXISTS?!
SHUT UP AND DIG -- YOU LIAR!
-GASP!- WE'RE POOPED ... ANY IDEAS FER FOOLIN' THIS TWO-BIT CAP'N BLIGH, CAP'N MICK?
-PANT!- NONE! I'M SO EXHAUSTED, I CAN'T THINK!
HEY ... THERE'S A STRAY CHARM HERE!
I KNEW IT!
DON'T KID YOURSELF! IT PROBABLY FELL OFF QUEEN KALHOA AS SHE ESCAPED! IT'S THE ONLY SURVIVOR!
SHUT UP! DIG IN THAT SPOT! DIG!

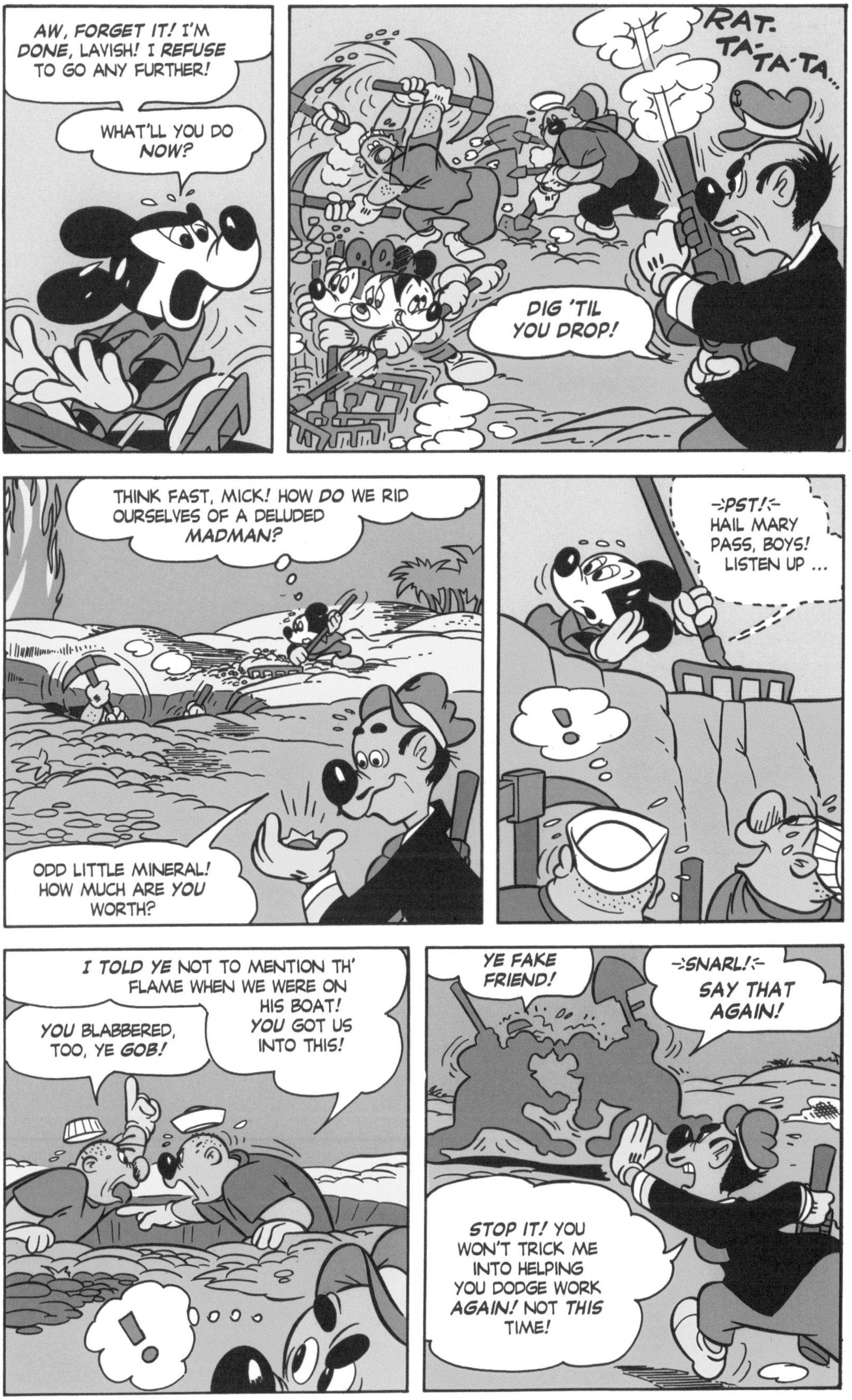
AW, FORGET IT! I'M DONE, LAVISH! I REFUSE TO GO ANY FURTHER!
WHAT'LL YOU DO NOW?
RAT-TA-TA-TA...
DIG 'TIL YOU DROP!
THINK FAST, MICK! HOW DO WE RID OURSELVES OF A DELUDED MADMAN?
ODD LITTLE MINERAL! HOW MUCH ARE YOU WORTH?
-PST!- HAIL MARY PASS, BOYS! LISTEN UP ...
!
I TOLD YE NOT TO MENTION TH' FLAME WHEN WE WERE ON HIS BOAT! YOU GOT US INTO THIS!
YOU BLABBERED, TOO, YE GOB!
!
YE FAKE FRIEND!
-SNARL!- SAY THAT AGAIN!
STOP IT! YOU WON'T TRICK ME INTO HELPING YOU DODGE WORK AGAIN! NOT THIS TIME!

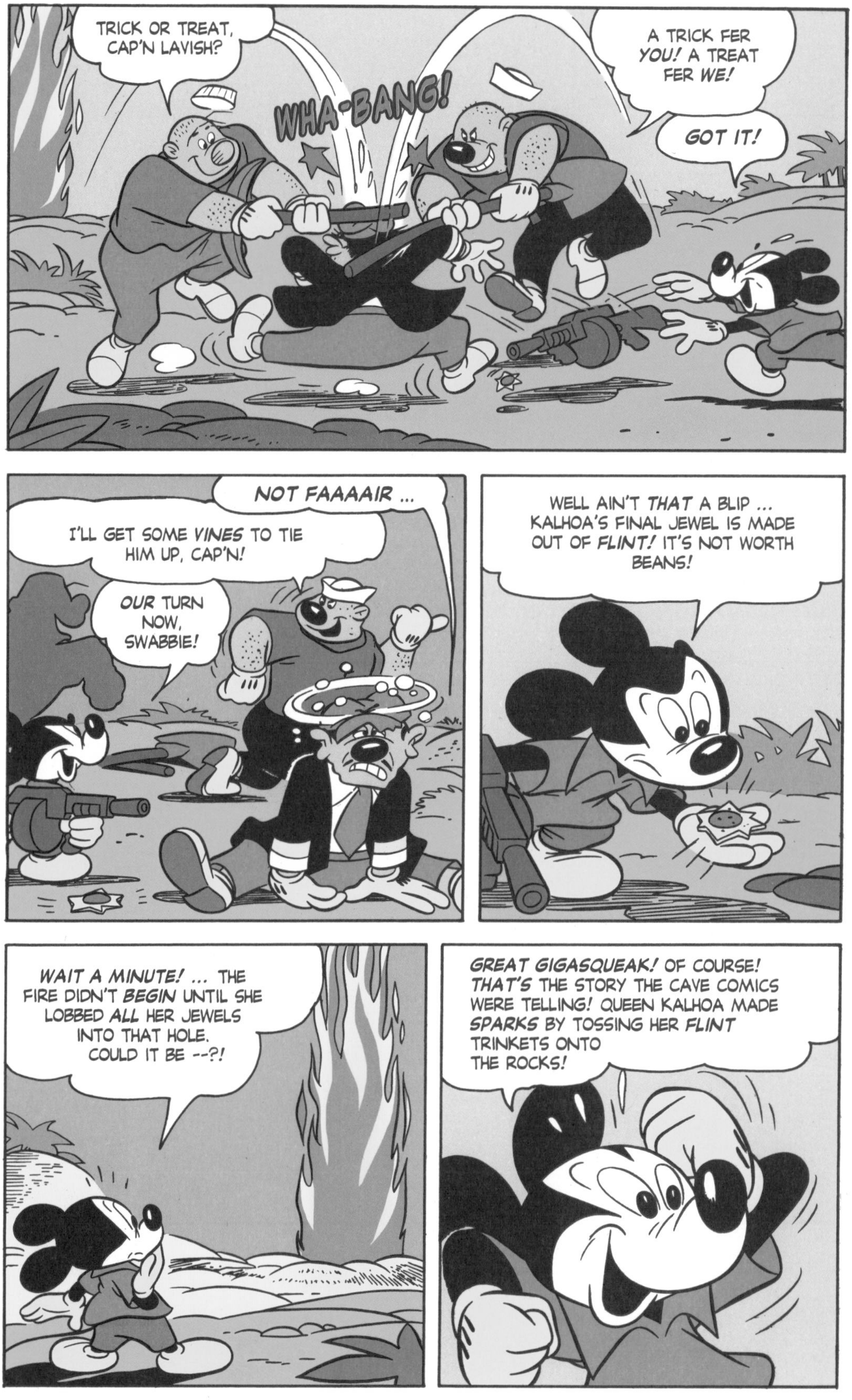
TRICK OR TREAT, CAP'N LAVISH?
WHA-BANG!
A TRICK FER YOU! A TREAT FER WE!
GOT IT!
NOT FAAAAIR ...
I'LL GET SOME VINES TO TIE HIM UP, CAP'N!
OUR TURN NOW, SWABBIE!
WELL AIN'T THAT A BLIP ... KALHOA'S FINAL JEWEL IS MADE OUT OF FLINT! IT'S NOT WORTH BEANS!
WAIT A MINUTE! ... THE FIRE DIDN'T BEGIN UNTIL SHE LOBBED ALL HER JEWELS INTO THAT HOLE. COULD IT BE --?!
GREAT GIGASQUEAK! OF COURSE! THAT'S THE STORY THE CAVE COMICS WERE TELLING! QUEEN KALHOA MADE SPARKS BY TOSSING HER FLINT TRINKETS ONTO THE ROCKS!

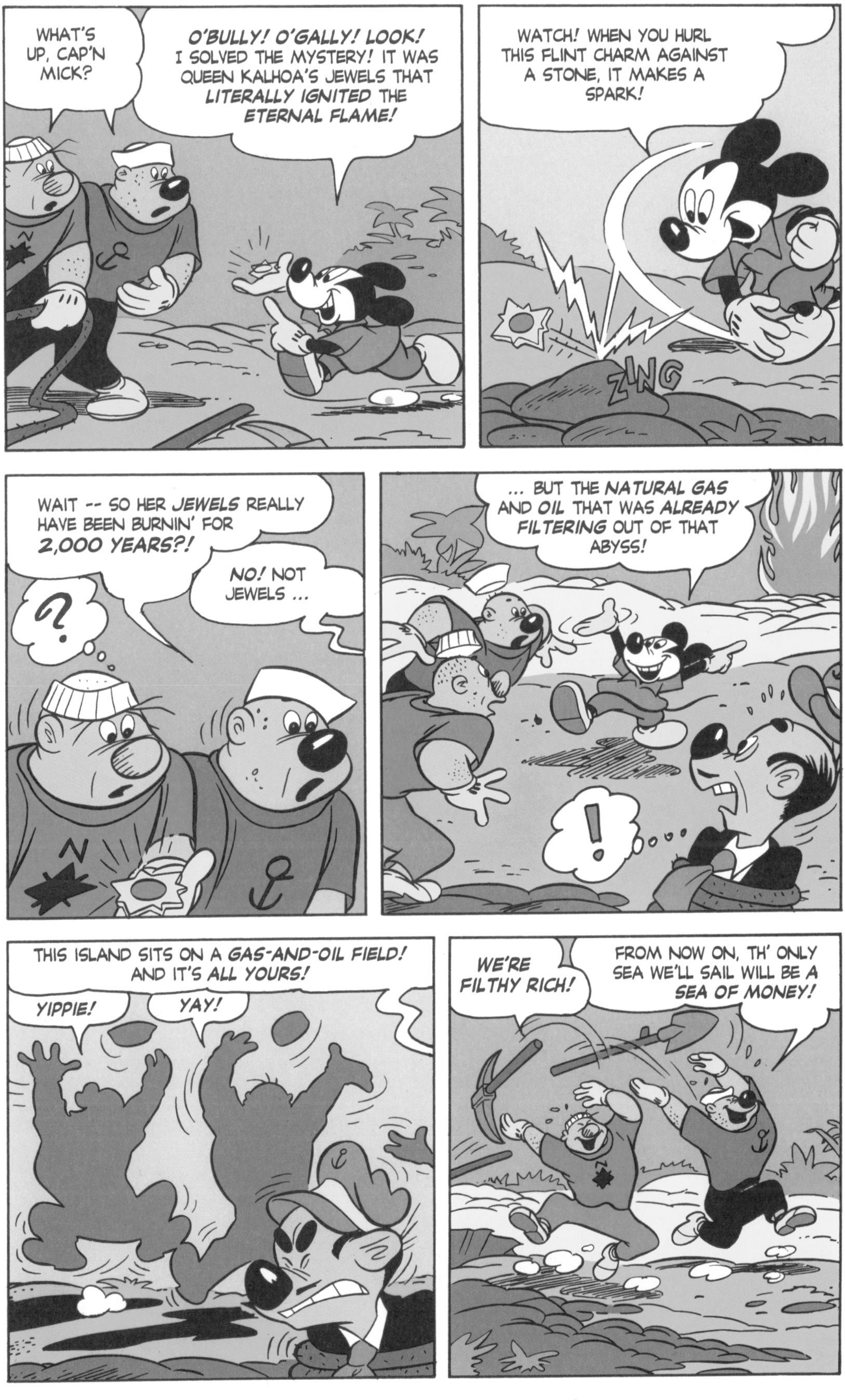
WHAT'S UP, CAP'N MICK?
O'BULLY! O'GALLY! LOOK! I SOLVED THE MYSTERY! IT WAS QUEEN KALHOA'S JEWELS THAT LITERALLY IGNITED THE ETERNAL FLAME!
WATCH! WHEN YOU HURL THIS FLINT CHARM AGAINST A STONE, IT MAKES A SPARK!
ZING
WAIT -- SO HER JEWELS REALLY HAVE BEEN BURNIN' FOR 2,000 YEARS?!
?
NO! NOT JEWELS ...
... BUT THE NATURAL GAS AND OIL THAT WAS ALREADY FILTERING OUT OF THAT ABYSS!
!
THIS ISLAND SITS ON A GAS-AND-OIL FIELD! AND IT'S ALL YOURS!
YIPPIE!
YAY!
WE'RE FILTHY RICH!
FROM NOW ON, TH' ONLY SEA WE'LL SAIL WILL BE A SEA OF MONEY!

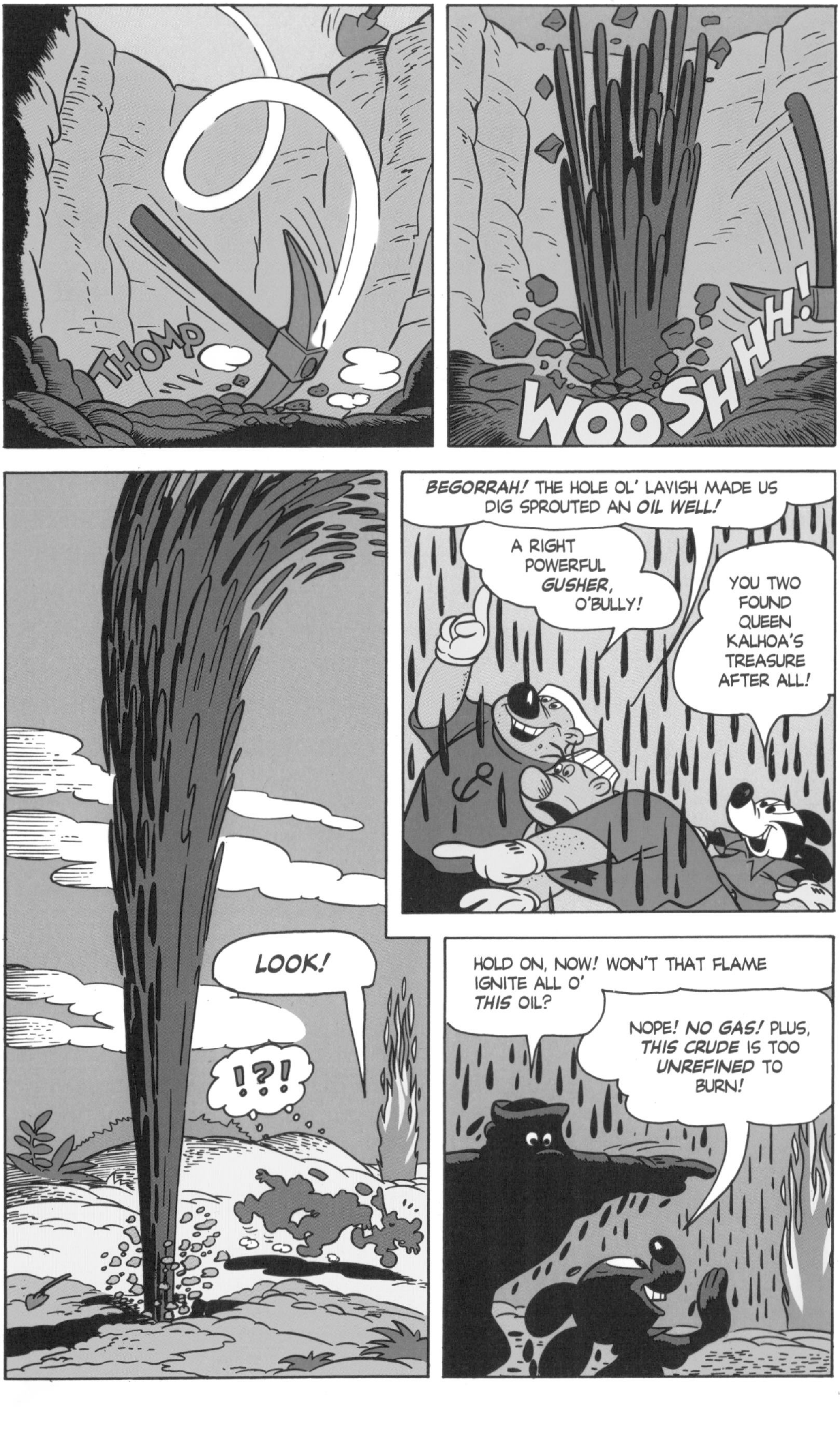
THOMP
WOOSHHH!
BEGORRAH! THE HOLE OL' LAVISH MADE US DIG SPROUTED AN OIL WELL!
A RIGHT POWERFUL GUSHER, O'BULLY!
YOU TWO FOUND QUEEN KALHOA'S TREASURE AFTER ALL!
LOOK!
!?!
HOLD ON, NOW! WON'T THAT FLAME IGNITE ALL O' THIS OIL?
NOPE! NO GAS! PLUS, THIS CRUDE IS TOO UNREFINED TO BURN!

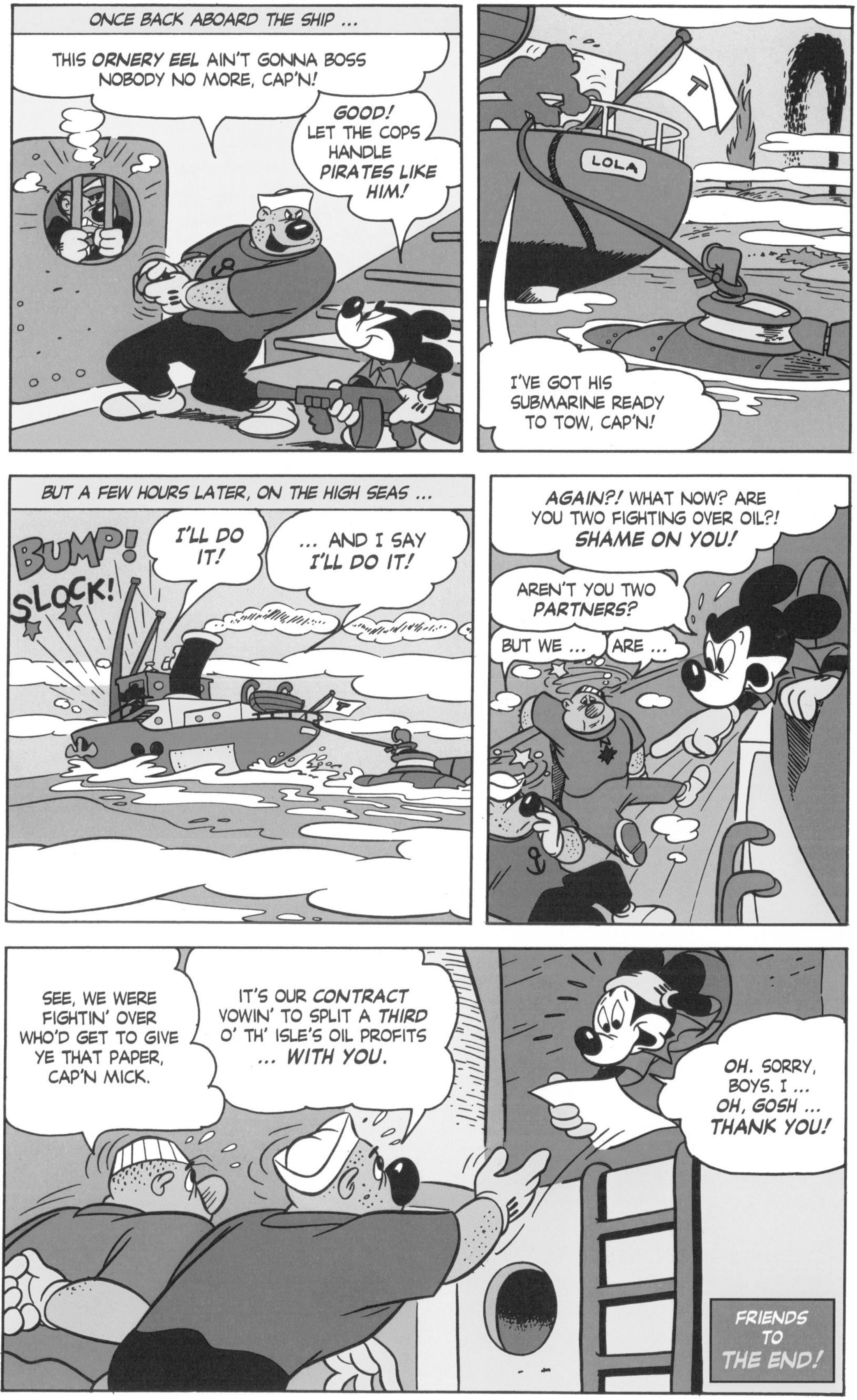
ONCE BACK ABOARD THE SHIP ...
THIS ORNERY EEL AIN'T GONNA BOSS NOBODY NO MORE, CAP'N!
GOOD! LET THE COPS HANDLE PIRATES LIKE HIM!
LOLA
I'VE GOT HIS SUBMARINE READY TO TOW, CAP'N!
BUT A FEW HOURS LATER, ON THE HIGH SEAS ...
BUMP!
SLOCK!
I'LL DO IT!
... AND I SAY I'LL DO IT!
AGAIN?! WHAT NOW? ARE YOU TWO FIGHTING OVER OIL?! SHAME ON YOU!
AREN'T YOU TWO PARTNERS?
BUT WE ...
ARE ...
SEE, WE WERE FIGHTIN' OVER WHO'D GET TO GIVE YE THAT PAPER, CAP'N MICK.
IT'S OUR CONTRACT VOWIN' TO SPLIT A THIRD O' TH' ISLE'S OIL PROFITS ... WITH YOU.
OH. SORRY, BOYS. I ... OH, GOSH ... THANK YOU!
FRIENDS TO THE END!

Romano Scarpa: Mouse Maestro

by FRANCESCO STAJANO AND LEONARDO GORI

AMERICAN COMICS FANS (and comics fans everywhere) have long admired the work of Floyd Gottfredson (1905–1986), the celebrated "Mouse Man" who, for two-and-a-half decades, created *Mickey Mouse* newspaper strip adventure stories that are still acclaimed around the world. (See, for example, the just-released Gottfredson collection *Mickey Mouse: The Greatest Adventures*, Fantagraphics Books 2018.)

But now, with this book, American readers can begin to understand for themselves the special place held by Romano Scarpa (1927–2005) among Gottfredson's successors — and as a pivotal figure in his own right. Among the comparatively few Disney comics talents who have both written and drawn their own material, Scarpa was the *maestro* who, more closely than any other, followed in

Romano Scarpa receives the Yellow Kid Award, a major comics industry prize, at the Lucca Comics convention in Tuscany, 1990. Photo courtesy Luca Boschi.

Gottfredson's footsteps in re-creating that unique atmosphere of "great adventure" for Mickey and his supporting cast.

Born in Venice, Italy, Romano Scarpa was the son of a baker who, rather than expecting his son to join the family business, allowed the youth to pursue his artistic dreams. As a child, Scarpa adored the Gottfredson stories he read in *Topolino* (*Mickey Mouse*), the Italian Disney comic book series that was at that time published in newspaper format. But he was even more fascinated by Walt Disney's animated masterpiece, *Snow White and the Seven Dwarfs* (1937) — which inspired him to try his hand at creating his own animated cartoons. With his father's support, Scarpa outfitted a small animation studio, gathered a young group of fellow enthusiasts (among them Giorgio Bordini and Rodolfo Cimino, both of whom would later also write and draw Disney comics), and began creating animated shorts and commercials. In 1953, Scarpa's team produced *La piccola fiammiferaia* (*The Little Match Girl*), based on the Hans Christian Andersen fairy tale.

Alas, soon after that project, Scarpa was involved in an accident that left him unable to stand for several months. That, and the meager financial return from his studio, led him to close the studio and set animation aside. (He involved himself briefly in a few animation projects in later years.)

He turned to comics and began work for Mondadori, the Italian Disney publisher. He soon found himself drawing a story written by Guido Martina featuring his beloved Snow White — for whom Scarpa's fiancée and later wife, Sandra Zanardi, posed as his model (see *The Return of Snow White and the Seven Dwarfs*, Fantagraphics Books, 2017).

From the start, Scarpa's artwork owed much to Golden Age animation, and one can see echoes of the work of Fred Moore (designer of the Seven Dwarfs) in Scarpa's pages — convenient for a Snow White artist, but propitious, too, for another reason. Master Disney animator Moore had famously streamlined Mickey Mouse throughout the 1930s. The better Scarpa learned to imitate Moore, the better he was also able to emulate Floyd Gottfredson.

It all came together when Scarpa got the chance to step into Gottfredson's shoes. In 1955, King Features Syndicate dictated a halt to the *Mickey Mouse* adventure serials and told Gottfredson to switch instead to gag-a-day strips. That move cut Mondadori off from a major source of popular *Topolino* content. Spotting Scarpa as an up-and-coming talent, the publisher drafted him, at first, to draw new Mickey adventures, then to write them, too.

The job was a labor of love. As a Gottfredson fan, Scarpa chose to mimic Gottfredson's style. Many Italian readers at the time thought, to Scarpa's delight, that Scarpa's yarns were actually the latest installments from Gottfredson.

After initially working from Martina's scripts, Scarpa soon started writing his own stories, creating suspenseful, elaborate plots similar in feel to the best Gottfredson long adventures, such as "Mickey Mouse Outwits the Phantom Blot," "Monarch of Medioka," and "Island in the Sky." Scarpa's own stories in the same spirit (including "The Delta Dimension" in Disney Masters Volume 1, *Mickey Mouse: The Delta Dimension* and this volume's "The Phantom Blot's Double Mystery") have equally powerful imagery — each is built upon several intertwining subplots that ultimately unravel in a dramatic conclusion.

Some Scarpa Mickey stories build new and original yarns atop plot devices, settings, or characters from the Gottfredson classics — the spy hides the secret formula inside an item that accidentally gets away from him; danger threatens either the weak sovereign of a faraway European kingdom or the enigmatic genius Dr. Einmug and his amazing scientific discoveries.

Other great Scarpa stories share no specific details with Gottfredson's tales, but still retain their epic Disney spirit. "The Chirikawa Necklace" (1960) is a Freudian masterpiece worthy of Alfred Hitchcock — and, indeed, is reminiscent of Hitchcock's *Vertigo* (1958) — in which Mickey must fight childhood nightmares and solve a long-ago crime in order to unravel a modern mystery. In the same story, Scarpa introduces Trudy Van Tubb, Pegleg Pete's brassy girlfriend, as the perfect companion for Mickey's archrival.

On that note, we should point out that Scarpa became, after Barks and Gottfredson, the most prolific creator of ongoing Disney characters for comics — and like almost no other writer-artist, Scarpa was equally at ease with both Mice and Ducks. From the aforementioned Trudy to Brigitta MacBridge and Jubal Pomp (respectively, Uncle Scrooge's hopeless love interest and his hapless business rival), Scarpa gave birth to an array of new characters who fit so naturally into Duckburg and Mouseton that other authors picked them up, regarding them as genuinely "Disney" as their Barks and Gottfredson forerunners.

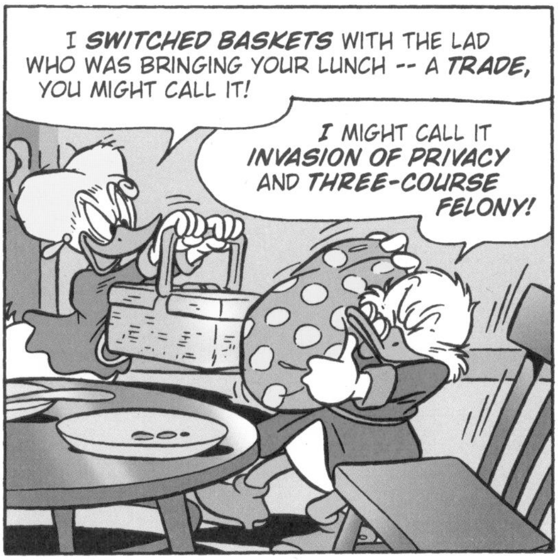
I SWITCHED BASKETS WITH THE LAD WHO WAS BRINGING YOUR LUNCH -- A TRADE, YOU MIGHT CALL IT!
I MIGHT CALL IT INVASION OF PRIVACY AND THREE-COURSE FELONY!

One of Scarpa's original character creations, lovestruck tycoon Brigitta MacBridge (who also appears in this volume) tries her best to woo Scrooge in "The Secret of Success" (1961; English version from *Uncle Scrooge* #338, February 2005).

Scarpa even created a figure in the mold of Eega Beeva, Gottfredson's wacky time traveler. As we see in this book, Atomo Bleep-Bleep — originally an atom, but magnified to human proportions by Dr. Einmug — picks up where Eega left off in terms of acting as a "superhero sidekick" for Mickey on some of his most memorable adventures (see the aforementioned Volume 1 for Atomo's debut appearance).

Scarpa's "golden age" was arguably his first decade of activity: 1953 to 1963, during which time he spared no effort to build meticulously crafted plots as suspenseful and surprising as Gottfredson's. Unfortunately for his avid fans, Scarpa, having become dissatisfied with the inadequate financial reward for his own elaborate scripts, gradually switched to only illustrating the stories of other writers.

He did, however, return to storytelling in full glory near the end of his career, when — as an explicit homage to Gottfredson — he created four special Mickey "strip stories" that recreated not only the spirit but the layout and structure of Gottfredson's daily strips, with cliffhangers and gags in the last panel of each installment.

Romano Scarpa's legacy, as both a Gottfredson protégé and as a towering comics talent in his own right, remains unsurpassed.

DISNEY MASTERS

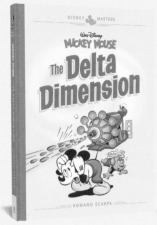

ROMANO SCARPA
Volume 1

LUCIANO BOTTARO
Volume 2

PAUL MURRY
Volume 3

**DAAN JIPPES and
FREDDY MILTON**
Volume 4

Plus...

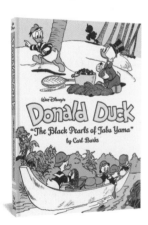

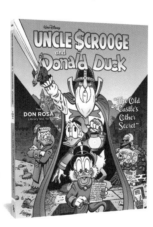

CARL BARKS

DON ROSA

FLOYD GOTTFREDSON